"I HAVE HEARD THE SONG."

"You shall not speak to me of the Wizard Dresh," Rebeke whispered softly. "If you try again, you will find yourself incapable of speaking to anyone about anything." Her voice grew stronger, defiant. "Need I remind you, any of you, that I am the possessor of the Relic? The last perfectly preserved body of a Windsinger born? Without it, you can start the transformation from lower specie to Windsinger, but you cannot complete it. You have not seen it, you cannot know how pathetically inadequate it makes all your carven images. Look at yourselves and look at me. Your bodies need the guidance of your mind and the Relic. But while you take this tone with me, you will not get even a glimpse of it. Until you can be made to see reason, I shall leave you to fumble your way along the path to being true Windsingers. I am nearly there . . ."

Other fantasy titles available from
Ace Science Fiction and Fantasy:

and much more!

THE LIMBRETH GATE

MEGAN LINDHOLM

ACE FANTASY BOOKS
NEW YORK

THE LIMBRETH GATE

An Ace Fantasy Book/published by arrangement with
the author

PRINTING HISTORY
Ace Original / July 1984

ISBN: 0-441-48358-5

Ace Fantasy Books are published by The Berkley Publishing Group,
200 Madison Avenue, New York, New York 10016.
PRINTED IN THE UNITED STATES OF AMERICA

THE
LIMBRETH GATE

ONE

A SLENDER red fissure appeared in the wall, dividing the stone like a snake cutting through water. The Windsinger had no breath to give the cry of relief she felt. Instead she gathered her strength again, and let it flow from her. The stony goddesses and bearded warriors in bas relief on the wall stared past her unseeing. The uncertain light of her fluttering lamp touched their high cheekbones and rounded arms, but left their eyes in darkness. Yoleth paid no heed to them. They had stalked the walls of Jojorum long before she was born, and would still be slowly weathering away long after she was gone. The creeping fissure split the smiling lips and smooth brow of a minor deity.

The city was still; Yoleth had lulled the wind to silence, and the crowing of cocks and the stirrings of market stall farmers were still hours away. The soft dust of the city streets lay as fine as talc over the ancient paving stones. In all the predawn city, only Yoleth was awake and striving.

A fine haze of sweat misted her lightly scaled skin. It damped the tall blue cowl that framed her narrow face, sticking it to her brow and the back of her neck. Her eyes, grey streaked with white, narrowed with the intensity of her effort. Her arms were folded before her, slender hands clasping one another's wrists within the voluminous sleeves of the blue gown that proclaimed her a Windsinger of rank. Her body was still but her mind groaned with effort.

She must not waver now. Carefully she blanked her mind again, losing her identity, letting her strength be tapped by the Limbreth on the other side. The seam became a jagged crack. The dark red light that glowed through it was like a fire seen

1

through treetrunks at night. The edges of the opening became regular, forming a tall thin rectangle. Her body steamed beneath her robes; the fine cloth grew heavy with damp. The rectangle stretched wider.

Yoleth struggled to remain apart from it. Curiosity broke and bubbled in her; she longed to peer through the opening Gate. But if the Limbreth were to be successful, she must not divert any of her mind's power. The Limbreth must control her vision and use her will to see the Gate from this side. She did not know how much longer she could support that need and remain standing. She banished the thought, trying for these moments not to think, not even to be.

The Gate was as wide as a Human now, and taller. But that would not be enough. She heard the hiss of her own breath between her teeth. With an effort that made the edges of the Gate waver, she returned her breathing to its deep regularity. The edges of the Gate firmed. The Limbreth stretched it wider. She felt herself drawn thinner with the effort. There. Surely that was wide enough now. But the Limbreth continued, drawing the sides of the Gate farther and farther apart. Her legs began to tremble, and she could not still them. Her strength was stretched thin as wire.

Slowly she sank to her knees, her robes wilting about her like the petals of a dying flower. Her proud head sagged forward. The Keeper stepped into the Gate, holding it, and Yoleth fell. The lamp beside her guttered, smoked, and went out.

The Keeper filled the Gate and held it. Yoleth's task was done; strength flowed back into her. She dragged herself to her feet, resuming a Windsinger's dignity. A trill from her throat brought a tiny breeze that cooled her skin. Withdrawing a small blue handkerchief from her sleeve, she dried her face daintily. She gave a short sigh; a flick of her hand stilled the breeze. "It's done."

"Yes," the Keeper agreed, his voice like stones falling into a still pool.

Yoleth regarded him with some curiosity. He was a squat and sexless thing, clad in layers of garments so ragged that they effectively concealed the shape of his torso and legs. His arms were lissome and shapely for all their grey color. His hands had three thick fingers that ended in squared-off nails. A shapeless hood hung low over his brow, but concealed no eyes.

Two slitlike nostrils flared as he breathed, and his mouth was a puckered seam. But he it was that filled the Gate and held it, his presence and training keeping open the rift between the worlds.

"I am Yoleth, of the Windsingers," she announced formally.

"I am the Keeper of the Gate, servant of the Limbreth." Whatever name he had ever borne had been swallowed by his duty. "Where is the one who would go through the Gate?"

"She has not yet reached Jojorum," Yoleth said hastily, surprised by his directness. "Her route is not a straight one; bad roads may delay her. But I thought it best to have the Gate ready before she arrived."

"Your snare is set, then, but the prey has not yet arrived." The Keeper chuckled sonorously. "By trickery and by treachery do they come, those who go through my Gate. Is she a fool or a victim of her trust in you?"

"That is none of your affair," Yoleth rebuked him haughtily. "My agreement is with your master, and your duty is to honor it."

"As I shall. I shall sit within my Gate and wait. When you are ready to use the Gate, you have only to bring your victim here. I will be ready. I have already selected the one from our side that will enter your world to keep the balance."

Yoleth frowned quickly, the Human lines of it wrinkling strangely the alienized contours of her face. "But I understood that you would call her in for me; that I had only to tell you that she was within the city, and you could call her through the Gate."

The Keeper snorted. "Your tales of us must be old indeed. As well ask me to call a particular bird out of a flock in the sky. I can call one through the Gate, yes. But the choosing is not mine when I call one from your side. I can but call, and those unwary ones within the range of my call must answer."

"Unwary?" Yoleth echoed. Her web, so beautifully simple, was tangling to uselessness with his every word.

"Surely you know what I mean. The ones who have let go the reins of their minds; the drunken, the grieving, the mad, or the extremely weary. Those I can call at random, and do, sometimes, for the sake of balancing the Gate, or to find a new mind to amuse my Master. But I cannot call one of your choosing. You must set your own trap; I can but spring it.''

"Once sprung, will it hold?" Yoleth doubted bitterly. "This is not the bargain I made. It is not what I thought your master offered. What else will you tell me is different? The Limbreth said that once she was through the Gate, I need trouble about her no longer. Is that true, or is there a string on this as well? What assurances do I have that this Gate of yours will hold her in, or others out?"

"You have our word on these things," the Keeper replied stiffly. "I can call the unwary through the Gate. And the Gate is impassable, unless I will otherwise, for I am the Keeper of the Balance and the Matcher of Worlds! The Limbreth, with your aid, can open the Gate. But only a Keeper can reconcile the meeting of two worlds. Their differences alone are enough to seal the Gate against most passage; I am enough to seal it against anything else."

"Prove it!" Yoleth snapped out the words.

The Keeper drew himself up straight. "I know not why my master would have doings with those who doubt my words," the Keeper grumbled. "But if the Limbreth has agreed, who am I to refuse? Wait, then, and watch. Speak no word. I will wastefully spend the one already chosen from our side; I will reach and call for one from yours."

The Keeper went silent. He stood unmoving within the rectangle of the Gate, his dark bulk limned by the deep reds behind him. Yoleth gazed past him in suspicion. She saw nothing but the red background that framed him, but it was an ever-shifting curtain of reds and umber shadows. Through the Gate, she knew, was the Limbreth world, a place that just touched but did not border the world of the Windsingers. Rumors of it were many, and old tales spoke of it; but what could be truly known of a land that no one returned from? Yoleth leaned forward, peering, but could see only into the Gate, not through it.

The dull thudding behind her of hastening hoofbeats pressed her back against the wall. She flattened herself against the stone hem of a goddess's robe, looking back, away from the Gate, and was still. The hoofbeats faltered, hesitating, and then a black warhorse cantered round the corner into view. A young Brurjan was high in the saddle, swaying gently with her mount's movements. She was dressed all in black leather, and the small round shield at her saddle bow carried the device of a yellow wheel in flames. A Rouster by profession. And all Brurjans were fighters by temperament, notoriously disrespectful of all authority. Yoleth eased even closer to the wall.

But the Brurjan made straight for the glowing Gate. The red of it filled her eyes and was reflected in them. It stroked her short dark fur to a crimson sheen. She slid from her saddle to stand before it, swaying slightly as she caught up her mount's reins. Yoleth smelled the sourness of cheap wine. But when the Brurjan spoke, her voice was clear and steady, though oddly accented.

"I dreamed me a Gate," she intoned. "A Gate red as spilled blood, and beyond it a treasure in flickering gems, calling for any bold enough to take them. I dreamed I rode toward it, and woke to find myself standing by my saddled horse. He knew the way, Black did. And I am the one who is bold enough to take."

"The Gate is for you, then." The Keeper was not at all surprised. "Enter slowly. Take your beast if you care to."

Yoleth watched, silent as a stilled breeze. The Brurjan, with the short swift steps peculiar to her folk, led her horse into the Gate. She slowed suddenly as she entered it, encountering an invisible current. She plowed determinedly on. The red Gate framed them all: the Keeper, the Brurjan and her battlesteed, and, from the other side, a small boy. His pale hair was tousled, his eyes dreaming still. A short pale green garment left his arms and legs bare. His skin was a golden brown. His dream made him smile.

For two breaths all were framed there, limned against the redness. Then the Brurjan and her black horse went on, fading through the Gate, while the boy emerged, stepping suddenly from the redness into the dusky streets of Jojorum. He stumbled as he emerged, as if he had leaned against something, only to find it suddenly gone. As his hands met the dusty paving stones, the dream left his face.

He crouched bewilderedly, staring about the streets in confusion. "Mother?" he called softly. "Mother?" A note of panic entered his voice. "I was following you as fast as I could. Don't go to the dancing without me! Mother?" The boy glanced back at the Gate, and then at the unfamiliar grey city

walls that framed it. He stumbled to his feet. The City must
have been foreign to him indeed, for he immediately went to
the Gate.

"Did my mother come this way?" he asked of the Keeper.
But the Keeper turned his squat back on the boy, crouching
down in the red of the Gate. "Mother!" the boy called again,
and began to venture back through the Gate. It stopped him.
Pressed against the wall, Yoleth could see no barrier to his
passing, but his fists drummed against something like rain
pattering on a stretched hide. It did not yield, even when he
scrabbled at it with bent fingers. The Keeper did not stir.
Perplexed, the boy looked around.

His eyes snagged on the Windsinger. Yoleth did not move
nor speak. His eyes beseeched, but hers were stony. A moment
longer he gazed into her granite eyes. Fear disfigured his face.
"Mother?" he called again, and began to trot off down the
street. His small face was lined with worry. His fine hair
floated on the dawn air as his head swiveled from side to side,
seeking a familiar form.

He trotted round a corner and was gone, except for his small
cry floating on the morning like the call of a lost calf. The
Windsinger stepped again from her place against the wall.

"It works," she conceded calmly. "Our agreement can be
fulfilled. But dawn comes soon to this city. Folk will be stirring. Where are doors that will cover this entrance from un-
friendly eyes?"

The Keeper swung his head slowly from side to side, marveling at her ignorance. "The Gate is here only for those who
know where to seek it, and come to seek it. It will be here
when you need it. And when your need is over, the Gate will
close of its own accord."

"I see." Yoleth digested this information. "And what of
that child?"

"He was necessary. If one comes in, one must be cast out to
keep the balance. Only thus can I hold the door. He is not a
threat to you. He will tell no one. Your white sun is deadly to
him. He will not last the day, and any who hear his raving will
put it down to the disease that ravages him. The Limbreth is
wary. He would not make an agreement with you if he could
not keep it."

Yoleth drew closer, eyes hungry. She lowered her voice.

"And he agreed that if I sent him Ki, there would be a gift for me."

The Keeper was bored. "If the Limbreth said, then he will do. If you can keep your side of the bargain. You have still to bring her to the Gate."

"I see," Yoleth repeated slowly.

"Mother!" The small cry floated distantly on the still morning air. A speculative look sprang into Yoleth's eyes. She was suddenly in a hurry. "It is agreed, then. You know who you are to watch for. Admit no other. Give your master my courtesies."

Yoleth stepped away from the Gate and began to hasten, in a dignified manner, up the dusty street. She glanced back once at the Gate. It was not there. The stony-faced goddesses and heroes gazed at her blankly, denying any knowledge. She stepped back again, scanning the wall, until suddenly the Gate winked back into view. She blinked at it as it teased her eyes. Its width appeared to be perpendicular to the wall. But when she stepped nearer, it opened right before her. The Keeper stared at her in bored competence. Yoleth nodded once and turned away again. Her lips pulled into a tight line. When she had been a Human, it had been a smile. It still expressed her satisfaction with her night's work, which perhaps she could make tidier still. She detested loose ends.

She hesitated at the first cross street, but the child's miserable call wailed out again. She hastened toward it. The light of dawn was tingeing the sky; too soon folk would be up and about. She wanted her task completed and herself far away before that time. Let no one even wonder about a Windsinger hurrying down a dawn street in Jojorum.

At the next turning she caught sight of him. His pace had slowed to a walk. At every step the boy glanced about fearfully, but most often he turned his eyes up to the sky that was fading into blue. A rosy blush was rising on his golden skin. He rubbed at his bare arms as if they stung. "Mother!" he cried again.

"Boy!"

He turned to the Windsinger's call, his eyes going wider in fear.

"No, boy, don't be afraid. I've come to find you. You're to come with me."

"No. I want to go to my mother. I was following her, and then suddenly she was gone. I must catch up with her. I don't like to be in this place alone."

"What's your name?" The Windsinger's tone demanded an answer.

"Chess."

"Exactly. Chess. I knew it was you. Your mother has sent me to find you, and take you to a safe place. She wants you to wait there for her, and do as I say, and she will come for you as soon as she can. Come along now."

"Why doesn't she come now?"

Yoleth shrugged eloquently and took a chance. "I don't know. She did not tell me. Does she not sometimes tell you to do things without saying why?"

Chess nodded slowly. He rubbed again at his arms, and then hugged them to his sides. He glanced worriedly from Yoleth's face to the blue sky above her.

"Then come with me. I have no doubt that when she comes for you, she will explain everything. But for now, she wants you to do as I tell you."

Giving him no time to consider her words, she rushed him down the street, striding so swiftly that he trotted at her heels. The innmaster would want a few more coins for this. Well, no matter. He was already too well bribed to say no. It made all her arrangements more certain. They came swiftly to where a signboard depicted a white duck in a blue pond. The boy's skin glowed rosily, and he cried aloud when Yoleth gripped his shoulder. She ignored it.

"Take this," she instructed, pressing a tiny blue stone into the boy's hand. "Give it to the man they call innmaster. Tell him you are come to help at the inn. You are to work nights at tables, and to sleep in the cellar by day. You are part of the bridegroom's jest. Do you understand?"

"Yes, but . . ."

"Repeat it, then."

"I give this thing to the innmaster and say I am come to help him, and work on tables at night, and sleep in a cellar all day. I am part of the bridegroom's jest. But why are you leaving me? When will my mother come?"

Yoleth stifled her impatience. "She will come when she can. And I must leave because there is a place I have to be soon, if I am not already late. The innmaster will take care of you. Do all he tells you, and your mother will be very pleased with you when she comes. You want her to be pleased, don't you?"

Chess nodded, but his small mouth was ajar with uncertainty.

"Good." Yoleth pushed him, not ungently, through the doorslats of the inn. With a glance up and down the street, she hurried on her way. Her lips were once more stretched tight on her face.

"I am growing impatient." Rebeke spoke coldly. "Did not Yoleth and the others know the hour set for this meeting?" Rebeke stood motionless upon the black stone floor of the High Council chamber. She refused to pace, or even to shift her feet. If the High Council wished to be so discourteous as to deny her a chair, she would not let them enjoy her discomfort.

Five of the nine High Council Windmistresses returned her look. Their eyes were emotionless. They could have been statues gowned in deep blue and placed upon white chairs. The dull white High Council table was shaped in a half circle. Rebeke stood at the focus of all eyes, surrounded by stony gazes. She turned her head slowly, meeting each set of eyes in turn.

"When will the others arrive?" she demanded again.

Shiela shrugged. Her seat was to the right of the center chair, which was empty. "How can we say? You gave us little enough notice that you wished to speak to us. Your action is unusual enough, to say nothing of the hour you have chosen. Dawn hasn't even warmed the fields. Besides, the High Council is accustomed to summoning the Windsingers they wish to address. Not the other way round. Lately, any summons we have sent to you has been ignored. Will you pretend surprise that others return your rudeness?" Shiela sniffed delicately through her narrow nose.

Rebeke did not flinch. She met Shiela's words silently, staring her down. The faces of the Windmistresses were impassive, but Rebeke could feel their uneasiness like a small cold wind. They did not like to look at her. She was more Windsinger than any of them. She had left her Human form behind like cast-off clothes. The shape of the ancient race was nearly fulfilled in her, and their legendary powers as well. She possessed already what they still strove after. But it gave her no beauty in their eyes.

Her blue cowl was tall above her brow. The blue and white of her eyes had gone flat. A swelling in the center of her face was a memorial to a once patrician nose. Her mouth was lipless, the corners nearly reaching the hinges of her jaws. The lissome movements of her arms within her loose sleeves suggested that the structure of her elbows and wrists had changed. The High Council could have forgiven the changes in her physiognomy. But they could not forgive the power that thrummed through her voice when she uttered the slightest word. Rebeke made certain they did not forget it.

She let the silence vibrate. "Yoleth," she said at last, "would certainly take pleasure in refusing to meet with me. But Cerie and Kadra and Dorin; were they even informed of my request?"

Shiela stiffened. "It is not the place of a Windmistress to question the High Council. Nor do we have to account to you for our whereabouts. You wished to speak to us. We have a quorum. Speak."

"I shall, but not because you command it. I will speak because I have no time for your petty intrigues. I have other things to attend to. Yet well I know that if I do not speak now, you will later plead ignorance, and make me out to be the unreasonable one. So I will speak swiftly now, and you will listen. Listen and remember."

Rebeke stared slowly around at the semicircle of hostile faces. "At least I need not wonder if I have your attention," she said mirthlessly. She lifted her right hand abruptly and took a perverse pleasure in the flinching of the two Council members nearest her. "The wind has brought me rumors. Do not think I jest or exaggerate when I say the breezes bring me news. . . ."

"Superior abilities are never an excuse for the misuse of power!" Shiela cut in angrily.

"Silence!" Rebeke's voice was gentle, but its power rocked the room. Shiela went white as if she lacked air. "Ignorance is never an excuse for rudeness. As I was saying, the wind has brought me rumors. There is the Romni teamster, called Ki. You are all aware that she lives and travels under my shadow.

Not my protection, nor my indulgence. My shadow. She is mine to rebuke, or mine to ignore. You have been warned to leave her alone. But the wind rumors say that you plan to do her evil. Will any of you deny this?''

Shiela took in air, but could not speak. A slender Windmistress, one of the young ones at the far edge of the table, shifted uneasily. Rebeke put her gaze upon her. Lilae was the newest of the Council members, with the face of a young Human maiden, lightly scaled. Her lips were still full and rosy with the blush of Humanity. ''I will speak for us,'' she ventured timidly. ''Unless there is another who feels she can speak better.'' She glanced about the table, but no other Windmistress moved or spoke. Shiela stared at the white table surface.

''Please speak then,'' Rebeke invited her courteously. Her tone was markedly more tolerant as she looked upon the young Windsinger. Lilae drew in a deep breath; her eyes darted to Shiela, and then back to Rebeke.

''The matter of Ki the Romni has been brought before us. Shiela spoke of it at the last calling of the Council. We are aware that Ki was your''—Lilae fumbled, seeking a word for what she wished to express—''servant, in the recovery of the sole Windsinger Relic. We suppose you feel some debt of gratitude to her for aiding you to recover so important a treasure.'' Lilae was becoming more certain of herself with every word. ''But perhaps you have not considered the other side of the coin. With the wizard Dresh she was able to force her way into our halls. She was a party to the slaying of Grielea, a Windsinger much honored among us, if not beloved to you.'' Rebeke's smooth brows knit, and Lilae's voice shook slightly as she hastily continued. ''And it is said that she helped you to regain the relic, not to please us, but to spite the villagers that would not pay what they owed her. Or would not pay her friend. The reports aren't clear.''

''They work as one,'' Rebeke said portentously. ''A lesson this High Council could learn from them.''

''Perhaps!'' Lilae agreed recklessly. ''And perhaps you can tolerate their disrespectful ways. But have you remembered she is Romni? For that is what disturbs Shiela. Though she and this Vanjin—''

''Vandien,'' Rebeke corrected.

"She and this Vandien may most often travel by themselves, but they do frequent the Romni campsites, sometimes to share a day or two of that life. The man is a skilled storyteller. All the Romni know what happened in your halls, and at the sunken temple. The story is spreading, for the Romni have made a song of it. Typical of them, the song is little related to the facts, but boasts only of a Romni and her man who tweaked the noses of the Windsingers, put them in their debt, and walked off without a scratch. Need I remind you that the Romni do not stay in one place? They move about, they meet other Romni, they move on again. The song is spreading. It is known in most of the major towns now, and is becoming a favorite. We cannot tolerate this kind of thing. A properly respectful attitude toward us is the necessary foundation for . . ."

"Ridiculous!" Rebeke did not laugh, but her voice was full of scorn. "You would kill her for a song. Perhaps you need the other races groveling at your feet, but I do not. And I have told you before: Ki travels under my shadow. If there is such a song—and I have not heard it—it bothers me not at all. Ki will continue to go her own way, unmolested. If we stoop to slaying her, it will not kill the song. It will only increase our reputation as humorless tyrants. Folk cannot be stopped from singing."

"I have heard the song," Shiela croaked. Her face was still white but her eyes blazed. "And it is more than disrespectful. It smacks of outright rebellion. Perhaps you fancy being the butt of a joke, Rebeke. We do not. Stick to pet wizards and leave the Romni to us."

No one could breathe in the thick silence. "You shall not speak to me of the wizard Dresh," Rebeke whispered softly. "If you try again, you will find yourself incapable of speaking to anyone about anything." Her voice grew stronger, defiant. "Need I remind you, any of you, that I am the possessor of the Relic? The last perfectly preserved body of a Windsinger born? Without it, you can start the transformation from lower species to Windsinger, but you cannot complete it. You have not seen it, you cannot know how pathetically inadequate it makes all your carven images. Look at yourselves and look at me. Your bodies need the guidance of your mind and the Relic. But while you take this tone with me, you will not get even a glimpse of it. Until you can be made to see reason, I shall leave you to fumble your way along the path to being true Windsingers. I am nearly there. And I have acolytes in my hall who are closer to true form and purer of voice than most here who call themselves Windmistresses. I am not going to force any of you. You can come around to my persuasion and join me. Or you can stay as you are, and be surpassed, outsung and outgrown, until you are unnecessary to anyone.

"Perhaps Ki and Vandien were not my willing tools in the recovery of the Relic. That matters little to me. I have it. And it was by Ki's voluntary aid that I was able to contain the wizard Dresh, and so control him that you now dare to refer to him as my 'pet.' So. I shall give you a few instructions. Let her disobey who dares. Listen well. Neither Ki nor Vandien shall be killed. Nor shall I agree to their lives being indefinitely postponed, as you so politely refer to it when you place one in the void. Send your singing Romni a storm or two. Blow in the roofs of a few taverns where this song is sung, if you feel that will prove anything. I have no time to watch your every move. For while you are wreaking your trivial vengeances, I am training the Windsingers who tomorrow will rise up, to show this world what Windsingers used to be. The time will come when we shall rule, not with harshness, but from the fullness of our generosity, and the gratitude of a wind-blessed folk. I fear no singing Romni."

Shiela looked down once again at the table. Pale lids hooded her eyes, teeth met her lower lip. "I regret the rift that has grown between us," she said in a low voice. "Of what use is the High Council, when the ranks of the Windsingers are sundered? Only under one authority can the winds of the sky blow in harmony. Yoleth is not here, but I think I can offer you this. I give you our word that Ki shall not be killed, nor put in a void. Nor Vandien. Does that satisfy you?"

Rebeke spoke slowly. "It would." Some thought she was reluctant to be reconciled, and some thought she was mistrustful of the sudden proposal.

"And, again, though Yoleth is not here, I will be so bold as to ask this. Under what circumstances, what agreements would you allow us access to the Relic? Let your words be tempered by this thought; when you deny us, it is not only the High Council that lacks guidance, but also many young and promising Windsingers in our halls. Will you let the calf die of thirst because the cow has displeased you?''

"Do not think that has not troubled me," Rebeke said, and her voice, for once, was empty of her power. "Your words are fair, your request equitable. But I cannot answer it without thought. When I return to my hall, I shall give my mind to it. The High Council will receive a list of what agreements I think essential for the Windsingers to be once more united. Your keeping of your word regarding Ki I will see as an omen of your good will.''

"You will." Sheila was gracious but reserved.

"I will leave you now. I am trusting that my words will be passed on to Yoleth, and to Cerie, Kadra, and Dorin. Please let them know that I missed them.''

"We will.''

Rebeke left them without another word. She stepped through the portal of the audience chamber and they listened to her footsteps fading down the hall. The silence that drenched the room was ominous. Shiela was the first to speak. She lifted her eyes from their contemplation of the bare table and aimed them at Lilae. Small fires burned in them.

"Mark how graciously she leaves us, without even a formal farewell. Do not think, Lilae, that I have overlooked your part today. You speak loudly for one so young, and not well. Shiela tells us this, and Shiela says that. I shall remember.''

Lilae was visibly flustered. "But I waited for another to take that part and speak for us. I did not want Rebeke to think we had no reasons for our plan other than to spite her.''

"Spiting that one would be reason enough for any number of plans. But I shall accept your word that it was only stupidity and not malice that drove you to blather on.''

"Have I missed Rebeke then?" All eyes turned to the portal. Yoleth posed there, looking well pleased with herself. Secrets simmered in her eyes.

"You have. Such a shame. She was so entertaining.''

Yoleth's eyes roved across the chairs. "Dorin, Cerie and Kadra; have they left already, also?''

"They never arrived." Shiela's eyes met Yoleth's and traded secrets. "Perhaps their summonses went awry.''

"Perhaps. It is just as well. They are too easily influenced by Rebeke's boldness. My errands, at least, went well.''

"But we must not!" Lilae sat up, going whiter. "Rebeke knows all! She says if we harm her Romni, she will never let us look upon the Relic. She says—"

"What a child!" Shiela's voice held no tolerance. "Rebeke knows all! It's a bluff. She knows nothing, not for certain. 'The breeze brings me news!' Sheer frippery! Only a fool would be taken in by it. No doubt she has heard something, for some tongues in this room wag overmuch, and out of place. But our plans need not change."

"You gave your word." Lilae was shaken but determined.

"We aren't going to kill the teamster, nor put her in a void. And that's all I gave my word for." Shiela looked away from Lilae. Her eyes locked with Yoleth's and they reached some agreement.

"The High Council is dismissed," Yoleth announced perfunctorily. "You all have acolytes to see to; a better occupation than sitting here and fretting over shadows. And Lilae?" The young Windmistress turned to look at Yoleth reproachfully. "Do not be upset. You are young, and full of ideals. I am old, and full of necessities. But one of my necessities is that I keep Windsingers like you by me, to temper my cynicism with your trusting ways. Put the Romni matter from your mind. Let it be upon my head, not yours. Sing with a clear conscience today. May the wind rise ever obedient to your call."

"As to yours," Lilae replied formally and left.

After a few moments, Yoleth checked the hall to be sure it was empty. She drew close to Shiela and spoke softly.

"Exactly what does Rebeke know?"

"She knows you don't like Romni singing. She seemed to accept that as your reason. But I would still like to hear the real one."

Yoleth measured the other Windsinger speculatively. "Not yet. But soon I shall tell you all. Be flattered that you know as much as you do."

Shiela appeared to be on the point of speaking. But she swallowed her first words and only observed, "It is hard to put trust where one is not trusted."

Yoleth only smiled at her.

Two

VANDIEN pinched the heavy weave of the fabric between thumb and forefinger. He gave the vest a shake, and the bright colors almost flashed in the afternoon sun. He raised one eyebrow at the woman in the stall.

"You know my price!" she reminded him firmly. "And you can see it's worth it. Try it on, and feel the weight of it."

Vandien obeyed, slipping it on over his loose linen shirt. He rolled his shoulders in it, and tugged the front even. "It fits well," he grudgingly admitted. "But . . ."

"But he can't possibly be serious." He turned his head sharply at the amused voice behind him. Ki stood there, her mouth puckered in mock dismay, her arms laden with supplies.

"I am. And why not?"

"Blue *is* your color. And green, yellow, red, and black as well. But not all at once."

"Not usually. But last time we stopped with the Romni, Oscar told me that a man who dresses as simply as I do is like a cockerel without feathers. What do you think of this?" Vandien pulled the front of the vest down straight so that the embroidery of birds, flowers and vines could be admired.

"I think Big Oscar is right. If you wear that vest, no chicken could resist you."

He met her laughing eyes with no amusement. "I think I like it."

"Walk about a bit and think it over before you buy. If you still like it, I am sure it will still be here." Ki made her suggestion in a practical voice.

"I suppose." Vandien took off the vest slowly and replaced

it on the piles of merchandise. The woman in the stall shrugged at him and rolled her eyes. Vandien gave her a grin she had to answer, and then turned away to Ki.

"Take some of this stuff, will you?" she demanded, and began to unload into his arms. "Help me carry it back to the wagon. Can you think of anything else we need?"

"What do you have there?"

She inventoried as she loaded it into his arms. "Smoked salted fish; red pomes; tea; honey in that brown pot; that's a string of onions over your shoulder; lard in the wooden box; cheese; and a square of leather for new gloves."

Vandien stared down at his load. "It all sounds very practical and essential." Disappointment dulled his voice.

"What did you want? Pickled chestnuts and peacock feathers?" Ki was nettled. She spoke over her shoulder as they edged through the busy market. When Vandien did not reply, she glanced back at him. He had paused at a stall aflutter with gay scarves. Belatedly he remembered her and fell in behind her.

"No. Nothing like that. I'd just like to see you be a little more impulsive. Enjoy life."

"You're impulsive enough for both of us," Ki pointed out.

Vandien shifted his load. They were out of the main press of the market, but Ki had left the wagon and horses behind the inn. Curly dark hair sagged forward onto his brow and fell into his eyes. He blew up at it, but it only tickled the more. "You're just jealous of me," he accused her gravely.

"Indeed." Ki juggled her own parcels and slowed to walk beside him. They were nearly of a height, and their eyes met with sparks. "I suppose next you will be saying that I secretly desire to wear a vest with trees and birds sprouting all over it."

"No, not my taste. You're jealous of my ability to enjoy life. You tiptoe through your days, worrying about warm underwear and axle grease, while I stride through mine singing. You've lost all your edges, Ki. You nibble at the dry corners of your life."

"Instead of cramming it all into my mouth at once, like some folk we know."

"Exactly." Vandien bowed his head to acknowledge the compliment. "This afternoon—I am quite safe in predicting—you will drink exactly and precisely the three bowls of Cinmeth you permit yourself to consume in a public inn, while I take down as much Alys as they have and I can afford. Isn't that true? What can you say to that?''

"Only that I'm glad the wagon is right in the innyard. I detest dragging you through city streeets in broad daylight.''

"Oh, that's funny,'' Vandien snarled.

"Truth stings.'' Ki grinned at him smugly. As they reached the wagon, she turned and added her burden to the items he already carried. She climbed up the tall yellow wheel onto the plank seat, and reached back down to receive the supplies from him. ''Come up here and help me put this stuff away,'' she invited.

"Do it yourself,'' he growled as he climbed up beside her. She slid open the cuddy door and climbed down into the living quarters of the wagon. The front half of the freight wagon had been closed in to resemble half a Romni wagon. Ki stood in the center of the tidy little cabin and put things away as he passed them to her. A platform covered with hides and blankets was the bed at one end of the room. The cuddy walls were a patchwork of shelves, cupboard, nooks and hooks. A small table folded down under the single tiny window with its greased skin pane. It took only moments for Ki to place every item on its shelf or in its bin. She looked up at Vandien sulking on the seat. She tried to straighten her face to match his.

"You're disgusted with me.''

"I am.''

"Because I am such a practical, mundane, boring person. Because I go through life immune to impulses and idiocy. Because there is never anything about me the least bit unpredictable.''

"Well.'' Vandien quailed before the harshness of Ki's self-indictment. "No. Because it's all there, bubbling beneath the surface, and you refuse to let it out. I'll tell you what I'd like to do.'' He stepped down into the cuddy and seated himself on the sleeping platform. ''I'd like to make a day for you such as I'd make for myself.'' Ki raised her eyebrows questioningly, but he plowed on determinedly. ''We'll do this.'' He suddenly became almost shy, and covered his hesitation by brushing the curls from his eyes.

"Yes?'' Ki said encouragingly.

"Stop interrupting me. How can I think and talk at the same

time if you keep interrupting me? We'll do this. We'll find a public bath; an old city like Jojorum must have some baths worthy of the name. And we will loll and soak until your little toes are as pink as your nipples.'' He grinned at her, suddenly wicked as his own fantasy carried him away. ''We will hire a body servant to put up your hair in long soft curls, and weave it all through with fine gold wire and pearls. We will drape you in one long length of cloth of gold, and put slippers on your feet of finest gleaming leather. Green stone earrings to match your flashing eyes, and three plain silver rings on each of your hands.''

''And then what?'' Ki asked gently when the pause grew long.

''And then we shall walk through Jojorum together, with your arm about my waist, and folk will gaze on us and remember when this city was young and lusty.''

''They'd only be admiring your vest,'' Ki teased gently, but she moved to stand close before him, and put her hands on her hips. ''You know we don't have the coin to do any of that, other than the bath.''

''I know. But when I want to do it, I know I want to do it, while you go about pretending you don't want to do it, because you know you can't afford it. And that's the big difference between us.''

''That makes us good for each other,'' Ki amended. She slipped one hand into her skirt pocket. With the other she caught a handful of the thick dark curls at the nape of his neck. Her gentle pull bowed his head to her. She drew her free hand out of her pocket and shook out a circle of chain and looped it over his head.

''What's this?'' Vandien pulled her down to sit on the bed beside him as he fingered the fine silver chain curiously.

''It's an impulse. From a friend who doesn't have many. I knew it was yours when I saw it in the jeweler's stall.''

Vandien slipped the necklace off to look at it. The chain was silver worked in tiny loops. Suspended from one larger loop swung a tiny hawk. Spread wings, talons and open beak had been chipped in fine detail from some black stone that glistened even in the cuddy's dim light. A chip of red was its sparkling eye. Ki knew she had chosen well at the sigh that escaped him.

He looped it again about his neck. The length of the chain let it rest well below the hollow of his throat.

"It's almost lost in the hair," she observed.

"I shall shave that spot on my chest to properly display it," Vandien promised.

"You will not." She kissed him so suddenly that her rare token of affection landed only on the corner of his mouth and his moustache. But when he would have been more thorough, she gently freed herself from his embrace.

"You just remembered you forgot to buy harness oil," Vandien guessed sagely.

Ki laughed ruefully at his accuracy. "And I need to refill the team's grainbox. I'll have to take the wagon to fetch that."

"I've errands of my own, nearly as dreary."

"Such as?"

"Warm underwear and axle grease," he told her solemnly. He rose, keeping his head bent under the low cuddy ceiling. "I found a nice little tavern, and left my horse tied in front. It's called the Contented Duck. As nearly as I could find by asking about, it's the only place in Jojorum that serves both Alys and Cinmeth."

Ki nodded. "I'll meet you there, then. But, Vandien." He turned back to the sudden worry in her voice. "We cannot tarry long. I've heard an ugly thing in the streets today: A juggler on a street corner warned me of Rousters. 'I can put a long coat over my motley,' he told me. 'But a painted Romni wagon is a harder thing to hide.' We'd best be clear of this place before nightfall."

"Rousters?" Vandien looked at her blankly.

"We've been together too long. Sometimes I forget you are not Romni born. The merchants of some towns are not pleased to see a Romni caravan arrive. They call us thieves and worse. But it's not just the Romni. It's any traveler with wares to sell that may be cheaper than their own, be he tinker or trader. So the merchants hire Rousters. They'll come on a wagon in the dead of night, beat the adults, terrify the children, disable the team if they can, set fire to the wagon if they can't; all in the name of moving on the thieving vagabonds and keeping their fair towns pure."

Vandien's dark eyes went black as Ki spoke. Her face held an expression he seldom saw on her. Her green eyes were unseeing as she remembered more than she spoke about. He touched her gently on the sleeve and she was suddenly back with him.

"Surely they won't bother us," he reasoned. "We're only one wagon, delivering freight."

"They don't care." Ki's voice slashed in, low and savage. "They don't care if you're selling lace or juggling at a crossroads or doctoring horses. You can just be begging. They roust you along, and not gently. I don't usually do business with towns that keep them. I'll be glad to watch the dust of Jojorum settle behind us, and get back to our regular hauls."

"All right." Vandien agreed so meekly that Ki turned to him in wonder. He gave a snort of laughter at the look on her face. "Just as you had your impulse for the year, I am indulging a spree of practicality. We'll meet at the Duck, have but one drink each, and be on our way. We'll be clear of Jojorum before nightfall."

They clambered out of the cuddy and Vandien watched Ki stride off to the innyard's corral to fetch her team. He shook his head silently. Rousters. He had never thought he would see Ki leave a town with no cargo to haul, and an inn room paid for and not slept in. He turned his own steps back down the dusty streets to the market again.

Just this morning they had arrived, and they would leave before nightfall. A pity. Jojorum had seen better days, but as downtrodden as it was, an old glory peered from its corners and teased Vandien's curiosity. Ki's wagon had rolled into the city through a towering arch whose lines were slightly obscured by the many mud swallow nests that clung to it. The tall yellow wheels of her Romni wagon had rolled smoothly over the pavingstones some ancient ruler had thoughtfully laid down for her. A blanket of dust shrouded the street and muffled the hoofbeats of her team. Weeds and grasses sprouted from the cracks between road surface and building fronts. Tall stone buildings frescoed with the faces of forgotten heroes were diminished by the mud brick houses that huddled between and against them, reminding Vandien of the swallow nests. Three of the five fountains they had passed were cracked and dry, but at the fourth one, folk were drawing water and at the fifth, laundry was being sloshed under the watchful eyes of seven marble water spirits that helpfully spewed down the clean rinse

water. The last fountain had been set in an ancient courtyard.
Dead harp trees were mute before the fallen mansion. Jojorum
was a melancholy city that had outlived its days of joys and
dabbled now in licentiousness.

Vandien wandered back to the clothing stalls.

"You've come back for the vest, then?" the proprietor
asked.

A gleam of mischief came into his eyes. "Have you one that
is similar, but smaller? One that would fit the friend that was
with me earlier?"

But he was cheated of his jest, for she had nothing gaudy
enough to satisfy him. For the second time that day, he gave
the merchant a regretful shake of his head and stepped from her
booth. He strolled through the market, enjoying the noise and
bustle. The long peaceful days of the last haul had chafed his
quick spirit. Now here were people and new things to see and
buy, and a handful of silver in his purse. He bought a bright
yellow scarf to knot about his throat, and a paper of dried
spiced fruit to nibble as he wandered from one stall to the next.
"Pleasure for coin?" a young woman in pink asked him. He
gave her a politely appreciative smile and a slow shake of his
head. He meandered on.

At a T'cherian stall he bought and devoured tiny greenish
cakes of vegetable bread. A length of yellow ribbon for Ki
caught his eyes, and a little pot of soft soap scented with
clover. A new leather pouch bound with thongs of red and blue
next seduced him. But this last purchase left him with only a
few copper bits to put into the new pouch, and thus he knew his
shopping was finished. He turned his slow steps back toward
the tavern.

"Pleasure for coin?" The same girl, or her sister in an
identical pink robe. Again Vandien shook his head politely and
tried to step past her. But she blocked him, coming so close
that he smelled the spicy fragrance of her breath. "Pleasure for
pleasure?" she offered him in a softer voice.

Vandien raised his brows at her. He was not an ugly man,
though most looked twice at the long scar that made a fine
seam down the center of his face. He knew the power of his
dark eyes and charming smile, and wasn't above using them to
his advantage. But an abrupt offer like this of such flattering
nature was outside his experience. The adolescent portion of
him crowed.

"I'm a fool," he admitted to her. "Or a crazy man. Perhaps I'm just happy with my present luck, and won't risk changing it. But I'll thank you for thinking of me." With a regretful shake of his head, as if he himself could not actually believe he was refusing her, he stepped past her. A needle of pain ripped into his thigh. Even as it raked up his spine, he lost the power to cry out. He staggered two steps and fell.

"My brother!" the woman exclaimed hysterically. "He's having one of his attacks! Please, someone, help us!"

Vandien lay in the dust stupidly, watching the feet mill around him. Dust was in his eyes, and he was breathing in dusty air, but he couldn't blink or sneeze. He could hear, and the woman was ranting on about her poor brother and begging for aid. Her sweet voice was sharp enough now to scale fish. Vandien was not surprised when someone decided finally to help her. It was easier than listening to her.

His mind should have raced as he was hauled to his feet, and his arms draped across the woman's shoulders and her benefactor's. But he found himself oddly complacent, an observer rather than a participant in this peculiar play. The woman lived several streets over and up a flight of stairs. He rather resented the way he was dragged up them with no thought of his shins and ankles as they whacked across each step. It was distasteful to be plopped onto a stained couch and covered with a dirty blanket, and offensive to have to listen to the benefactor noisily taking his reward. He did not watch, for they had laid him with his face to the wall, and he could not move. His eyes ran tears to wash out the dust he could not blink away. Even more annoying was that he could not close his eyes and sleep as he so longed to do. He stared at the cracked masonry wall before him, and finally drifted into an open-eyed sleep, or an unconsciousness very like it.

Ki stared down into her bowl. At most there was a swallow or two of the rosy Cinmeth left. After that she would have to reach a decision. She could take her wagon out of the city and trust that Vandien would figure out she had gone north, back to her regular trade routes. Or she could leave a definite message with the tavernmaster for him. Or she could take her wagon back to the innyard and spend the night at the inn, trusting to luck that her wagon wouldn't be burned in the night. Or she could walk through the evening streets, calling Vandien's name at every corner.

She quaffed down the Cinmeth, and held her bowl aloft for more. She would wait just a little longer for him. She would have just one more drink, and if he was not here by then, she would decide what to do. She watched the tavern boy pour the spicy liquor into her bowl. It was her fifth. So let Vandien come and find that she could be as impulsively reckless as he. She could trust her luck just as he always did his. But that was the trouble with his damn luck. It was always good, cushioning his falls, so that he never learned a lesson or two of cautiousness. Nor punctuality.

A rattling sound turned her head in surprise. The serving boys were letting down the windowslats. One boy was making the rounds of the tables with a tray full of little candles on clay plates. He kindled one for Ki and set it carefully before her. Ki stared at him curiously, for he was not the usual tavern boy. They tended to be stout little lads picked for their sturdy bodies and tough little legs that could jog up and down from the cellar all evening. But this lad was slender and delicate, appearing nervous and fearful even of the candles he was kindling. His grey eyes were faintly luminous in the semi-dark of the tavern. His hair was pale as moonlight, as were his brows and lashes, which stood out against his mellow brown skin. Despite his coloring, the bruises of hard fingers were plain on his small wrists and thin arms. The boy caught her staring at him, and his fearful eyes were almost accusing. Ki raised her bowl and drained off half the potent Cinmeth to wash away that look. Where had the child learned so immense a wariness?

But when Ki set down her bowl, the boy was standing right before her, the tiny candle flame dancing reflected in his eyes. He glanced fearfully all about before he spoke. The words came as carefully phrased as an actor's.

"Do you wait for a man with a line like this?" He drew a thin finger down his face, starting between his eyes and running beside his nose to his jawline.

"Perhaps," Ki parried warily. Her hand went to her coin purse, but his eyes did not follow it. Her answer had left him uncertain. He glanced around again, as if to take encouragement from someone, but found no one there. His eyes were panicky when they came back to hers.

"I've a friend marked like that," Ki admitted hastily.

The boy sighed out loudly in relief. He licked his lips and picked up his lines. "Then I've a message for you. He's had a bit of trouble. He sent a man to the tavern to find you, but the man couldn't stay. I do not know why, but the Rousters have put him out the Gate. He waits for you there."

Ki shook her head in disbelief. But it had to be true. That would explain why his horse was no longer tied in front of the tavern. Damn his impulsiveness! She wondered what he had said and to whom. She hoped they hadn't hurt him.

She gulped down the last of her Cinmeth, and made a small coin ring on the table for the boy. He looked at it, but did not move. With a sigh, she added another. Even the tips in this town were more than she could afford. "Take it!" she told him a bit testily, and he slowly picked up the little coins. She rose quickly, but her head spun. Damn and damn and damn. See what happened when both of them got impulsive on the same day, she chided herself. She dreaded what she would find. Vandien would fight back. She *knew* he would. But his rapier, which made him the equal of many a taller, huskier man, was on its hook inside her wagon. Ki had seen the Brurjans the city kept as Rousters. They were hulking, quarrelsome beings, their faces dark with fur. They painted the hooves of their horses red. Ki had reached the door before she remembered.

"Which Gate?" she called across to the serving boy.

With a stricken look he hurried to her side. He pointed out into the street and gave her the count and directions of the turns. "It's called the Limbreth Gate," he ended in a small voice. Then, as if he were speaking a family motto, he added, "If you are looking for it where I tell you, you will find it. But you must be looking for it."

"I will." Ki reached to tousle his hair, but he flinched away so wildly that her heart squeezed within her. He scuttled away from her. She was almost tempted to go after him. But he was likely bound into service, and buying him out of it would be a lengthy affair, requiring the presence of his parents and much haggling with the tavernmaster. She would keep him in mind, she promised herself, and perhaps do something about it after she had found Vandien. She wondered if the Rousters had broken him up much, and hastened her footsteps.

The cool night air soothed her skin and eyes and made her

feel steadier, but it could not calm her worries. She forced herself to move slowly and confidently. She had no desire to call the attention of any Rousters to herself. It was full dark in the strange streets. At least the Cinmeth had not made her head pound as wine did. It floated airily above her shoulders.

Ki walked into the side of her own wagon before she saw it. She grumbled at the blackness and made her way by feel up onto the seat. Inside the cuddy she groped through the familiar space until she found her lantern. Senseless to drive the team in this blackness. She would have to walk before them with a light, at least until she reached the Gate.

Friendly Sigmund nuzzled against her in greeting. She gave the huge grey horse an affectionate slap on the shoulder. But surly Sigurd turned his head aside and shifted his feathered feet in the dust. He considered it no treat to be left standing in harness while his owner refreshed herself. When she chirruped to them, they both leaned into their harness readily enough, following at her heels like huge dogs. The wagon came ponderously after them, the sounds of its passage muffled by the dust.

The night city eluded her eyes. Every familiar landmark was just beyond the reach of her lantern circle. She moved down nameless streets in what could have been any town, hearing only the creak and jangle of her wagon. She counted intersections, praying that she would not mix streets with alleys. If she made one wrong turning, all the boy's directions would be useless. At least the streets were paved well. Squat mud brick houses crouched at either side of them. Mōst of them were dark. Here and there a dim candle glow seeped from one of the small windows or through worn doorslats, but it was not enough to illuminate the streets. Ki paced on in her own small circle of light.

She took the last turn in her instructions. Now, if the boy had given them correctly, and if she had followed them accurately, the Gate should be straight ahead. Ki walked on slowly, resisting the urge to keep step with her thudding heart. He would be all right. If he had been alive enough to send a messenger with directions, then he could not be badly injured, perhaps not at all. She gave a small shudder as she thought of the Brurjan Rouster she had glimpsed earlier. He had worn a black leather harness, with the hated emblem of a burning wheel upon it. She could have made two Vandiens from his bulk, and still had material left over. She hoped he hadn't met that one.

The city walls loomed suddenly before her. Ki cursed. There was no Gate. All was blackness below the parapet, and black with stars above it. She had missed the Gate. She'd have to go back. She could follow the wall and hope to find the Gate that way—but follow it in which direction? If she chose the wrong one, it could be hours before she knew it, and then she would have to retrace her steps. Damn the man! He wished she were more impulsive, did he? Well, if she followed her impulses when she found him, his ears would ring for a week.

Ki calmed her temper and steadied her breathing. Just as she was halting the team to decide which way to go, her eyes caught a glimmer of ruddy light. She turned toward it and saw nothing. But this time a light caught her eye from the opposite corner. Puzzled, she turned back more slowly. There was the Gate.

Her heart settled into her belly. Some trick of the wall's projection, or the Cinmeth, had shielded it from her eyes. Now the rectangle of torchlight grew larger as she led her team toward it. But as she drew closer, she saw that the Limbreth Gate was lit by no torches she could see. Ki's lantern did not even illuminate it; rather, the light of it bounced back to her as if it could not penetrate the stone that outlined the Gate. There was no portcullis, indeed, no barrier to entry or exit that she could see at all. It was larger than the North Gate she and Vandien had come in by. She wondered how she could have missed it. A vague uneasiness about this Gate roiled in her belly; she closed her eyes tightly for a long moment and then opened them slowly. Damn Cinmeth. No guards leaned against the wall, but a single watcher crouched in the center of the Gate, blocking her path.

Man or woman, Ki could not tell; it wasn't even a race she was familiar with. The ragged clothing that swathed it could have been white or grey or pale blue. The red glow of the Gate baffled her eyes, making shapes of shadows, and shadows of shapes. The Keeper stared at her, unspeaking. Hidden eyes bored into her despite its veiled features.

"Is this the Limbreth Gate?" Ki's tongue felt thick and even to her the question sounded inane.

"If you come seeking it, then you know that it is." The voice was as deep as a rumbling from the earth itself. The phrasing was as peculiar as the tavern boy's words. For some reason Ki felt nettled by them.

"Well, I came seeking it because I intend to go through it. Are you going to move or look at the bottom of my wagon?"

"Are you Ki, the Romni teamster?"

She stiffened. She did not like the idea of giving names at midnight gates, especially when he classed her as a Romni. Were there Rousters waiting beyond the Gate? But he had called her Ki, so perhaps it was Vandien who had been so free with her name. "I am," she snapped, feeling suddenly reckless.

"We have been expecting you. All is ready for you to pass through the Gate. Enter slowly."

Ki frowned. Every muscle in her body tensed as she saw his tri-fingered hand wave a signal to someone. Rousters or Vandien? Too late to flee if it were Rousters. Heightened awareness battled with drink as she led her team under the reddened lintel. The red light was like peering through a fog. For an instant she caught sight of another figure within the Gate. A tall woman, robed in pale green, her eyes swollen with weeping. Ki thought she shook in fear as she stumbled forward, but it could have been a trick of the wavering red light. She saw her for only that instant, but her resemblance to the boy in the tavern was great. The same pale hair flowed upon her shoulders, and she had the same fragile bones and skin. So perhaps someone did care for the boy. Ki hoped so.

A spasm of vertigo passed through Ki, so that she felt she swam forward through thick warm water. Cinmeth, she thought, half closing her eyes and striding doggedly on. Never again. It passed in an instant and she opened her eyes to the night outside the Gate. The air had changed. Even the horses tossed their heads in a flurry of manes and blew out approvingly. The air washed over them all in a warm wave, with the barest tinge of a cool edge to soothe weary eyes. Ki smelled the perfume of night flowers and the warm mossy scents that woods breathe out at midday. How different this from the dusty, stony city!

"Vandien?" she called questioningly. She lifted her lantern high. Its light touched slender grey treetrunks. Trees? The

North Gate had entered the city from a barren plain of yellow grass. But she had forgotten how old Jojorum was. Had not she heard that it had once been fabled for its gardens? Perhaps these were they, long untended and come back to dominance. At least the road remained good. Moss crept in soft tongues across it, but it was flat and straight, not buckled nor heaved with age. Her wagon rolled silently behind her, the hoofbeats of her team cushioned now by moss. There was moisture in the air, and peace. The very night seemed less dark around her.

So where in hell was Vandien? Even if he were lying senseless by the road, his horse should have whinnied to her team. If they had left him his horse. "Whoa!" The team stood. "Vandien!" Her worried voice sounded shrill in the friendly night, muffled by the peace. She walked around her wagon, back toward the Gate. Perhaps the Keeper could tell her something of Vandien.

The Gate was a fiery rectangle against the darkness, its brightness obscuring all else. Ki felt her eyes water as she stared at it, and she was finally forced to turn her eyes aside. "Gatekeeper!" she cried. "The man who told you to watch for me; where is he?" She risked a glance at the glowing Gate. The Keeper was a darker huddle in the center.

"Go down the road." His voice was fainter than the distance explained. "Just follow the road toward the lights on the horizon."

Ki swung her eyes away from the Keeper and Gate again. It had not seemed so bright from the city side. She focused her eyes on the black ground, letting them readjust to the darkness. Her own small lantern seemed dim after the Gate. It was as she was looking down to let her eyes clear that she saw the tracks of a single horse, its hoofprints cut in the moss and all but obscured by the heavy marks of her team. Ki moved back to the front of her team and walked slowly down the road. No sign was on the road itself, but here and there were marks that cut right through the moss to the road's black surface. The horse was heavy with a rider, and the rider had been in a hurry. Well, at least he had shown that much sense. She was glad he had gotten clear of the city before waiting for her. The farther they were from the Gates, the less likely that Rousters would bother them. She felt relief that he was healthy enough to ride, and annoyance that she had been so worried.

She clucked to her team and they came on again behind her. If she had not had Vandien to fret over, it would have been a pleasant stroll down a silent road by night. The soft moss that cushioned the road was kind to her feet. The cool breeze stroked her face. She swung her lantern beside her, flinging light ahead to stretch over the hoofmarks she followed.

Ki paused. After a moment of hesitation, she snuffed her lantern. She had been right. Away from the suffocating walls of the city and its dark old buildings, the night had become a friendlier place. There was enough light to see by, though the sky had become overcast. Enough to drive by? She shrugged and halted the team to clamber up onto the box. She took up the reins and slapped them on the wide grey backs.

The road ran straight and true before them, slicing through the forest as cleanly as a knife. The moss that coated the road seemed tipped with silver, making it a long ribbon that ran away from Ki, dwindling to a thread in the distance. Gone were the familiar jerks and jounces of potholes and gullied roadbeds. The wagon moved on in near silence, smooth as a ship cutting through water.

The forest cupped her in its hands. Friendly night trees leaned over her road in a near arch. Luminous white blossoms decked them, filling the dark with a sweetly elusive scent. At intervals the forest drew back from the road, to give Ki a view of a pasture, with a small cottage at the back of it, or just a patch of wild meadow. Some pastures seemed to be tilled and bearing crops. No lights showed in the cottages.

Twice Ki halted and checked the road, to find the hoofprints still leading her on. Each time some small discomfort nibbled at the back of her mind, but the glow of the Cinmeth warmed it away. If she took a deep breath of the night air, she could taste its spiciness still. For a moment she idly wished she'd had the foresight to bring some along. But then she contented herself with the cool night air. Reassurance grew in her slowly. If Vandien had ridden this far, he was most likely not injured at all. Perhaps they had only shaken him up; or perhaps his glib tongue had slid him past trouble. If that was his case, as seemed more and more likely to her, then he had gone ahead to find a good stopping place for the wagon. She'd come upon him at any moment.

Or, and she frowned in amused tolerance, he had trusted to

his message to bring her after him, and had ridden ahead. He did that often enough when the ponderous movement of her slow-rolling wagon became more than his short patience could bear. It was not unusual for him to be gone a day or a week when the need for solitary exploring hit him. Ki did not resent it. She would welcome a rest from his sharp tongue and restless ways.

She let herself slip into a waking dream. The wagon rolled on through the night. Ki floated through a dream on a sweet wind tinged with flower breath and Cinmeth. The wide pastures that spread in sudden clearings in the forest shone dark green. The sky behind a cover of clouds shone like opal through smoke along the horizon.

Ki lost all track of time. Could the glow ahead be dawn? No, it didn't feel like dawn. There was no hushed expectancy, no last calls of night birds. There was only the peace of the settled night. But there was a definite glow along the far horizon. The glow was gentle and even, speckled here and there with points of blue and green and red. Ki rubbed at her eyes, wondering if the specks were only fatigue. They remained above the hilltops, steady and unmoving. She was distracted from them by the diminishing thunder of some small hooved beasts.

She pulled herself up straight on the wagon seat and shook the reins slightly. But in a moment she was slumping again. The harmony of the night drew her in and comforted her. It was like slipping into a sleep when freshly bathed and between soft warm blankets. She could not resist it. "I drank too much," she chided herself, but found no regrets now. Her worries over Vandien settled like chickens gone to roost. The peace of the clean open country settled over her aching body and soul. The night soaked into her. Ancient anguished memories within her lay down, and the sweetness of those times came to her instead of the bitterness. Pieces of herself she had thought long dead turned over in their sleep and murmured promises to reawaken someday. Her thoughts touched Vandien gently, and she suddenly felt pain that she spoke to him so seldom of what she so often felt. In a haze of sentimentality, she promised to change all that. "From now on," she promised him solemnly, "I shall match you drink for drink. I see now why you do it."

Far ahead she made out the twisting silver of a rivulet that crossed the road. There was the dark shape of a bridge, wrought with a skill that surpassed any Ki had ever seen, and the wonder of it did not diminish as she drew near, but increased. It arched extravagantly to cross the small water, far beyond need of its span, and ornate parapets graced it. Ki could imagine that some being had spent its entire life to achieve that bridge, to express in solidity the joy it had felt in the land and the water.

She had already decided to stop by the bridge for the rest of the night, but she crossed it for the sheer pleasure of feeling how well the wagon took it. On the far side of the bridge, she guided her team off the silvery road and onto the dark soft turf. Even in the dark, her fingers seemed to fly over the buckles of the harness, accomplishing with ease what was usually the last trial of the day. Sigmund walked about with dignity, whiffling at the new grass. Sigurd dropped ponderously to his knees and rolled with all the abandon of a colt.

Ki smiled at his foolishness and resisted the temptation to join him. Instead she seated herself next to the wagon on the cushiony turf and leaned back against the wheel. Within her she felt no need for a fire, or the warmth of her sleeping skins. She ran her hands gently over the ground at her side. Short soft-leaved plants were thick on it, and replete with round plump berries. She plucked one and held it up against the undark sky. It was black, but might have been purple or blue in the light of day. She garnered a handful of them from the grass beside her and filled her mouth with the fruit. They were sweet and juicy, and as warm as if the afternoon sun had just left them.

She could not recall a time when she had been so immensely comfortable with so little effort. She rose and crossed to the edge of the stream. Crouching on the mossy bank, she leaned her face down to the water, to draw up long sweet draughts of it. It did not lose its silvery appearance, even when viewed from only inches away. It was cold and heavy; she felt it slide down her throat and spread through her as if it were alive. She lifted her face and watched a few drops fall from her chin to the moving surface of the water.

She sat back on her haunches, and then stretched out on her back, a pleasant little chill running over her. She felt her heart thump more slowly. The waters of the stream rippled through her, spreading through her limbs a delicious chilliness. The liquid flowed through her, heavy, silvery, dense as mercury. Ki had never been so aware of her own body, so alert to the flow of her blood in her veins. She gazed about at the beauty of the night. It filled her with a longing to stay here, by the bridge and the silvery water.

"Vandien?" she asked him softly. "Why would you pass up such a stopping place? I don't want to get up and chase you down the road tonight. I want to rest here. And I think I will, my friend. You say I never have impulses. Well, here is my third one today. As you so often bid me, I will act on it." Ki settled back on the grassy sward.

"She went through." The Keeper's voice was dark as midnight.

Yoleth nodded from the shadows. "It was the one bait she would never refuse. You have done well. Your master will be as pleased with you as I am. Now the Gate may be closed, for we are done with it. After, that is, you have given me the small token agreed upon."

The Keeper slowly swung his oddly shaped head. "Not yet. She may be through the Gate, but she is not the Limbreth's yet. You will have your reward when they receive her. Besides, the Gate is not yours nor mine to close. The Limbreth can open it, and I can hold it so. But the Gate must close itself, slowly as a healing wound."

Yoleth shook her cowled head angrily. "You made no mention of this when our bargain was made! Does the Limbreth know that she is through the Gate? Go to him and tell him!"

Again the Keeper shook his sightless head. "I may not leave my post, not until the Gate begins to close. Until then I guard it. But you would send me on a fool's errand. None can pass the Gate without the Limbreth knowing. To the Limbreth she will be drawn. When she arrives, the Limbreth will keep any bargain you have made."

"I don't like this!" Yoleth drew herself up. "Your master should know that as well. The Limbreth spoke of no such delays."

"Would you have the teamster back? I can call her." The Keeper made his offer blandly.

"No. No. The Windsingers keep their end of a bargain,

however the Limbreth may quibble over his. They can have her, and we will wait for our token. For the sake of the ancient friendship between our races, to be renewed with this offering.'' Yoleth drew herself up. Her dark blue robes swirled around her ankles, whipped up by a breeze that eddied the dust at her feet. She nodded to the Keeper, the awesome contents of her cowl bobbing slightly above her forehead. The Keeper was unimpressed. Yoleth turned from the Gate and was gone into the night, the dust, and the wind.

Three

"Come, lover. It's full dark and the moon's over the Herald's Tower. That's all I promised your friend."

Vandien felt hands upon him. He was rolled onto his back. He blinked up stupidly at the woman that leaned over him, trying to pull him into a sitting position. He didn't remember her. He didn't remember any of this. He scrubbed at his strangely tingling face with sleepy hands. And did remember. He swung his feet to the floor and sat up so suddenly that the woman overbalanced and sat down hard. He glared at her wide-eyed look.

"What's going on?" His tongue felt as fuzzy and dirty as the blankets he sat on. The woman licked her full lips and tried a smile on him. Vandien stood, caught himself as he tottered, and then found balance. One leg was still numb. He gripped that thigh and massaged it; it roused back to life with tingling pain. His whole hip on that side was tender, except for a dead spot right in the center. He touched it gingerly; dried blood cracked under his fingerprints.

"It's just a tiny jab!" The woman dropped her smile and raised her hands as she fell back before him, not attempting to defend herself but only to ward off as much of the beating as possible. "Your friend said you could appreciate a good joke. It's a common enough one. Don't waste your time on me! The wedding will still be waiting for you, it's not all that late. If you hurry, that is."

"You don't make one damn bit of sense," Vandien growled.

She began to whimper. "Well, you know. The other appren-

tice, Jori, he paid me to do it. Said you'd done the same thing
to a friend not three moons ago. Just a little jab with a dose of
numbweed, and the bridegroom's a little late for a wedding. It
was just a joke!'' she cried out before his murderous look.

''On the wrong man. Do I look like an apprentice, or a
bridegroom?''

She quailed and accused together. ''Well, you're wearing
the hawk, and you've got the scar. Oh, this is always my luck,
it is! Look, don't be angry! If you haven't got a wedding night
to go to, stay here, and I'll make you think you've had one.
Only don't hit me and break up my things! Please!'' Tears
welled, exposing the child, and Vandien was disarmed.

''That's all right,'' he assured her, backing away. ''It was
just a mistake. Don't do anything so damn foolish again.
Didn't you wonder what kind of a man would set you up to
bear the brunt of another's anger?''

''He gave me three times what I asked,'' she said defensively, and Vandien saw it was useless.

''I'm going,'' he replied, quite unnecessarily. He limped
from the room, his leg still bending strangely whenever he put
weight on it.

The darkened stairs were a challenge he nearly didn't meet.
At the bottom he stopped to catch his breath and get his bear-
ings. His head was as hazy as a drunkard's. He would find his
way back to the market, and then to the tavern. Ki was going to
be annoyed at waiting so long for him; until he told his story.
Then she would be amused. Neither appealed.

A horse snorted in the darkness. Vandien froze, letting his
eyes adjust. His horse. Still saddled, and tied to a bush outside
this seedy building.

He tried to make sense of it. Someone had made a very
thorough mistake in identifying him. Not likely. Ki had set it
up as a prank, complete with hawk necklace. It was more
likely that Ki would hire an assassin. So. Your head is fuzzy
and you won't find any answers here in the dark. Get you to a
tavern.

He mounted with difficulty. He had to grab the knee of his
bad leg to get it properly placed. Once he was up, it was better
than walking. Ki had chosen this animal for him. It was taller
than one he would have picked, and uglier. But she had assured him that once she was finished with it, he would be able

to trade it for whatever he wished. He had been skeptical. But now that she had wormed it, and her oil and herb mixture was improving its coat, it was a decent-looking mount. He was just lucky it hadn't been stolen while it was tied there. That was another thing Ki would never have done: she would never have left a valuable animal and saddle standing in the dark. No, it wasn't Ki.

Her wagon wasn't under the sign of the Contented Duck, and she wasn't inside. Cursing the strange turn of his luck, Vandien limped to a table and sat down to think. He ordered Alys to clear the thick taste from his mouth, and sat rubbing at his tingling leg. The dead spot in the center of his hip still bothered him. He could not resist tapping a finger against it. Nothing. His finger could feel the outline of the small wound, but his hip didn't know it. He wondered how long before that would pass.

A dark and sullen boy brought Vandien his Alys. Vandien held up the coin to pay him, but did not release his grip on it. The boy glowered at him.

"I need to ask you a question. I'm looking for a woman, a little shorter than I am, green eyes. . . ."

"I know a man named Sidrathio; he can get you any kind of woman you fancy, short ones, tall ones, ones that . . ."

"No." Vandien broke the boy's litany. "I am looking for a particular woman; I think she was here earlier. Green eyes, brown hair worn loose, a yellow blouse . . ."

"The tavern has been very busy. I could have seen her and not noticed."

Vandien's hand went to his coin purse and the boy's eyes darted after it. Vandien set the money for the Alys on the table, and a second small coin atop it. "Yellow blouse and a blue skirt and boots."

The coins vanished. "Sidrathio's women will dress any way to please you, and know skills that . . ."

"Go!" Vandien waved him off in disgust. "I wonder," he mused softly to himself, "if the age of a city has anything to do with how much rot runs through it. Or do I look so salacious and deprived. . . ?" Even as he spoke, Vandien realized he was still rubbing his leg under the table. He broke off with a woeful laugh.

Despite the serving boy's claim, the tavern was not busy. It

was past the hour for casual drinking. Only determined drink-
ers and local sots filled the chairs. Vandien raised his glass for
more Alys and wondered which group he belonged with. He
forced his muzzy brain to think. If Ki had not been here, or if
she had gone, it all came to the same thing. Either she had left
without him in a fit of pique at his tardiness, or she had been
rousted out of town. Where would she go? If rousted, probably
to whatever Gate was closest; if she were allowed to choose.
His mind balked away from the thought of her in trouble. If she
had chosen her own direction, which way would she go? Perhaps to the southwest, with its rumors of spices and rare woods
to haul? For a moment Vandien's fancy galloped down strange
roads in pursuit of her, through foreign landscapes and cities of
strange folk and customs. Then he reined it in, and with a sigh
he knew she would go back north, to her regular routes, where
she knew the quirks of the roads and merchants were eager to
hire her. So he had best ride out the North Gate tonight. Unless
she had been rousted and forced out on another road; unless she
were in danger even now.

Vandien growled softly in frustration. His serving boy stared
at him speculatively. Vandien traded him a glare. If Ki had
been rousted from here, then surely someone had seen or heard
of it. Again his eyes roved the tables. None of the patrons
looked likely to volunteer information. The innmaster himself
was a leering brute of aggressive hairiness. The other serving
boy . . . perhaps. He had been polishing the same spot of table
for a full five minutes, with his eyes more on the door than on
his work. He was a slight and pale youth, his thin shoulders
bowed forward in a permanent cower. Vandien flipped up a
small coin and let it fall ringing on his tabletop. The boy didn't
turn to the sound of it. So strange a behavior was this for a
serving boy that Vandien wondered if he were deaf. Hastily he
tossed down the rest of his Alys and held up the glass.

"Lad?" he called.

The boy flinched and turned at the same instant. He came to
Vandien's table as reluctantly as a kicked dog. Vandien liked
Jojorum less and less with each passing moment.

"I'm looking for a friend," Vandien began gently. The
boy's eyes went wide, his pupils filling them with blackness.
"If you haven't seen her, tell me so. I won't be angry. She is
slender, a bit shorter than myself, green eyes and brown hair,
wearing a yellow blouse."

Already the boy was shaking his head in a terrified manner, so that his fine pale hair stood out around his face like a halo. His eyes whipped back to the door, but his danger came from another direction.

"Wretch! Don't shake your head, fill his glass! He didn't come here to look at it empty, and I don't feed you to deny the customers. About your work, or do I take a fist to you?"

The boy's whole body jerked in apprehension, his face crumpling into tears even as the promised blow fell. There was a solid smack of flesh against flesh, and a loud grunt of surprise from the innmaster. Vandien's capable fingers tightened on his soft white wrist until the flesh stood out between them in red bulges.

"Child beatings always detract from the pleasures of drinking. Do not you agree?" His tone was conversational, but Vandien's fingers continued to tighten until the innmaster made a sound, half grunt, half gasp, of agreement. The boy was white, sagging against the table, his shock at being defended almost as stunning as a blow.

Vandien rose without releasing the innmaster's wrist. The man still stood half a head taller than Vandien, but Vandien was road hard and whiplash limber. For the space of three breaths the innmaster's eyes met his. Then they dropped before his black stare, to dart about the table legs.

"The little snake has always been trouble to me. Don't let his sweet looks deceive you. I give him a bed, clothes to his back; he repays me with lies and trouble."

Vandien picked up his empty glass. He held it before the innmaster's nose. "Innmaster, my glass is empty. See to its refilling. And bring a glass of red wine for my friend."

The Innmaster wanted to snarl at the boy, but he was stopped by the coins in Vandien's free hand. Vandien kicked out a free chair and nodded the boy into it. Seating himself again, he dropped his landlord's wrist as if it were a piece of fresh offal. For a merest blink the man stood still, rubbing at his smarting flesh and eyeing Vandien. But Vandien smiled back at him affably. It was late at night; none of his regular patrons were willing or sober enough to aid him. To summon the city guard at this hour would require a bigger bribe than the innmaster was willing to pay. He turned and strode back to his kitchen, trying not to hurry. Moments later, the other serving boy appeared at the table, filling Vandien's glass and bringing a goblet of red wine as well. He picked up Vandien's coins and then stepped well away from the table.

"Begging your pardon," he said softly. His lips trembled, but he glanced at the kitchen door and went on. "My master bids me to tell you this. If you want the boy, he has to be paid for, same as anything else in this tavern."

Vandien gave him a level stare, and a wolf's smile. "Actually, it's your master I lust for. Tell him I bid him to come to my table, so I can pay him what he's worth."

The boy nodded stiffly, and scurried away. Vandien turned his eyes to his white-faced companion. The lad was on the edge of his chair, nearly slipping away.

"Sit down," Vandien told him. "And drink that down. It may give you some color. Now. Before we were interrupted, we were talking. I was telling you I was looking for a friend."

Again the boy's eyes went wide, and Vandien saw his error. "No. Nothing like that. There is a woman I travel with, a Romni woman I was to meet here. But she seems to have left without me. She has green eyes and brown hair. . . ."

The child put his head down on his arms and began to sob softly. Vandien looked at him, sighed, and swallowed half his Alys. "Well, we can talk about my friend later, perhaps. Don't be upset, now. Listen. Have you ever heard the story of the woman who walked to the moon by following its shining path across a lake?" The boy did not stir. His sobs were only slightly less. Vandien drew his story-string out of his pouch. "I'll show it to you. See, here is the moon. . . ." The string looped and settled on his fingers, forming his people's sign for moon. Vandien began telling his story softly to himself.

Four stories passed. The boy's head was still pillowed on his arms, but he looked about, and Vandien had talked half the wine into him. He seemed calmer. Vandien began another story, but his voice dragged. He kept losing his place in it. His story-string tangled on his fingers. He picked at the knot, trying to remember what story he had been telling. He could no longer taste the Alys he quaffed. That numbweed was potent stuff indeed. It mattered little now if his hip were numb or not. He wouldn't have felt a dozen small jabs. He continued to work at the knot.

His forehead bumped the table. He jerked himself upright and forced his sandy eyes open. The boy regarded him gravely from across the table. "Why do you keep doing that?" he ventured to ask.

"It's either too much to drink or not enough sleep," Vandien told him fuzzily. He couldn't tell if the boy heard his reply or not. His grey eyes had strayed back to the door. "Now it's my turn to ask," Vandien ventured. "Who is supposed to come in that door soon?"

"My mother." The boy's voice went flat and dull. His eyes were beyond pain as he turned them to Vandien. "That's what she promised me. The blue woman said that if I told her to go through the Gate, my mother would be able to come in and find me. So I did. She was looking for you, and I sent her through the Gate. I'm sorry."

"What?"

The story came slowly, in bits and tatters. Vandien felt his jaws tighten. He forced himself to nod and tried to keep his fears from the boy. The boy's description made the blue woman a Windsinger. Ki had been sent through a gate on a ruse. Into what? Rousters? Windsinger's magic? Or simple death in the dark?

"Tell me again about the Gate," Vandien urged. "Why didn't you just run home to your mother?"

"The Keeper wouldn't let me. And my mother couldn't get through the Gate either. I tried once. I crept away from here once and ran down to the Limbreth Gate. My mother saw me and ran to meet me. But we couldn't get through. We couldn't even get into the Gate. Then the terrible light came, and my mother told me to run away, back to shelter."

Vandien straightened himself, alarm horns blaring in his mind. This was no nightly ritual of waiting for his mother, nor a question of Rousters keeping his mother out of the city. His sleepiness drained away; a touch of sobriety rebuked him.

"My mother even offered to trade herself for me. She told the Keeper that she would come in the Gate, if he would let me go out. To keep the balance. But the Keeper wouldn't let her. He was afraid folk on this side would believe my mother's words. They pay no heed to one such as I."

"What could she tell us that would so upset the Keeper?"

The child leaned forward to whisper the great secret. "The Jewels of the Limbreth are not for this world. Only for ours.

One of your kind cannot seize the Jewels and bring them back here as a treasure. For your kind, the Jewels seize.''

"My kind seize the Jewels?" Vandien was wishing desperately that his head was not so fumed with Alys and the drug dart. Into what had Ki been sent?

"No! No, the Jewels seize them," the boy said, as if reciting a well-known story. "They have no moderation. They do not bask in the peace and revelation of the Jewels. The Limbreth smiles upon them, and the Jewels seize them. But it is not an unpleasant thing for them. They are then inspired to do some great work. It may be wrought in metal or worked in stone. It may be the making of songs of far places the Limbreth has never seen. Their work is a joy to the Limbreth. But those who touch the Jewels of the Limbreth never return to this side of the Gate.''

Vandien shook his head as if clearing his ears of water. He picked up the empty Alys goblet, and then slammed it back to the table. His mind was fuzzed enough. He had listened, and now he had best act.

A sudden gust of cool night air flowed into the tavern. Vandien turned stinging eyes gratefully, seeking the source of the welcome draft. The door was open, and a woman was framed in it as she held the slats to one side. Her eyes glowed pale grey, and her green garment clung to her like fog on a morning hillside.

"Mother!" The boy collapsed under the table and scuttled past Vandien's tall boots. He immersed himself in his mother's long skirts.

Vandien pushed free of the table, tossing down a few coins for payment. If she were here, then Ki had gone through. His heart began to hammer, and his head to spin when he stood too rapidly. When he regained himself, the woman and boy were gone. He limped to the doorway and stood there, steadying himself on its splintery framework. The streets were dark and empty. His quick ears caught the sound of a light and hurried tread.

"Wait, woman!" he called into the night. "I must speak to you!" The patter of feet paused, then resumed more rapidly. Vandien cursed to himself. He stumbled slightly over the doorstep and then went after them.

The darkness closed over him like a cupped hand. The thick

dust of the street cloaked the sound of their fleeing footfalls. Vandien hurried after them, swinging one leg stiffly. Once he slipped in fresh slops, windmilling his arms for balance. He trotted on, his own thudding boots obscuring the sounds he tried to follow. A crossroads opened before him and he halted. A fool's errand. He would get lost in the city and never find this peculiar Limbreth Gate. The thing to do was return to the tavern, get his horse, and make a swift round of the walls. But then he heard the boy's voice, lifted querulously. Someone sternly shushed him. Vandien turned softly toward the sounds.

This was a poorer section of Jojorum, the mud brick houses built on the crumbled foundations of older, nobler buildings. The smaller dwellings were ready to tumble down; the narrow alleys between them were clogged with debris. Vandien's fogged brain cleared as his wariness reasserted itself. This would be a fine place for an ambush. There was a whisper of fabric and Vandien spun to it.

"He's only the man from the tavern, Mother." Mother and son emerged from the shadow they crouched in.

Vandien's shoulders sank and he let out a short breath as his arms unclenched. "That's right," he said softly. "It's only the man from the tavern."

The woman had a low voice like wind over a meadow. "My son tells me you were kind to him, sir. It seems it was the first kindness he was freely given since he so foolishly left my cottage. I did not mean to leave you unthanked. But my time is fleeing. I must return to the Gate before your light comes."

Vandien took the boy's hand. "Then we have the same errand. I, too, must pass that Gate tonight. As I do not know the way, would you guide me there? And I would ask, rudely perhaps, how a child as young as this comes to be working alone in a tavern such as that."

The pale gown of the mother was a blur before Vandien as he followed her down the narrow street. "Chess is a willful boy. He is not one to stay at home around my feet as I do the chores and work the land. Always he is off by the stream, or up in the trees on the hillside, or loitering by the Limbreth's road. I did not worry when he was late for our meal. I saved up the scolding I had for him. But the time for second meal came, and he did not come. I went seeking him. A neighbor told me he had seen Chess speaking to a Gate Keeper. The Keepers are deceitful, honorless ones. I knew no good could one wish my Chess. I hastened to the new Gate. But even before I got to the Gate, I saw a stranger coming up the road, attired as one from this world. I knew she could not come in unless one had gone out. 'Where are you going?' I asked her. She gave me a cold look and no reply as she rode past on her black beast. Then I knew she came seeking to steal away the Jewels of the Limbreth. I hurried to the Gate. But the time was past, and the Gate led to hot deadly light. Too late to pass now, even if there had been one willing to change places with me. The Keeper vowed he had never seen my child. I knew he lied. He stood safe within his Gate and lied to me.

"I have haunted the Gate and waited. Once Chess came, but we could not pass. So I had to wait. Until now, when a woman drove animals and a cart through the Gate and the Keeper let me through to balance her. Our chance of returning to our side is slight. But I have regained my Chess. Whatever we face, we face now together."

"She went on without me," Vandien muttered dully. His abused mind could not absorb the full import of her words. "What has she been lured into?"

"She seemed not at all like others who have come through," the woman commiserated. "Yet I fear the Jewels will seize her nonetheless. It's a pity. She seemed to have her heart in this world. Yet she went off down the road that leads to one end without a backward glance, a fool like the rest. Still, I shall not speak ill of one who let me through to my Chess."

"I will," grumbled Vandien. "She chooses her companions recklessly, and takes foolish advice. She makes more haste than sense."

The darkened streets were deceptive in their turnings. Vandien was not sure if it were darkness or Alys that made the way so tricky for him. The game leg did not help. The mother and son preceded him, her pale garments and hair floating before him in the blackness. They seemed to find the way clear and familiar, stepping past the potholes that Vandien stumbled in, and turning at crossroads down streets that led only to darkness.

Vandien followed them like a led beast. Once he found Ki, he'd fumble his way back to the tavern and his horse. For now he had to get through the Gate and catch her before she went too far. The moon grew paler in the sky.

They turned an abrupt corner, Vandien stumbling hastily after them. He stepped on the hem of her garment, for she had halted before him. He pulled himself up and looked past her. The Limbreth Gate glowed before them.

It struck Vandien as no more than a rectangular hole in the city walls. It was difficult for him to make out the country beyond it, and yet the Gate itself was strangely clear to his eyes. It was as if the darkness itself had been pressed back to make a space for this red Gate. No bars or portcullis hampered the way. Only an old gatekeeper in grey robes. Vandien put a gentle hand on the woman's shoulder to urge her forward. Even intoxicated, he felt sure he could handle the old wretch. But under his hand her muscles were tight as a hunting cat's.

"So you have returned, have you?" the Keeper charged her. "What will you do? Haunt me from that side now? By now you know I am beyond your reach. How can two of you ever expect to enter? No two will ever wish to leave, and the Limbreth has told me to let the Gate close. Folly. You should have returned to your farm, woman, and mourned the child as dead."

Vandien tightened his grip on her clenched shoulder muscles. With a courtliness that was only partially the Alys, he stepped past and in front of them, placing them in the shelter of his body.

"Why do you seek to bar these two from returning to their home?" His tone was of reasonable curiosity. His fingers did not even venture to the worn hilt of his belt knife. There was nothing in his stance to suggest a threat, but every muscle in the set of his face promised it. It was a disparity that Vandien cultivated. He smiled hard, letting his scar pull his left eye into a sinister squint.

But the Keeper was not daunted. Instead he seemed to be staring past Vandien, considering the skyline. He smiled blindly and nodded toward it in a superior way. After a moment, Vandien's eyes unwillingly followed his gaze. There was nothing to be seen. Only that the moon was a little paler in a sky that was venturing toward dawn.

"What is it?" the woman behind him whispered in awe.

"Nothing!" snorted Vandien. "It's an old trick, supposed to unnerve us by implying he has comrades behind us. Pay no attention."

He glanced back at the Gate Keeper. The Gate was harder to

see in the growing light. Its red glow had paled and faded to
match the stones of the wall. Vandien heard the boy whispering to his mother.

"The world is going away. It does that here, Mother. A
great heat and whiteness descends. If you remain out in it, as
once I did, you are blinded and burned. We must seek shelter
from it now. It may be hard to believe, but it becomes much
worse than this. This is only the beginning, what they call
'dawn.'"

"Tavern man! Where can we go?" Vandien turned to that
piteous plea. Chess had hidden his face in his mother's gown,
and the woman had thrown her arm across her eyes. They
wilted like daffodils in a drought.

"You must let them through!" Vandien cried, understanding only vaguely what was happening. But the Gate, that had
been before them a moment ago now eluded him, first winking
wide, then showing only as a narrow rift in the wall. It hid in
the growing light. He glimpsed the Keeper's toothless grin. As
Vandien sprang forward angrily to seize the mocking creature,
his outstretched hands met a forgiving resistance, as if he
pressed against the air bladder in a fish. He pushed against it,
ignoring a stinging tingle like nettles. So far would his hands
go, and no farther. The Keeper's laughter did not reach their
ears, but Vandien had a glimpse of his mirth as he battled with
the evasive Gate.

Behind him he heard cries as the first rays of sunlight
touched the city. At the same time, his fist scraped the old
stone of the city walls. He pulled back his hands and stared at
the coarse stone of the solid wall before him. Gate and Keeper
were gone like mist in the sunlight. He spent a few futile
seconds pushing against this and that stone of the wall, seeking
some hidden catch or loose stone. The carved figures smiled
down at him condescendingly. He pressed his hands against
the wall, weaving his hand from side to side like a blind thing.
The Gate would glimmer for an instant, and be gone before he
could see it. Vandien cursed, clawing mindlessly at the stone.
Then he felt a fumbling at his cloak.

The woman had sunk to her knees, her face huddled across
her crossed arms. Chess had crept across to him, to tug at him
piteously. He crouched, whimpering wordlessly before Vandien. The morning sun colored his hair between blond and

grey. It fell forward over his bowed shoulders, baring a slender neck as brown as wild honey. Vandien looked at the solid wall and shook his head in bewilderment. His brain rattled sharply inside his skull; the first stabs of an Alys-inspired headache jabbed him.

He eased himself down to untangle Chess from his cloak. Any sudden movement or violent activity would trigger a truly memorable headache. He knew he should turn his efforts to finding Ki. But he couldn't just leave these two here. "We'll go to the next Gate and circle around," he promised them.

As he unhooked each of Chess's small hands, they fell unresisting to the dusty street. He continued to whimper as if he wished to cling to Vandien but found the effort beyond his strength. His high-pitched keening and the deeper sobs of his mother pierced Vandien's brain like arrows. "What has happened to the Gate? Will they open it again?" he asked them gently. There was only the rising and falling of the boy's wailing as a reply. Vandien felt needles at the back of his eyeballs. "Chess, stop that, please. I can't help you if you won't talk to me."

More keening. Vandien reached for the thin shoulders, repressed just in time a violent urge to shake the child into silence. He looked down in pain and consternation at the small head bowed before him. His eyes widened and his own throbbing head was forgotten.

Small watery pink blisters were rising on the back of his exposed neck, popping up even as Vandien watched. His belly tightened and he started to back away from whatever unsuspected disease this was. Where the hair parted on the boy's skull, more blisters were popping up in a neat row like seedlings after a rain. Chess's eyes were screwed tight shut in pain as he raised his face to Vandien. The skin of his small brown face was pure still, but as soon as the morning sunlight touched it, the blisters began to swell.

"The light! The hot light!" Vandien looked at the mother struggling to rise. "How can it be endured? We shall die here!"

She lifted her once proud head and staggered a few steps closer to Vandien. Her eyes were squinted to slits. He saw the blisters rise on her nose and high cheeks as she groped toward him. She fell to her knees, her hands seeking blindly before her. The green of her airy garments began to brown and crumple in the morning light like leaves seared in a desert wind. Pink blisters popped on her exposed hands and arms.

He did not understand why, but he comprehended the need. With a sudden movement that brought demons to dance in his skull, he whipped the cloak from his own back and floated it down over the woman. It covered most of her, and as soon as she sensed its protection she drew her arms and legs neath its shelter. "Chess!" Her agonized moan came from beneath the garment.

The child at his feet whimpered in reply but didn't move. The brown ragged garment from the inn covered most of his body. He had the sense to crouch with his arms and legs drawn up beneath him and his face averted from the sky. The cloak would not cover both of them. Vandien was tugging off his shirt when he heard the scuff of a footstep behind him.

He twirled, wincing at the pain this cost him. A portly man, the worse for his night's revelry, regarded the group with a carefully uncurious eye. As Vandien rounded on him, he became even more disinterested; his careful walk proclaimed that the woman huddled under the cloak and the child that whimpered and scrabbled at Vandien were invisible. A true city dweller, he gave them only an oblique glance that never reached Vandien's eyes.

Vandien knew the courtesy of the city forbade him to look at the stranger or express any need, but his splitting headache and the peril of the young boy before him banished politeness. He dragged himself free of Chess, to clutch at the man's sleeve. "I need your cloak, man! The child is burning up!"

The man opened his bloodshot eyes a trifle wider. He belched, and pulled his arm free of Vandien's frantic grip, even though the tug nearly cost him his balance. He staggered a few steps sideways, drew himself up gravely, and shot Vandien with a haughty and disdainful look. But as he shrugged his cloak back even about himself, his eyes took in the blisters on the child's exposed arms. With a speed surprising in one so large, he ripped the cloak from his back and dashed it down into the street.

"My thanks for your mercies." Vandien stooped to take up the cloak.

The man's mouth opened wider than Vandien supposed it

could. His eyes were distended and suddenly sober. "Pox!" The word blared from his mouth like a blast from a hunting horn. "Pox bringers!" he screeched again.

Vandien flung the cloak about Chess as aroused citizens began to stir. A door slammed somewhere. Heads began to pop out of doors in the side street. A young woman stepped from a door near the corner. She halted at the sight of Vandien with the bundled child in his arms and the body huddled under a cloak beside him.

"Pox bringers!" She took up the cry lustily and the man made it a chorus. Stooping to the street, she grabbed a loose stone. Vandien flung up his arm to shield his face, but the fist-sized rock bounced instead off the woman. It brought a sharper cry from under the cloak. The streets were filling with people awakened by the cries of "Pox bringers!" Head and heart pounding, Vandien stooped beneath his burden of the child to seize the mother by her arm and drag her erect. The cloak fell away from her face as she came up; the stone throwing woman gave a shriek of horror. The blisters were rupturing. A watery flow shone on the woman's face and dripped from her chin. Screaming with pain, she dragged the cloak over her face again.

And then they were running, with stones skipping and bouncing past them. Vandien received a solid thunk from one that hit between his shoulders, but no more flew true after that. Mentally, he cursed the gods for his luck, and in the same breath thanked them that his pursuers were city bred and poor in skills of aiming and throwing.

Chess jolted in his arms as he tried to keep a hand free to guide the woman along. The cloak blinded her and the pain crippled her. Their run was little more than a hurried hobble; they had no chance of outdistancing their pursuers. His rapier was in the wagon with Ki; but he had no hand free to draw it in any case. He had only his belt knife against a fear-crazed crowd.

He glanced back to check their numbers. But though they shook fists and hurled stones, they had given up the chase. Perhaps they only wished to harry the pox bringers out of their area; perhaps they feared getting closer and becoming contaminated. Vandien realized now why the man had parted with the cloak. And he had thanked him.

"I cannot go much farther." Chess's mother panted from under the cloak. Vandien cast about for shelter. But no inn would take in two marked with oozing blisters, even if Vandien had possessed sufficient coin. It was early yet, and few folk were about; but they could not rely on that for long. As soon as they were seen, they would be stoned again. He steered them down an alley.

He half dragged them past the windowless backs of squat mud brick dwellings. He was staggering under his double burden, uncertain of what type of shelter he was seeking.

They scuttled across a street that interrupted the alley, and back into the shelter of the next alley. This one appeared a little more run down. Dry yellow grass grew against the backs of the houses, new green sprouts pushing up in their shade. Another street was crossed, and Vandien found himself in an alley where the weeds and trash choked the footpath. He gave the woman what trodden surface there was, himself hopping over the tufty grasses, bits of broken furnishings and crumbling piles of rain-melted mud bricks. Chess was silent and limp in his arms.

A wooden porch jutted into the alley, clinging haplessly to the crumbling wall of a fallen-in house. But as Vandien cautiously skirted it, he realized it was not a porch. Chicken feathers and dung crusted the floor. A splintered wooden door hung crookedly on sagging leather hinges. There were no windows nor any door into the abandoned house it clung to. The dung cracked dryly under his feet as he dragged his charges into this dubious shelter. As soon as he halted, the woman sank down onto the floor. Mercifully, she became silent. He deposited his motionless bundle beside her and turned back to the door. It looked as if few folk passed this way, but it would be a bad place to be cornered. It couldn't be helped. He dragged at the door and it scraped toward him, to wedge tight half a handspan from being closed. It could not be tugged farther. His stubborn efforts only wrenched the doorframe and threatened to pull it loose entirely. It would have to do. Vandien sat down wearily on the filthy floor. The dryness of dust, old dung and chicken feathers tortured his mouth and throat. He lowered his throbbing head into his hands, and wondered unhappily how yesterday's pleasures had gone so wrong. Dust motes danced in the narrow wedge of light that slipped through the door's crack. The random sounds of an awakening city came distantly to his ears.

He lifted a corner of the cloak that covered Chess. The boy's breath was light and shallow, his eyes still squeezed shut. His face was not as badly blistered as his arms. But when Vandien lifted the cloth higher for a better look, Chess cried out and scrabbled deeper within its cover. At the sound, his mother stirred and crept closer to him. "Hush, Chess. Hush." She raised a corner of her cloak to peer out, but dropped it as soon as the dim sunlight reached her. "Are we safe here?"

"For now. What manner of Humans are you, that cannot bear the light of day?"

"Day." There was wonder and dread in the muffled voice. "It is more fearsome than any legend warned. I thought it only a myth, a tale to warn adventuresome fools who could not satisfy themselves within our own world. Each Gate, they say, has a terror beyond it. Some murmur that the Limbreth should not open Gates. But who are we to question the Limbreth?"

Vandien's pounding head ground small sense from her words. She implied the Gate was more than a passage through the wall. Well, he had heard of stranger things, and seen a few of them proved true. He made a futile effort to cough without jarring his head.

"Will you feel safe here if I go to fetch water? And some food, perhaps, if I can manage it. Your blisters might be calmed by cool water. And I've a thirst that this chicken dust only torments."

"We will be fine here, man from the tavern. You are very kind not just to leave us. You seem different from the other folk of your world. Do you belong here?"

"I wonder?" he mused bitterly. "Vandien," he offered her then. "My name is Vandien. And I am not all that different. The folk who stoned us were terrified; they thought we had brought pestilence into the city. Fear breeds cruelty. And I can't let you think I am so unselfish. If I am to catch up with my partner, I need to pass through your Gate. Doing that may require your assistance. It is like no Gate I have ever encountered."

Beneath the cloak he saw the motion of a shaking head. "It cannot be passed. Not unless a like number of folk were willing to come out. The Keeper calls it the balance. But I will try to recall all I have ever heard of the Limbreth's Gates. It will not be much. I was content in my land, tending my own farm, and didn't listen to foolish tales of the Gates. Not until Chess was lured through one.''

"I will be back as swiftly as I can. Keep silent while I am gone.''

"Jace.''

"What was that?'' Vandien paused with his hand on the crooked door.

"My name is Jace, Vandien. We shall be silent until you return.''

The splintery door scraped earth and sod as he forced it open and then shoved it closed behind him. He dusted the dirt and feathers from his clothing and stretched. His eyes blinked and watered in the bright sunlight that stabbed his eyes. The day would be hot. Day, he mused to himself, and started back to the inn and his horse.

When he returned, the sun was reaching for noon. The alley was still empty. Vandien led his horse down to the chicken coop and tethered it to a scraggly bush. He slipped off the worn bridle so the horse could graze. The saddle he left in place. It was small burden to his horse. If the tethered animal did attract curious folk, Vandien intended to be ready to retreat with Chess and Jace.

He took the still cold and dripping waterskin from the saddle. The new pouch was empty now. But he had found two small loaves of bread at an early baker's stall and flat slabs of red salt fish at a fly-buzzing fishmonger's. These purchases he balanced awkwardly in the crook of one arm. He kicked lightly at the door of the chicken coop. There was no stirring within, no reply of any kind.

Vandien set down the waterskin to jerk the door open. Then there were sounds, gasps of pain and a quickly smothered cry from Chess as they dove under the cloak covers again. Vandien entered hastily, dragging the door shut behind him. But the small shaft of sunlight still squeezed in the door, and neither Jace nor Chess emerged.

"Just for one moment,'' Vandien promised as he took up the corner of Jace's cloak. She gasped in fear as he whisked it from her and stuffed it into the gap left by the faulty door. The portly man's cloak was a fine one, its weave heavy and costly. The bright fibers shut out the sun. Vandien had plunged himself into a hot and dusty darkness. He wiped sweat from his forehead with the back of his arm.

"That's so much better," breathed Jace. Vandien heard her sit up in the darkness beside him.

"I can't see a thing," he complained, but as his eyes adjusted, he found that was not strictly true. The pale green of Jace's gown almost glowed, and there was a sheen to her hair and eyes that even the darkness could not quench. Chess at last unrolled from the cloak and ventured out. Vandien distinguished his pale eyes and fine hair in the darkness. He proffered the waterskin to Jace and she seized it gratefully.

Chess drank first, taking in long gasping gulps. Vandien moved his tongue inside his mouth. He had drunk his fill of cold water at the public well when he filled the skin, but the fine dust and feathers sucked the moisture from his mouth. Sweat trickled down his back in the closeness and heat, but he said nothing. He watched Jace drink, more quietly than the unabashed boy, but with equal eagerness and relief. She then damped the corner of Vandien's cloak and soothed the blisters that had begun to break and run on Chess's face and arms.

"I never saw a people so affected by the sun," Vandien observed.

Jace damped the corner again and began easing the sores on her own face. "And I never saw a man so blind, and yet so easy in his movements. When the hot light came, neither you nor the folk of your city cried out or were burned."

"Where does that Gate go?" Vandien asked the question that gnawed him, thinking of Ki who had gone ahead.

"To my home," Jace replied with childish inadequacy. "I wish I could tell you more. There is only this. When the worlds are in alignment, the Limbreth can make a Gate. The Gate can be used as a passage, as long as the balance is kept. Through the Gate the Limbreth calls folk to bring it new ideas and joys. Out of the Gate pass those discontented in our own world. Those who come in walk the road that leads to the Limbreth, to be blessed by the Jewels."

"Your legends leave little hope for us to get through the Gate."

"Legends do not always tell all there is to know."

"The innmaster's cellar was cooler than this place." Chess

broke the conversation. "I liked being down there during the day. Usually he left me alone down there for all the hot light time. I wish I were there now."

"Hush!" Jace rebuked him. "At least we're together now. And we have a friend."

The silence that followed weighed awkwardly on Vandien. He fumbled in the darkness, found the loaves of bread and the dried fish. "I brought food," he announced in a falsely hearty voice. "I thought you might be hungry."

Chess immediately reached for a loaf and broke an end off. He was already nibbling at it while Jace took a piece of salt fish from Vandien's hand. He heard her sniff at it cautiously.

"What is this made from? I do not mean to seem ungrateful, but it smells spoiled."

"Let me see it." Vandien nibbled a piece off, swallowed it. Immediately his drink-soured stomach offered it back to him, but he managed to keep his throat closed. After a moment's struggle, "It's fine," he managed. "Smoked a little heavily for my taste, but good river fish. This spring's catch, or so the monger claimed."

"You ate a fish?" It was Chess's shocked voice coming in the brooding silence. "You ate a moving, alive thing?" There was horror in the voice, and hurt.

"Such is our custom." It sounded stiff, even to Vandien. But how could he have known that there were Humans who ate like Dene, refusing all food that didn't grow from a root? Vandien heard a scuffling as Chess crept to his mother's side.

"He's as horrid as the rest of them," he whispered hoarsely. "As bad as the innmaster . . . who sometimes did *not* leave me alone in the cellar."

To Vandien the stuffy little coop was suddenly as cold and dank as some evil well. "I . . ." he choked. "Among our people, it is *not* a custom . . . not acceptable to force . . . never a child . . ." He could find no words of defense and his own bile rose at what Chess had implied. Soured Alys and acid scorched the back of his throat. He wished he could be sick, alone somewhere. But he could not open the door and let light fall on them. He breathed deep, his lips and eyes tight. He heard Jace whispering words of comfort to her son, but for his own soul there was no comfort. He got up, paced two steps and flung himself into the far corner of the coop. "I am sorry."

Empty words. "There will always be those who prey on the defenseless. There will always be the occasional one who is twisted, a disgrace to the whole species."

"Not in my world." Jace's voice was firm now, but Vandien sensed the thinness of her control. "Not in my land. I hunger so for its peace now. This is horror and evil beyond my wildest fears. My Chess will have much to forget. If he can. I know I cannot."

Vandien sat silent in his corner, wondering where he had come in. He had been trying to find Ki. These two had shown up. He had helped them escape being stoned to death, found them shelter (such as it was), brought them water and food, and now he sat apart from them in their darkness, an object of disgust, a member of an immoral and unclean species.

And yet. . . . Damning his own empathy, Vandien followed the thought to its end. What betrayal Chess must be feeling, to find that his "rescuer" was a beast who dined on the flesh of living creatures? What antipathy must Jace feel toward him and those others of this world so debased as to turn on their own young? The giddy circles of his own thoughts dizzied him as he took both sides against himself. He wished he had either drunk less Alys last night, or had more to dose himself with now. He was suffocating in this darkness and heat. He was on the point of figuring a polite way to leave when he felt a touch on his forearm, light as moonlight. He turned his head.

Jace knelt beside him. Her pale hair fell like a veil of silk. Her head was bowed, and the rippling hair sheltered him from her lambent eyes. Her long fingers were warm where they rested on his arm, but somehow they lessened the discomfort of the coop.

"Chess sleeps."

"Oh." He sensed her overture of peace.

"Have you ever gathered mushrooms, man of the hot light? Do they have them on this side?"

"When I was a boy, I did. I remember little of it, other than the peace of the very early morning in a dim forest, carrying a basket on my arm, and being, for the moment, an equal with the other boys in my family's holdings. Why? Did you want me to bring mushrooms? The sun is too high for them now, and the weather of this summer too hot and dry."

"No," sighed Jace, and Vandien heard a trace of humor and

warmth. "I was trying to find a basis for an understanding. That is what came to me. In my place, we gather the orange milk cap."

"As we do here." Vandien felt an unreasonable pleasure at recognizing the name from his childhood. "If you scratch the gills, a milky liquid comes out. That is one way to know it."

"Yes. An excellent food. Do you also have here the fool's deceiver?"

Vandien shook his head in the darkness, but she picked up his response.

"Well, we do. It, too, will leak milky fluid from its gills if scratched. It, too, has the orange and green mottled cap, lacking only the orange circle inside the cut stem to be twin to the orange milk cap."

Vandien's headache returned. The mycology lesson seemed moot to him at this time, other than an interesting comparison of what kindred worlds might share. He shifted under her touch; the pressure of her fingers increased lightly.

"I'm not good at putting thoughts into words. Chess and I live alone on the farm. For two as close as we are, words and explanations are not often needed. We are with each other so much, that I can tell you the origin of every thought in his head. Or could, before." Jace sighed, and Vandien expected her to fall silent and withdraw from him. But she cleared her throat and went on. "In my world, we have the two kinds of mushrooms, so similar in form. One is a delight to the palate, a food to be found when others fail. The other is rarer, and likewise delights the tongue, until its slow poisons begin their insidious work. Yet I do not cease gathering the one for fear of the other. I just remember to be cautious. Nor do I think the less of the good mushroom, because the one that mimics it is harmful."

"Your words take you to your meaning by a very round-about path."

"You are right. I will say it simply. I will not judge you by the evil of your fellows. But neither shall I shed the caution I feel need of here. That I will keep as a cloak to protect me until I am safely home."

"That would be .wise." What manner of world had this grown woman come from, that she would phrase out to him so carefully a lesson known by the smallest street child? He thought of Ki in such a place and shook his head. How long before she realized she had been duped and came back to the Gate?

Jace's cool fingers were still resting on his arm. He covered them for a moment with his own callused hand. She snatched them away, as if even this friendly pat were a thing to be wary of. Vandien could not blame her.

"Rest now," he advised her. "At nightfall, I want to try this Limbreth Gate again. Do you think any have ever forced a way through? Without another coming to change places, I mean."

"I think not." Jace hesitated. "The Gate is hard to see when your world is white. And no one may pass unless the Keeper allows it. Then the way opens."

"I didn't see it closed last night."

"You felt it. Like a fine cloth barring the way, did you not?"

"More like the birth membrane on a calf."

"I have never seen the birth of a calf. But doubtless you are right."

"You've never seen a calf born?" Vandien was skeptical. "You let your cattle birth alone, in the fields?"

"We keep no cattle."

"You eat no meat."

"How can a sentient being put the carcass of another living creature into its mouth? It is an abhorrent idea. It defies all righteousness, all sensibilities."

Vandien ignored the insults. His mind went back to chew at the Gate. "If the Gate is impassable when closed, why have a Gate Keeper at all?"

"Perhaps he is only a cruel man that loves hurt."

"Perhaps, but not likely. Jace, any Gate that opens and closes may be forced. Or tricked. He let Ki's wagon pass. Did he look within it?"

"He would not need to. Nor need he search. One cannot evade his knowledge. Eyeless he knows."

"Bunk!" Vandien leaned back against the rickety wall, unmindful of the shower of dust it loosed down his back. "There's never yet been a city Gate that I couldn't pass when I found needful. This won't be the first."

His dark eyes narrowed, and then closed completely. Jace stared across at him, her luminous eyes puzzled and faintly revolted. "You have no respect for rules, for the rightness of things and the balances that must be kept." She made the observation as if noting that he smelled peculiar.

"None at all," Vandien admitted freely. "A balance is an invitation to a finger on the scales. Tonight I'll be that finger. If you'll ever let me sleep long enough for the plan to hatch."

He slumped a little deeper. Jace stared at him, and moving slowly as if she were caged with a beast, she lay her own body down between Vandien and her child.

FOUR

Ki was awakened by a whiffling near her ear. She pushed Sigmund's big muzzle away. Her eyes slid open and she lay still, staring up into a soft sky of deepest grey, one shade from black. Dawn's edge, perhaps? Yet she felt oddly rested and revived, as if she had slept for more than a night. Dreams tattered at the edges of her mind and she tried to knit them back together, but they unraveled before her waking eyes. There had been a castle at the foothills of the sky, trimmed in lace of light. She had known that Vandien was there, and not only him, but all her heart's desires. She had only to follow the road to the shimmering glow on the horizon. She tried to remember more detail, but could not. The dream eluded her conscious mind, seeping into deeper parts of her.

She sat up and stretched; hunger nibbled at her. Well, her last meal had been only berries and cold stream water. Before that, the Cinmeth at the tavern. That took it back to yesterday morning since she had really eaten. The only wonder was that she wasn't ravenous.

She mounted the seat of her wagon and slid open the cuddy door. The dark cuddy was full of the homey smell of Vandien, stored food and their possessions. She ducked past smoked sausages swinging from the rafters to climb down into her small home. She moved easily in this familiar clutter, drawing her belt knife and reaching for one of the dangling sausages.

No. Not meat. Ki set her knife down on the shelf and stared at the sausages. Why had she never truly seen them as dead flesh before? She was filled with disgust. She ran her hand down the front of her long skirt to erase the smell of the oily

59

meat. Some dried fruit and a wedge of cheese, she found, were all she wanted. Tea would be nice. She picked up her kettle. But the thought of building a fire by the side of that silvery stream, of roasting to death all the small plants and deep moss for the sake of a hot drink made her shrink. She thought, too, of bright orange flames stabbing the soft night, licking away the gentle darkness. She put the kettle back.

The silvery darkness outside the cuddy welcomed her back. It electrified her now as it had earlier soothed her. She nibbled alternate bites of fruit and cheese as she wandered around her wagon. The team was as restive as she. They came begging for a bit of the dried apple. Sigurd, rude as ever, nipped at Sigmund's face to try and claim more than his share. But she parceled it out evenly, with only a rebuking tap to Sigurd's velvety nose. She finished the last of the cheese and drank deeply from the stream.

An eagerness filled her. She wished Vandien had waited. Why had he gone on? The road ahead of her was silent and the sky just as grey as ever. The glimmer on the horizon was not dawn, but the same jewel-like glow she had noted the night before. A man on horseback could be far ahead by now. If she was going to catch up, she had to start now. At least there was no mistaking his route; she'd passed no crossroads. She wondered idly how the folk reached their cottages she had glimpsed earlier, and then shrugged it off. It wasn't her problem, though she could understand their reluctance to pound the sweet mosses into a hard-hearted road.

She whistled softly and the team came. They drifted into their places like great grey ghosts. As Ki reached and stretched for buckles and straps, she was unusually aware of their huge sleek bodies under her hands. Even the snappish Sigurd was unusually benign. The harnessing finished, Ki felt a surge of elation. She was on her way, to Vandien and whatever else awaited her. To those glorious beckoning gleams of mystery that fringed the horizon. Limbreth Jewels, her dream echoed softly. Ki smiled at the fancy. She was not sure what waited there, but it mattered less every moment. Vandien was only a part of it now.

Mounting her wagon she took up the reins. The team reached for the smooth and softly shining road before them. The wheels unrolled their journey upon it, the rumbling muted by the evenness of the surface. Ki felt the vibrations like music in her body. She leaned back against the door of the cuddy, the reins lax over her fingers. The hooves of the team neither rang nor clopped; there was only a thud, thud, thud of their easy pace. They passed gently swelling pasturelands, and then fields, obviously cultivated, but bearing no crop she recognized. The plants grew in even rows, bushes with a healthy bluish-green sheen to their leaves even in the darkness.

The placid grey twilight curled warm about her. It seemed to have no end; she no longer watched the sky for signs of dawn. The horses plodded steadily onward, seeming as dogged in their purpose as Ki herself. She lifted her eyes to the intermittent gleams at the base of the sky. A comparison occurred to her. She closed her eyes and pressed lightly on her eyelids until she saw lights against them. When she opened her eyes again, she was both pleased and justified to find that the lights and patterns matched exactly. They were hers, those far lights, intended for Ki. It was unthinkable that she not go to them.

Then Sigurd balked, very slightly, and Sigmund was forced to echo him. The team carefully detoured around a heap of objects in the road. One tall wheel bit gently into deep moss as the team skirted the obstacle. Ki glanced down to see what they passed, expecting to see a basket of produce tumbled from some farmer's cart, or the like. Her involuntary start of surprise tugged the reins and brought the team to a halt. Ki stared down, leaning over the side of her wagon. Habit made her set the wheel brake and wrap the reins about it before she dismounted. The shield of a Rouster stared up at her.

It was like a sprinkle of water on a dreamer's face. She found herself dragged unwillingly back to the edges of her normal world. Before her were all the accouterments for a warrior and horse. It was a riddle she didn't wish to consider. Yet here it was, too strange to be ignored.

Dubiously she lifted the padded chemise from the top of the pile. It unfolded from her hands and fell past her knees. A large warrior. Ki glanced about the empty night, expecting to hear someone cry out to leave the things alone. Nothing moved; no one spoke.

Beneath the creamy chemise was a light but finely wrought mail shirt, a sweet jingling ringing from it as it swung from her fingers. Here were heavily padded leather trousers and padded tubelike garments that Ki deduced to be arm protection. Spurred boots leaned against a saddle of black leather. The saddle's peculiar design made it look singularly uncomfortable. A bridle of matching design was looped over the cantle. Other strapped items and metal pieces beneath the saddle appeared to be light armor for a horse. The sword was a stiff and heavy affair, made in an unfamiliar style; its stained and worn scabbard of dark leather banded with metal testified to regular use. And the shield burned with the hated Rouster symbol.

Ki let the bridle slip from her fingers. She backed away from the pile. But before she put a hand on her wagon to hoist herself up, she stopped. It was offensive. Not just to herself. That pile of warrior's gear, so foreign to this peaceful world, was a blot upon the smooth roadway. Like a dead pig in a fountain.

She rubbed the back of her neck uneasily. It belonged to someone. It must. But there was no one in sight, and she knew no reason why a warrior would pause, strip self and horse, and then proceed again. She couldn't even conceive of a warrior being on this road.

She couldn't leave the armor there in a heap. Again she peered about, feeling strangely guilty. She gathered up the pieces and dumped them in the wagon's freight bed. Not stealing; tidying up, she told herself firmly. Let no filth from Jojorum pollute this countryside. She wiped the smell of them from her hands and mounted her wagon. The journey resumed, the team pulling effortlessly as the wagon began a very gradual downgrade. The road, so long straight, bent now into a gentle curve. Ki lifted her eyes to find the lights on the horizon still directly in front of her and beckoning. So it was all right. She was still on her way to the Limbreth lights, and Vandien would meet her there. She had only to follow the road, just as the Keeper had said.

But the road was blocked. A hulking shape stepped from the darkness to bar the way. Bigger by far than a Human, it loomed silent upon the road before her; but it was the wrongness of the creature that overwhelmed her. She couldn't identify it. She studied its dim outline as they approached, totally perplexed by it. A deep trepidation stirred in her.

First Sigurd and then Sigmund raised whinnies of greeting to it, and as the creature answered them it became only a horse. It didn't gallop off at their approach, but advanced, as if it found itself lonely and as strange to this place as to Ki's eyes.

As the wagon drew abreast of it, two thoughts occurred to her. This animal was hard to see, as dark as her own beasts in the soft perpetual twilight; it possessed no inner luminescence to mark it a creature of this place. The second thought was more unnerving. This was the horse whose tracks she had followed; and it wasn't Vandien's.

It was a heavy beast, a strayed plow animal perhaps. A closer inspection showed fine legs, built strongly but not as chunkily as her own horses'. Its back and sides bore none of the marks of a pulling harness, but only one long and narrow white scar against its black coat. A scar such as a glancing spear might leave. Here was the naked warhorse whose trappings were in the back of the wagon.

Not Vandien's. The thought was strangely hard to absorb. She glanced over at the horse that kept pace with her team as they went on. If it wasn't Vandien's, then . . . Ki struggled to focus her mind on what it meant. Then it meant Vandien had gone to Limbreth's on foot. She frowned to herself. That didn't seem right. There was something wrong with that solution, something that chafed her mind. Why would Vandien go ahead without her when he could have waited and ridden in comfort? When she caught up with him, she would ask him. But she would have to hurry now to catch him. She slapped the reins on the greys' backs and they obediently lengthened their strides. The black horse still kept pace.

It was a relief to go back to watching the black road uncurl before her. She found herself breathily humming an old Romni tune that blended pleasantly with the cadence of her team's hooves. The strange horse beside her seemed pleased with it as he flicked his ears to catch her voice; the darkness glinted off his rolling black eye.

The tune died in her throat. She listened to a peeping chorus that came from one side of the road. There the flat surface gave onto a boggy stretch of reedy grasses and white and yellow flowers. The standing water about the reeds was a shining black mirror for the sky. Beyond the bog was a rolling field, and at the back of it a hut. Ki watched a figure emerge from it, stooping to clear a low doorway and standing up straight and tall.

Man or woman, she couldn't tell at this distance, but it was Human. Or close enough. Shimmering hair with a yellowish sheen reminded her of the woman she had glimpsed at the Gate. The figure took a tool from the wall of the hut and started toward the fields. She was suddenly seized with a desire to speak to someone, and she reined in her team and leaped up to stand on the seat.

"Halloo!" she called, swinging her arms over her head. Her voice sounded thin and improbable in the dark; Ki felt suddenly foolish. Here she was, standing on her wagon and waving as if she were not the only visible object on the flat smooth road. Anyone who looked her way would have to see her. She sank back onto the seat, but kept a hand raised in greeting. The figure advanced toward the field and the wagon. Its long robe fell past its knees and caught the strange light of this place and cast it back with every step. But it didn't speak to her, or even turn eyes that way.

"Hey!" she called again. She meant it to be louder than her first call, but somehow it came out fainter, as if her own shyness conspired with the peace of the night to still her voice. The person had reached the first row of the hummocky lines of crops. The tool rose and fell, rose and fell, with a steady beat. She heard the scrape of it across the soil.

"Hey!" Ki called again, as loud as she could muster. Slowly it turned to look at her. The gleaming yellow hair fell back from its face and the light of eyes fastened on her. For a moment the glowing eyes regarded her as she waved, an idiot smile upon her face. Then they dropped back to the soil and the hoe began to rise and fall again.

Her raised hand fell to her lap. So eloquent a dismissal needed no words. She felt a sudden pang of rejection, such as she had felt as a child when village children had been called away from her, shooed off by parents that didn't want their youngsters around a wild Romni girl. This was the same, again; she was visible but not to be recognized. Tears stung in the inner corners of her eyes. She slapped the reins on the horses' backs. The riderless beast beside her again matched the team's pace. What was this nonsense? she scolded herself. Had she not outgrown this vulnerability before she was even a woman? This midnight road had stripped away her protections as easily as it exposed her to the long ago simple joy of being alive. Did the two always have to balance one another?

A sudden thirst assailed her. She slid open the cuddy door, reaching for the waterskin that always hung just within. Then she remembered the cool silver of the flowing water and could be satisfied with no other. She stirred the reins, hastening the team again. Bog water such as rimmed the road now she would not touch, no matter what her thirst. Bog water, the Romni said, was fever and flux water, waiting for the unwary. But where there was bog there must be soon found the streams and trickles that fed it. And such moving water, she thought, would be cold and silver and *helpful*. As wine was sometimes helpful, and the more potent and spicy Cinmeth. Ki, who did not often yield to cravings, felt a pang of unease. She silenced it quickly. So she desired the cool and clear water of a flowing stream. Did that make the impulse somehow dangerous?

"You spend your days denying yourself, fearful that if you take joy in something, you will not be able to endure life without it afterwards." Was not that how Vandien constantly chided her? But look at him, that marvel of self-indulgence. Money in pouch was money gone. How many times had she seen him empty his purse at some roadside fair and come away with no more to show for it than a sweet cake and the memories of tumblers and minstrels? She envied him that, in a way she could never admit to him. She wished she could forget all caution, her wary habits, for an afternoon and be a child that did not have to plan for the morrow. So generously he spent his life and coins, how amazed and absorbed he was by all things. The seasons of their companionship had taught her that his giving to others never diminished what he had for her. At times it seemed as if half her feeling for him was a joy that he existed as he did, moving so carelessly through the world, taking no precautions, but always landing on his feet. He balanced her. She liked the way his life wove through hers and affected it, led her into dares she would ordinarily refuse, even as she defended her stability against his foolhardiness.

She leaned back on the door of the cuddy, letting the cool breeze of movement cool her. Had there ever been a night for the thinking of such thoughts as these? Like some moonstruck girl child, she was savoring her affection for Vandien as if their friendship were new and miraculous. She found herself smiling over his hawk-dark eyes; the fine straight nose; his lips, so mobile when he laughed, so expressive when his soul was touched; his dark and unruly curls, always growing too fast; his soft moustache; and the smell of his body, that even in a sweat reminded her of crushed ferns and sweetgrass. Her heart swelled. Never had she so indulged her fondness for him, letting it sweep away from her thoughts all the inconveniences and dilemmas that their strange partnership heaped upon her. She unwrapped her cherished memories of him, gifting herself with moments when her eyes had caught him silhouetted by her fire, candlelit times in the cuddy when his face glowed damp with the heat of passion, the sensory memory of his shoulder muscles playing under her hands.

Ki swallowed, and sudden tears of longing flooded her eyes. Vandien should be here beside her, and she would finally speak aloud of how she felt. A single tear traced down her cheek. She wallowed in emotional indulgence. Something was happening to her; she didn't know what, but it was a relief to finally empty the secret closets of her heart. The soft night shared and sorted her thoughts, easing her away from worries. She felt healed; but so terribly thirsty.

The hooves of the greys rang hollowly on wood planking. With a sniff and a start, Ki came out of her reverie and realized she was crossing a narrow bridge. This one was as plain and functional as the first had been airy and fantastic. The warhorse wisely dropped back to let the wagon cross before he followed it. Ki looked down onto a larger stream than the first she had crossed; this one verged on being a young river.

On the far side of the bridge, Ki pulled her team and wagon up onto a stretch of rounded gravel. A silence flowed in after the halting of the wagon's creaking. Then in the silence she heard the water's whispering rush over the gravel riverbed. Shifting stones crunched under the black horse's hooves as he made his way down to the water. At the sight of him drinking, the team tossed their heads impatiently, tugging at the reins Ki still held. Reminded of her duties, Ki jumped down to free them of their harness. She slid the straps from their warm grey backs and the two headed for the river. She walked upriver to drink herself.

Here there were no reflections, no silvery shimmer of mirror water. Here the water rushed and boiled forth over the gravel, foaming and shining in the darkness. She knelt, and suddenly too eager to cup her hands and drink, plunged her face into the water and opened her mouth. The water rushed into it, too fast and powerful to be drunk. She opened her eyes but saw only a silvery bubbling as the swift water washed the weariness from her eyes and filled and refilled her mouth with coolness. Her hair had fallen past her face into the torrent; she felt the tug of it as it streamed with the water. She knelt for a long time, hearing the windy rush of the water only a finger's breadth from her ears, feeling it alive and moving. Then a building pressure in her chest reminded her that she needed air as well as this coolness to survive. Reluctantly she drew her face from the water, to take in a deep breath of the warm night.

Now she cupped her hands full of water and drank deep. Its taste was beyond description; Ki's cares dropped away from her. There was only the joyous heaviness of the water in her body, and then the desire for sleep and rest. It was almost too much trouble to fetch a blanket from the wagon, but she did. She spread it on the gravel by the wheel, doubling it to cushion her back from the rocks. The rush of the river seemed to create its own wind, rich with the smells of water and plants. She teetered on the edge of sleep.

Light footsteps crunched quickly over the gravel. Another time, Ki would have whipped over onto her belly and come to her feet to face the intruder. But another time she would have built her campfire by now, and had food cooking over it, would be indulging in tea, and carefully planning for tomorrow. She would have been fretting over Vandien.

The thoughts trailed off and faded from her mind. So another biped (by the sound of it) had elected to join her; was it not just as simple to assume they were harmless and friendly as to assume otherwise? Ki stretched fractionally, enough to enjoy the feeling without pulling any muscles. She did not speak; neither did her visitor. The steps came closer, quick short steps. Then there came a whicker, but not from her team. It was the black horse, coming eagerly over the gravel to greet the stranger. Ki made the effort of turning her head and opening her eyes.

The warhorse was nuzzling the stranger, rubbing his nose against her shoulder. Ki watched idly. The stranger spoke low to her horse in a tongue Ki did not know, and scratched his favorite spots behind his ears. She was naked and the soft fur of her hide matched the horse's. She was taller than Ki by a head, and twice as wide. Ki guessed at the blackness of her eyes in the moonlight. Her dark scalp hair was swept back from her forehead and over the top of her skull, barely reaching the nape of her stout neck. Ki tried not to stare at the strangeness of her features. The stranger's own eyes were bold on Ki's face, her ears pricked slightly forward. With this sign of focusing, the hair on her skull rose in a crest, with a soft rattling like a porcupine's quills. Ki thought she knew; almost.

"Brurjan," Ki murmured.

The stranger shook her head and replied in a Common that was only slightly and pleasantly accented. "Brurjan-Human. I'm a mule."

And that explained it. It made sense of the soft belly fur that rose almost to the tilted breasts, though the muscular legs were turned more like a cat's than a Human's, and sheathed in more of the soft dark fur, and her feet were small and round like a camel's. As she advanced toward Ki, she set them in the swift, short steps that were typical of the Brurjan. Soft fur cloaked her hips and loins, but her supple back and arms were only slightly more furry than Ki's own, and she was too small to be pure Brurjan, her nose too prominent, her fingers too long. Ki pitied her suddenly, for she could pass for neither Human nor Brurjan. Ki knew of only three other species that could comfortably sustain a sexually companionable relationship with Humans. Yet it was only the Human and Brurjan joining that occasionally resulted in a pregnancy. On the rare event of the child surviving the birth, it was, as she so aptly put it, a mule.

She stood over Ki, looking down on her. Ki returned her gaze calmly. This dark visitor was one with the night, as much at peace as Ki was. She showed no indication of the notorious Brurjan ill humor.

"You're a Human, and from the other side of the Gate."

Ki nodded. "My name is Ki."

"Hollyika."

She turned from Ki and headed to the river. Ki listened to her progress over the stones. The tiny Brurjan steps fell quickly, but covered little distance. Ki's keen ears even picked up the sound of her lapping water. She drank long, and Ki began to doze off. She heard the footsteps return and awoke just enough to see that Hollyika had taken the black horse's saddle blanket from the back of the wagon. She shook it out flat on the gravel beside Ki. They slept.

FIVE

JACE gasped and cowered as Vandien thrust the stubborn door open. But no white sunlight flooded in to scald her; instead there was the still warm air of evening, and beyond the door the shadowy alley and the night sky.

"Thank the gods it is passed," Jace breathed. She vented her relief in a long sigh. Easing forward, she leaned against the splintery doorframe and peered out. Chess crept forward to peek out under her arm. Their eyes stared up at the strange stars.

"Time to move." Vandien spoke with satisfaction. "We have a lot to do while this night lasts." Stooping, he gathered the waterskin and the cloak that Chess had lain on.

His horse was as he had left it. Wadding the cloak into a bundle, he tied it behind the saddle, and added the waterskin. He drew the bridle out of the tangle of dead branches he had hidden it in and began fitting it to the horse's head.

"He does not appear to enjoy that," Jace said reprovingly as the horse tongued away the bit Vandien tried to force between its jaws.

"This horse never appears to enjoy anything," Vandien replied dryly as the horse bared yellow teeth at him. "It's just his nature. He's a master of understatement."

"I do not find this a matter for levity." Vandien felt Jace's hand fall light on his arm. Her other hand clutched the bridle firmly. The horse snorted and shifted as Vandien tried gently to free it from her grip. Jace held on, her eyes frightened but determined. The horse took advantage and shied his head free of both of them. Vandien expelled his breath in a rush through his nose. He let the hand holding the bridle fall to his side.

"I take it you do not use beasts for carrying things in your wondrous land beyond the elusive Limbreth Gate."

"No. We don't." Jace shrugged off the annoyance in his voice, but Chess's eyes grew wider in the darkness. Vandien's shoulders slumped in defeat. Much as Jace was beginning to irritate him, he would do nothing to give the boy more fear. He plainly expected that Vandien would strike Jace for disagreeing with him. No guessing what he had seen in that tavern.

"Just how the hell do you live over there?" he demanded pettishly as he flung the bridle over the saddle. He stooped to unfasten the tether line.

"We are farmers, most of us. We tend the earth, and harvest what we invite to grow there. From the trees we receive fruit and nuts. From the plants we take the leaves and buds they can spare, and later the seed, fruits and tubers. From our ocean the waves yield to us the salty curling plants of the deep, and bring to us the floating bulbous kelp."

"You keep no cattle for milk and flesh? No flocks for eggs and meat?"

Jace turned from him in disgust. "You speak of leading a life founded on the death of innocent creatures."

"And I suppose the wolves and Harpies of your world graze upon grass or browse upon willow leaves?"

"Wolves rend flesh there, yes, but no sentient being does. When you say 'Harpies' I know not what you mean."

"Well, Ki will be grateful for that. A world without Harpies would suit her fine. Tell me, Jace, do you condemn the wolf that brings down the deer to feed?"

"A wolf is only a beast. Such is its nature."

"Then consider me a sentient wolf. Predator I am, Jace, and not ashamed of it. I am no less than the wolf in that I kill for food only."

"And no more," Jace replied succinctly. She turned her back on him in a whirl that sent her gown rippling about her. "Come, Chess. Let us seek the Gate and see if there is any way for us to enter."

"I had thought to rush it on horseback, while you distracted the Keeper." Vandien fell in behind them dispiritedly. "Won't you consider trying it?"

"It is not natural to bestride a living creature. Nor is it proper to try and upset the balance of two worlds. Entering and leaving the Gate must be done in harmony."

"Not even to get Chess back to his own side, and away from what he has suffered here?"

"Shall I reinforce the evils he has seen here, teach him that it is all right to behave incorrectly if one stands to gain by it? Vandien. I can imagine what you think of me. But our ways are not yours. Much as I long for my own world, and despise the Keeper who tricked my son, I cannot condone what you suggest. If Chess and I are patient, sometime we will regain our world. Somehow."

Vandien stopped and the horse halted behind him. After a few steps, Jace paused and looked back at him. Chess clung to her hand. Even in the moonlight, Vandien could see the despair in his wide grey eyes. The mother knew little of what she spoke of so serenely. Meanly Vandien thought that if only Chess were safely on his side of the Gate, he might be tempted to let Jace sample the life Chess had found here. But there was Chess.

Vandien slapped at his clothing. His purse was flat and empty. Most of his possessions were in Ki's wagon. There was nothing on him he could easily trade for coin. Except. . . . He flinched. From his neck he lifted the chain of fine silver links. The tiny black hawk winked at him regretfully as it swung. Ki would forgive him for parting with her gift sooner than he would forgive himself. Stepping forward, he put the hawk into Jace's hand, the horse's tether into Chess's.

"I will presume your folk do some trading, and you will know how to bargain these for coin—though I doubt you could ever get what that hawk is worth to me. Still, it will be enough, from hawk and tack, to get stable space for the horse and a cheap room at a decent inn. Be sure and ask for a cheap room; then you'll surely get one with no windows."

"You abandon us." Tears edged Chess's voice.

"No. I go to do for you what you won't do for yourselves. I'm going to force your Gate, and return with Ki. That will be two coming in and two going out . . ."

"It will take three exiting to restore the balance if we two enter," Jace began to correct him, but Vandien shook his head at her.

"I'll do what I can. Keep the boy safe. And come to the Gate at least once every night. I don't know when I'll return. Ki makes better time in that wagon of hers than you might suspect. Much as I hate to admit it, she may like your world.

But I'll talk her into coming back. There's little, wise or foolish, that I can't persuade her to try. When I bring her back, be
waiting for us."

"And if we run out of coins before you return?" Chess
asked practically.

"Sell the horse. Ask thirty silver bits, but don't take less
than twenty."

"We cannot sell a beast into slavery!" Jace objected.

Vandien looked at her despairingly, and turned to Chess.
"Perhaps I should be telling you to look after your mother. Do
what you can, Chess, and what you must, to stay alive. Remember to come to the Gate at least once every night. You
will?"

Chess nodded once, and looked up in awe at the beast he
led.

"Don't worry about him. He'll obey you perfectly, as long
as you don't ask him to work. He'll love your mother. They'll
get along well."

"You think me an ungrateful fool, Vandien, but—"

"The night slips away, and the Gate goes with it. If I fail,
we can talk all day about what we think of one another. If I
succeed, it won't matter. Be careful."

Vandien could take no more of it. He stepped up silently to
claim his cloak from the saddle.

"Take your waterskin also, and fill it before you go," Jace
urged him softly.

"Your land has no water?"

"It is not safe for you to drink. It will affect you. . . ."

"I've a brass-lined stomach, friend. Water in strange lands
has never given me the cramp or flux."

Jace shook her head impatiently. "It's not that. The water in
our land flows to us from the hills of the Limbreth. With it
flows wisdom and peace. You would lose your determination if
you drank it. You would begin to see the higher goals you
might set for yourself. No outworlder has ever passed the first
stream without drinking from it. Its call is said to be undenia-
ble. No one is ever unchanged by it. After the second bridge,
you never need fear the stranger. That is how our saying goes.
The peaceful waters of the Limbreth quench their fiery
thoughts and hot lusts. It brings to the surface whatever sweetness is hidden within. They become enlightened and seek the

Limbreth, to be cured forever of restless ways and dissatisfied hearts. Then they are given a task that is to them a joy, and is to the Limbreth a lasting monument.''

Jace's heart was in her words and her words were worshipful when she spoke of the Limbreth. Chess lifted his face to his mother and his shining eyes echoed the peace his mother spoke of. Not even Vandien was immune to it, despite his quick, hawklike nature. Peace. Contentment. How often had he scoffed at those goals—as Ki had, with her roaming Romni attitudes. What had that old priest called it? Sour fruit.

They had given the priest a ride on the wagon one spring when they overtook him, footsore and weary, upon the road. His wooden chest of healing herbs and potions Ki had lifted into the back of the wagon. Gently she chided such an old man for wandering so far from his kin that cared for him. But all he spoke of was the peace and contentment of poverty and service. There was a joy in binding up the running sores of a beggar, or mixing the potion that lifted delusion from the mad. Ki and Vandien had smiled at one another over his white head. "Peace," he had chided them then, "to you two will always be sour fruit. You long for what you cannot reach, and so you pretend to despise it. You run from the aches in your hearts and the scars on your bodies. I would that I had a potion to cure you, but you are beyond such skills as I have.''

His words had quelled all talk; Vandien had not been disappointed when he left them at the foot of a pass. He and Ki had kept the image of sour fruit, and made it a secret bandying word between them.

Vandien gave his head a shake, aware that they were both staring at him. He could see their secret fear; he would find peace in their world and forget all about them. "Do not be afraid," he told them lightly. "I'm immune to contentment." He made those words his farewell, lifting the waterskin from the saddle as he went. Let it be a sign to them and a talisman to himself. Once he glanced back. They both were looking after him, holding horse and hawk in their hands. He hoped to the gods they would have the sense to follow his instructions.

He replenished the waterbag at an ancient fountain. Looking down at the moon reflected in the water he promised her never again to drink Alys in a tavern, and to beware of needy strangers. A drop of water from the bag's spout fell back onto the surface; the moon winked at him, knowing well he lied.

He slung the bag over his shoulder. This early in the night there were still people abroad in the streets, though not many. Cheerful light issued from many a window or door left ajar in the summer heat. He passed an inn where the sounds of revelry beckoned him. But he went on, threading his way through the unfamiliar streets. Lacking a knowledge of the city's land-marks, Vandien relied on his sense of direction to take him back to the city walls. He soon found himself on a street he remembered. There was the house of the woman who had called him a pox bringer. The flung stones were still scattered in the dusty street. But of the Gate there was no sign.

The gods striding on the walls of the city looked past him in disdain; the heroes went on their heroic tasks. The wall was innocent of any Gate or opening or crack as far as he could see in the gloom. No one was about. Vandien went quickly to the wall, running his hands over it. No cracks, no loose stones to push. The wall was solid. Rapping his knuckles on its thick-ness did nothing but skin them. The wall emitted no sound, hollow or otherwise.

Stretching to his full if unimpressive height, Vandien ran the tips of his fingers over the wall again. He grimaced to himself in the darkness. It was no better maintained than any other city wall he had been up against, but its basic construction was sounder. The bas relief figures offered little purchase for climbing. But it was not impossible. He did wish he had kept the horse with him. Its back would have given him a place to start his climb from.

Stooping, he unfastened the buckles of his knee boots. Kick-ing free of them, he stood barefoot in the dust of the street. He flexed his toes and feet in the dust, and rubbed his hands down his shirt to free them of sweat. Once more he stretched and ran his hands over the wall. A kneeling goddess offered him a leg up. He gave a final glance about for guards; the last thing he wanted to do was flee barefoot down these streets with a pack of guards after him. The dusty streets were hot and empty. Vandien started up the wall.

From the goddess's knee he found a grip on her torch. Vandien cursed the unknown artist admiringly. Purchase places were few, and they were shallow, nail-bending, knuckle-scraping ones. His chest dragged against a hero's face, and he wished he had left behind the friction of his shirt. A third of the way up, one foot slipped from its spider-splayed grip and he nearly tumbled back. He heard his knuckles pop and felt a toenail tear. But he did not fall, and after a moment resumed his ascent.

The city had confidence in its walls, or no longer cared. At the top were no jagged potsherds or broken wooden spikes. There was only a wide flatness big enough for a man to lie on. Vandien panted for an instant, then wiped his sweat and the dust from his eyes. He looked over the wall.

Nothing. Well, nothing different from what Ki and he had seen approaching the North Gate. A flat expanse of yellowish plain interrupted by scraggly trees and thorns. Nearly out of eyeshot in the darkness were the humps of houses and low growing masses that indicated a farm kept alive by well and bucket irrigation. Only to the north of the city could one glimpse the far shining band of the river that brought the trade and kept the city alive. During late winter and early spring the river became a flowing plain of water, bringing new soil and fresh life to the farms by it. The long hot summers shrank the river into submission. Farmers that chose to live closer to the city walls rather than endure the annual flooding had to turn to buckets and wells to survive. It was a harsh land he looked down on; Vandien could not imagine calling it home.

He lay flat on the wall and hung his head over. The ground looked hard, the sand and dust blowing across it loosely. There were no marks of a wagon's passage, or any sign of regular passage of folk through a gate. Vandien was perplexed and still as he let the slight dry wind ruffle the damp curls on his forehead and cool the sweat on his back. Over the wall, he conceded, was not the same as through the Gate. If only he could find the damnable Gate.

The city streets were still empty. Vandien swung his legs over the side and scrabbled his toes for a hold. His raw toe bumped and he stifled an oath. As he inched his body backwards off the wall, he considered making a light and catlike leap down into the street below. Then he considered lying in the street until morning with a broken ankle, and eased his body a little farther down the wall. He went from having his ribcage hooked on the edge of the wall to hanging by his forearms, and then to a crumbly and wrist-straining hand grip. His feet skidded down the images, rubbing grit into his raw toe and scraping ankles and shins. But at last one toe got a precarious grip on an exposed lip of stone. He braced himself on it and let go with one hand, to ease another questing foot farther down.

But suddenly there was no wall at all beneath that foot: it swung forward into an empty but only semi-yielding space. Finger grips and toenails failed; Vandien fell, back first, in a gut-wrenching downward arc. He landed on a lumpy mass that collapsed under him. He lay still, trying not to be sick. The wind had been knocked from his lungs, he had struck his jaw against the wall and the front of his body was scraped raw from the slide. His joints crackled as he closed his hands. Whatever he had landed on was still poking him in the back. A red haze of pain obscured his vision as a nettlelike tingling singed his skin.

When he could, he began to move. But his muscles seemed to resist his will. He was able to straighten his legs, but slowly. He wondered what damage he had done to himself. The very air seemed to resist him, as if he were entangled in a giant but invisible spider's web. With a gasping heave he hauled his body to a sitting position. Dazedly he looked about.

He was sitting on the threshold of the Gate and the lumpy mass beneath him was the Keeper. Vandien's mind swung. There had been no Gate here when he climbed up, but he had fallen into the middle of it. It was impossible. The Keeper groaned and began to stir. Vandien tried to roll off him; he was lucky he hadn't broken his neck. Then, as his sense came back to him, he realized he was sitting in the opportunity he had sought.

A force was gently pushing him back to his side of the Gate; Vandien fought it. He leaned against his invisible bonds, striving to push them to their limits. The tautness of them against his face was like a smothering stretch of fine linen. The tingling grew worse, nigh unbearable. Vandien eased back a trifle and felt it follow him. He also sensed the easing of the force. The more he pushed, the more it resisted.

It felt like a membrane; so, he reasoned, why not treat it as he would a stubborn birth sack that was strangling a new calf? Vandien leaned forward against the force, stretching it to its full limit, and then drove his fingers stiff against it. His hands were small for a man's, no larger than Ki's, but the callused palms and scarred knuckles attested to their usefulness. He tried to get a grip on the barrier, tried to twist his fingers into it and rip it. But it was thicker, heavier, slicker and stronger than he expected. It eluded his grasp and his fingers could not rip it.

The Keeper was stirring now. Any second he would return to full wakefulness, and then Vandien would have two opponents to battle. If he was going to break through, he had to do it now. One outstretched hand kept the tension on the wall; the other reached for his belt knife.

He stabbed the blade into it. He had expected to plunge the point of his knife through it. But his initial stab bounced back into his hand. He tried again, pushing the blade in steadily, leaning on it with wrist-cracking force. The haft began to burn against his hand, but the blade sank in. He forced it to the full length of the blade, gasping at the effort it took. The barrier showed no sign of parting. Vandien tried cutting with a sawing motion. But his blade was smooth, lacking the serrated edge for this to be effective. The Keeper raised a hand to his head and groaned dully. Vandien sawed frantically.

His knife suddenly went through and his hand followed it. The sensation was the same as puncturing a large skin of cool water. His hand plunged into the coolness; he felt more of it ebbing and squirting out at him.

The Keeper rolled over with a sudden gasp, as if the spattering coolness had revived him as well. "Stop it!" he shrieked wildly. "You've broken the seal! You'll unbalance us!"

Unheeding, Vandien pushed his forearm into the other side while he worked the fingers of his other hand into the rupture as well. The Keeper clutched at his bare feet. Vandien kicked at him, using the gained impetus to force his second hand the rest of the way through. The thick nails of the Keeper's hands scraped down Vandien's legs as he kicked free of him. Like a diver preparing for very cold water, Vandien steeled himself with a deep breath of air. He butted his head against and then into the torn wall. The sensation was unpleasant in the extreme, like plunging his face into a congealing gut pile. He could neither expel nor take in breath. His vision wavered. He struggled, bucking his body, feeling the Keeper finally get a good clutch on one of his ankles.

Vandien was suffocating. What if this wall never let him
through? What if he became entrapped between, like a fish in
aspic? Panic was inspiration. The Keeper had captured one of
his feet. Vandien shot out the other one in a tremendous kick
that caught the Keeper in the chest, breaking his grip and
propelling Vandien forward.

Vandien felt the vague stirring of birth memories, and then
cold air on the top of his skull. He felt his shoulders constricted
by the wall. With a wiggling surge, he forced his way out into
the cool dark air. His chest was squeezed, and then he was
falling, hands braced to catch himself as he somersaulted
through the Gate. He tumbled into an awkward heap on a
smooth straight road.

From behind him came a muffled cursing. Vandien leaped to
his feet, ready to run. He had a dim vision of the Keeper trying
to hold closed the torn curtain between the worlds. His ragged
clothes were stirred as if by a powerful wind; his hood fell back
to reveal a band of white and wrinkled skin where Vandien had
expected eyes. The torn barrier fluttered with a snapping sound
backed by a rushing noise like a river heard through wind-
stirred trees. Vandien felt the motion as it rushed past his face
toward the tear. At least he need fear no pursuit; for a time the
Keeper would have his hands full. He slid his knife back into
its sheath and turned his steps down the long straight road.

Barefoot, and a night and a day behind Ki. The grey team
always made their pace look easy, but Vandien had more than
once tried to match them on foot. Even their most leisurely
pace had a way of devouring the road. He gave a sigh and
broke into a wolf trot. The road was smooth and cold beneath
his bare feet. He rested one hand on the waterskin that hung
from its shoulder strap to rest at his hip. He had never been so
poorly prepared for anything. But the night air was cool and
clean against his face; the arching trees garlanded with pale
flowers beckoned him on. An unbidden smile came to his face.
It was a fine night for running.

As his eyes adjusted to the darkness, he could make out the
signs of Ki's passage. The heavy wheels had left long grooves
cut in the tongues of moss that stretched here and there across
the road. Vandien trotted doggedly on, his eyes fixed as far
ahead down the road as he could peer. His body worked
smoothly and independently of his mind. His mind chewed at

the little information he had, letting the lovely night scenery slip by him unnoticed. Chess had indicated a Windsinger had set up this whole ruse. But why? They had lured Ki through this Gate, but she had met with no foul play as far as he could tell. The Windsingers had no reason to love Ki, but one at least, Rebeke, had reason to treat her with courtesy. As for Ki herself, she had never spoken of the Windsingers with anything but distrust. Her dislike of them was founded on her father's old hatred, which blamed them for the untimely death of Ki's mother. Ki had inherited that theory with no facts to back it up. Yet there had been a time when Rebeke would have fallen prey to the wizard Dresh, had Ki not intervened. It was all a most interesting tangle when viewed in the abstract. When considered while trotting down a black road with the aftermath of a hangover bouncing in one's skull, it was positively unsettling. But it was also as irresistible as prodding at a loose tooth.

His legs and feet had begun to ache dully, and he had been running in the moss beside the road for some way when the bridge came into view. He let his trot ease down to a walk, but the bridge demanded more. He stopped and gave it a full share of attention. He had no comparisons for it; rather it was like the first glimpse of a natural wonder. Like the mountain from his childhood that would always be The Mountain, or his first dimly remembered glimpse of the sea, this bridge would stay with him the rest of his days. It was the pure essence of Bridge, the perfect form that all such structures sought to attain but never did—till this one. He could spend a night looking at it, a week touching its graceful curves and still not have absorbed all the beauty of its lavish arch. If only he had the time.

But he did not. His bare feet throbbed, his shirt stuck to him and his trousers chafed him. Unstoppering the waterskin, he swung it up for a small mouthful. He let it wet his mouth and trickle slowly down his throat. One more small swallow and he regretfully put it away. Much as he would have liked to gulp the water, he could not run with a sloshing stomach, nor did he know how long the water would have to last him. He looked longingly at the stream that chuckled and slid beneath the elegant bridge. Its cool freshness changed the air. He rubbed the back of his sticky neck and looked about at the night that gave no clue as to the passage of time. The wagon was far ahead of him now. He had found no traces of a cold campfire, nor any signs left by the road Romni-fashion. If Ki had not stopped here, then he could ill afford to. But his throbbing feet decided him. Jace had told him not to drink the water; she had said nothing about bathing in it. He trotted heavily on toward the water, pulling his shirt over his head as he went.

The delightful chill of it eased his feet, making their hot throb an unpleasant memory. He lay full length in the shallowness, letting it flow past and over him. He had not known how much he ached until he felt the moving fingers of water soothing it away. Tipping his head back, he let it saturate his dark curls. When he shook his head briskly, he was amazed to find his headache completely gone. The water shattered from his hair in a silver spray. When he slowly rose from the water, it clung to his body in a silver sheen. The night air closed over him like a robe of silk as he moved lazily to the moss and soft grasses of the shore. He slowly rubbed his hands over his face and stubbly chin.

Abruptly he dropped his hands to stare at them. The flesh stood in white ridges on his fingers and palms. Had he really soaked that long? An inspection of his feet showed even their callused surfaces were soaked into tender wrinkles. He lay back on the moss, feeling foolish and relieved. Foolish to have lain so long, and relieved that he couldn't resume his run just yet, because his heels would crack and lame him. Besides, he needed rest. No telling how far he had come from the city. No lights showed behind him, and the glowing of the horizon was as distant as ever. Ki was probably camped somewhere by now anyway. She likely wasn't getting any farther ahead of him. He rolled over on to his belly to relax, and froze.

Just a simple thing. Just a set of wagon tracks that led off the road and then back onto it. Vandien rose hastily to snatch up his clothes. He bent over the tracks, squinting at them in the dimness. Ki had paused here. Here were the cuts of the team's great hooves. But the grass and small plants in them had already struggled upright again, save those broken outright. Vandien straightened to stare down the road. Ki had come through the Gate looking for him. She had stopped here, but made no fire, and had gone on. Something was wrong.

He lifted his eyes to the horizon and the pulse of lights thronging it. Jace had said they had a pull, a lure for the unwary. He looked at them and felt only a mild curiosity. A nameless urgency laid hold of him. He began to drag clothing on over his damp skin. He gave the bridge a last admiring look and took up his trot again. He would have to gamble that he would reach Ki before he lamed himself. Unwillingly he glanced again to the horizon. What in hell was a Limbreth anyway?

Six

"WOULD that you had taken your courage into both hands and come to me sooner." Rebeke's voice was gentler than her words, but Cerie still bent her cowled head before them. On the black stone floor of her own hall, Rebeke Windmistress was showing little formality or humility toward this High Council member who had come seeking her out. But for the darker blue of Cerie's robes, an observer would have thought Rebeke the Singer of rank chiding a negligent acolyte. Stranger still was that Cerie accepted this new role.

She spoke softly. "I thought long before I came. I thought it likely you were already aware of these events. I feared my coming would be a finger on the scales, overbalancing some carefully contrived gambit of your own. But at last I decided I dare not chance that you might be ignorant of all that had transpired. So I came. I did what I could to keep my coming a secret, but if the High Council wishes to know of it, they will. Well I know there are those among my acolytes who would gladly whisper any secret of mine, in exchange for a robe of darker blue."

"And that is what weakens us, or them, I should say. Political skills are rewarded more readily than true ability to sing the winds. What do they think we will come to, when their Council is full of voices that can sway a crowd but not stir a breeze?" Cerie quailed before Rebeke's glowering eyes.

Rebeke flung out her hands as if discarding the entire High Council and began to pace the bare hall, robes swirling about her ankles. There was little to impede her stride. The shining black floors were bare of rugs, as the walls were innocent of pictures or windows. A tall black stool for Rebeke, a scattering of coarse straw cushions for the lesser Singers of her hall; these were the scanty furnishings of the room. The very austerity of the setting gave an ominous importance to the blue-curtained alcove at the end of the hall. Cerie felt her eyes stealing to it, and drew them back to her feet.

"So Yoleth has dared to put Ki through the Limbreth Gate? That one has ever been wont to sing a breeze both warm and cold. What did she think? That I would never find out? That I would find out and pretend I hadn't? Or is she hoping to force a confrontation with me? Oh, I have no time for this! I should be bending my every effort to train my Singers, to make of them what the Windsingers of old were! Or is that Yoleth's aim? To hamper and distract me from that duty? Does she sense that her days of power dwindle with every Singer I shape?" Rebeke turned a sudden glint of eye on Cerie. "Do you know her purpose? Has she been so blatant to the High Council?"

Cerie shook her head mutely. Guilt filled her eyes as she raised them to Rebeke. "To the Council she has said nothing. She has breathed no word since that last meeting, except to Shiela."

"Then how do you know of it?"

Cerie gave a sigh of regret for lost innocence. "I overheard, in a way said to be impossible. You know I am entrusted with a speaking egg?"

Skin moved on Rebeke's face in a parody of eyebrow raising. "No. I did not. Go on."

"But you are familiar with the use of one, I am sure. I was seeking to reach Yoleth on an unrelated matter; on the production level of Dowl Valley. What happened should not have. I reached Yoleth, but she was speaking through an egg to Shiela. They were unaware of me. I listened."

Rebeke stared at Cerie, at her eyes cast down in shame. She breathed out slowly. "There is more you have not told me, isn't there?"

Cerie turned pleading eyes on her. "There was much I didn't understand. The eggs speak not with words, but with knowledge. I think I would have been happier knowing less."

"Go on."

"There were two things, besides that the Romni woman had been lured through a Gate. She went, yes, but a Keeper was there who held the balance. No sign was left of a Gate being used. But the man, Vandien, did what is believed impossible. He forced the Gate. It has created an imbalance, a rip between worlds. The Limbreth world bleeds into ours.''

"Fools!" hissed Rebeke, and Cerie knew she didn't mean the teamster and her friend. "Just as our strength begins to blossom again, they draw attention to us. A ruptured Gate is like a blazing signal fire. Do they think the Gatherers will ignore our tinkering? Do they not realize that the Gatherers would prize this as highly as we do?" With a few sweeping steps, Rebeke drew the blue curtain aside. Cerie gazed in wonder at the Wingsinger revealed.

The white flesh of the petrous body seemed to glow against the plain black back curtain. The sole complete fossil of the extinct race gazed out at her with eyes serene in their complete whiteness. Cerie let her eyes and thoughts feast upon the sight, let her body take new direction and inspiration from the Relic. Thus would she be when her transformation was completed: the multi-jointed limbs, the high domed skull with the ripples that cascaded down the spine, the smooth lipless mouth, the face immaculately cleansed of emotion. Like all children chosen by the Windsingers, she had imbibed the powdered bone and flesh of such creatures, had sought a metamorphosis into the form of the ancient race that had ruled the winds. But the most intricate changes could only be guided by knowledge of the original. For long had all complete Windsinger bodies been lost to them, until Rebeke had recovered this one—incurring no small debt to the Romni teamster Ki in doing so. Rebeke had used this image to shape her own transformation more swiftly, to give to her voice and wind songs more power than current Windsingers deemed possible. This power had brought her the enmity of the High Council.

"The Gatherers would take this from us, if they guessed we had it," Rebeke said in a low voice. "We would be powerless to stop them." Cerie stirred in her reverie, hearing the words but unable to draw her full attention away from the revealed body. Already she felt a new strength in her joints, the thinning of her Human lips as she stretched her jaw to a new alignment. "The Gatherers tolerate us, are even amused by our attempts to take power for ourselves in this little fishbowl world. But they would not tolerate too much success. They tolerate nothing that upsets their balances and checks. No race may gain ascendancy; does not the Moon rule it so? True religions are those that let the races live in harmony; does not the Moon rule it so? And whence comes our Common language, pronounceable by every sentient creature upon this world, lipped or beaked or snouted? From the Moon, of course. And to whom does the Moon belong?''

"To the Gatherers." Cerie whispered that most secret of Windsinger doctrines, stunned to hear Rebeke speak it aloud.

"The Gatherers." Rebeke snorted. "We are to live in peace, to harmonize, to remain pure in our separate species, in our balanced worlds, for their entertainment."

"Blasphemy!" cried Cerie. "They keep us in peace and harmony. They protect us and cherish us. They give us their just laws. . . .''

"Common sense." Rebeke refuted her. "They do all you say, of course. But they do it because it amuses them. We ourselves are but a pitiful mirror of their image. We bring the winds that spread the grain pollen, we shepherd the rain clouds away from the ripe harvest standing in the field, we bring the wet winds in the drought years. Why? Because we are the Windsingers, and it is given to us to bring the weather that will make the earth fruitful for the tillers of the fields and the keepers of the flocks. Because of our great wisdom and goodness and fondness, we watch over the little folk. And because without our percentages extracted from them, our halls would be dreary places indeed. Why wear coarse cotton when the wind moves more sweetly against blue silk?" Rebeke caressed the loose folds of her robe.

"What will you do?" whispered Cerie.

"Do?" Rebeke gave a short bark of laughter. "Nothing. Who can rebalance the worlds? It is too late to do anything. I will run away and live as a peasant in a little hut in the woods, with anemones under my window, and a wizard to warm my bed." Rebeke's blue and white eyes had gone fey and wild. Cerie shrank from her strange words. "That would be at least as useful as anything else I can do. Yoleth has unleashed it. All we can do is attempt to stand before a wind not of our singing. I shall do my best to be a guardian." Rebeke's hand swished closed the curtains of the alcove.

"I fear I have come a long way, in what some would say

was an act of treason, for very little good." Cerie put her lightly scaled hands to her face and rubbed at where her temples had been.

"No journey that ends in the finding of a friend is without good." Sanity and control had returned to Rebeke's voice. She came to Cerie and touched her cheek with a hand that asked forgiveness for her wild words. "For myself, I shall be glad to know that I do not stand before the blast of the Gatherers alone. That is a comfort to me."

"To me also. And there are others: Dorin and Kadra at least. The High Council guesses that you have our sympathies, and so they were elaborately careful to summon us late when you requested a Council hearing. They know what we feel; that while the Windsingers function best under a single authority, the High Council that exists now is not the only possible answer. Others might lean to us. Yoleth rules the hands of most of the Council, but she has no one's heart—unless, perhaps, Shiela's, if she has one."

"It is good to know of your support." Rebeke had calmed. She found her stool and perched on it to think. "I lied to you, a moment ago. It is easier to say, 'I will do nothing,' than to admit I do not know what I can do. But act I must. There are sources I can question to find out if there is a way to seal a Gate and hide this imbalancing of the worlds. Perhaps together we can forestall the storm of the Gatherers. Jojorum, you say? Yoleth would put her Gate in a pit of filth like that. I will go there, and gather knowledge of this Gate if nothing else."

"There is yet the second thing," Cerie began hesitantly.

"It cannot be worse, so tell me of it," Rebeke said with a shade of humor.

"Better or worse, it made no sense to me, but it was clearly acknowledged between Shiela and Yoleth. Yoleth, at least, insisted on it when they spoke, and Shiela accepted her thoughts as true. She referred to Ki as a renegade Windsinger."

Silence rose cold around them, drenching them. Rebeke spoke at last with an effort. "Those words make no sense together. And Ki is no Windsinger. You must have somehow taken separate thoughts out of context."

"Not three times," Cerie insisted, but quietly. "It was quite plain that this is the root of Yoleth's hatred for her. The Romni song was a blind. She speaks of Ki as a dangerous traitor."

"Impossible."

"As impossible as rupturing the Gates between the worlds, or listening on another speaking egg."

Rebeke's face rippled with conflicting emotions, anger the strongest. Then she smoothed it blank again. "I will think no more on that, nor speak of it, until I have gathered facts. There is one, I think, who will know what basis there is for Yoleth's words. One who can be persuaded to talk to me."

Cerie smiled at her. "I marvel at you. You make me feel I can safely lay it all in your lap, and go back to sing my winds. You have gone far beyond us. What is it like, Rebeke? To be as close as you are to being fully a Windsinger."

Rebeke chuckled in spite of herself. "Ask a candle what it feels like to be nearly a bonfire. We can never attain it, Cerie. The more I grow, the more I know that is true. Yet what we will become will be enough for us; indeed, it will be all we are capable of holding. There is so much they left us, when they left us the knowledge of how to change. They knew they were dying, Cerie, vanishing forever. The Windsingers left us a legacy that is both a gift and a responsibility. We have fallen from their standards; our physical faults are the least of it. You will learn things beyond my words to tell you. They left messages for us written on the winds themselves. Each breeze has a name, given by them, which it comes most swiftly to. It will be as if I had called you Windsinger all my life and only today came to know you as Cerie. They knew every breeze as an individual." Rebeke sighed, her own breath a small gust of wind. "We have lost so much along the way. Thrown knowledge aside because we were more concerned about what percentage of crops we could ask from a given region, and too busy arguing over whether to threaten or punish when the farmers rebelled. We learned how to count our coins, and forgot how to read the winds."

"Will we ever regain what we have lost?" Cerie asked in a small voice.

Rebeke smiled wearily. "We may. If Yoleth and Shiela let us survive that long. We may."

SEVEN

KI's eyes had reopened of their own volition. She lay staring up into the dark and finally realized she was awake. She rolled her head to one side to stare at her companion.

Hollyika slept peacefully on her side, slightly curled. The outlines of her features were shadowed by night and softened by a light overlay of downy fur. Ki examined her face with some curiosity. The dim but omnipresent light of this land divided her face into halves, one silvered and exposed, the other hidden by shadows. The exposed eye was as large as a horse's. A horizontal row of stubby lashes across the center of the eye marked the juncture of the two lids that hooded it. Her nose began, not between her eyes, but slightly lower than their inner corners. It was broader than a Human's nose, with the nostrils more clearly defined and useful. Even as she slept, they flared softly with each breath to bring her the olfactory news of the night air. Her short upper lip was split and rounded like a cat's. The mouth beneath it was extremely generous, the corners reaching nearly to her jaw hinges. Only the front portion of it was used for speaking. Ki estimated that if she opened her mouth to its widest capacity, she could easily engulf a rabbit's head. Ki gave an uneasy squirm as she recalled rumors that this was precisely how the Brurjans dispatched their meat.

Little hands were curled peacefully beneath the impressive jaw. For all Hollyika's height, her hands were no larger than Ki's. Her fingers were thicker, lightly furred on their backs with thick black nails that curved slightly over the tips. The plumpness of her fingers and their tininess in relation to the rest of her made her hands look soft and helpless. Ki would wager it was an illusion.

She looked again to her sleeping face, but Hollyika's eyelids had parted in the center, to reveal a horizontal slit of eye. She focused on Ki and opened her eyelids fully. Then she sat up slowly, stretching and rolling her muscled shoulders. When she yawned wide, Ki stared in helpless fascination at the double rows of pointed teeth within that impressive maw. Hollyika surged up to her feet in one effortless movement.

"It's time to go," she said softly. "I can feel that it's time to move on again. Can't you?"

Ki nodded. She did feel it, an urging to rise and once more seek those distant glimmers that beckoned so temptingly. Peace was waiting for her at the end of this road; the very thought made Ki hungry for it. Rising she tossed her blanket into the back of the wagon. Hollyika dropped hers in as well, but when Ki turned to lift the team's harness, Hollyika put a restraining hand on her arm. "How can you practice beast slavery in this place?" she asked accusingly.

Ki recoiled a little from her touch, but Hollyika remained as she was. She was not menacing or angry, Ki decided; only rebuking. "All my life I have driven a wagon. It is what I am, a Romni teamster."

Hollyika shook her head. "That is as foolish as if I said that I have always been a warrior and a rider of horses. That is only true of my life on the other side of the Gate. These lands opened my eyes. Odd to think that in the darkness I finally saw. I must war no more, nor put a beast to my tasks. Nor must I partake of meat."

"So you left your harness upon the road, and left your horse to stray where he would."

Hollyika nodded. For the first time Ki noted how her softly furred hide hung from her arms and paunched emptily upon her body. She had never heard of a Brurjan eating anything but meat, or grain cakes moistened with blood. She did not look as if she were adapting well to her new diet. She looked pathetic, or as close to pathetic as a Brurjan could look. "Why have you left your clothes behind as well?"

"Shall I wear leather, the hide of another creature ripped from its bleeding body? Besides, the cloaking of my body was a false modesty. I shall no longer hide what I am. On the other side of the Gate, my body was a stranger to me, for it is neither Brurjan nor Human, and clothing myself was a denial of myself as both. But with the help of the Limbreth, I have accepted myself, and so should you. Be rid of the disguises you wear; cast them aside as you cast aside the harnesses that enslaved those poor beasts. Can't you feel the truth of what I speak?''

Ki could not meet Hollyika's eyes; she shook her head slowly, feeling vaguely ashamed that she didn't wish to comply. Like cool water rising around her, she began to feel the righteousness of Hollyika's words flood through her body and mind. She *had* been wrong to bind animals to her will. She must stop. And it was also time to shed all clothing and weapons, to cast aside the outer shell she had accumulated in the stained world beyond the Gate. She was coming home now, to peace and fulfillment. Would she come as a dirty, willful child? Did she want the Limbreth to find her unworthy? Ki pulled her blouse over her head and shook her hair free down her back. She stepped out of her long road skirt, kicking her boots after it. She stretched, warm and glowing in the night's caress. Hollyika beamed on her.

"I have been here longer than you, so the river has taught me more. But don't be discouraged, for I will help you. I learned that from the river already; that we must help one another if we are to reach the goal. The stretch of road ahead of us is the final test of our worthiness.''

"But . . . I thought you were coming back. I did not pass you on the road.''

Hollyika shook her head. "The road leaves the river here. It goes a long dry way, and I carried no water with me. I walked and slept and walked again. But no water did I find, only a dried-up streambed. Without the waters of this world, I couldn't go on. I had to come back to the river. We must carry our own water if we are to go on. We can't do without it, for a dryness assails one that is more than the thirst of throat and tongue. It is a very shriveling of the spirit.''

"The water casks on the wagon are full," ventured Ki. "If we took the wagon and team . . .''

Hollyika's hand flew up in a forbidding gesture. "The water cask we can take, rolling it on before us.''

There was something wrong with that idea, a fatal silliness, if only Ki could pinpoint it. But the logical and rational parts of her mind had abdicated. Lacking other ideas, she followed Hollyika to the wagon. Ki began to unfasten the heavy straps and buckles that held the cask in place, and Hollyika stooped at her side, ready to assist in lowering the gurgling weight. Her nostrils flared wide and pink-rimmed in the darkness. She drew back from Ki and the wagon, her hands drooping in disgust. Ki glanced over at her in puzzlement. Then her lesser nose caught it, a cold stench like the reek of night mist off a poorly drained graveyard, or the noisome damp that rises at night from black-flowing city gutters. Hollyika spoke in a strangled voice. "It's the water cask. The water's gone stagnant, or was bad when you took it on."

Ki opened the tap a trifle. No more than a mugful escaped before she shut it, but the putrid smell of it as it stained the river gravel made Ki gag. She backed away from the wagon, flapping a hand in front of her face.

"We will have to dump the cask, scrub it clean with river sand and refill it," Hollyika said. Ki shook her head.

"Water that bad can't be scrubbed away. It soaks into the wood. The cask will only spoil whatever we put in it."

"Then what will we do?" Ki heard the soft rattle as her plume rose and fell in agitation.

"We carry water in something else. In a waterskin or a jug or something." Ki felt unreasonably pleased with herself for thinking of this. Not only would it be easier than rolling the cask along, it was . . . it was. . . . She had lost the end of her thought. No matter. Her thoughts had a way of floating away from her lately, of beginning in strange places and ending in the middle. But even so, she knew that the thoughts she managed to hang onto were better thoughts than she had ever had before. Her ideas were changing, becoming tuned and perfected to harmonize with the better world she traveled through, and Hollyika was experiencing the same purification.

Ki scrabbled about in the darkness of the cuddy, seeking for a container for water. The waterskin she usually kept on a hook by the cuddy door was gone, and she could not remember where. Most of her food stores were of the dried variety, kept in boxes and cloths and paper wrappings. The two crocks she kept were wide-mouthed awkward things, fine for balancing in a rattling wagon but too wide to carry comfortably.

She gazed again around the cuddy interior. If only her mind would focus. She let her eyes roam, hoping for inspiration. She glanced over the sleeping skins wrenched from living creatures, at the dried smoked carcasses she had once fed upon, at

the sheathed rapier for the shedding of blood, at Vandien's soft
leather shirt. . . .

Vandien. There was something about Vandien, something
she had to remember. She fumbled and found it. She was so
fond of him. He had taught her to follow her heart, and she
would ever cherish his memory because of that. Something
else?

Ki sprang forward with a cry. She had bought him a second
gift before she left Jojorum. She fished a jug of brandy from
under the pillows. She had hidden it for a surprise, for it was
not the usual cheap sour wine they kept to clear the road dust
from their throats at the end of a day. This was potent stuff, the
heady spirits of . . . somewhere. Ki found her memories about
the brandy fading. What had she been thinking, to put it under
the pillows? Ridiculous storage place. As Ki picked up the jug,
it gave a questioning gurgle. She tucked it firmly under her
arm.

Hollyika loomed over her, watching impassively as Ki carefully worked the stopper free of the narrow neck. Ki gave an
appreciative sniff. Hollyika's nostrils flared as she caught the
scent. The flames of righteousness dimmed in her eyes as she
licked her lips.

"It seems a shame to pour it out," Ki observed to her.

Hollyika seized the jug in her stubby fingers and raised it;
her brow wrinkled and her plumes clattered as she inhaled. She
started to hand the jug back to Ki. But then, as if doubting her
first judgment, she took a second cautious sniff, gave Ki a
quick look, and took a short nip from the jug. She blinked her
eyes slowly; Ki watched fascinated as her lower eyelids rose to
meet the falling upper lids over her large and shining eyes.

"It does seem a shame," Hollyika agreed with her after a
deep breath. "Yet we must have a vessel to carry the water in.
This one seems to be our only choice." She began to tip the
jug, but Ki caught her hand and righted it before any sloshed
out.

"Would you profane the grounds of this world by pouring
onto it the product of that world beyond the Gate? Even as I did
not leave your saddle and clothes upon the road on my way
here, lest these traces of our evil origins offend others, so too
we should not infect this pure earth with this drink."

Ki took the jug from Hollyika's clutch to tip a little of the brandy into her own mouth. She tasted the warm sunny day in some far orchard where the stuff had been born. A tiny warmth kindled in her belly, a memory of the sun on the trees. Ki felt oddly divided. The sun-warmth of the brandy in her throat and belly contrasted strangely with the cool but urgent desires of this night-wrapped land and its swiftly flowing waters. Ki took another mouthful, both to savor the moment of division inside her and to be scared by it. She closed her eyes, feeling the elements battle within her body, scarcely aware of Hollyika taking the jug from her hand.

When she opened her eyes a moment later, it was to see Hollyika lowering the jug from the delicately pursed lips of her impressive mouth. Ki took the jug back. She noticed how comfortable Hollyika looked, seated with her back against the yellow spokes of a wheel. Joining her, Ki tipped up the jug again, and then set it carefully in the gravel between them. Had drink ever been so stimulating in such a curious way? Ki knew she hadn't the great capacity for it that some of her Romni companions did, but she was accustomed to drinking with dignity and control. Whether the brandy was more potent than she knew, or because it battled with the river coolness inside her, Ki felt the world tilting around her, gently swinging in a manner at once delightful and alarming.

She felt Hollyika's hand on the jug and relinquished it to her. "I did not think that Brurjans drank, other than water, milk, and blood," she observed genially. "But then I thought them totally carnivorous as well. Goes to show you should never believe rumors about another species until you actually get to know one."

"True." Hollyika spoke after a longish interval.

"What's true?" Ki had lost the string of the conversation. She took up the jug that was leaning against her hip.

"True you shouldn't believe rumors. True Brurjans don't drink wine, or eat green stuff growing in the dirt. Don't lick our fur, either."

Ki was pleased with herself for drinking and listening at the same time. She gave the brandy just a few moments to slide all the way down her throat and curl up warm and cozy in her belly. It drove the caressing chill of the river water into her extremities, making her fingers and toes tingle with icy sparks. The sensation was well worth paying attention to. But don't forget manners. One must converse with one's guest. "Never heard that Brurjans licked their fur," Ki replied companionably.

Hollyika set the jug down on the gravel between them with a thunk. "They don't!" she said in a less than amiable tone. "Stupid rumor, probably started by a Kjeetan. Kjeetans. Now there's a species with disgusting habits. You know that whenever they shed a skin, they boil it up in a soup and *eat* it?"

Ki wrinkled her nose in distaste, and took a mouthful from the jug to chase such unpleasant thoughts from her palate. She frowned a bit, for the jug felt substantially lighter than it had a moment ago. She turned to watch Hollyika drink. She was a large being, and a mouthful to her was a mugful to Ki. But Ki did not begrudge it. There was plenty. The warmth of the brandy filled Ki's body, a small sun warming her from within. But all over her body was a layer of coolness, the coolness of this sunless land. She shivered delightedly in the contrast.

"But!" Ki suddenly said as a radical thought took over her mind. "But you are a Brurjan and you are drinking brandy! How about that, huh?"

Hollyika set the jug down carelessly. It tumbled onto its side, but was no longer full enough to spill. Ki set it meticulously upright anyway, pushing its base into the gravel to make it stand.

"Not a Brurjan!" Hollyika was now as mournful as she had previously been annoyed. "Part Human, you know. Mother always said it meant I could indulge in the vices of both species. So I did. But no more!" she suddenly promised the overcast skies. "No more! Hollyika eats meat no more. No more making a poor old horse do what I want him to do. I let him go. He can go roll on the grass or chase mares or just stand around and do nothing. I let him go. Even though I love him. Damn old horse. He's all I got, Ki, and I don't have him anymore. I let him go, you know. And I threw away my sword and my armor and my clothes and everything. I'm only going to eat green stuff and drink cold water from now on, until I find the peace of the Limbreth."

"Me, too," Ki murmured. Their hands met on the jug. Ki graciously let Hollyika drink first. She regretted it a moment later when she had to turn the jug completely up to collect the last swallow. She set the jug very carefully down and lay back on the gravel.

The coolness of river water danced and tingled over her entire skin, but the warmth of the sun was inside her; Ki did not shiver. Idly she raised both hands and brought the tips of her two index fingers together. On the third try she actually made them touch, but was disappointed when no cold spark of river energy leaped between them. She let her hands fall back to her side and expelled a long sigh. Hollyika was talking beside her, her voice so close to Ki's ear that Ki surmised she, too, must be lying flat on the gravel.

". . . Picked its shell off a little at a time. How it whistled, and its feelers rattled against its carapace. Yellow foam dripped from its mouth parts. I was sick for days after. But it talked. Oh, yes, it talked. I believed in them then. They said it was a clear choice and I would have to make it. I could either wring the truth of its battle plans out of it, thus harming one creature, or I could let hundreds of my own ride to certain death. It seemed such an easy choice then. This one T'cherian would die slowly, with every imaginable pain, or hundreds would be slaughtered. I took it as a number problem, Ki. Which is greater, one or a hundred? But at my hands, perhaps, that one T'cherian suffered more than one hundred Brurjan warriors would suffer by wounds inflicted in open battle. I never thought of that until I came to this place. But now I think of it, and it saddens me. Yet I know that the thinking of these thoughts is a necessary if painful part of my preparation. Peace will be mine when I reach that horizon we see glimmering. It is not unlike seeing a physician; before he can help you, he must prod every hurt, even the ones that have closed over and you think healed. This is what the Limbreth is doing to me. Prodding open the festering wounds on my spirit; not to be unkind, but to let them drain of their foulness. Have you not felt it so, Ki?"

Ki felt strangely lethargic and little else. But she was willing to talk and listen. "My sins are of a different kind, I fear. I have loved well, but without embraces or words. Tender feelings I have dissipated with a jest. I am chary of my feelings."

"Your crimes are a child's crimes," Hollyika declared with a snort. "I could wish I had so little to regret."

Her indulgent tone nettled Ki. A child's crimes, were they? Her competitive spirit stirred and she began to search for other, worse things to admit, things at least as bad as slowly picking a T'cherian to pieces. In her newly found penitential spirit, she dredged up old acts, ones scarcely regretted by her before, but suitable to air as crimes. "Two Harpies have I slain by my own hand," she intoned darkly. "And caused the death of their clutch of eggs. One Windsinger have I slain." She was neglecting to mention that the first deaths had been a matter of self-preservation, and the second caused more by ignorance than malice. Why spoil a shudderingly evil list of admissions with a set of extenuating circumstances?

But Hollyika was not to be outdone. "Death! You make of execution the greatest crime? Would I still had your innocence to bear before the Limbreth!! Death I have done a hundred times and more, in the heat of the battle or the stealth of back streets. Shall I save my greatest regret for deliberately ending a life probably started in the fever of mating rut, coincidental to release? I have lived all my life as a mule, Ki; to buy acceptance, I have performed the most base of deeds, ones that blacken my mind to recall. To prove myself a Human, I have betrayed Brurjan friends. To prove myself a Brurjan, I have feasted on the bodies of the slain, even when I did not know the reasons for the battle. To prove my affection for a Human beloved, I once plucked the sacred teeth from the still-warm jaws of dead Brurjan comrades, the teeth they needed to enter the Hall of Feasting Eternal. And when I found that Human later in the embraces of a slender and hairless Human female, I did not let past affections sway me. I alternated my slow attentions between the two. I taught each to hear the screams of the other as music, for while he screamed, she was spared my talents, and while she wept and begged and gibbered for mercy, his flesh could know no new torment."

"Why do you tell me this?" Ki asked in a low intense voice. She did not wish to hear these things from Hollyika. Neither the cool peacefulness of the twilight land nor the sun glow of the alcohol in her belly could completely numb her to such words. Ki wanted Hollyika to remain a chance met companion, a fellow pilgrim on the trek to the glowing horizon. She was going to peace and fulfillment, an end of her troubles. Why did Hollyika have to remind her so fully of the pains of the world she had left? All those deeds had been done on the other side of the Gate. She wanted them to be left there.

Hollyika did not speak again for a long time. Ki heard the rushing of the river, the shifting of the horses as they moved about cropping the dark grasses. From deep within Ki came a wish for sunrise, for the illumination of all dark things by a friendly light. Before Ki could follow the thought further, Hollyika spoke.

"I tell you so that I am honest; because I felt that if you did not know, you would like me. That would be a pleasant experience, but I would be deceiving you for the sake of it. In this land, I must make no deceptions lest I lose all. Had we met before, on the other side of the Gate, you would not have liked me, Ki. A month or so ago I would have ridden up on your wagon in the darkness to put a lance in your beasts, to smash your kettle on the campfire and set flame to the rest."

"A Rouster." Ki had long known it without admitting it to herself. Now a chill went over her, a cold as horribly unlike the delightful chill of the water as death is unlike the daydreaming.

"A Rouster," Hollyika confirmed, and the darkness went darker. " 'For a fee, merchant, I will keep this town free of Romni vermin. An honest man like you need not compete with wandering tinkers and tradesmen like these. For a fee, I will terrorize their children, cripple their teams, destroy their wagons and scatter their caravans. For a fee.' "

Childhood memories of terror in the dark stirred in Ki. They rustled about the back of her mind like lizards, but she refused to let them come to the front of her thoughts. Repressed long ago, the memories could only scuttle in the dark corners of her past. Hard hands had fallen on her in the dark, and she had screamed. . . . She felt a curious suspension of all feeling for Hollyika. She teetered on a balancing point in her mind. She could think about the Rousters and all they had meant to her in her past life, and as the lethargy of the brandy slipped away, she would hate Hollyika, perhaps to the point of a physical confrontation. Or she could go to the river, drink deep of its cooling and peaceful water, and be cured of hatred and memories. Never before had Ki sensed such a control over her emotions.

Hollyika rose with a grunt. Ki watched her silhouette sway slightly against the deep grey sky. She looked at the half-Brurjan profile from that delicate mental balance and found a striking beauty in the strangeness of her body. "Where are you going?" she found herself asking.

"For more water," Hollyika reluctantly replied. "I find I

crave it now as much as when I first returned to the riverbank.
And for the same reasons. The thirst of the soul. Is it not
ironic, Ki? Since I came through the Gate, I have finally begun
to see myself. This land has given me a true vision of myself as
I am. To make that vision bearable, I must drown it in the river
water. Drown it or myself. Perhaps that is one and the same
thing.''

Ki listened to the peculiar rhythm of her steps as she moved
over the gravel, and looked at the Limbreth lights. Hatred and
friendship teetered in her mind. Why hate? Because of what
Rousters did to the Romni. Why friendship? Because she had
come in peace out of the night, and shared Ki's pilgrimage.
Selfishness decided Ki. If she chose to hate, she would have to
pursue that course to its end. Its end was not in the promising
glow of the Jewels of the Limbreth, and their peace was what
she needed. She rose and followed Hollyika to the river's edge.
She took the empty jug with her.

Ki knelt over the water. A short way downstream she could
hear Hollyika gulping the river with an endless thirst. Ki put
her face close to the rushing surface. Stray droplets of water
flung up by the river in its flight misted her forehead and
cheeks. She felt the cool whirl of its passage, smelled its
freshness. Still she hesitated. She was not one who drank to
become drunk, or ate for the taste of the food. She lived life
sparingly, too wary to indulge too deeply. Her eternal caution
infuriated Vandien, but had often restrained him from more
trouble than he found on his own. He was one who would
wallow in every pleasant sensation. Ki was a taster, a sampler,
a shy child standing on the edge of her life and learning by
watching others.

Now she was going to drink, was going to drown her wariness and hatred of this former Rouster in the cool sweet waters
of this dark world. The river called her, whispering and roaring
in her ears, and she listened. She put her lips to it.

They sat again by the wagon for a short time. The damp jug,
now heavy with river water, rested between them. They didn't
speak; each was focused inward, on the new sensations fizzing
within their bodies. The river water extinguished the brandy
sun; the heat of it fled from Ki's body as earlier the water chill
had. She felt it leave her belly, briefly rise in a flush of heat that
suffused her skin with a rosy glow; then it was gone. The

coolness of the night cloaked her, drawing her back from any excesses, of hatred or of love.

It hit her, sudden as a gut spasm. Time to go. Time to be back upon the road that led to the Limbreth, to peace and satisfaction and an end to all goals. Like twin marionettes pulled by a single puppeteer, Ki and Hollyika came to their feet. Ki lifted the bottle, but Hollyika took it and tucked it under a river-sleeked arm.

Sigurd and Sigmund lifted their heads to watch Ki go. They would not follow, for home was the wagon. If their mistress wanted them, she would have called them and put them in their harness. Hollyika's black was less decided. He whinnied after her and trotted up to the gravel bank to stand on the smooth road looking after her. But there was no whistle, no clap of hands to beckon to him. He shook his head. After one more questioning snort, he returned to the other horses and the sweet grass.

Ki found it strange to be on the road afoot. She was not used to striding along for miles, let alone barefoot. But Hollyika's short quick steps set a pace she could match. It was, Ki reflected, a bit like taking a stroll with a chicken. There was no sound in the night but the brisk pad, pad, pad of Hollyika's round feet on the road beside Ki. The road bent swiftly away from the river with its incessant muttering; for the first time Ki became aware of the distinctly upward slope of the road. It had begun the ascent to the hills. Ki turned her eyes up to the beckoning glow. Staring at the lights, Ki found that she did not even have to watch the road or her feet upon it. It was easy, easier than anything she had ever done in her life. The river water rushed through her, enervating her, and Ki smiled.

Eight

CHESS watched in trepidation as Jace worked loose the final strap on the saddle. She slid it from the horse's back, letting it fall to thunk in the dust at her feet. The horse shied away.

"Vandien isn't going to like this," Chess predicted.

Jace turned on him. "What would you have me do? Continue to enslave this beast, perhaps trade its freedom to feed us?" Worry entered her voice. "What's come over you? Before, you would have been the first to weep at the cruelty of one creature enslaving another."

"It is the custom here," Chess replied. His eyes flickered uneasily. "The horse will only wander the streets until someone catches it and puts harness upon it again. It will gain nothing by us setting it free, and we will lose the food it would bring." He gestured toward the chicken coop. "The bread Vandien left us is gone. We have to find a market and get something to eat soon."

Low drifting clouds cast a blue haze over the moon. A dry wind whispered down the alley, stirring the grasses already brown, and sucking the moisture from the green ones. Jace ran her hand across the back of her neck. Sweat damped it and dirt and old skin rolled under her fingers. She pushed tousled hair back from where it stuck to her face. She longed for cool water and green banks of grass, for the peace of her farm. And Chess scared her.

"Do you think of nothing but your stomach, then? Does hunger make you forget what is right and wrong?" Jace bored her eyes into his.

The boy squirmed. "But how can we be sure that what is

wrong in our world is wrong here?'' he asked stubbornly. ''Might not different worlds have different rules? In our place, we have no beast slavery, nor burning day. Here they have both. If day is right for this place, perhaps . . .''

Jace gripped Chess's shoulder, pulling the child up straight and still. ''Hush!'' she said savagely. ''What has this place done to you? Will you ever be as you were? Oh, Chess, Chess, if only it could all be undone.'' Her words ran out and she stood looking down on her son's bowed head as if she were looking at a sadly broken toy. She could find no more words or reason to utter them. ''Come.'' She took his limp hand. ''We have this he gave us to trade. We will go to the market and trade for food. You will feel more yourself with something fresh and green in your stomach. Come.''

He plodded along beside Jace unresistingly. He spared a single glance for the horse, who didn't comprehend his free-dom. He was grazing quietly on the grass in the alley. His tail gave a long, slow switch.

As soon as Vandien had left them the night before, Jace had brought him straight back to the hovel. They had nibbled dry bread together and huddled in the hut, talking little but com-forting one another. When the dawn began to poison the night sky, they had hastened within, to shut the door and stuff the cloak into the crack. ''At least now we know how long the darkness will last in this world,'' Jace had told him.

In spite of last night's vigil, neither really trusted the darkness of this world. The very fact that it could be eaten by the day made it a treacherous thing, not the kind eternal dusk of home, but a turncoat friend that would lure them from shelter to betray them.

''First we shall go to the market,'' Jace was saying to him. ''Then we will go to the Gate.'' He could hear the light tremor of her voice and knew she was telling her plans aloud to make them more firm in her own mind. Chess cast his mind back to home and market time. He frowned in the hot darkness as he trudged along. It seemed so long ago; memories of that time seemed foreign and hazy, as if dust-covered. He remembered the market meadow by the darkly flowing river and the high calls of farmers greeting one another as they converged there. The rush baskets strapped on their backs were heaped with the specialties of their farms. Kallen, his uncle, would spread out a

woven grass mat at his regular place, and from his deep basket
he would spill a heap of ripe red quorts, their skins as hard as
tree bark. Always he saved the largest and sweetest one for
Chess. His big thumb would pop a hole in the skin, and he
would hand it to him. Chess would sit on his own mat, sucking
the cool juice and soft pulp from the quort as he tended to
trading. Heaped about him would be the bundled produce of
their farm; radishes, turnips, and rutabagas, their roots
scrubbed to gleaming and their leaves crisp and green. The
produce left on the mat at the end of market time, Chess would
press upon their friends, laughing at their mock refusals and
receiving from them their own excess. Market time was a time
of plenty and sharing. The thought of a market, even in this
barren world, cheered him. He hurried to match Jace's stride.

The huddled mud brick houses lining the dusty street peered
menacingly at them. Jace flinched away from the yellow window lights at first, but soon came to find that they were tolera-
ble, if she kept her distance and didn't look directly at them.
They raised no blisters on the skin, but gave to everyday objects an unpleasantly sharp appearance, making their muted
colors flat and harsh as they threw confusing shadows. Jace
took Chess's hand and pressed it reassuringly, but felt no confidence herself. The street grew wider and they passed wide
open doorways, with yellow light spilling out in wide bars.
Loud voices, raucous or angry, surged out; Jace hurried Chess
on. They did not walk close to the lighted buildings but kept
well to the center of the street, hastening through the puddles
of light as if they were slop spills. They turned a sudden bend
and Jace dragged Chess into the shelter of a tall cart's shadow.
They had come to the market, lit by dancing torches and
thronged by such folk as did not do their business by day.
Some, it was true, only preferred to shop in the coolness of
evening, but many were there whose transactions would not
bear the light of day.

Jace peered out around the corner of the cart. Her eyes
widened and her nostrils tightened in horror and disgust. She
was crouched behind a butcher's cart, its wood stained with old
blood. Even the dark of night had not abated the cloud of flies
that buzzed about it. The butcher himself stood tall on the
cart's seat, loudly proclaiming the freshness of his wares. Jace
swallowed down sickness. Her hand rose to cover her nose and
mouth as she drew Chess on.

But now there was no shelter from the flurry of the market. They were caught in the tide of people coming to pick through wares or to set up their own stalls. Jostled by rough-looking strangers attired in the furs and feathers of fellow creatures, they were propelled into the whirl of the market. The invisible push and sway of the crowd took them from stall to mat to cart. Eager merchants held up swatches of cloth, snapped whips over their heads and flapped slabs of smoked fish before them. Jace felt bewildered and sickened by the coarseness of the shouting, by the belittling exchanges between merchant and customer, the bickering over prices and values. Somewhere in this din she must find sustenance for herself and her child. She stopped, forcing the crowd to flow around her. She fumbled with the hawk pendant Vandien had given her, looping the chain about her wrist as she clutched the bird in a damp palm. With dazzled eyes she squinted about for a place to trade it.

Of coins and money she had only the small knowledge that Chess had picked up in the tavern. It seemed a dubious exchange at best, to barter this bit of jewelry for pieces of carved metal that she would then exchange for food. Jace could not fathom the complications of it, and so she decided to bypass it entirely, and trade the hawk directly for whatever it would bring her. Gripping Chess's shoulder, she steered him through the press of the crowd.

Each stall was a nightmare and a revelation. Here were chickens, their legs tied together, lying in bedraggled feathers upon a mat. Squealing piglets were caught up and thrust head first into sacks and pressed into the arms of buyers. Here a metalsmith dangled bright earrings set with gaudy stones, there a woman displayed a swirl of scarves on her arm. Past eggs stacked in unstable heaps on mats, past piles of hides both raw and cured, past shadowy folk who urged them to venture closer and see secret and mystic wares, the two tottered on. Jace finally caught sight of a stall hung with herbs both green and dried and festooned with strings of onions and roots. Just past it a gnarled old woman crouched on a mat among heaps of variously withered vegetables.

Jace battled her way to this backwater of the market and then hesitated, torn with indecision. She had only the one item to trade. She wished she had a better idea of its worth. Vandien had held it in high regard, but that gave her no indication of what she should ask for it. Ornaments of cold metal she did not know or desire, but she equated them vaguely with carved wooden beads for a child, or the garlands of sweet herbs the young men sometimes wove into their hair. She decided on the old woman with her heaps of vegetables; not only did she offer a greater variety of what Jace recognized as food, but there was a homely, familiar air to her in the way she crouched on her mat. Her long greying hair hung loose to her shoulders. She wore a simple sleeveless garment that would hang to her feet when she stood but now bunched about her on the mat. Jace was hopeful at the sight of the pale metal bangles on her wrist. Perhaps she favored these metal ornaments.

As soon as she paused before the old woman's mat, she was fixed with eyes as bright as stream pebbles. "Fresh greens?" the woman creaked hopefully. "Plump juicy root plants, pulled just this morning? Calms the stomach and soothes the bowels!"

"I wish to trade, yes," Jace replied artlessly to the woman's chant. "What will you give me for this?"

She opened her hand and dangled the tiny hawk before the woman, who scowled at it. This was not honest coin! Her old eyes darted suspiciously over Jace's strange garb and pale eyes.

"Don't need no fancy trinkets!" the old woman declared. "Get along now!"

"Please!" Jace begged in confusion. "It's all I have. Vandien said we could trade it for food. Please!"

But the old woman wouldn't even look at her. "Fresh greens!" she cawed hopefully at a passing man.

"Please!" Jace begged again, proffering the tiny hawk. Both hand and voice shook. The old woman folded her lips and shifted on her mat so that Jace and Chess were out of her line of vision. Chess tugged at his mother.

"May I see what you have there?"

The soft voice fell on Jace like warm rain on a dry garden. A young girl leaned on the wooden counter of the herb and onion-string stall. She was smiling at them, her white teeth gleaming in the darkness, a slender hand extended to receive the hawk. Jace breathed out in relief and stepped quickly up to her. The girl's dark eyes widened and then narrowed again as she held the tiny bird aloft so that it hung from its chain. Her free hand pushed thick chestnut hair back from her eyes. She touched her full lips, then pursed them speculatively. "It's not very big, is it?" she commented in a carefully neutral voice.

Jace shook her head. "But it's all I have. Please, we have come to trade for food."

"Why did not you take it to the jeweller's stall, to see what he would give you?"

"I am not familiar with the custom of coins. I would rather do my own trading in my own way."

"You do not come from this city, do you? In fact, I would wager you have come a long and weary way." The hawk hung heavy from its chain as it swung over the girl's free hand.

Jace gazed on the hawk with worried eyes, comparing its tininess to even one of the onions in the stall. "But it is very cunningly made, and Vandien valued it greatly," she countered timorously.

The girl smiled as if accepting an apology. "No doubt. Well, such trinkets are valued by those who enjoy them. And it is cute. Thank you for showing it to me." She offered it back to Jace.

Jace drew her hand back quickly, ignoring Chess's tugging at her sleeve. "Please! It has no value to me, except what food it can bring. Will you not give us something for it?"

"Well," the girl said reluctantly, as if caught between charity and the shrewdness of a bargain. "But you can see I am a simple girl, with no use for such adornments. Besides, it is not at all what a girl would wear. See, it is nothing but a plain black bird on a bit of chain." She shook it gently in front of Jace and set it back on the counter.

Jace shook off Chess as he grasped frantically at her arm. "But see how brightly its little red eye winks! Can't you give me something for it?"

"Well." Again the pursed mouth and the sigh. "I am a softhearted fool, but I can't let a child as sweet as that one go hungry. But mind! and don't go telling it about that Verna at the herb stall will take such gewgaws for her wares, or I'll be besieged by an army of folk who would cheat me out of my living." Swiftly Verna's hand swooped and fell on the tiny hawk; it vanished into a fold of her skirt. "What would you like for it?"

"Only whatever you think is right?" Jace offered humbly.

Chess had ceased to grab at her. He stood beside his mother

with a downcast face, his hands clinging helplessly to each other. He watched as Verna gathered together a small bundle of the limpest roots and driest herbs. She freed a few onions from a string and added them to the pile. It was enough to sustain them for a day, at most two. He bit hard on his lip as Jace caught them up in a fold of her sleeve, giving the woman repeated and grateful thanks. And then he was following his mother down the dusty street.

Night was deep now, and the crowd was thinning. Wheels creaked and boards clapped as merchants folded their stalls and hauled goods away. The evening trade was done. Only a few stalls, mostly dealing in weapons, potions and semi-legal merchandise, would remain open now to garner the trade of those folk that lived by night. Jace felt the air of furtiveness that seeped through the night market now. She hurried gratefully into the darkened streets, away from the blowing torches that lighted what remained of the market. Now they passed doors closed and dark. A few inns and alehouses still lifted their voices in the night, but Jace rushed Chess past these, keeping him to the safety of the shadows.

"That woman cheated you," Chess said suddenly.

"Shush!" Then, "What do you mean?"

"I have seen it in the tavern where I worked. It is the custom of this world. You offer what you have to trade, then you belittle the other's goods. Each seeks to get as much as possible for what he offers. She expected you to say that her roots were withered, her herbs without potency, her onions gone to rot."

"As they are," Jace conceded. "But I would not be so ill-bred as to mention it. You must realize that what we gave her had little value to her. We must not complain that she gave us the least of her wares; to her, it was as if we wanted to give her a stone in exchange."

"Mother!" Chess's voice rose a notch. "That is how they barter here! She only wished you to believe she had no use for the necklace. In that way, she could give you as little as possible and you would feel grateful."

"So swiftly you have grown hard and suspicious in this place. You would turn a cold eye on the food she gave us, food that will keep us for a day or so, in return for a trinket that was not even appropriate for her to wear."

''Yet it was a good enough 'trinket' that it was the only one Vandien wore!''

Jace hesitated, uncertainly considering what he said. But her faith in her own years and experience won out. One hand was gripping the sleeve that held the vegetables. But she caught Chess's hand in her other hand and held it tightly.

''Let us go to the Gate,'' she said softly, letting the wind blow away their previous words. ''Maybe Vandien will be there. Maybe he has made a way for us to go through. Think of that, Chess! We might be home safely tonight. Come.'' Privately Jace resolved that if Vandien had found a way for one to pass the Gate, that one would be Chess.

They came to the street that followed the city wall. With a quick glance to be sure all was clear, they darted into its shadow. Like mice they scurried along the base of it. When they sighted the dull red glow of the Gate, they slowed to more cautious steps. If Vandien had indeed won through to the other side, the Keeper would be looking angrily on all comers tonight.

Jace halted them completely at the low mumble of voices. A few more silent steps and the words came clear to her, but she paid them no heed. For at the same instant a breeze, so fresh and pure that it seemed a living creature, rushed up to her and enveloped her in its embrace. The clean scents of her home filled her nostrils, and she tasted the peace of the meadows and streams. It was like nourishing broth to starving children. Its moist kiss was no kin at all to the sterile dry wind that swept through the city streets and stirred the yellow dust.

Only gradually did the voices penetrate her mind. Jace had closed her eyes in the breeze's caress. Now she opened them and peered hopefully into the Gate.

But no Vandien watched to beckon her on. Instead she saw the grey-draped figure of the Keeper, his robes fluttering in the breeze. The hood had blown back from his face. Dark hair streamed from his flattened skull. An eyeless band of wrinkled flesh writhed above his nose ridge. But that which stood talking to him was no odder. ''Windsinger,'' she breathed to herself, remembering old legends. For there was the long blue robe, the mysterious tall cowl and the scaled skin. Worry and frustration emanated from the Keeper, but anger alone lined

the Windsinger's face. Their voices came to Jace in broken
snatches, their words blown away by the wind.

"How could he get through?" the Windsinger demanded.
"Of all the mortals on this side, why did you have to permit
him?"

"Permit!" The Keeper spat out the word. His arms moved
and his long fingers gripped at the night itself, striving to heal
it. "He was violent! You made no mention of any attempt like
that! The Limbreth was totally disgusted. He broke contact
with me to avoid the contamination! You gave no warning
about any such as he! He ripped through! Do you understand
what that means? Can you begin to grasp it? The balance is
gone, our world bleeds into yours. The Gatherers have but to
look and they'll know what we have done here! You fret about
this man, but when the Gatherers come for you, will you even
remember him? They can feel it. A breach like this cannot be
hidden."

Jace watched them silently. The anger was gone from the
Windsinger's face, replaced by fear and wonder. The blowing
wind came from beyond the Gate. It fluttered the Windsinger's
torch to a red glow and a streamer of straggling yellow. The
Keeper leaned against the wind as he worked, but Jace could
not see what he struggled with. His actions were strangely
difficult to follow as he was alternately hidden and revealed by
flapping rags and tatters as scarlet as the torch and as black as
the night. His hands and bared arms were thrust aloft, his
muscles straining against invisibility.

"Do the Gatherers really care?" asked the Windsinger. "Do
they really take an interest in such as we?"

"They do," the Keeper grunted out as he wove up the night.

"How long do we have before they discover us, then?" The
Windsinger's voice was hushed.

"Who knows?" the Keeper growled. "While the Gate is
here, it shouts aloud to them."

"But if it should close? You said it would, but it seems no
smaller than last night." There was more than disappointment
in the Windsinger's voice; there was dread.

"We don't know if it can close. The Limbreth doubts that it
can heal against such an imbalance." The Keeper's voice held
no sympathy. He was too immersed in his own misery and
fear. "Our world bleeds into yours. Who knows what damage

it does us? Your day is stained with our blessed darkness, our winds of peace waste themselves in your streets.''

"You are the one that let Vandien through!" The Windsinger's voice denied his accusing tone. She changed her tack. "What about Ki? Does the Limbreth have her yet? If they are satisfied with her, I should like to at least settle the rest of our bargain. A calling gem was promised to me. . . ."

"Is it not enough that my Master has taken her from your hands? Our Gate is torn, and a rogue loosed in our world, and you come begging and whining for that which you could scarcely use properly. If I had the voice of the Limbreth! But I do not, and he bids me now to be respectful to you.'' The Keeper paused, lapsing into a listening stance. The Windsinger shifted impatiently but waited. At last the Keeper turned his eyeless face back to her. "Ki has not reached the Limbreth yet. The one you insisted we admit before her to test the Gate has slowed her progress. This is your own doing, so you must wait until it is settled. Once Ki is before the Limbreth and is proven to be suitable, all bargains shall be fulfilled. Does that suit you?''

"It sounds to me as if you hope that the Gate will close before then! Tell your master to be wary of cheating a Windsinger. I shall be back tomorrow. I want the gem then. Tomorrow will be the last time I speak gently.''

The rest of her words were gusted away by a blast of wind that drove the Keeper to his knees. He fought it as it rolled him onto his back and his grey legs waved bare and skinny as a stork's. The street grew suddenly darker, more fragrant, cooler. Behind her, Jace heard Chess snuffling in long breaths of it, gulping the air down as if he could drink it.

". . . Do about the dark seeping into this world?" demanded the Windsinger into a catch of silence. The Keeper shot her a venomous look that was no answer but a denial of culpability. Jace watched as the Keeper battled his way back to the center of the Gate, to once more lift his arms overhead and begin his incomprehensible weaving motions.

"Vandien isn't here," Chess pointed out hoarsely.

"I know. Hush.''

"But I'm hungry," he protested. "Can't we go home now?''

"Home?" It took a moment for Jace to realize Chess was

referring to the hovel they hid in. She felt a moment of panic.
The boy was dangling over an abyss and slipping inexorably
away from her. She took her son's hand, but knew she could
not hold him. Not long. Not here. She gazed with longing at
the Gate, but something obscured her vision. Even a glimpse
of her own land was denied her.

"Come along," Jace whispered, and they slipped away,
moving from shadow to shadow as they wound their way
through dusty streets back to the alley. They stopped only
once, to drink water from a public well. Jace cringed at drinking the flat lukewarm stuff, but Chess drank deeply of it. After
he had finished, he drew up another bucketful and laved his
dusty face and arms. Those thin arms gave Jace a pang. The
sun blisters had pocked them and privation had thinned them to
bone and tendon and skin. Jace remembered them as round and
plump, a little boy's arms. Now he looked like the few other
street children she had glimpsed tonight, down to the ragged
brown garment. When she touched the coarse cloth of it, he
glanced up at her inquiringly. It was almost as if he didn't
know that he suffered. His eyes went to the sky and he
frowned.

"It will be coming back soon," he warned her. And it was
Chess who took Jace's hand to draw her down the street and
into the alley, to the safety of the tumbled-down coop.

Nine

VANDIEN wakened to the growling of his stomach. Uncurling only stretched its emptiness. He thought back to the nibble of bread and dried fish he had eaten in the chicken coop. That had been his last meal, and it had been little enough. He unstoppered the waterskin and took a small swallow. The water was flat and cool and lonely in his stomach.

Habit made him glance to the sky to see how long he'd slept, but the night and the overcast were unreadable. It didn't matter. When he had trotted as far as he could without rest, he had slept. Now he was awake, and it was time to head down the road again. Yawning, he rubbed a hand over his bristly face. Back to the road, he commanded himself sternly. He took up his endless trot, staring ahead down the black ribbon of road. It was endless, he realized as he dropped suddenly into a walk. His feet and legs ached, his stomach flopped inside him and the whole quest was stupid. He strode along berating himself for the futility of it. Walking and hungry, he could never hope to catch up with Ki. He had found no signs of her stopping and camping. Unappealing as it was, he had to accept Jace's premise, that Ki was under some kind of Limbreth madness and was already making her best time for those far hills. Vandien imagined her standing on the seat, the greys whipped to a gallop, the wagon wheels rumbling as they spun along this smooth and perfect road. And here he came, footsore and empty-bellied behind her. It was pathetic. But he kept walking.

He wished for his boots, for his horse, for a package of traveling food. He wished for clean clothes and a hot cup of tea. He wished for a chance to grab Ki by the shoulders and rattle her silly for not waiting for him. He grinned stiffly to himself as he imagined the aftermath of that action. He'd probably be wishing for teeth.

As his mind chewed, his eyes wandered and his legs carried him on. There were cultivated fields to either side of the road now. The cottages on the far sides of them were humpy little shelters barely distinguishable from the rolling hills that rose beyond them. His belly grumbled again and Vandien swallowed. Crazy to go on walking hungry until he dropped. He began to scan the rows of crops as he passed them, but saw nothing he recognized. It would take him too long to walk to one of the cottages and beg for food. Besides, from what Jace had told him of her world, no one would begrudge him food. A neat row of bushes lined the road. He scanned them eagerly for fruit, but saw only long narrow leaves hanging from twiggy branches. Well, perhaps it was a root crop or bearing time was past. He strained his eyes, peering ahead through the dimness.

He kept walking. A gentle breeze stirred the crops, and the earth breathed a rich fertile smell in the darkness. The black road was smooth under his weary feet. Ki was probably making excellent time over it, he reflected sourly. Another and separate hunger began to stir in him, harmonizing with the one in his belly. Why the hell couldn't he be on the wagon seat beside Ki, swaying gently to the rhythm of the turning yellow wheels? There had been a few balmy nights like this, cool traveling weather through hot lands, when the wagon seat was a place to share companionable silence and wedges of cheese and apples. Those were the best times, he reflected, when errands were done, or deadlines not yet pressing, the long days of unhurried and shared solitude. They were rare days, never strung so closely together that they became boring. A hundred times more frequent were the hot days of choking dust, the blustery days when the icy rain slapped at them and the team's great hooves skidded in the mud, or the days when Ki drove them all from daylight to past dusk, cursing herself as she harried her weary horses on to meet some delivery date. And now there was this rare evening of fine weather and excellent road through a mysterious and fascinating countryside, and Vandien was padding along on bare sore feet like an abandoned cur.

Vandien stopped and looked down over the fields. The road

bed was elevated slightly, just enough at this point for him to
see past the line of twiggy trees into the fields beyond. The
trees were only a border: beyond them vines lay untidily along
the ground. Vandien thought he could see dark shapes like
melons resting on the ground beside the big leaves.

Beside the road was a fringe area of deep moss, then a
pebbly embankment that bruised his bare feet. The coarse grass
at the bottom of it sliced into his bare ankles, leaving shallow
stinging wounds. When he tried to push through the row of
bushes at the edge of the field, he found them not twiggy but
thorny; long raking thorns pierced carelessly through his
clothes to drag long scratches over his flesh. Another man
would have been happy to return to the smooth road bed and
limp on, but to thwart Vandien was only to make him more
determined. Protecting his face with an upflung arm, he pushed
doggedly through. He hobbled out into the field on the other
side, both feet so painful that he couldn't decide which to limp
on.

Hissing softly in pain, he lowered himself onto the cultivated ground beside one of the vines. A red globe rested on the
ground within his reach; smaller ones decked the stem of the
vine. Vandien let his eyes roam. Nearly all of the vines were
heavily laden with the globes in various sizes. A few from such
a bountiful yield would scarcely be missed; he took one as big
as his head into both his hands. A gentle twist snapped it easily
free of the plant, and he turned it over in his hands.

"No fruit I know, but no farmer would grow such a thing
unless it could be eaten. Like a big red egg." He puzzled
aloud, tapping a cautious finger against the thing's shell-like
rind. Drawing his knife from the sheath, he rapped its pommel
against the globe, and the crust gave way. Vandien picked off
bits of it to form a hole. A sweet smell rose. Hunger did not let
him question it and he raised the globe to his mouth and sucked
at it.

A thin layer of pulp came free in his mouth and then a gush
of juice, thick as fresh milk, sweet, but tart enough to be
refreshing. It brought him to a full awareness of his hunger.
Too soon the fruit was an empty shell in his hands. He twisted
off another and popped a hole in it with his knife.

As he lowered it, he became aware of eyes on him. He had a
glimpse of a woman's startled face, and then she fled from

him. "Come back!" he called in Common, but she only ran faster. He cast the empty rind from him and pelted off after her. The vines caught at his feet. He heard her breath in shuddering gasps. "Stop!" he cried when he could nearly touch her. With a shriek she darted away, leaping over the vines, fleetness powered by terror.

Her legs were longer than his, and she knew the lay of the ground. He was at the edge of the dooryard when he heard the slam, and a thump of something piled against the door. Vandien approached the door but didn't touch it. "I won't hurt you!" he called through it. He thought he could hear the frightened sobbing of small children within. "Please! I'm a stranger here! I only wish to beg food of you, and to ask if you have seen my companion coming ahead of me down the road. On my honor, I wish you no harm."

There was a scuffling inside, then silence.

"Please!" he cried again, but in vain. Reluctantly he set his hand to the door handle. He put his shoulder against the door.

"Get away from the door, Dark One!" The courage of the man's words were little marred by the shaking of his voice. He advanced on Vandien, the stick in his hands held awkwardly. But when he raised the pole, his intention was as unmistakable as his inexperience. Vandien could have disarmed him in a moment. But a scuffle was no way to gain their confidence. He backed away from the door, holding his hands up wide.

"Please. I mean you no harm. I only come to ask for food."

The man kept his pole at the ready. His eyes gleamed palely in a golden face outlined with shining hair. "Drink of the water, Dark One. It will be enough to sate you!"

Vandien sensed the test in the man's words, but didn't know what answer would clear him. "I cannot drink the water of this place. I have been warned against it. I come from beyond the Gate. My friend came before me through the Gate, and I have come to fetch her back."

"Silence your lies, Dark One! Did you think to find fools here?" The man made the pole whistle through the air. Vandien retreated a few steps.

"I will not ask even food then. Only this: Have you seen my friend, driving a wagon and a team of grey horses? Tell me, and I will go. I mean to do no harm."

"Your being here is harm enough! The wrongness of you

cries aloud in our ears. You are a corrupter, a seducer of innocents, come to charm our young ones into venturing through the Gate.''

"No! I swear it! By my coming and my going, I seek to make a way for two of your own people to return. For Jace and Chess! Do you know those names? Jace told me she kept the farm near the Gate. Chess is her son.''

The rod cut the air and Vandien fell back before it. Muscles flexed under the man's tawny skin with each swing. He handled the rod in a strange way; Vandien could not tell now if it was skill or foolishness. He did know now that he could not predict how the next swing would come; this man feinted by no rules Vandien knew. "Get back, Dark One! Back to the black road! Stay to the way that is made for you!"

The scrape of heavy wood and the opening of the door came to Vandien's ears. He looked back to find the woman framed in the doorway, but the glance nearly cost him, for the rod whistled suddenly past his ear. Vandien stumbled backwards through the vines. "Back!" the man roared, following him as he retreated.

"But he spoke of Jace!" the woman called hesitantly. "And Chess, long gone from us.''

"He is a Dark One, and a rogue as well!" the man roared back. "What did the Limbreth say to us? We were warned of him. Do not listen to him, though he comes to you with honeycombs in his hands, and the moon's own words on his lips. He is dark and unclean, not touched by the Limbreth and the Jewels. He will defile us! Back!"

A fanatic, Vandien decided. And decided too that he would not be fool enough to fight him, for there would be no winning. Even if he downed and defeated the man, neither he nor the woman would willingly part with any food or news of Ki. Best to take what little advantage he could. This time when the rod swished by, Vandien was ready for it, stepping in with a ready grip and a wicked twist. The rod went flying, the man leaping after it. Vandien did not attack, but turned and fled, leaping over the vines. The distance he gained let him stoop and rip free one more globe, although the man had regained his rod and was again in pursuit, and he was large and long-legged. Only Vandien's iron-willed leap through the thorn bushes saved him, for the rod whistled over his head close enough to stir his curls. Vandien scrabbled back up to the road and then looked back, grinning and panting. The big farmer would go no farther than the thorn bushes.

"My thanks for the food, and the pleasant talk! Now will you tell me if you have seen my friend go by, upon a tall wagon with yellow wheels?"

"Damn you to the darkness of the black road! The Limbreth knows of you already. Unclean you come into his lands, no pilgrim but a plunderer! He knows of your coming and upon you his wrath will fall. By no intent of mine have you taken the food of this land! Do not spatter me with your thanks!"

"The team was grey?" Vandien called, sweetly inquiring, but the man stumped off, his rod still cutting the air. "May as well eat it now as later," Vandien advised himself, and sat on the road to do so.

When he resumed his journey, his feet were dead clods on the ends of his legs, but at least his belly was full, and the road was downhill now. Marsh began to edge it, and he trotted on, hearing the mutter of water.

The sound of the cool running water rapidly became a torment to him. His scratches stung, his clothing clung to his sweaty body and he could smell himself. He wished he knew, in days, how long it had been since he had been able to drink his fill of cold water. The aftertaste of the fruit in his mouth had become cloyingly sweet, and a sip from his waterskin did nothing to dispel it. Worse, he could smell the running water; it smelled of purity, coldness and the night. It occurred to him that he might have to try a mouthful of it. The amount left in his waterskin would not be enough to take both him and Ki back to the Gate. Perhaps he had best try it now before he was completely out of water. Vandien thumped that thought flat and gave his head a vigorous shake. He limped on.

He came to a bridge and paused to gaze longingly at the white rush of water that foamed past beneath him. Its damp breath rose to bedew his skin, teasing and soothing his face. He thought of going down to the brink, of letting his sore feet and scratched legs trail in it for just a moment or two. "Like last time?" he asked himself sarcastically. "Onward!" He raised his eyes to the faint damnable glow of the Limbreth. And saw the wagon.

"Ki!"

His feet forgot their lameness. The two grey horses raised their heads, and a third horse trotted a few paces uneasily. Vandien wanted to laugh aloud with rel ef as he skipped and cursed his way over the stretch of river gravel to the wagon. "Ki!" he bellowed again, feeling joyous, triumphant and righteously annoyed with her. She didn't answer. Probably sleeping, while he wore his feet out chasing her. He sprang up to the cuddy seat and slammed the door open. The cuddy was dark.

He didn't need to see the empty bed; the inside of the cuddy smelled dank and abandoned. He rose on the seat to stare around in all directions. "Ki!" he bellowed into the whispering rush of the river's song. But he saw no sign of her, heard no answering whistle. She was gone.

He crouched on the seat again, taking in the sight of the strange horse, Ki's casually abandoned camp, harness dropped on the ground and left there. Fear squeezed his guts slowly. None of this was like Ki. She wouldn't go off and leave her wagon like this. Vandien ran a hand through his hair; practicality asserted itself.

Dried fruit and hard bread were in the cupboards. He chewed mouthfuls as he rummaged through his corner of the cuddy. Reluctantly he pulled clean clothes on over his sweaty body. He was more determined than ever not to bathe in that mysterious rush of water. He gingerly dragged soft low boots on over his tender feet. His face was grim as he groped for the rapier on its hook and buckled its belt about himself. The weight of it was oddly reassuring. He had seen nothing in this land that he would use it on, but it gave him a sense of readiness and competence.

The food and plenty of water from the casks comforted his belly and throat, the clean light clothes were fresh against his skin, but his weary mind still whirled. Where was Ki, and why had she left the wagon? He had never known her to leave it willingly, and certainly she wouldn't have left it this way, untidy and unsecured, harness growing damp on the ground.

Sigurd and Sigmund had come to stare curiously up at him as he perched on the cuddy seat. Sigurd lipped at his boot toe and Vandien absently parceled out dry fruit to them.

"Where'd she go?" he asked them, and Sigmund flicked his ears in reply.

When Vandien leaped down from the seat, his foot caught

and he fell. Cursing, he snatched at the sodden mass of cloth he had stumbled in. Ki's skirt. It slipped from his suddenly nerveless hands as ugly fears raised their hissing heads. He lifted it again gingerly. Ki's skirt, made heavy by the constant dew off the racing water; beneath it, her blouse. Slowly he spread the garments before him. No rips or blood. Ki had removed them voluntarily. He wadded them up and tossed them into the back of the wagon. And here was another riddle: more garments, but these were strange to him, as strange as the battle harness beneath them. He looked at the warhorse that still kept a cautious distance. "You and me both, my friend," he told it. "But this time she's the one on foot and bootless. Where would she go? Not far over these river rocks barefoot; not if I know Ki. Not back to the Gate, for I would have passed her. If she went by boat, I may as well forget her. There's no way for me to follow. No, my friend horse, I think she's gone on down the road, and with your rider, if I read these signs rightly. Naked as the dawn. I'll be damned."

He leaned back against the wagon and began to laugh. It had hit him suddenly; this was how he made Ki feel when he took off on one of his ridiculous side trips, on a moment's impulse with the explaining saved for later. But somehow it wasn't sporting for her to turn the tables on him like this. Well.

For only a few breaths longer he leaned against the wagon. Then he gave a whistle, and the greys raised their heads. Sigurd put his ears back and bared his teeth as well.

"Fine," Vandien agreed affably. "Then Sigmund can have all the grain when he comes to harness." Vandien reached over the lip of the wagon and flipped open the grainbox. He stirred the contents, letting it rattle through his fingers. Sigurd's ears came forward and he gave an anxious whinny. "I thought you might see it my way," Vandien observed.

TEN

"MOTHER!" Chess shook Jace's shoulder. The woman came awake more slowly than the boy. Her maturity and stoicism helped her to substitute sleep for food. She had lain down at the coming of the light and slept deeply, although it was not a refreshing sleep. Chess had no such patience. He had tossed restlessly in the dirty smelly hovel, creeping often to the door crack, until the air flowed in cool and moist and he smelled the night. His belly had kept him awake all day; now it bade him seek food.

"Mother!" He shook her again. "It's gone again. It's safe for us to go out."

Jace sat up slowly and looked at Chess sadly. "There's no hurry, child. We have all the dark before us, and only one errand: to check the Gate. I have no hopes that tonight will be any different. Vandien won't force his way in, and we shan't force our way out. It is time for us to talk, Chess; the time is upon us for setting aside of false hopes, and the accepting of what is."

"I'm thirsty," Chess interrupted. "And hungry. I wish we hadn't let the horse go."

"Aren't you listening?" Jace demanded sharply. "Chess, we have no more food. And if the horse were still with us, I should still give it back its freedom. Hunger and thirst do not change right and wrong."

"Wrong and right do not change hunger and thirst, either," Chess grumbled softly to himself. "I'm listening, Mother. You are saying it is time for us to give up and die."

Jace sighed. "Must you put it so? Why be angry about what

we have been given? Sometimes the fruit is sweet, and sometimes it is sour. It is always fruit, and we eat it. So it is with the
days we are given. Some are sweet, and some are not. If the
last of our days are not as sweet as some have been, they are,
none the less, the days that are given to . . .''

"Words! Words, words, words! You cover up our life with
words, and our deaths too! Mother, I am thirsty! Those are
words, too. Don't you hear them?''

But Jace didn't hear. She caught hold of Chess abruptly,
pulling his face close to her own and sniffing at him. "You
have a foulness to your speech and a foulness to your breath as
well!'' Suspicion lit Jace's eyes, but she couldn't bring herself
to voice it.

"I ate it!'' Chess's voice was fiercely defiant. "When my
belly wouldn't let me sleep, my nose found it. And I ate it. It
gagged me and it made me thirst, but it gave me enough in my
stomach to let me sleep. And why not? Vandien ate of it, and
he is not the only one I have seen. At the tavern I saw men and
women eat plates full of it, steaming and hot and running with
juices.''

"Ah! Ah! Ah!'' The hoarse gasps frightened Chess; then her
grip loosened, and for the first time in his life, Chess felt his
mother push him harshly away. Shock made his knees go weak
and he fell to the dirt floor. Drawing in his knees, he stared up
in sudden terror at the amazing spectacle of his mother towering over him in rage.

"How could you?'' she demanded. Tears streaked her dusty
face, but rage gave her control of herself. Her voice was steady
and hard as stone. "You have eaten the flesh of another creature. What will you do next? Will you kill? Will you—but it is
beyond me to imagine what one such as you will do! You are
incomprehensible to me! No one could hunger enough to jus-
tify what you have done, not even one whose bones were
pushing out through the flesh. That fish was a creature as alive
as we, it knew the joys of leaping up a stream, of feeling the
cold water rush against its flanks, of breeding to create more of
its kind to enjoy the water. It possessed a moving life, no less
sacred than your own, and it . . .''

"Happily gobbled up other living moving things to sate its
hunger!'' Chess pushed up from the floor. He faced his
mother, standing as tall as his nine years would let him, fired
with an anger as great as hers.

"*It* is not sentient!" hissed Jace.

Chess glared at her, having no reply. He whirled suddenly. A bash of his shoulder flung open the rattly door and he fled into the night. "Chess!" Jace wailed after him, but his steps did not even pause. He was angry and hurt and ashamed, his child's mind filled to bursting with conflicting thoughts and feelings. He had eaten the body of a fellow creature; his mother valued the life of a fish over his; his mother could never forgive him for the atrocious thing he had done; his mother would rather see him starve than let him eat a fish that was dead anyway. The salt and fish taste filled his mouth as he ran panting. He found himself at the public well.

He flung himself at the water, to drink and pant, and drink again. But the taste of his sin wouldn't go away. Long after his thirst was slaked, he drank the lukewarm water, drank until he felt it slosh inside him. But still the taste of the salt fish filled his mouth like an obscenity. He rose and walked heavily away.

He scarcely noticed where his steps took him. He could not go back to the coop; in his mind he saw the door closed and held against him. He would not risk confronting the unbearable reality of such a thing. Unconsciously, his steps strayed toward the homey sound of folk talking and laughing.

The harsh glare of torches stained the darkness. He found himself at the edges of the market square. Huddling in the soft shadow of a wall, he peered out at the folk that laughed and talked so loudly. His water-heavy stomach muttered sadly at the sight of fresh melons piled in heaps. Sweetness flavored the air as the farmer split one open to display its juiciness. Another farmer paused to speak to the melon merchant; his donkey shifted restlessly at the delay. Its panniers were heavy with a soft orange-fuzzed fruit that Chess didn't know, but the warm aroma tantalized his nostrils. He hunkered down in the shadows, holding his belly tightly.

A woman's sudden shriek of laughter spooked the donkey. A toss of his long-eared head and a hitch of his rump were all it took to send half a dozen of the ripe fruit tumbling from the overladen panniers. The farmer swore bitterly and with a jerk led the beast on to his own stall in the market. Chess remained crouching in the darkness, staring at the half-squashed fruit in the dust. The man did not want it, and no others seemed interested. He darted out of the shadows to snatch them up.

Like a mouse with a crumb he fled back to the wall's shelter with his loot.

The juice ran stickily over his chin and his teeth grated on the rough pit. He ate eagerly, ignoring the dust and grit that adhered to the squashed side. Two and then three he devoured before he felt his hunger ease. Three remained in his lap, and belatedly he thought of his mother. Conflicting emotions still stormed in him, but love decided him, love as much a habit as a feeling. He would risk his mother's wrath to share with her this bit of fruit, warm and sweet as a memory of their soft dark world. He rose with the fruit jumbled in his hands and slipped out into the street.

"Ho!" came the shout just as a heavy bootshod foot came down on his small bare one. With a cry of pain Chess dropped his fruit and hopped out of the way. But a heavy hand settled on his shoulder and gripped it before he could slip away into darkness. He smelled the sourness of wine and stared up in terror into a heavy grizzled face. Large brown eyes measured him shrewdly, but softened suddenly.

"Did I break your foot, little man?" the stranger asked, and the kindness in his voice was unmistakable. Chess could only shake his head, wordless. He stooped to retrieve his twice-bruised fruit, but a swipe of a large hand knocked it back into the dust. "No, little one, it's all spoilt now. But don't think old Mickle will send you home to face a scolding and a slap. I stepped on your foot and spoiled the fruit. So I'll be the one to put it to rights. So!"

The heavy hand on his shoulder turned him about. Mickle leaned heavily on him and propelled him through the market to the stall of the fruit merchant. Chess was speechless with fright. He had no inkling of what the man intended, and could only think of his mother alone in the dismal hut, and the rising of the terrible sun that must come eventually. If the drunk's hand had not been so tight on his shoulder, he would have squirmed away and vanished into the darkness, to seek his mother again, no matter what scolding and disdain he might find. But Mickle's grip was tight.

"A dozen of your plumpest!" he told the merchant loftily in a drink-furred voice. "Hold out your basket, boy!" When Chess just stared at him helplessly, Mickle leaned down and squinted at his empty hands. "So that's the trouble of it! No basket to hold out. No wonder you spilled the fruit, darlin'. Hold on to those peaches, farmer. We'll be back.''

The next few hours passed in a sort of delightful horror for Chess. Mickle purchased a basket, large enough to hold a dozen peaches and to spare. The room in the basket seemed to trouble him, so that he added a melon and two crusty loaves of warm bread. And then a bit of cloth, to cover it over and keep the dust from the fruit and the warmth in the bread. And a pair of sandals for Boy, so that the next time his feet were trod upon, they would have some protection. And then a brush, to smooth the wildness of his hair. When it was smoothed, so neat a head of hair deserved a hat, and a feather or two to make it perky. But then the tunic was too ragged for such a fine head, so Mickle must have a blue cloak to cover over the ragged brown garment. From stall to stall he wandered with him, with many a genial belch and lurch. His hand was ever on Chess's shoulder. Mickle carried the heavy basket; Chess's hands were curled defensively against his thin chest under the soft blue cloak.

Mickle bought him gooey sweets that the vendor passed over to him in a curled leaf cup. After Chess had eaten one, he found his tongue and courage to ask, ''Why are you so kind to me?''

''What else should I be to a puppy like you? Eat your sweets, boy.''

''I must be going home soon,'' Chess whispered, half afraid that this strange man would keep him against his will.

But Mickle only stirred as if awakened, and with a glance at the night sky, agreed that he certainly must. With a gaspy belch, he looked about in sudden puzzlement. ''Which way is home?'' he demanded of Chess.

Chess's heart thudded to stillness, and then went away at a gallop. Mickle's hand possessed his shoulder. His buried memories of the innmaster broke upon his mind like fresh welts. But looking into Mickle's drink-softened features, he saw no lust or secrecy, only the mild confusion of drink. After an instant of hesitation, Chess turned them from the market and toward the Gate. A certain craftiness, new to him, rose up as he asked, ''Shan't I carry the basket? You've carried it all evening and it must be getting heavy.'' Shame flushed his cheeks, so trustingly did Mickle hand it over to him, but the darkness hid his blushes. For now they were beyond the reach of the market's torches, moving down the quiet wall street that led past the Gate. For Chess must visit the Gate, as he had every night since Vandien had left them; he still hoped Vandien would find a way to open the Gate for them.

"Down Dark Street we go?" Mickle asked questioningly. "So folk are calling it now, did you know? There's a leak in the wall that lets in the dark and the cool, day and night, though none can say from where; even by day it's grey here, and night brings blackness. But there is a marvelous coolness and freshness to the air. Some folk have moved away, saying the darkness is demon's work, but as many have moved in, saying the coolness and freshness is a blessing from gods we have forgotten."

Chess nodded, scarcely noting his words. He waited for some unevenness in the cobbles, some stumble to loosen the grip upon his shoulder. Then he would be gone. Adrenaline hastened his breath; his leg muscles felt rubbery with readiness.

When Mickle did stumble, his grip only went tighter on Chess. Chess's heart sank into his roiling stomach. How long was it until light and heat? The Gate loomed up on their left before Chess expected it. But, no, it was not a Gate anymore; no red glow lit it. The sweet coolness of the air increased, and Chess smelled the flowers of his home; but the Gate was now only a rent in the solid wall of the city, exactly as if the stones had torn like scraps of weathered cloth. No Keeper stood within it, and the tear was too narrow to admit or release anyone.

Chess drew closer to it, unmindful of Mickle's hand on his shoulder. Rags of darkness fluttered from the edges of the rent, coolly insubstantial to his reaching hand, but the night flowed out of the rent, thick and strong as gushing water. He forced his hand into it, feeling his skin tingle in gratitude for its fresh moisture. He leaned forward, pushing. Past his elbow, up to his shoulder. He had forgotten Mickle and the basket now. He turned his slender body sideways and tried to slip into the crack. His chest and buttocks rasped against stones, he butted his head against rough rocky edges. He would not fit.

"It's too small!" he wailed, drawing away from it. "No one can get through that! We can never go home!"

"Hum?" Mickle's questioning noise suddenly recalled him to mind. The grip that still rested on his shoulder was the clenching fist of this hateful hot place. Chess whirled on him, his small teeth bared in a sudden grimace of hatred. "Why won't you let me go?" he screeched. "Why are you keeping me here?"

His anger forsook him and his strength went with it. He sank sobbing to the hard cobbles of the street, feeling the wind of his home wash over him without comfort. Even the tears he shed in this place were hot salty things that left stiff tracks down his face and stung his chapped lips. He huddled himself into a little ball, rocking. He had no home, his mother hated him, nothing was right, and he couldn't understand why any of it had happened.

Mickle knelt awkwardly beside him. He patted him clumsily with huge rough hands. "There, lad. There. It happens to all of us, sooner or later. It's sooner for you, that's the shame of it. Just when you need to go home the most, you find that you can't. Well, I won't claim to understand it. So you came from the other side, is that it? I've heard tales of folk that did, not loudly told, but I've heard. Home. Well, there are homes and there are homes. I won't say that mine is much of one, but it's all we've got tonight." With a grunt, Mickle raised him in his arms. The basket dangled from one of his hairy wrists. He wrapped the new cloak clumsily about the boy. Chess found he had neither the strength nor the will to struggle away. He dropped his head against Mickle's shoulder, smelling his beery breath and sweat.

"Don't let the sun shine on me," he whispered. "I won't," Mickle promised solemnly. So thin this boy, and so scared. What, he wondered, would the Windsinger be wanting him for? And where was the other one?

Jace could call no more. Her dry throat was rasped raw, but her mind still whispered. "Chess, Chess."

No sooner had Chess disappeared from sight than Jace's anger had vanished, too. Her heart was heavy, her belly cold as she sat down on the step of the hovel to await his return. Anger was a rare emotion for Jace, and she was not accustomed to apologizing for words said in its heat, especially not to Chess. But now she groped, trying to think what she would say when

Chess returned. But he did not return. Ashamedly, and then with rising fear, Jace had called him. She had made her way back to the tavern where he had worked, thinking perhaps he would return there for shelter and food after she rejected him. Sly peerings at the door and window cracks had discovered no Chess, and when she made bold enough to tap at a kitchen door and ask if the boy was there, the innmaster had flung foul words and a bowl of slops at her. She had fled, and then began a fruitless combing of the dark streets and alleys, calling Chess softly but with urgency. Twice she had visited the Gate, or the crack that was left of it. No Chess. The herb stall woman had not seen him. She did not know where else to look.

Jace turned her steps back to the hovel, pausing one last time at the Gate and again at the public well. But there was no trace of him. Dawn began to stain the sky and Jace hastened for shelter, promising herself that Chess would be there, that he would have returned and be wondering where she was. The early morning light tickled and then stung her skin. Her eyes began to water in its grey glare, her breath to come in gasps. Then the hovel in the alley was before her, and she flung herself in the open door, crying "Chess?" But she found only dust motes dancing in the horrid bitter light. Jace wedged the door shut and huddled trembling and alone in the dark.

ELEVEN

REBEKE's heart was shaking in her chest. She stood still in the empty corridor, listening to the silence that pressed in on her ears. She longed to hurry past this ordeal, but haste was the mother of error. So she stood motionless before the plain door, stubbornly waiting for these foolish vestiges of Human emotion to wear themselves out.

She came here seldom; only dire need could force her to it. She had lain awake and restless all the night, draining her thoughts of emotion, trying to let logic guide her. She was here because it was necessary; she had no other source for that which she must know. She could scarcely go to Yoleth and ask her for the secrets of the Gate and how to contact the Limbreth, and there was only one other who might know such things. That was why she went to him; she insisted to herself that this was the full truth. She rejected the notion that when all others turned against her or were as helpless as herself, she returned for comfort to her earliest alliance. Pride scoffed at such an idea. Pride would have made her forsake whatever bitter longings she might appease behind the door. Within that chamber, she would find no companionship nor loyalty, no help given for the sake of friendship. Dresh would never again give her any of those things. What he might have for her was information, if she asked correctly, and if he were weary enough of the void.

No locks hampered this door. Rebeke set her mouth close to it and breathed a melodious word before she set her hand to it. The word was all she needed to enter, and all that was needed to keep others out. For behind this door she kept a wind of hurricane force, leashed, but ready to blast out the open door at any intruder. This the acolytes of her hall knew, but none dared to question what she kept behind so formidable a guard.

The room was as barren and stark as any in Rebeke's hall. The same black walls and floors framed it, there was the same sparse sprinkling of furniture: a small table and chair in one corner, a tall black stool in the other, and that was all. She set the basket she bore on the table and turned slowly. In the center of the black floor, with no curbstone or cover to protect the unwary, a round well gaped. The blackness within the well was darker than the walls of stone. Rebeke stepped to the lip of it and looked down. She didn't sway or become dizzy, for she knew what to expect: a long cylindrical shaft of nothingness, with tiny shimmering lights at the far end filling a circle no bigger than a clenched fist. Within that far circle, blotting out some of the lights, floated the shape of the wizard Dresh. She sighed as she took a coil of fine blue rope from the sleeve of her robe and stared down at the spread-eagled body that rotated ever so slowly. She arranged the rope carefully in a circle around the well, finishing by making a loop at one end and threading the other through it. A wizard snare.

The simple melody she sang now was as soft and sweet as a breeze over anemones. The wind that stoppered the shaft flowed up to greet her song, and the suction of its movement drew the floating body of the wizard. Rebeke stood at the lip of the well and looked down on him. His grey eyes were open. She looked deep into them, but he stared past her, bemused by whatever thought his mind had held the last time she had reimprisoned him. His chiseled lips were parted as if they still held words for her. Fine black hair floated softly around his face. Rebeke knelt and gripped the shoulder of his black doublet, and pulled him with ease to the lip of the well.

As his hand brushed the brink of the well, he gasped loudly, a swimmer finally reaching air, and scrabbled violently for a grip. "Please, Reby!" The words pealed out of him before his eyes regained comprehension; Rebeke's soul twisted at the pain in them. For a moment both froze; then Dresh was dragging himself up from the well as Rebeke stood up and stepped back.

He spoke no word as he clambered up, nor even looked at her until his boots were clear of the well and set on solid stone.

Disdaining to stand, he drew his knees up and rested his arms upon them. "Well?" he asked coldly. "Come to gloat again?"

The splendid control of his voice had faded from disuse. How long since he had spoken? Rebeke cast her mind back to the last time she had called him. For him those months in between had passed as one long undreaming moment. How his heart must seethe still with the anger and despair of their last meeting. How many more times could she draw him up from the well for speech before one day she confronted a madman? Rebeke pushed the thought away. She did not do this out of any petty vengeance or pity; she did it out of need, and need must be answered.

"I've come to ask questions, Dresh."

"Hmm. And you expect answers?" His laugh was brittle. "You amaze me, Rebeke. You haul me up to answer questions, do you? But the sooner I answer them, the sooner you will banish me back to that nothingness. So ask away. But expect no answers."

"I see. You have saved us both a great deal of time." Rebeke stooped to pick up the end of the blue noose.

Dresh remained as motionless as a bird before it breaks cover.

"I will confess I hadn't expected to find you so reticent, Dresh." Rebeke continued to draw up the cord, and Dresh watched his circle of freedom contract. "I even brought food and wine for us, for our talk might have been a long one."

His grey eyes did not leave the line on the floor. "You know as well as I that within the void I have no needs. I do not thirst, nor hunger, nor dream. I do not even belch or piss." His eyes flickered to her to see if she would shrink from his crudity. She did not. "Within the void, I do nothing and am nothing. My life is suspended. Think of it, Rebeke; I may live for thousands of years, with generations of Windmistresses coming to my well to haul me out for consultation, then lower me back into storage. I may become a legend to the acolytes, the secret councilor, the . . ."

"You shall not live beyond my life span. I have promised you already that your torment will not go on forever. I know what I have done to you, and you know who forced me to do it. Those topics are past discussion. I know your body knows no wants; I would not torment you with hunger or pain. But the

senses can long for stimulation, after being so long disused;
a sip of wine, a slice of spiced fruit, a bit of bread and
butter. . . ."

Wolf lights gleamed in Dresh's grey eyes. He clasped his
hands together to still their trembling and looked at Rebeke.
Silently. The room tilted slowly for her until she looked up into
those eyes. His mouth was soft and grave and would be warm
under her lips. Rebeke snatched her gaze from his.

"Damn you! Try no tricks here, snake! I want to know all
you know of the Limbreths, how to make a Gate into their
world, how to close such a Gate, how to pass it, how to make
first contact with a Limbreth before the Gate is made. And
anything else you know that may be helpful." Dropping the
end of the rope, she crossed to the small table. From the basket
she drew out two peaches. One she bit into; the other she
tossed once, catching gently its warm fuzzy weight. She
strolled back to the circle of the rope and drew her stool up to
it. Stooping she took up the loose end of the line and set the
untasted peach in her lap. "Well?"

Dresh swallowed. "The Limbreths, or Limbreth. No one
knows which. How did you ever get to be a Windmistress and
remain so ignorant? The answers are all easy, requiring only
that you forget your fixed ideas of how the world is made." He
caught the peach she tossed him and bit into it immediately. He
sighed and chewed slowly, swallowing reluctantly. "The Limbreth world," he resumed, "touches ours in one place, but that
place can be nearly anywhere you desire it to be. Don't ask me
how I learned all this; you would shudder and be scandalized
and throw me back down the well before I finished my peach."
He took another bite. "To continue. We touch and yet are
infinitely far apart. Not unlike ourselves, eh, Rebeke? To contact them is easy, however. Tell me, Rebeke, if you had an
important thing to say to a Windsinger far away, what would
you do?"

She shrugged. "Summon her here with a messenger."

"No imagination; it was always your curse. And you were
always chary of using power where simple brawn would suf-
fice. *A speaking egg.* Just because you use them only from
Singer to Singer, do not imagine that that is the limit of their
power. They are very draining to use, I am sure you know; the
farther away the egg speaks for you, the greater the strain upon

you. But it does not strain the egg. Not at all. That egg could speak to a thousand worlds, ones that do not touch ours at all. The egg is only limited by the will that commands it.'' Dresh finished his peach in two juicy bites. ''I think you may have the will to reach that far. It will strain you, and you will ache for days afterwards; but if you have to, you can.''

''Tell me about Gates.''

Dresh turned his head and stared pointedly at the basket. This time Rebeke brought the whole basket back to rest beside her stool. She reached into it and brought out a small plate. A little brown crusted loaf rested on it beside a small ball of butter and a wedge of cheese. She set a wooden knife beside it, and, stooping, she set it within the circle and pushed it toward Dresh. He drew it to him with a little sigh, then looked up at her and for a moment malice didn't shine in his eyes. ''I never thought I would be bought for a little loaf and butter and cheese.'' He gazed at his plate thoughtfully. ''You know, I can never look on an uncut loaf without thinking of Mickle's little shop, and the heat of the ovens in the yard behind it. I used to stoke those ovens even on the hottest days, all day, for a loaf of bread and a place to sleep at night. Mickle always gave me more than that, of course. He was never a niggardly man. But I remember how I promised myself that someday my day's work would bring me more than that. And now . . .'' He gave a short laugh and then flashed his eyes to Rebeke's. But her expression was blank, not unguarded.

''The Gate,'' she repeated coldly.

Dresh shrugged and began to break the loaf with his fingers. ''The Limbreth will make the Gate, if you are willing to assist it. It needs your help to visualize it on this side. And cooperation usually involves an exchange of gifts.''

''What sort of gifts?''

Dresh was buttering bread and spoke around a mouthful. ''Nothing a Windsinger can't afford. Any person you happen to be getting rid of. They take wizards, I understand.''

The laugh burst from Rebeke before she could control it. Dresh grinned up at her, and for an instant the air of the room changed and she looked down on him almost fondly. But slowly she shook her head and the light went out of her eyes.

''What do the Limbreths want with such gifts, and what do they give in return?''

"The Limbreths," Dresh mused, cutting cheese. "Limbreths are fascinating creatures. Or is a fascinating creature. No one can figure out if there's one or many. But a few facts are known. They have great intellect, but no physical ability and few of the needs or hungers belonging to physical bodies, at least not that we understand; only a hunger of the soul. They long to create, but have few artistic media of their own. It is said that once they created poetry and tales and song, and were contented with them, but that was before we corrupted them. Limbreths use the creatures sent through the Gates as tools for other kinds of creating. The only drawback is that they use them up quite completely. Drawback to the creatures, that is. It's quite convenient for the ones who send them through the Gate."

"It may already be too late, then," Rebeke muttered to herself. "And what do they give, Dresh?"

"I'm thirsty."

Rebeke busied herself with opening the wine and pouring. She rose to set the glass within easy reach of Dresh's hand. He raised the glass and looked at her gravely over its rim in a silent toast. He sipped and went back to his subject. "Limbreths give anything you ask of them, if they have it. But ask yourself what they are likely to have that you might want? They don't eat or drink as we do, they don't dress or collect jewels, nor hoard precious things of any kind. What would you ask a Limbreth for?"

Rebeke pondered, watching him drink. "Poetry? Are their songs compelling in any way?"

"Quite the opposite. Obscure to any but another Limbreth— if there are any other Limbreths. I heard one once. Bored me to distraction."

"Have they any powers? Favors they could do?"

"The favor they do is to remove the unwanted person from our world. It always struck me as insufferably bold to ask them for a gift into the bargain. But some do."

"But what do the Limbreths give?"

"You guess. It entertains me while I am eating, and it takes longer. I am in no hurry to be back in my pit."

"Dresh!" Rebeke warned him, taking up the end of the noose.

He sighed. "The Limbreths give useless things, with good

intentions, or so they would have us believe. Example: a draught of their water, supposed to bring sweet dreams and peace and inspiration. It gave an insatiable desire to see the Limbreth in person and be fulfilled in him. It.''

"And what else?"

"My dear Rebeke, you flatter me. Do you suppose I have had any personal dealings with them? That is a bit tawdry, even for me. No, all I can give you is the rumors of them I have gathered. The rumors say that no one ever got anything worth having from a Limbreth. Unless you count getting rid of someone.''

Rebeke pondered. Dresh finished his bread and cheese and nodded toward the basket. "Is there more?"

"Is there more?" she countered.

"It depends on what you have in the basket."

"Mushroom and onion pastries."

"If one must have a worst enemy, it is best to choose a former lover, who will know best how to tempt and torment. Pass them over. The Gate itself. Now there's a tricky thing. The Limbreth creates it, opening a place between the worlds. But it cannot be left open to all passers, for the things of their world and ours cannot be mixed without discretion, which might alert a Gatherer. So the Limbreth puts in the Gate a Keeper, a servant, to prevent unwanted ones from using the Gate, and to keep the Gate from closing before the Limbreth is finished with it.''

"If the Gate is forced?"

"Not likely," Dresh mumbled around a crumbly mouthful. He was taking his time eating. "Not likely at all. Even if the Keeper weren't there, you must take into account the differences between the worlds. The light in their world, for instance, is dim and filtered, and the folk of their world are strange and unpredictable; they seem as soft as silk but they can be dangerous. So, to protect both worlds, the Limbreth seals the Gate. It's hard to describe, rather like the membrane on a fish egg. If the Limbreth wills it, it softens to let one through.''

"What if it were ripped, or forced?"

Dresh drained the last of his wine. "Impossible. While fighting off the Keeper?"

"It's happened." As soon as Rebeke had revealed it, she

regretted it. It had slipped from her as they sat talking as if they were old friends, instead of prisoner and Windmistress. To confide in Dresh gave her some small vulnerability to him; and he seized that bit of power remorselessly.

"Then I think you have a problem. A pity you have no friend to help you with it."

"Yes. Tell me what happens when a Gate is ripped."

"It's never happened before. Let me see. There would be a flow, from one world to the other, and who knows what nastiness might pass through. But that is minor. The important thing is that the Gatherers would know of the Gate instantly, and would know that someone had been tinkering where someone had no business."

"What would they do?"

"Who knows? The ones who make the rules don't have to reveal the punishments. Maybe nothing. Maybe they aren't really that interested in us. But if they did anything, I would say it would be something nasty. Nastier than we can imagine."

Rebeke was silent, staring off as she tried to picture them. The Gatherers had created this world and peopled it according to their desires, and given them rules for living together. Dresh looked up from picking the last crumbs of cheese from his plate.

"Who ripped it?" he asked shrewdly.

Rebeke looked at him through narrowed eyes. But what could it hurt? "Vandien."

"Vandien?" He was incredulous. Then laughter burst from him, filling the chamber. "With Ki's help, no doubt! Those two will be the death of us yet!" His voice held the warmth of a doting parent for errant children. Rebeke looked at him in amazement. With a gasp and a sigh, he controlled his laughter and met her eyes. "Come, you can't be surprised! If you leave sharp tools lying about, someone will get cut. First me, now you. Evens the score a bit, doesn't it?"

"Dresh." Rebeke cut through his merriment. "What is it about Ki?"

Dresh smiled at her. "Don't gull me, Windsinger. We've both used her, haven't we? You know full well, or you wouldn't have put her through a Gate."

Rebeke stared at him silently. He looked deep into her blue and white eyes, reading her. She let him.

"Oh, ho! So you didn't put her through. This bit of gossip gets juicier all the time. What is it about Ki? I don't think you have anything in that basket that could buy that secret from me."

"The basket is empty," Rebeke admitted.

"I've other senses you could indulge," he suggested lewdly.

"Dresh. Don't push me."

"I've never cared for scales, but it might be interesting."

"Don't be snide."

"I'm not. I have something to sell, and I'll wait for your best offer."

"Then ask for something I can give you."

"My freedom."

"No!"

"Then it appears we cannot bargain." Dresh shrugged and hugged his knees.

"So it appears." Rebeke stooped and took up the rope. Almost casually she began to coil it. Dresh's circle shrank.

"That's not sporting!" he hissed when the rope nearly touched him.

Rebeke stopped. "It's not a game."

"At least give me something for my secret. How's this? My secret for yours. Tell me what is going on, completely, and I'll tell you what I know of Ki."

Rebeke glared at him, but she began a terse recounting of her situation. Dresh grinned at first, but then the smile faded. She could almost see his mind begin to work in its old trails of deception and subterfuge. When she finished he was rubbing his hands slowly and staring down the well and the look he flashed on her scared her.

"Now is my time, though it comes in a way I could never have foreseen. I shall bring the High Council down. Oh, it will be your doing; the dress will fit you well, Rebeke, but I shall cut the pattern. They stole you from me and I vowed they would pay. But I never thought you would be my weapon."

"You are stepping beyond your bounds, wizard," she warned him in a flat voice.

"Of course I am. And so are you, with your wizard in a well and your Relic to blackmail the High Council with. Fun, isn't it? Now listen to me; I shall have to be brief. Once, long ago, wearing a face you wouldn't know, I spent an evening in a

Romni camp. There I heard many Romni songs, but one was
very different. It told of a woman who had died in the act of
stealing her little girl back from the Windsingers. I asked about
the song and a strange thing happened: a whole caravan of
Romni had nothing to say. No protestations that the song was
true; no knowledge of who first sang it. Intriguing. And, in
spite of their silence, the song told me much. The woman's
name was Wisteria. The Windsingers' killing tool had been a
Harpy. And the baby had survived."

"Preposterous!"

"The best strokes of luck always are. So it was possible that
somewhere there existed a child that had been Windsingered
but then regained by its parents."

"How long did we have the child?" Anxiety stained Rebeke's voice and lined her face.

"The song didn't say. Listen, and stop asking questions. I
pursued a lot of avenues. I spoke to Harpies; I spoke to old
Romni who knew the genealogy of the tribes. I followed old
scents, and lost them a hundred times. I managed to narrow it
to a handful of young Romni women, but the Romni became
more jealous of the secret the more I pursued it. Soon I came to
realize what they feared; that the Windsingers had not forgotten the child. The Romni are nothing if not thorough and I soon
came to believe that the secret was so well kept that not even
the girl involved could betray it, for she didn't know either. I
was reduced to keeping tabs on the young women; not an easy
task. And then luck struck again.

"The Windsingers hadn't forgotten. Or so I guessed when
the husband and two young children of one Romni woman
were murdered by Harpies, apparently for sport. It was a tenuous premise, of course. But add up my facts. The father of
this girl, one Aethan by name, had never permitted her to take
any of the young Romni to husband, although by their standards she was more than old enough. And, after the father
died, no young Romni approached her for an agreement, even
though she was a likely enough girl, with a wagon and team of
her own. What made her untouchable? She did take a man, but
he was not Romni, and she did have two children by him,
normal as far as anything I could hear. Then the Harpies
widow her and kill her children. Coincidence? Perhaps. But
what followed was not. Ki took her vengeance against the

Harpies, resisting not only their physical violence, but proving strong against their other powers as well. I became convinced she was the one.''

''It well explains a lot of strange things,'' Rebeke cut in with a dreamy look on her face. ''You need tell me no more. You disguised yourself by merging your aura with hers, when she shouldn't even have had one. When she swept your runes away that night in the inn and set me free of your power: that should have killed her, or at least crippled her. It but stunned her for a moment.''

Dresh nodded, a bitter look on his face. ''My carelessness; I left a sharp tool lying about. I know more of her than I can tell in one night, for I made quite a study of her. I have ridden on her wagon more times than she knows of, for she has a habit of picking up weary strangers.

''So there you have it. Ki is a Windsinger that was never shaped. She's ingested your potions, but hasn't changed physically. Some in the High Council must have known of her, but only watched her, removing her mate and children when it seemed expedient, lest the children have some inherited tendencies the Council couldn't control. But Ki? All she seems to have is a predilection for evading magic. Not a power; more an immunity. When I found her and used her, I suppose it scared the Council. So they decided to put her out of the way. A Gate.''

''Why didn't they just murder her outright?''

''I suspect that for a long time even the Windsingers weren't certain just what baby they needed to kill; and by the time they knew, they also saw the possibilities. They hoped she would be useful, in time.''

''What have we sunk to?''

''You could answer that better than I. Come, now, Rebeke. Plot with me how best to turn this to our advantage.''

Rebeke shook her head absently. She sat silently staring at the black floor in front of her, her mind ranging over the possibilities.

''You're finished with me, aren't you?''

Rebeke came out of her reverie to find his grey eyes looking up at her pleadingly. He did not wait for her reply.

''Please, Rebeke. Not the void again. Anything else, for, like you, I can imagine nothing worse. Chain me, cut off my hands and silence my tongue, take my sight and hearing, and still it would be better than the void, for I would be *real*.''

Rebeke picked up the line, trying not to hear him, for she dared to do nothing else with him. He was treacherous, she reminded herself, a man who stored little hurts for years, a wizard who would never forget that she had mastered him once.

"I loved you!" He flung the words at her like stones. "I loved you and you turned from me to the Windsingers, with never a word of explanation. How could you expect me to feel anything for them but hate? Yes, I plotted against them, I did them all the damage I could! But it was against them I acted, not against you. You were what they had stolen from me, the Rebeke I loved.''

She burst out: "You didn't love me, Dresh; you deceive yourself. You loved mastering me. You bent my young powers to your hands, and it satisfied you. You loved me like you loved a fine hawk on your wrist; I was a tool, as sharp as Ki. But you no more loved Rebeke than you loved a wild hawk sailing down the wind.''

"Damn you! That's not true! I would have taught you things, made you my equal as soon as you were ready. You were impatient, like a child clutching at a flame. I kept from you only the things that could hurt you, and punished you only as a parent would punish a child that put herself into danger.''

Rebeke was not listening; she forbade her ears to hear. Slowly she drew up the rope, the blue circle shrinking. He rose to his feet, still talking, as it crept toward him. He balanced on the edge of the well, arms windmilling as he shrieked at her: "You hate me because I mastered you and commanded you! But what do you do to me now? If commanding another is such a grave fault, how will you atone for it?''

He did not scream as he fell; the void took him too quickly for that. He drifted away like an autumn leaf falling, and Rebeke watched him go, coiling the rope to replace it in her sleeve.

"I am a Windsinger," she reminded herself. "What was is no more." She rubbed grudgingly at the eyes that ached because they were no longer structured for tears.

Twelve

"I CAN go no farther." Hollyika abruptly dropped down on the road. She settled on her haunches, her massive head drooping onto her bent knees. Ki halted in surprise, for the Brurjan-Human mule had showed no signs of weariness before this. Their pace had been steady, the lights drawing them on as smoothly as line run over a pulley.

"Do you need water?" Ki asked. She sloshed the jug she was carrying. In tacit consent they had been drinking sparingly, for they knew they had a dry way to go. But Hollyika shook her head slowly.

"It would help," she admitted. "It would ease me. But it would be an easing only, not a cure. I am weak. It is my own foul nature that dooms me, that makes me unfit to tread this road and drives me to my knees. I have tried, Ki. Since I drank of these waters and my mind was cleared, I have taken no creature that breathes to be my food. Water only have I drunk, no rich warm blood. Grass I have eaten, to be as innocent as the horse I once enslaved, though it caught between my teeth and strangled me as it went longways down my throat. My body betrays me; it was never designed for this life, but for a life of baseness on the far side of the Gate. My strength came from my evil ways and now that I have forsaken them, my body will not carry me to the Limbreth. The better path is denied me."

A terrible sympathy welled up in Ki. She wanted to comfort her, but had no words, for the truth could not be compromised. Slowly she sank down beside her. "Drink then, and be eased."

Hollyika reached for the jug, then slowly put her hands back on her knees. "No. You will need it to reach the Limbreth. If I drink now, we shall both be lost. I am going to die here, Ki, on this road, and I will never see the Jewels of the Limbreth. The doing of any great deed is denied me, but I am left the chance of not doing a foul one. I will not drink and by not drinking, I shall be sending you on to the Limbreth. Whatever peace you gain when you reach the Limbreth, think of me."

"I shall." Ki did not try to sway her. The longer she was in this land, the more often she drank its water, the clearer her path became. Old patterns of thought and behavior were sloughing from her like outgrown skins and in their stead she was finding wisdom that welled up in her as effortlessly as the silver waters welled up from the land. Decisions no longer troubled her; she did not seesaw at crossroads, nor torment herself with wondering. The better way, the right way, was clear before her like a shining silver thread to be followed. Hollyika was doing the right thing in denying herself that Ki might go on. In any other place and time, Ki would have tried her best to dissuade her, would have felt by friendship bound to do so. But her new wisdom taught her better. Hollyika was not designed to live in this land, and for Ki to force her to strive on would be a cruelty, a giving of false hope. Both of them had grown beyond that.

"I will stay with you," she said softly, "for a while, that your candle will not burn out alone. Then I shall go on to the Limbreth and the Jewels, and in their peace I shall hold your memory."

Hollyika looked up at her with great brown eyes full of wisdom and sorrow. She knew, in the same way Ki did, that her decision was correct. She nodded slowly. "I shall not keep you long," she promised. "My strength was ebbing before I met you by the river. Since then I have traveled on the reserves of my flesh, burning what the Brurjans call the oil of the last lantern. My body follows most closely the way of that folk; to be strong and to strive, until the very last moments when there is no strength left. Death, now, is not far off." She lowered her head slowly until her broad forehead rested again on her knees.

Ki sat beside her in the midst of the strange land they had traveled together. The air was keen, but the chill no longer troubled her body. The water had seen to that.

The wide lustrous fields of the farmers had been left behind as the road climbed straight and true, and now it threaded hilly country, ungrazed by any save wild flocks. Small yellow and white flowers shone out in the grasses like stars come to earth; and even the bare bones of this place, where the rocks thrust suddenly from the verdant hillside, seemed to scintillate coldly with a light of their own. Hollyika alone was a dark and huddled thing, a lightless lump in a place of glowing life. To be so strange and alien in this comforting place was lonesome enough; but Hollyika was dying in a world where living was peace. Ki reached over and took her hand, holding it loosely and companionably in her own. She stroked the downy fur on the back of the hand and looked down on the clean black nails that thickened like claws.

"Ki?" Her voice was muffled. "For all the Romni, will you forgive me?"

"I will." Ki gave no thought to the words, for the decision was plain. "For all the Romni, I forgive you." It was so simple, with the water running cool within her and the black road running straight before her; it was all so very simple and easy and good. The pale far lights of the Limbreth blinked at her, letting her stay for now, but waiting for her.

Without warning Hollyika fell over on her side and lay slightly curled in the road. With each softly expelled breath, she made a "kah" sound. She looked terrible, with dry crusts forming around her eyes and her breath foul with dying. Ki set her hand down gently against her breast and stroked the dry fur, once sleek, that covered ribs beneath scanty flesh. If she had seen Hollyika as a Brurjan, she would have known from her first sight of her that she was starved to the edge of death. But Ki had imputed her lack of bulk to her Human side.

Ki rose, stretching. As she did so, she looked down at her own body and was amazed at how ribby she herself had become. She could not remember when she had last eaten, but no pangs of hunger stirred in her. She unstoppered the jug and took a tiny swallow of water. Even that small sip spread coolness and comfort through her, and she was able to see Hollyika's death in a calm, clear light. The poor creature had tried to set aside her martial ways and become a seeker of peace, but her body could not adapt. Her death was not upon Ki's head, and she basked in the comfort of that knowledge—

and then realized how foreign it was to her former way of
thinking. Even as she startled at it, she realized it was the
Limbreth reaching into her mind and bringing order out of the
chaos that years of unguided living had created. The Limbreth
were to guide her now. She sat down upon the road again,
hugging her knees, letting their wisdom flow through her.

Dimly she became aware of a sound: hoof thuds and the
creaking rumble of a wagon. Whoever was driving was in a
hurry; only a fool would drive so rapidly in the dark. But he
was yet a long ways off; she seemed to feel the sounds through
the road rather than hear them with her ears.

Slowly she moved to the side of the road. She thought about
Hollyika lying where she would be trampled, but the Limbreth
wisdom touched her, and she saw it did not matter if she died
of starvation or was trampled to death, for death was her goal.
Ki should give her no grief, nor any further thought. Hollyika
had been her guide, and in following that vocation she had
risen as high as was possible for her. Her death would be a
peaceful one, no matter how it came, for in her own heart she
knew these things. Her honor had been to prepare Ki for the
path that lay before her. And now Ki must come, for she was
ready. Come.

The sound of the wagon and team distracted her. They were
still far away, but the sound came to her clearly, and it stirred
something in her. *Come now* a voice within her cried, and she
received an impression of terrible danger. She rose to her feet,
feeling for an instant woozy and unsteady; then the night
snapped into clarity. In the new Limbreth darkness, she saw
with a clarity her eyes had never enjoyed in the harsh brightness of sunlight. The subtlety of shades of colors came to her
and new insights flooded her. She was able to see how the
leaves held up the branches of the trees; she understood for the
first time that a mountain was a place where the substance of
the sky had withdrawn and the earth had risen to fill it. All the
immense things that made up the world, the mountains, the
rivers, the forests, were actually very tiny things bound together in a common purpose, just as her life was a very small
and finite thing, a tiny being coming into a place where a tiny
bit of non-being had withdrawn. She was made not merely of
flesh, but of moments of time, and of a greater purpose she did
not know, any more than an individual leaf knew its tree.

Anything she ever wanted to do, she must do now and at the risk of failure, for the length of her life was not revealed to her: she might be called at any time to surrender her life spark. All she could be sure of accomplishing were the things she had already done.

That last thought galvanized her. She had not yet attained the Limbreth. At any moment, all chance she had of reaching them might be snatched away from her by her own mortality. Unlike Hollyika, she did not have even a minor goal attained that would let her die in honor, and by her own slothfulness, she would have sullied Hollyika's attainment of guiding her. It all rested on her now.

Ki began to tremble. She raised the jug of water and drank hastily, hoping to quell her sudden terror, but her desperate purposefulness was only increased by it. She stoppered the jug and hugged it tightly under her arm, and ran. No time to waste in saying farewell to a dead thing on the road; Hollyika would not want goodbyes that wasted precious time. She must go to the Limbreth.

As she ran, her body became lighter. The water within her now did not slosh in her belly like ordinary water. It rippled through her limbs like a stream dashing down a hill, lending her the swiftness of running water. The road unfurled before her and her bare feet poured over it. She felt a dew of sweat damp her skin, oiling her muscles, letting her run as smoothly as fish sliding through silver water. There was no effort to this motion, and it took no time at all. Time was stilled, breathless in an eternal night, as Ki ran to the Jewels of the Limbreth.

Only twice in that long uphill run did she fall. Even as she lay motionless with her face against the road's hard surface, she could feel the Limbreth flowing in her, urging her closer. Each time she fell she drank more water, and the second time she finished it and cast aside the jug. After she drank, she could rise again, renewed, to run on. The glimmering lights were closer, and still closer. The soft air bore her up and the smooth moss of the road was warm underfoot. When she finally halted to breathe after the long final rise, she felt she teetered on the brim of the valley below her. Awe washed over her.

The glowing lights of the Limbreth, viewed for so long from far off, were more than brilliant here. They clustered as if on the brows of stony giants. There could not have been more than a dozen in all, but their very massiveness made them seem legion. The road flowed down from her feet and spread around them in a massive puddle of smooth blackness. A ridge buckled up from the center of this dark plain, and on this ridge they were rooted. Immense steep-sided pillars they were, featureless as black water, until her eyes touched their crowns. The lights glimmered upon them, and Ki felt them as eyes, though she could not believe they saw her. Beings such as those must spend their sight upon less finite things than a mere Human. She envisioned them gazing eternally up into the shrouded skies of this place, seeing through the perpetual overcast to the stars that lurked beyond. Her skin shivered all over her flesh. She was moved in a way too deep for a Human to tolerate. Joyous tears stung her eyes, but she wished to scream in terror.

"There is . . . too *much* of them." She could barely bring the words out of her mouth. It was beyond her to wonder how she knew of their vast sentience. Enough that their age and wisdom filled the valley before her like wine fills a goblet. Her breath came and went in a constricted throat.

Her first step was hesitant, but then her feet flew. She was coming home, her heart told her, home! She laughed aloud. Even as she looked on the Limbreths, they changed before her marveling eyes, so that they were ever new and wondrous. They, and then, no, *it*, she realized, they were one and many at the same time, but it was their unity that had called to her. With every step she took toward them, she was bedazzled with revelations, until she felt her skin sparkling with new knowledge. She bubbled with their effervescent miracles. Her feet lifted and fell tirelessly on the road and peace flowed through her.

"Come!" called a sudden voice, a voice like nothing Ki had ever heard; if metal had been given a tongue, so it might sound. But her wisdom told her it was the voice of the Jewels that crowned the Limbreth. She ran to them, down the last bit of hill and across the dark plain.

The Limbreth loomed before her, and she approached it eagerly, awed but urged on by the inner knowledge that she was now fit to confront it. When she had entered the Gate, she had begun a time of preparation; the many layers of her false world were stripped away from her like a dry husk from a ripe seed. It humbled her that the Limbreths had seen fit to so purify her. Without them, she would never have come to this awakening of self.

Understanding burned her like a fever. For all the time she had been coming to the Limbreth, it had been beside and around her; she had only to open her eyes and see. The hard smooth road beneath her feet was a part of the Limbreth, as was the cooling water that flowed for her. The path of purification and the waters of awareness, others had called them. This the Limbreth let her know, for they were kin now, and it could speak in her mind.

At the base of the Limbreth, Ki sank down to rest in blessed peace. The sheer sides of the Limbreth rose in a pillar too large for even four Humans to circle with joined hands; its surface was hard and smooth as the road, but unseen beneath it seethed and bubbled the same silvery waters as flowed in the river. Its lofty crown of the flickering, glowing Jewels pulsed gently with the emanations of the Limbreth's thoughts, shining into Ki's mind as they dappled her flesh with glowing colors.

"I am here!" she told it, rejoicing.

"And I am here, as I always have been." In the Limbreth's simple reply, Ki felt its years; it had always been and it remembered all. It would remember her always, also. Whatever else might happen to her, this moment gave her immortality in the Limbreth's memory. She felt a touch on her mind and that touch took up her sentience and gave it back to her, reordered and refreshed. "Rest now and think," the Limbreth instructed her. "Go again through your life. Ask me what you will and I will answer you. Know yourself as well as I know you. You will be able to see how your own choices have always destined you for me."

Ki let her mind drift lazily on the current of her thoughts, marveling at all she had known without knowing. The Limbreth had charted all her moments and correlated all her knowledge in those brief moments, flowing through her consciousness, leaving its shining trail through all her memories. She looked back over her years and felt the Limbreth at her shoulder as she did so; the Limbreth explained the feelings that had baffled her and cataloged the needs that had gnawed endlessly at her, and gaps in what she knew about herself were filled.

Even her most private moments and thoughts had been gently handled and brought to order. Ki looked back over a life that was suddenly a harmonious whole, no longer a string of events that varied from dull to shattering. She saw how they all fit together, and how unknowingly she had shaped the most devastating of her tragedies. Saw, but no longer flinched from seeing.

Memories too painful to recall were given back to her, their poison drawn. Then one fine spring morning rose into her mind, and it was like seeing the keystone of the arch. The weather had been mild and the small campfire long cold on the morning she had arisen and toddled from her blankets. She had wandered away from the caravan encampment, drawn by sweet singing, and followed the blue-gowned stranger.

The Limbreth numbered for her the days among the Wind-singers. She saw them through her baby eyes as immensely tall and gracious beings that cared for her and dressed her in a little white robe. Then her mother had come, wearing Ki's own adult face, to steal her back. Ki remembered her joy at the reunion, and then knew terror again as her mother and a scarlet Harpy fought over her to their mutual deaths. Then Aethan came for her, to take her home to the wagon.

It was only one memory, buried under the callus of years, but it gave order to all others. Had she not gone to that sweet call, the Windsingers would not have known her. They would not have sent the Harpies to kill Sven and her babies nor would she have had to face a blue Harpy in the Pass of the Sisters; Vandien would never have scarred his face taking its claws in her stead. Dresh would not have used her as a pawn against the Windsingers. Nor would the Windsingers finally have disposed of her by putting her through a Gate—if only she had not followed the singing. But all those things were as they had to have been, in order to lead her to this moment before the Limbreth.

The Limbreth was silent, but Ki felt the quiet as a probing question. She puzzled, waiting for her emotions to rise. She thought of the callous ways in which the Windsingers had twisted her life. She should resent them for separating her from her husband, children, and friend, and finally setting her adrift from her own world. They had sent her here as a gift to the Limbreth, as if she were a cow or a sack of beans. She should be full of plans for vengeance.

Nothing. The peace of the Limbreth flowed through her. All of that was past. No action of hers could alter the past; but she could shape her future, take her exile by the Windsingers and turn it into a thing of beauty and wonder, and her life would have a meaning.

"That is good," the Limbreth told her. "You are ready."

"I am ready," Ki assented.

"You know yourself. Now I must teach you the world."

Another touch upon her mind, this one soft as melting butter. Ki saw all as the Limbreth knew it, and the Limbreth was old and unchanged since the Gatherers had first brought it here. Its own far world had gone into rosy darkness and then deep cold, and the Gatherers had brought it here that the Limbreth need not perish. The Gatherers, free of time and space, took from every world a few of each kind of being, and brought them to these linked worlds, putting each with kinds similar enough to share a world, and bidding them only to keep their species intact. To the simpler races they did not make themselves known, but to the old beings, such as the Limbreth, the unchanging ones who knew something of the scope of time, they occasionally came and spoke. The others lived out the days of their lives in their own ways, unaware of the miracle of their continuance. Ki saw that now, and her concept of the world was enlarged and renewed just as her memories of her life had been. She knew herself, and she saw again her niche in the order of things and the insignificance of her brief life. To the Limbreth she was a moth newly hatched, and doomed to die before the night ended. The knowledge freed her. What were wagons and cargoes, coins and friendships, when set in such a framework? Like the tailings of an earthworm, in a moment they crumbled back to common dirt and could not be distinguished from it. Nothing so brief could hold any obligations; but she might freely choose to pay her debt to the Limbreth, to the extent that her small being was capable of.

The bridge she had crossed to come here had been the work of one from beyond a Gate, called by the Limbreth to a higher goal. Wrought from the very stuff of the Limbreth itself, it was as eternal as they were, a monument of that fluttering moth to the black night of time. The essence of a mortal being had been poured into that structure and physically immortalized by it.

"What will you do?" the Limbreth asked her gently.

The night held its breath as she sought for her answer. "I would like." She stopped.

"Yes?" prodded the Limbreth.

"I would make a garden. A garden of life, not merely a garden that lives. A garden that grows from the seeds of wisdom you have given me. One would pass through it on the way to the bridge. That is what my soul would do, but . . ."

The Limbreth shone gently upon her. "Do not be daunted. I am neither stone nor water, as you perceive me. The vision shall be yours and the working of it. But the skill will come from me, as will the material to bring it to life. I am the fertile soil, the rains, and the wind that spreads the pollen. Go, now, and begin."

Ki started to step away and then felt a glow of warmth from the Limbreth upon her back. She waited.

"You have given me a new story, one that pleases me greatly. I am old, and the older I get, the more every new thing is savored. I shall not forget an instant of your life, Ki. You have been but an instant, but you have filled it full. Your garden will reflect it."

Ki turned eyes onto the road that went back up the hill. She had not rested, and her journey had been long. And now she had as far to go again, to return to her chosen spot. She felt the amusement of the Limbreth. Was not this its world? Did not the road do as it was bid? Let Ki follow a new path, one that would take her back swiftly to her destination, avoiding all distractions.

The new road unrolled before her feet like a flung carpet. Moss carpeted it for her as swiftly. It flowed like a shining stream, an effortless straight path to follow. Weariness fell from her and a desire to reach her chosen spot and begin blazed up in her. She would pour herself into it. She sprang away as lightly as a hart, racing down the road as she had never run before.

Thirteen

YOLETH crouched by the dark Gate; little remained of it. Stooping, she peered through the fissure in the wall. Her knobbed cowl bobbled as she bent to put her mouth to the crack, and her sharp-edged whisper cut the peaceful night. "Keeper!" she hissed. "I know you must be there. Answer me!"

She waited for a reply, the night silent but for her harsh gasps of frustration. The dark breeze from the other side of the Gate was gone. Yoleth burned to know how balance had been restored. If they had forced Vandien or Ki back out of the Gate, they should have told her of it. She rocked slowly back on her heels, her joints cracking. It was a strain to crouch here and an insult to her position. She was a Windmistress and a High Council member, hissing through a crack like a lovesick peasant courting a housemaid. "Keeper!"

"Yes?" The oddly sexless voice was calm. "You had no need to call so often. I heard you, but I had a distance to come. My Master says that so small a crack has little need of guarding, for what could venture through? The worlds have found a new balance, and perhaps if we leave it alone it will close now, though it shows no signs of it yet. My Master says that perhaps the crack will remain open between our worlds. An interesting thought, don't you agree?"

Yoleth did not agree. She had no patience for this Keeper and his crack. "I am come to finish our business. That the worlds balance is good, for the Gate will not draw the Gatherers now, and it is one less thing to hinder our settling."

"There is no need of abject thanks. You may rise. My

Master has completed all you asked. It is always pleasant to be of service to another sentient species, and to interact with strange cultures.''

"I did not come to thank him!" Yoleth raged.

"Indeed." The single word was an accusation of execrable manners.

But Yoleth was not to be cowed by social protocol. "No! I am here to demand my payment! Your master has had his new plaything long enough! Do not pretend that Ki was accepted only as a favor to me. There is the calling jewel that they promised to me. You have put me off long enough."

"A calling gem?" The Keeper's voice wondered that she dared say such things.

"Yes, damn you! The jewel the Limbreths use to call ones of their choosing to them. I would have one of my own. They agreed to that, when first this bargain was struck, and together we opened the Gate. Ki was to be their toy, and in return I was to get a calling gem."

"That is not how I understood it! I am the Keeper of the Gate, and know such things. You begged the Limbreth to aid you! The Limbreth opened the Gate, testing it once on a Brurjan totally unfit for any of our purposes, and then took Ki out of your way. It was a favor between peers."

"Liar!" Yoleth was rabid. "You spoke of it here to me. We talked of it before, and you promised that when the Limbreth had Ki and was sure of her suitability, the jewel would be delivered! How dare you claim no memory of it!"

"Yes, we spoke of such a thing. But as a possibility only. I am staggered that you dare ask for it so brazenly, as if it were a tinker's trinket. But, be still! My Master speaks to me."

Yoleth fumed at being so addressed by such a lowly creature. She swallowed her words and peered through the crack at the Keeper. The Keeper huddled like a pile of rags on the ground, its eyeless face gazing far afield. Yoleth stifled her impatience with a growl. She couldn't tolerate any more delay. Ki was out of the way, and the High Council was beginning to sway to her songs; but the calling gem could make her power certain. With the jewel, not even that insolent Rebeke would dare to stand before her. Once she had the knack of using it, she could call any before her and keep them there, until they knuckled to her will. The Relic would be hers, and Rebeke would learn to do as she was told.

Yoleth seethed as she measured Rebeke's ambition by her own. Rebeke wanted control of the High Council, to sway them to her ridiculous ideas. She would make them all slaves to the peasants in the fields. Ever she harped on duty and always she prattled of how generosity and gentleness would pay off in larger harvests and tribute given with a free hand. The fool. The larger the harvest, the less value each bushel had. The peasants were not the simple-hearted folks she painted but greedy sneaks, adept at hiding the true bounty of the harvests from the Windsingers who gave them the fair weather. Give them a golden summer and they gave you a bushel of wormy apples and some spotted tubers. But give them a few storms and a splatter or two of lightning to keep fear in their hearts, and they would yield up the Windsingers' proper due. No, Rebeke was a fool and a dangerous one, and Yoleth wouldn't wait until she had the Council at her feet. Yoleth would get that calling gem, if she had to sing a wind to blow through this damned crack and shred the rags off the Keeper. She would have it.

The Keeper stirred, coming out of a far meditation. Yoleth was secretly disgusted at the quivering of his body as he became aware of her again. "Well?" she demanded harshly.

"Long has my Master kept me, to make me understand what they wish." He bowed low to her, suddenly subservient. "I am rebuked for my discourteous words, and must ask your pardon. I am but the Keeper of the Gate, not the Mouth of the Limbreth. I have spoken beyond my station, and said words that must be taken back. I abase myself before you and beg that you will consider those words the mouthings of an ignorant churl, not the message of my gracious Master." The Keeper literally groveled in the dust on his side of the Gate. Yoleth regarded him with distaste as he writhed in the dirt, scooping handfuls of it to pour over his own head.

"Enough!" she cried. "I am sure you have learned not to interfere between your betters. I dismiss your words from my mind. Rise now, and give me the gem."

The Keeper leaped up in a flurry of dust. He curtsied low to her and crept close to the crack. "Of course! As my Master has agreed, so it will be done. It costs me a pang to part with it, so long have I held it for them. I will be honest. Jealousy flavored my earlier words. The highest honor this one has ever known has been the holding of this for my Master. But he has revealed to me that his will may be better served by putting it into your hands. What true servant questions the wisdom of the Master? I obey.''

Yoleth knelt in the dust to receive it. The Keeper slipped his hands inside his ragged robe, groping. He seemed to struggle; Yoleth made a wry face at his dramatics. Having said he was loath to part with it should have been enough for him, but now he was miming his own reluctance. She saw the sinews of his muscles crawl as he gripped something tightly, and there was a ripping sound, then a snap as if a cord had given way. He thrust the something at her, his own eyeless mask twisted into a mockery of agony. The jewel alone seemed to pass easily through the wall; she felt as if she reached into tar to take it. As soon as she took it from the Keeper's hand, he fell limply back into the dust. Yoleth gave one more disgusted look at his abject posturing, and rose with the jewel clutched in her grip.

She wiped it clean of his sweat on the cuff of her flowing sleeve and raised it to the pale light of the stars. It began to pulse and throb, gleaming so intensely she almost believed she felt a warmth with each blossoming of light. Her heart quickened to its beating; she felt a thrill of possession such as she had almost forgotten. It was hers, Yoleth's alone, to master and use. Did the High Council think that she would do their dirty work for them and have nothing to show for it? Fools.

She began to slip it into the pocket inside her sleeve. A dark stain on her cuff caught her attention. It smeared darkly on her fingers with a coppery smell. Puzzled, she stooped to peer again through the crack in the wall. The Keeper lay as she had last seen him, his eyeless face a grim mask; no breath swelled his chest. Instead, a dampness spread in the dust beside him.

Yoleth rose, her thin lips pulled even tighter. The Jewel in her hand pulsed at her fondly. She knew the speaking eggs of the Windsingers, living creatures so like stones, but brimming with life and thought. They might be used to communicate, if one were trained and dared risk the tremendous energies involved. But this calling gem was not like them. She gazed into its lights, wondering what dangers were in it. Would the Limbreth or Keeper have warned her? Was there any real need for it? She had thought there would be some formula given, some series of meditations to attune oneself to the gem and focus her calling. But the Keeper, who could have given such instruction, sprawled beyond the Gate, senseless or dead. Perhaps she would be wiser to put this thing from her hand, to thrust it back through the Gate and ask for some other favor, a lesser boon, a trinket. Yoleth gazed into its shimmering depths and knew the Limbreth possessed nothing that was the equal of this, and that she would take nothing less. She could learn to use it; a bold hand need never fear power. She gripped the gem tightly, feeling its surging warmth flood her. Sliding her hands up inside her long loose sleeves, she strode away into the night.

Jace stood in the shadows watching her leave. The Gate was little more than a crack now and she wasn't much more than a shadow herself. Her past few nights had brought her no food, and her constant wandering and calling for Chess had taken a toll of her energy.

She could not have explained what drew her back to the Gate, for it no longer held any promise for her. If Vandien were going to return, he would have done it before; now it was too late. She was not really surprised that he had not come back; would anyone, given a choice between her world and this one? No, she was not surprised, but she found that she could blame him. A week ago she would have had the equanimity to accept it, to see his decision to stay over there as his only sane choice, not as betrayal or abandonment. Her cool logic would have told her that he had been given a chance for a better life, and had taken it. She would have felt glad for him.

But that was before Chess was lost to her. It changed everything. Where were her fine thoughts now, the words she had pelted Chess with? Regretted and swallowed, every one. But she could not call back the ones Chess had carried off with him. Like thistles in his skin, they would dig in deeper and spread their poison. Wasn't it odd, now that Jace had no weaker companion to exhort to acceptance and inner peace, her own had fled? ''I could accept it, I could lie down and die peacefully, if only I knew that Chess had also done so. If only I knew that he was safe from this world and beyond its corruptions, I could breathe out my last breath calmly. But I cannot do so, if it means leaving him here alone without aid. I can't. But I may have to.'' Jace whispered the words aloud to the rough stones she leaned on. Her strength was nearly at an end. Much of the cool darkness that had leaked into this part of the city remained here still. Perhaps tonight she should stay here, and see if the day was diluted enough not to harm her; she feared that if she tottered back to the hovel one more time, come the next night she might not have the strength to leave it. She no longer hoped that Chess would return on his own. He had been driven forth too thoroughly, too callously. But the Gate might draw him back.

Jace slid slowly down the wall. She turned her eyes back to the Gate, hoping for his small shadow. The only caller this night at the Gate had been the Windsinger. Jace had watched her with dulled curiosity. She had understood little of what had passed at the Gate, save that the Limbreth had chosen to call Ki to their hallowed valley. Ki would be blessed by the Limbreth and given a vocation. She would pour herself into her new-found work with joy and vigor until her days ran out.

A little hunger nibbled at Jace's heart. Once she had dreamed she would be so called; she had fantasized that she would awaken from her sleep hearing the pure call of the Limbreth to take the pilgrim path to the Jewels. Some few there were who went thus, clothed in a plain white garment, bare of foot and head, with a smile of gladness that shone like the Jewels themselves. Those ones did not return, and no word was heard of them, save in rumors of a new and beauteous thing rising in some far part of the peaceful world. It did not seem fair to Jace that sometimes the Limbreth would hunger for ones from other worlds to enact a vision. The Limbreth would open a Gate and one of those rogues would enter, wild and violent and ruthless, until the spell of the Limbreth worked and the waters of peace soothed the outlander. But from those strangers came the works of awesome power that were sometimes seen, like the first bridge, which was no part of the peaceful world it decorated; it had been born in this world. It pleased the Limbreth and made him hunger for more extravagant minds and iron wills for such tasks. From what Chess had said of Ki, the Limbreth would like her. Yet it ached in Jace that for such a fancy she and Chess had been exiled from their world.

Jace let her head tip forward to rest on her huddled knees. Her pale green garment had gone brown, like dead leaves, and was rent and stained; her glossy hair was now coarse as a pony's tail. She rummaged about in herself for the will and the strength to rise, but found neither. Slowly she let the knowledge sink in. The Gate was too small to use. There was no chance of Vandien coming back. Even if she found Chess, they could never go home.

"Wake up!" The hand on Jace's shoulder was callused but not unkind as it shook her. "It's nearly dawn, and you have to be the one from all he has raved. Hurry up, woman!"

Jace forced her weary head up. Her eyeballs felt dry, her lashes gummed and grainy. She stared up at the man who shook her so boldly. His heavy jowls bristled with black and grey stubble above a beard that fringed his jawline. His eyes were dark brown, his hair a willful tangle of loose curls that frizzed out on his forehead and bushed above his ears. A working man, she decided, but even Jace had been in the world long enough to see that his clothes were wrong for that part. They were too fine of cloth and cut, even though he wore them carelessly, not minding where dust or wine had left a blotch. They smelled of wine, but his eyes were sober and alert as he shook her again, and then dragged her firmly to her feet. She could find no resentment for the stout arm he put about her waist. She staggered along at his side. "Come on, then. Boy needs you. He's sick. Just like a child, to stand tough as brambles through all hardship, then, the second he had a bed and a bite, to give up and go sick on me. Feverish. He raves a lot, and mostly he calls for you. It was hard for me to find out from his words what you looked like or where to seek you. But the dark Gate came into his talk so often that finally even my slow wits made the connection. So I came to find you. Odd. I thought you would know what to do for him, once I found you. But you don't look too healthy yourself. Like as not, I'll have the two of you on my hands and under my feet now."

His words didn't convey any of the annoyance they suggested; Jace suspected him of enjoying this. She let her thoughts drift. Chess was ill, but in kindly if not skilled hands. So was she. She would see Chess again soon. The homely kindness of the man beside her soothed her bruised spirit. He clucked and nagged as he helped her along. There was a purpose to his movements that did not match his slovenly clothes. She sank gratefully down into the comfort of someone else taking charge.

Mickle wound up carrying her the last stretch of the road to his home. He moved silently through the rooms he kept

darkened for Chess's sake, to settle Jace into his own soft bed.
Then he hurried about the room scooping most of his debris up
and trundling it out of sight. He hummed softly to himself as he
floated a coverlet down over Jace and pulled a heavy curtain
closer across the window. He touched the woman's lax face,
but she didn't even stir. Well, he had chicken broth simmering
on the hearth, and healing roots mashed and ready. He could
bring them both out of this. He cocked his head, thinking he
had heard Chess call from the other bedroom. But all was
stillness in the snug little house.

Mickle bustled his way back into the kitchen, sighing with
relief. His sigh was cut short as he gazed at Rebeke perched on
his tall baker's stool, and he blew out the rest of his breath as a
snort and started in on her before she could speak.

"A fine mess you've made of things, and no thought to the
nuisance for me, I suppose. Here I am now with a house full of
sick folk and no one but myself to care for them. I don't
suppose you gave any thought to that, did you? And here you
come to poke at them. Well, they're both run into the ruts of
the wearies, and I won't let you trouble them. No, save your
glares for someone they impress. This is my house, Rebeke.
Bought with your money, perhaps, but mine nonetheless, and
here I am master."

"Do you forget to whom you speak?" Rebeke asked
sternly.

"No. And neither should you. I'm speaking to that street
brat Reby, who's gone from being under my feet begging for a
sweet cake to barging in here and filling up my bed with sick
folk. Look what you've done to an honest baker and a pretty
little maid. Here I am a disreputable man of leisure, and you a
grotesque spectacle and skinny as a rail. You must be hungry.
What can I fix for you?"

Rebeke surrendered with a chuckle. "Tea. And save your
good-old-days routine; neither one of us would go back.
You've found them for me, Mickle, and I thank you. I know
they'll be in good hands until I need them. But I warn you, not
out of harshness, but to save your tender old heart. Do not get
too attached to these waifs. When I need them, I must take
them from you. So cherish them and heal their hearts, as
always you had a knack for. But don't tie their lives too tightly
to yours, lest your heart bleed when I tear them away."

Mickle had bustled about as she spoke, poking up his hearth fire and clattering mugs and filling the kettle so carelessly that water spattered the floor. If he had heard one word, he gave no indication. "It's heartless you've become, Rebeke," he scolded her. "Heartless. Oh, you may remember an old man who was kind to you when you had no one, and so you throw him coins, more than are good for him. But I should like to know what's become of my little miss with the big blue eyes in her thin little face? I grew you up to be a lovely thing, and just when I thought I had you settled with that lad . . . what was his name? Grew up and became the herbalist's apprentice?"

"Dresh," Rebeke breathed unwillingly.

"Just when I thought I could look forward to babies crawling after crumbs in my shop, what do you do? Disappear one day without a word. Time passes, and I think you're dead. Then money begins to come to me, but no words to go with it, just a tragic rumor. That you'd gone to the Windsingers, even though all know that the Windsingers prefer to steal babies to grow up their own way, and you near a woman grown. Then a few nights ago, you give me the turn of my life when I walk into my kitchen and find you here. Nearly gave up drinking on the spot. Well, missy, just you know this." He poured tea into the heavy mugs and set one on the table before her. "I've done as you bid me. The honey's in that pot. But let me tell you, it wasn't the money you've sent me all these years that bought you my services. No. These buns were fresh this morning. Eat one, don't pick at them. It wasn't money. I did that for Reby's big blue eyes, that you've made all blue and white, and I did them for the hunger and pain I saw in the boy's eyes when I found him."

Rebeke shifted on the stool, setting aside the bun he had pushed into her hand. "What does it matter?" she asked him gruffly. "You found them."

"It matters to me," Mickle insisted. He looked at her long and expectantly, waiting for a reply, a sign. None came. Rebeke merely looked at him gravely over her mug's rim. "What do you plan to do with them?" demanded Mickle suddenly.

Rebeke set down her mug. "I plan to send them home. I can't go into it, Mickle, not in detail, but I have to put things back as they were before."

"Nothing can go back as it was before," he warned her.

This time when he sighed he seemed to crumple, his shoulders drooping low as with a weight. "Reby," he asked softly. "Reby, how do I even know it's you? What have you left of yourself for me to recognize and love? When you vanished it near killed me, and that Dresh boy like to go mad. Turned him bad, some say, though I don't know what he became or where he went. Reby, why did you do it?"

"Care for them." The gold pieces made a heavy chink as she set them together upon the table. "And hire a servant for yourself, Mickle. This place wants looking after. You should treat yourself better."

"Why did you come back, if only to leave again?" Mickle asked, but he asked it of the clattering doorslats. Dawn light spattered briefly onto his floor, falling as softly as his tears.

Fourteen

"WHAT do you make of it?" Vandien asked the black war-horse that plodded easily beside the wagon. The horse snorted. His ears were pitched forward and Vandien saw a sudden tension shiver across his muscles. Giving an anxious whicker, he broke into a trot. The greys tried to copy him, but Vandien held them in. He peered forward through the dusk to where some bulky object had been dumped squarely in the middle of the road. The black horse was snuffling at it when he reached it, and Vandien took the wagon around it in a swerve. First team and then wagon left the smooth roadbed for the deep turf with a sway and a jounce. Vandien pulled them in sharply as he realized what he was passing.

It was not Ki. As he knelt over the body, he was torn between relief that she was not dead in the road, and vexation that he had not caught up with her. Surprise had made him recoil from the strange body when he first touched it. But now he bent to look closer. A Brurjan. Starved to death, by the look of her. The softly expelled breath of the creature before him sent a shudder through him. His common sense urged him to back softly away, remount the wagon and continue his search for Ki. A starved Brurjan was no business of his; wise Humans did not intrude themselves on Brurjan affairs. He drew softly away from her. She twitched, swallowing with a gulping noise. Unwillingly he paused to watch as she moved her black-ened lips and crinkled her eyelids in an effort to pry them open. Then he sprinted back to the wagon to fetch the waterskin.

Her large head filled his lap. The quills of her crest rattled dryly when he raised her shoulders. Gingerly he pried open her

jaws to bare her razor teeth clenched in a death mask. One
sudden chop of those jaws! Vandien silenced the thought and
trickled a little water between her teeth. It vanished, some
leaking out the corners of her mouth. Her thick tongue moved
behind her teeth, but the rest of her remained still. It was too
late for her. Suddenly she choked, sending a spray of water
into his face. He supported her shoulders as she struggled to
clear her throat. She was feebler than he had imagined a Brurjan could be. His only prior attempt to match strength with one
had proved that one didn't need to open a tavern door to leave
by it. He had breathed softly around cracked ribs after that
meeting. But this one was also thinner than he had ever seen a
Brurjan, and the more he looked into her wasted face, the more
subtly wrong it appeared.

Thin as she was, she was too large a limp body for him to
drag into the cuddy with any sort of gentleness. So he covered
her and pillowed her where she lay upon the road. She didn't
move again, but her breathing seemed steadier. And each time
he poured water into her, she resisted him a bit more. The
black horse hung over her like a ponderous guardian as he went
about making a simple camp. Vandien guessed she was the
mysterious rider, and the gear in the back of the wagon was
hers. But how it had come to be there, and where Ki was now
were questions still to be answered.

Fire, Vandien found, was damned hard to make here. For
one thing, he could find no tinder. If any sort of bush had ever
dropped a branch near the road, then someone had eaten it.
There wasn't a dry twig to be found, nor even a bush that
smelled resinous enough to kindle. Vandien in desperation
took the dried meat out of its storage box and wrapped it in a
clean cloth. The box became firewood. Then he struggled long
before he could persuade sparks to jump from his flint and
kindle the box shavings. When the fire did burn, it did so
grudgingly, giving out little light and less heat. Vandien
coaxed a pan of water to a fickle boil and warmed in it bits of
dried meat and finely chopped roots, hanging over it impatiently as the stew simmered. A mug of tea he brewed for
himself, taking a sort of strength from its warmth, trying to
resign himself to the delay. The greys, freed from harness,
cropped grass beside the road.

At last the stew was ready. With a thick wooden spoon he

stirred and mashed until it was a lumpy gruel. He let the pot sit on the ground and cool a bit while he gathered his courage and energies. He thought longingly of sleep, then took up his stew pot and closed in on the Brurjan resolutely. He set the pot on the ground and sat down close beside her, propping her head and shoulders against him so she would not choke. "Eat," he told her softly, wondering if she was alive enough to hear.

Her lips parted stickily. "No," she groaned.

"It will make you feel better. Try. Here."

A feeble flop of her arm knocked the spoon from his grasp. "No." It was a growl now. "Let me die as I am. You have filled my mouth with water gone bad, and I can smell what you would give me now. Stewed flesh. Gah."

Vandien retrieved the spoon from the grass and sniffed at the pot. Nothing smelled spoiled to him. He knew Brurjans ate meat; she was raving, or he had heard her wrong. He brought the spoon to her mouth again.

Her teeth snapped, taking off the wooden bowl of the spoon. He thought it a dying reflex, until she spat it out at him. She broke her crusted eyes open to glare at him balefully through the slits. "Leave me to die in peace!" she gasped. "If I cannot come to the Limbreth, at least let me know I died trying. Ki shall carry my name to them."

"What of Ki?" Vandien demanded, but with a last glare she shut her eyes and would say no more.

While he was not a patient man, he was seldom moved to violence against the helpless. But not only his logic but his curiosity had been strained to their limits, and impulsively he acted. He lowered her head to the ground and rose to stand over her. He flipped the spoon handle off into the darkness as he measured her, then took a breath and stepped across her prone form to straddle her body. She was big, and she didn't seem as weak as when he had poured the water into her. Maybe that had done her some good, though it would make his task harder now. Her eyes were sunken deep in her face and her flesh stretched over her bones in planes and angles. Well, live or die, he told himself and her. He dropped a knee neatly on each of her shoulders, pinning her to the earth.

Her huge jaws opened, the double row of teeth far too close to his flesh, but Vandien was ready and he set the edge of the bowl atop her lower teeth and tipped it. She closed her jaws with a snap, but the bowl was wedged in her mouth and Vandien had the leverage.

"Drink or choke, dammit!" he heard himself roar. She chose choking, and soup spattered them both; but he was adamant. He tipped the bowl up higher, and it was only when he saw the bottom of it that he released his grip on it and sprang clear of her.

Her arms, no longer pinned at her sides, came up at him in claws. Her eyes blazed red as she rolled onto her belly and tried to come after him. But she got no farther than her hands and knees before falling again. She spat at him and then sank down, gagging and gasping. "Bastard!" she hissed at him. "Nameless whelp of toothless parents! Bird bait!"

"Glad to see you're feeling better." Vandien brushed stew from his shirt front. For one so weak, her spitting accuracy was remarkable. He squatted down a cautious distance from her. "Where's Ki?"

"Gone on to better things than you, dropping of a sickly goat! My mouth stinks of carrion in my throat! You poisoned me with that warmed-over filth! And cheated me of an honorable death. Damn you, damn you, damn you! When I choked, I couldn't close my throat against it and it went down. I won't die!"

"Thank me later. Where's Ki?"

"Gone to the Limbreth. I told you that. Gone to better things than you or I shall ever know. Gah! Carrion all through my mouth and up my nose. I can't stand the taste. And only one thing to chase it away. Black!"

The horse came to her willingly, far more so than the greys ever moved to Ki's command. Nor did it shy away when she gripped its stocky foreleg and hauled herself up by it. She leaned against it, standing only by its strength. Vandien watched her with some curiosity. If she thought she was going to mount and ride off, he was betting against her. She'd never haul herself up onto its back with no harness.

She pressed her face against its neck. The animal gave a start, snorted, and then stood stoically again. Vandien stared at the motionless Brurjan, wondering if she wept, until he heard the soft sounds of lapping. He turned away and went back to his fire. Was taking blood from a horse that different from taking milk from a cow? Warm blood was a Brurjan need and he had heard their beasts were trained for its taking. Still.

"You said to thank you later." Her voice was gruff. "Now is later. Thank you."

"Welcome," Vandien told her shortly. He poured himself more tea and didn't watch her as she went to the water cask. She opened the spigot and let water fill her hands, scrabbling it over her face and snorting in it. She shook the water from her hands and closed the spigot. All Vandien's muscles tightened as he heard her coming back to the fire. But she only folded herself up and held her hands out to its puny warmth.

"It is nippy out, isn't it? This the best you could do for a fire? No, don't move, it's fine."

"Your clothing is in the back of the wagon."

"I know. Why do you bring it up, do I bother you?" She rubbed her hands over her face again. "What do you have to eat?"

Typical Brurjan, Vandien told himself. Rude, callous, and self-centered, but always honest. "Dried meat and fish." He didn't bother to list fruits and grains; Brurjans didn't take much interest in them.

"More of the cooked crap you tried to poison me with?"

Vandien shook his head. "Dried in the sun, salted and twisted into strips."

She gave a brief nod. "I'll take that, then. All you can spare. I'm famished."

When he came back out of the wagon, she had donned the linen padding she wore under her armor. It made her seem more massive. She took the cloth-wrapped meat from him without a word, crouched where she had stood, and began on it. Vandien poked without hope at his pathetic little fire and warmed himself a final cup of tea over it. He was still sipping it when she shook out the cloth and began to fold it neatly.

"I'm Hollyika, man. And I'm alive, and now that I know it, I do thank you for it. But, damn it, never again pour slop like that down any Brurjan. If I'd been any stronger and you a little slower, I'd have killed you. Boiled meat. That's one thing wrong with Humans, you know—the shit they eat."

"I'm Vandien. And one thing wrong with Brurjans is that I've never yet met one with any courtesy." He spoke recklessly, and then shrank back as she stepped up to him, but she only put the folded cloth into his hands.

"What the hell do you want of me? I didn't ask you to do it, so you did it because you wanted to. I've said my thanks—

twice, even. Shall I grovel and kiss your feet? Or am I supposed to offer to lie with you in my gratitude?"

"You could answer my damn questions, damn it!" Vandien
found his language matching hers. "Where in hell is Ki? I
thought I'd find you two together."

"Oh. Her." Hollyika fell silent for a moment. "You know,
it's peculiar. I was so set on going with her, and now she looks
like a damn fool to me. Yet I'm the one that spurred her on.
She's gone to the Limbreth; those blinky lights on the horizon.
She's gone to get a gut load of peace and fulfillment and
enlightenment. Isn't that a fist in the throat?"

"Yes," Vandien agreed morosely. "Why'd she go?"

"I just told you. Oh, you mean why does she think they
have buckets of goodwill up there. Damned if I know. I
thought they did too, and was all set to lie down and die
because I'd never get there."

"It's in the water," Vandien surmised, recalling Jace's
warning.

"Could be. That's likely, now that I think of it. But how the
hell did I get here? And when is dawn?"

"How you got here I don't know. I came through a Gate.
Dawn doesn't seem to happen here. It goes from grey to black
to grey again."

"Oh. Well, the road got me here, so the road can take me
back. I'll go a lot faster on Black. I'll take that fish with me, if
you don't mind. After I get a bit of sleep." Hollyika started to
move to the freight bed of the wagon where her possessions
were. She paused at Vandien's silence and turned back to him.
"What are you going to do?"

He shrugged. The whole grey roof of this world pressed
down on his shoulders. "I guess I'll sleep. I'm tired enough to
die. I've been chasing her for—well, I've lost track of the
days, with no light to go by. When I wake up, I'll hitch up and
go after her."

"Why?"

Vandien rubbed his hands over his face. His eyes were
sandy and the skin of his face felt like a hide left to dry in the
sun. "Because we're partners. Because, like you, I don't think
she'd choose to do what she's doing, if she had her own mind
about it. Because I promised some folks on the other side to
bring her back to the Gate. Because I want to."

Hollyika shook her head with a clatter of plumes. "You poor fool."

"Right." Vandien rose stiffly, to clamber into the wagon. He let his clothes drop straight to the floor and clambered into the bed to worm under the covers. "You poor fool," he sympathized once with himself, and then the pillows and darkness claimed him.

Some time had passed, but by the aching of his head and muscles, it hadn't been much. A heavy bulk settled onto the bed beside him. It was dark, but he sensed her looming over him. "What?" he demanded uneasily.

"Maybe I'm more grateful than I thought. Move over. Let's see if there's anything about you different from any other Human I've had."

Vandien took a shallow breath. All he could picture in his mind was her maw of teeth adjacent to his throat. It wasn't erotic. "Thank you, but . . ."

"But what? Put off by a little extra fur?"

"No. Just tired. I've been following Ki on foot, you know. And . . ."

"Boiled meat," Hollyika commented in disgust. She turned her back to him and settled in beside him. "This is a hell of a lot better than the grass or the wagon bed."

He could think of no reply. Her stentorian breathing filled the cuddy. After she had shouldered in beside him, her smell reminded him of new puppies in clean straw. She slept, but when he did, he dreamed of lionesses.

Fifteen

VANDIEN struggled up from a dream of drowning. He found himself wedged in a corner like a bolster, pinned down by one of the Brurjan's outflung arms. He shifted under it, seeking a more comfortable position, and was warned by a grumbling growl. He subsided, feeling oppressed and crowded. For a moment he tried to settle, calming his breathing and focusing on sleep. But then his quick temperament boiled up against the restraint and he bucked himself to a sitting position, snarling, "Let me up."

"So climb over," Hollyika told him gruffly, and when he had awkwardly done so, she stretched out with a deep sigh, filling the bed more completely than ever. She burrowed under the covers, showing no signs of rousing. Vandien scooped up his clothes and stumbled out the cuddy door, dragging them on as he went.

Sitting down heavily on the plank seat, he shoved his feet into his boots. His abrupt awakening had left him groggy and shaky. He glanced futilely at the sky, frowning in disgust. No way to tell how long he had slept. He considered trying to sleep on the turf, or in the back of the wagon. He shut his eyes in the warm dark of his cupped hands. But they opened again and he found himself irrevocably awake.

So. Fire and breakfast? Too much effort. He clambered stiffly down, gathering up the remnants of his untidy camp. The bedding he had spread over Hollyika was damp and chill. He threw it into the back of the wagon, knowing Ki would skin him for it later. Or would she? He stood in the dark, thinking. Ki had moved on, leaving him and the team and the wagon flung aside as carelessly as her clothing. Could she wink out of his life as suddenly as he had thrust into hers? He sat down in the back of the wagon to consider it. What if she had tired of him and his careless ways? A worm of insecurity gnawed at him. But they cared for one another. There was more to their partnership than work shared. They understood one another.

The grey half light suddenly put him in mind of another barren hill camp. Then it had been just past dusk, and rocks had gnawed at his ribs as he lay on his belly watching Ki. He could almost feel the hunger and cold again. His clothes had been too thin and worn for the weather in the pass; it had been a full day since he had managed to snare that bit of a rabbit, and he had been forced to eat the meat warm and raw, for the rain made fire impossible. He had lain in the shadows and waited.

All he had needed was a horse. His conscience had been a weary and broken thing, worn down by the nagging of his body. He was going to take only one horse from her. She could ride the other back down the trail and buy herself another. She looked to have the coin for it. What did she need of his pity? He could not keep the saliva from running in his mouth as he watched her putting together her simple meal. He had smelled the bubbling stew of dried roots and meats. He had watched her mouth as she drank the hot tea she brewed. The thought of that warmth had made him shiver.

He had known he could take her down. She looked fit, but no larger than he. And he had known she was not as desperate nor as hungry as he; desperation would give him strength. He could take her down, have the food, steal the horse, perhaps find a cloak or boots in her wagon. He shifted in the dark, and his own breath sounded to him like a growl. He had felt the strength rising in him, fueled by the thought of food. He had imagined his own pantherish charge, taking her with a shoulder in the belly, pulling her down and then . . . what? Choke her unconscious? Beat her head against the earth until she stopped struggling? Stand on her with both feet while he tied her up?

His grin had been narrow as a knife blade. Perhaps he could smother her with the reek of his long unwashed body; it was as likely. Even if his physical strength had been up to it, he didn't have the stomach for it. He would steal the horse tonight, after she slept, because he wanted very much to live, and he would slink off afterwards, feeling the taint of thief upon his name;

but he would not add blackguard to it. He had raised his head slightly, watching her intently.

Then the damn horse had wheeled, whinnying, and she had risen and seen him. Without a thought, he had sprung forward, knowing it was his last best chance to get a beast that would take him out of that forsaken pass and back to folk that knew him. But his heart hadn't been in the struggle. He felt an animal, a fool, gripping at her, trying to wrestle her down when he knew full well that was no solution. She had flung the kettle in his face; he had found himself on his back with a knife at his throat. He had frozen beneath her, her solid weight squeezing the air from his lungs, knowing he was looking up at his death. Not only his last hope but all his hopes were gone. But he had not closed his eyes, because it was the last moment of his life, and he was going to see it all, no matter how bad it was.

Their eyes had met. Hers were green, something he had not been able to tell from his previous vantage point; a rare color for eyes in this part of the world. She looked as if she had once smiled easily, but hadn't for some time. There was anger in her face now, seasoned with fear, but no killing lust, no sense of her total power over his helplessness. By the time he had realized all that, he had known also that she wasn't going to kill him, could no more draw the blade across his throat than he could batter her head in. She was as ridiculous as he. The absurdity of their present postures had suddenly rung in his mind as clearly as a great bell. He had laughed. She had scowled at him, knowing full well what was funny but refusing to let it amuse her—refusing him. That had been the challenge, for folk that could share a joke as ultimate as that one should share it, not perch on one another's chests and pretend to be as dull as the rest of the world.

"From that instant, I knew you, Ki." His own words broke him out of his reverie. He raised a finger to touch the smile on his face. "You'll have to think again if you suppose you can be rid of me so easily." But the irony of the situation was not lost on him. Then it had been Ki with the wagon, and he had been the needy stranger who moved in on her so casually, disrupting her life. Now he was the one sitting on the tail of the wagon, and within a stray Brurjan was snoring in the bed. How had Ki felt about him then? As annoyed as he felt now, he imagined.

He shrugged the thought off. This was different. Hollyika had
none of his charm, his warmth and wit, let alone his engaging
smile. His grin now was mocking. "In a pig's eye," he said
aloud to himself, and moved to gather up the kettle and bowl.

Bribed with grain, the greys came to harness. The black
horse came as well, nipping at the greys until they abandoned
both grain and harness position. Vandien was forced to shake
out a measure of grain for the black before he could calm the
team and get them harnessed. By the time he was finished he
was sweating and wishing he had stopped to cook breakfast.

Within the cuddy, Hollyika still filled the bed. Vandien
jumped down into the cuddy and began to rummage for a quick
meal. "I'm ready to leave," he told her back as he sliced
cheese and sausage on the small table. Bread and cheese and
sausage; well, it was better than what he had had before he
caught up with the wagon.

"So go." Her reply was muttered beneath the covers.

"I'm taking the wagon."

"Only a half-wit wouldn't."

"But you're still inside it. Are you going with me?"

"Damn it, I'm asleep!" Hollyika roared, shooting to a sitting position on the platform. Her head thunked neatly against
the rafter and she dropped back to the pillow. With a savage
Brurjan curse she rolled her great head to stare at Vandien with
red-rimmed eyes. "Humans!" she snorted.

"Don't glare at me! Yesterday you said you were headed
back to the Gate."

"Well, where the hell are you going after you catch up with
the Romni numbwit?"

"Back to the Gate."

"So what difference does it make?" Hollyika dragged the
covers back over herself.

Vandien shrugged, bewildered. "None, I suppose. I just had
the impression you thought of Ki as a fool."

Hollyika rolled back quickly to face him, a crooked black-
nailed finger pointing at him accusingly. "And that's another
thing that's wrong with Humans. They always want to know
what you THINK, what you FEEL, when all any sane creature
needs to know about another one is what it is doing. I'm in the
wagon, sleeping, so I must be going with you. Even a chicken
could have figured that out, without a lot of nasty prying."

Vandien leaned back against the wall and made a noise at her through his teeth. Words failed him. He turned to go and was halfway out the cuddy door when her voice stopped him. "Did you grain Black?"

"What do you think?" he asked her with savage satisfaction. The cuddy door slammed behind him.

Once he had the team and all four wheels back on the road, he stepped them up to a smart clip. The black kept pace with them easily. Vandien glared at him, but the horse nodded back at him as he matched the greys. Vandien leaned back on the cuddy door. Ki couldn't be far ahead, and she couldn't match this pace on foot. He just had to be patient. The cuddy door jerked open behind him and he fell back into Hollyika's arms.

"Shit," she commented dryly, looking down into his face. With a shove she restored him to his place. The greys, who had faltered in their pace, resumed the rhythm as his hands steadied on the reins. The Brurjan clambered out of the cuddy, squeezing out the narrow door to perch uneasily on the plank seat. The seat wasn't large enough for her; she dug in her nails to keep her place. Her breath smelt of fish.

"What's a Limbreth?" he asked her.

She barked a short laugh. "Damned if I know." She was silent for a while, mulling. Vandien let her take her time. "You know, you're right. It's the water. The longer I'm clear of it, the better I can figure." A frown wrinkled her brow and nose. "The Limbreth came to me in a dream. Last thing I remember of Jojorum is drinking with the Human Rousters in my company. The shank of the evening had been eaten, and we knew we wouldn't be called on to do much the rest of the night. So it was time to drink and then to sleep. I don't remember falling asleep, but I did, and I dreamed. I dreamed of a treasure of shining jewels. Funny jewels. I always think of reds and greens when I think of gems, bright individual colors that flash. But these were heaped in mounds and ripe for the taking, pastel glowing things, like fungus in the dark. The image doesn't even appeal to me now. But then it was like a magnet drawing me, and I had to go for it, fast, before someone beat me to it. So Black and I went." She paused. "Damned if you aren't right again. I went through a Gate, but not a proper one. I've been working Jojorum for the better part of a year now, and there's no Gate in the wall where I went through. But I went through one, and fast."

The silence lengthened to a stop in the talk. Vandien risked prodding her. ''That still doesn't tell me what a Limbreth is.''

She was unruffled. ''No. Well, in the dream, I knew that the gems had belonged to the Limbreth, but now they were for me. 'The Jewels of the Limbreth' I heard, plain as blood. Let me see. I remember a bridge, and we stopped for water. I must have slept there. That's when it becomes very muzzy. I can recall perfectly what I thought, but not why I believed it. I knew that the Jewels of the Limbreth were not gems, but were things like peace, joy, and fulfillment. Ha! But then it was a wondrous thing to have realized, for the Jewels were still expressly for me. All I had to do was come for them, showing myself worthy along the way. I think that's when I let Black go, and dropped my gear and started eating grass. Nothing makes much sense after that, but then, what would you expect, eating grass?''

''And Ki? I believe she passed through the Gate looking for me, supposing I had gone ahead of her. But now?''

''Now she goes to seek the Limbreth. Don't blame it on me, for it was only partly my encouragement. I believe that no matter why you come through the Gate, sooner or later, you seek the Limbreth. Have you felt no pull yourself?''

''No.'' Vandien hesitated, remembering his lassitude when he bathed in the stream. ''But I have drunk none of the water here, and eaten only a little of the fruit.'' Briefly he told her of his encounter with the farmers.

''Nice folk,'' she growled. ''If it had been me, I'd have crammed that stick through his ears and set his house afire. But then what can I expect of a boiled-meat Human? No spirit.''

Vandien looked sideways at her, trying to tell if her lips curled in a smile or in disdain. He gave it up.

''Why don't you whip up these nags a little?''

''I don't know the road. Once they get the wagon rolling, it takes a bit to stop them. Damn near ran you down in the dark, and it's not much lighter now. I'd hate to find Ki with the wheels.''

''Hm.'' It was as noncommital a reply as Vandien had ever received. He peered up the road. The grade was definite but steady. The team was pulling well; no sense in straining them. Ki had always cautioned him that they worked better in steadiness than in stress. Ki. What wouldn't he give to have her on the wagon seat next to him instead of this hairy Brurjan?

She poked him in the ribs, and Vandien wondered if she had guessed his thoughts. But she pointed ahead to the gleaming lights, suddenly larger and closer. They had crested the long rise at last and were looking down into the Limbreth's valley. The team checked of its own accord. Vandien stared down in puzzlement. Hollyika beside him was shaking her broad head in denial. "That's not how I dreamed them," she muttered to herself. "That's not right at all."

Vandien grunted. He slapped the wheelbrake into position, bracing his foot against it as he stared down into the grey valley before him.

The road ran as straight and true as ever down into the center of the valley. Tall black stones sprouted unevenly from a ridge in the fine cobbled surface of a flat central plain. Grass sprouted at their base, and ambitious bushes were thrusting up through cracks in the smooth cobblestones. The black stones were tall, but worn and weathered, and the glowing Jewels that crowned them seemed dimmer here than they had as beckoning lights on the horizon. Massive were the Limbreths, yes, but power and majesty had fled them; like the mummies of ancient kings, their royalty had seeped away.

"They weren't like that before," Hollyika growled. "They were tall and full of might, promises and secrets and wealth and joy; they held them all, and more beyond my mind to comprehend. They called to me, Vandien, with a lure sweeter than warm blood. Now this. Was it all a cheat, my long dreaming on the road here? Was it all a deceit of the water and the night?"

"Or is this the deceit?" Vandien wondered aloud. He turned to Hollyika, but she was gone. Her armor clattered harshly as she dragged it out of the wagon bed. The horse went to her guttural command. Vandien did not blame her. She had been teased on to see these Limbreths she had dreamed of. Well, she had seen. She had no call of friendship to answer, no promise to a child waiting outside the Gate. Almost he wished he could turn back with her. "Travel in safety," he wished her. She cursed rust and damp as she struggled with stiff leather.

"I damn well intend to!" she answered him suddenly. Her horse's scarlet hooves rang on the road. "Let's go!"

Massive as a mountain, she came from behind the wagon, mounted and armored. "Let's wake them up down there!

Come on!'' She didn't wait for him, but dashed forward, smacking Sigurd on the haunch as she went. The sloping road was before him and the black horse at his side spooked him. When the greys lunged, the brake screamed and gave way.

Long afterwards, that ride came back to Vandien in dreams, more awful than any dream of falling. The smooth road unwound straight before him, offering no resistance to the thundering wheels; the Limbreths grinned up at him like jagged teeth. The team raced away from the wagon, moving as fast as he'd ever seen them go; his soul shrieked out to them not to stumble. They gained momentum as they went, until scenery blurred away on either side of him. Steady in his gaze was Hollyika, perched on her saddle like a parrot on a limb, screeching as she charged ahead. Helmless, her crest was canted up and forward in the well-feared warning of Brurjan aggression.

''Moon's,'' gasped Vandien, ''blood,'' he finished, the wet reins sliding through his hands. The team wasn't slowing and when the wagon stopped, it wasn't going to be on top of its wheels. Its normal top-heavy sway had taken on an alarming skating quality. The Limbreths loomed, monstrous and near; he looked up to the glimmering lights and realized he was on the flats, racing across to the base of the Limbreths. His hands took a fresh bight of the reins and he pulled steadily, sawing a little to get the greys' attention; he thought he felt them respond.

But Hollyika's pace never slackened, the speed of her black belying its great size. She ripped her sword free of its sheath and swung it in a glistening arc; her strident war cry floated back to him. She was insane.

Vandien mastered his team; the wagon rumbled to a halt. He wanted no part of her mad charge against the Limbreths; as soon charge a mountain. But Hollyika's enthusiasm was unabated. She raced toward the center of the row of Limbreths that sprang from the ridge like young trees from a nursery log. He saw her swing her sword and heard it thunk solidly into the Limbreth. The impact sounded like that between wood and metal, but the Limbreth didn't even shiver. The sword remained embedded, but Hollyika did not remain in the saddle. The black horse raced from under her as she whipped around her own sword and spun through the air as prettily as a tumbler at a fair. Her armor clattered as she lit and rolled to a stop. Her horse galloped on, and came gradually to a halt, stiff-legged and staring about in surprise. Silence welled up to refill the valley.

Vandien headed the team toward the fallen Brurjan. She showed no signs of rising, damn her foolishness. He didn't need to be fussing over her right now. Here were the Limbreths and Ki was nowhere in sight. He wanted to give his mind to that, not to some crazed warrior.

When he reached her and knelt by her side, she was conscious and not much hurt; her thick hide protected her where her armor didn't.

"Anything broken?" he asked her gently before touching her. But her dark eyes stared up past him, her pupils dilated, and breath hissed between her parted teeth. In a supple movement that startled him, she flowed all the way to her feet. "Look at them," she cried brokenly. "Look at them!"

He turned his own eyes on the Limbreths that her spread arms encompassed. They were the same as they had been. But Hollyika was waving her arms and her face was bright. "I told you! This is how I dreamed them! That, up on the ridge, that was the deceit! Look at them!"

"Let me see your head," demanded Vandien, coming to his feet. She danced out of his reach, a mad look in her eyes.

Then he felt it. It seeped around him like a cool mist, a tenuous groping that was not physical. It slid over him, seeking for something he did not provide. He blinked, and for an instant beheld the Limbreths standing sleek-sided and momentous in their power; but as swiftly it was gone, leaving his vision blurred.

"Damn you!" Hollyika shrieked. She, too, had lost sight of them. "Liars! Cheats! You made me want to die for you!"

With a lunge she gripped again the hilt of her sword to wrest it loose. It did not come. A blue halo flashed around Hollyika and sword both, flinging her away. Vandien was on her as she tried to rise, heedless of her temper as he gripped her shoulders. "Sit still!" he hissed; suddenly he sensed the life that coursed through the monoliths, and his tongue was a dry stick in his mouth. It was not the massiveness of this being that froze him, nor this display of its peculiar powers; it was its foreignness. This Limbreth was more different from Vandien than he had ever supposed any living thing could be; it made Hollyika his sister by comparison. Even the grass at his feet was more kin to him than this creature rearing up hill-high.

"Your violence is not needed. I will speak to you if you wish it." The voice rang faint in their ears but clear. While the words were in the air, the Limbreths shone with power, but as the sound faded, they were no more than mossy pillars again.

"Speak, hell!" roared Hollyika. "I don't want you to speak at all, you pile of bricks! Understand only this: we have come for Ki."

"Ki is not here." No emotion, a flat statement.

"Did you think us as eyeless as yourself, rock? Where is she?" Hollyika's voice rasped.

"She is gone on, to better things than you could ever offer her." Even in his present straits, Vandien had to smile. Had not he heard those very words from Hollyika?

"Pumped full of peace and goodwill, no doubt," Hollyika snarled. "How can you say she is gone on to better things? What could a piece of masonry know of comradeship, or the lives of moving things?"

The chiming voice of the Limbreth became stronger in an eerie way, ringing more in Vandien's mind than in his ears. "What can a drop of dew like you know of the great world it falls upon? Ki came to me as a moth comes to the candle, knowing that to be consumed by my fire is not death but eternity. Are you jealous, little furred one? Your mind wriggles with nasty little uglinesses when I speak to you. No servant falls so low as the one who nearly attains the true path, and such are you. Will you try to turn Ki aside so that you can pretend that you lost nothing when you were seduced back to your petty organic survival? Both of you come here with your minds acrawl with temporal rubbish. Shall I make you a metaphor simple enough for you to comprehend? A child sits on a sunny doorstep, grasping at dust motes on a beam of light. That is the significance of your whole lives to one such as I. Ki at least shall have a chance to paint her thoughts from an enduring palette. Miniscule as they are, at least they shall last long enough for the great ones to peruse them. But yours shall wink out like the dust motes that vanish with the movement of a cloud."

Hollyika snarled in response. Vandien made his appeal.

"But this does not sound like Ki's own will. Won't you give her the chance to decide her own path, whether to remain with you, or come home with me?"

"Home?" the Limbreth mocked. "Home? A quaint idea. You have no home. It vanished in a puff of cosmic dust ages ago. Say, rather, that you will take her back to the niche of ecological and social pressures that the Gatherers designed for your kind. Ki's will has nothing to do with it. No one goes *home* from any world of the Gatherers. Why shouldn't she stay here and entertain me instead of them?"

Vandien was blasted suddenly by a vision of worlds beyond worlds; a sudden realization of his insignificance squashed him. When next he drew breath, he sucked in air as if he had surfaced from the bottom of a lake. Hollyika gazed at him curiously.

"Are you in health, man?" she demanded.

"I think, yes, I am all right!" Vandien gasped. "Didn't you see it?"

"I saw you look up like a fool and gape as your eyes went wide and dead, and the muscles stood out in your face and throat. I expected you to fall down dead, but instead you took a breath."

"But—what I saw—"

"Limbreth visions, huh? Never mind. Whatever you saw, you can't eat it or trade it for Ki. Thing!" she roared suddenly. "We want Ki back. Give her, or take our vengeance!"

"I cannot give her, nor can you take her. Seek her if you wish. It is all the same to us. Perhaps a last meeting with you would give a sharper edge to her final vision. Do as you will; it is all immaterial. But do not expect our aid or protection."

"Meaning you can't really stop us!" Hollyika taunted them.

They both felt the pause. Hollyika's sword clattered suddenly onto the plain. She was not swift to take it up. The horses pricked up their ears and tossed their heads, sensing a change. "What is it, what is it?" Vandien muttered to himself and suddenly knew. The Limbreth no longer harkened to them, no longer paid any attention at all; its thoughts and will were withdrawn.

Hollyika stared at the smooth side of the Limbreth. How had her sword clung when it had not even notched it? She shrugged and bent gingerly to retrieve her weapon. She sheathed it and looked to Vandien for a rare meeting of eyes.

"Do you really think it can't stop us from following Ki?" he asked her seriously.

"Who cares?" she replied, typically Brurjan. "Thinking, feeling, guessing, wondering," she muttered under her breath, flaring her nostrils at him. She caught her horse as Vandien clambered back to the wagon seat. They were going on. There was nothing more for them here; the Limbreths had gone, as if these stony bodies were not where they resided at all. The valley seemed empty as a tomb, and the Limbreths themselves monuments to forgotten wizards.

Hollyika stirred her horse. "Before you ask," she called back grudgingly over her shoulder. "There's only one other road out of here. We may as well follow it, for the Romni fool did. Come on, will you?"

With a sigh, Vandien slapped the reins on the broad grey backs in front of him. He could not quell a nagging feeling that something more should have happened here. The Limbreth should have told him more, should have done more, been more. But their attention had turned elsewhere, listening to voices he could not hope to hear. A brooding fear hung over him and sneered at him more harshly than the Brurjan. He no longer felt his life was his own; he had become a chip on a gaming table. The vision the Limbreths had given him still colored his thoughts, and he had a horrible prescience that when he found Ki, she, too, would know how insignificant they both were. How could she care? He watched Hollyika's straight back before him rising and falling steadily with the pace of her mount, and longed for her stoicism.

Sixteen

CERIE tried to shift quietly in her cushioned throne, but even the light rustle of her robe against the embroidered cushions made Rebeke shudder. Cerie froze, cursing herself for having disturbed the other Windsinger's concentration. As one entrusted with a speaking egg, she was aware of how it painfully heightened all senses in the user. A sigh left her silently as she resumed her long vigil.

She had left orders with her acolyte Windsingers that they were not to be disturbed, no matter what crisis loomed, until Cerie herself came to the door and ordered otherwise. All her attendants had been dismissed; lessons had been canceled for the day. The room looked bare without her white-robed students; the deserted looms hung heavy with half-finished tapestries and books lay in neglected heaps on the long trestle tables; nor was there the group of little white-robed Singers that usually clustered at her feet to learn their notes and letters, and fly to her errands. She regretted this interruption of their routine, but it was necessary, or so Rebeke had said, and she was inclined to believe. Even so. She swallowed vainly at the lump of unease in her throat. If they were caught; if word ever leaked out that she had loaned to another the speaking egg entrusted to her care; if Rebeke were clumsy or unskilled and damaged the sensitive little organism; Cerie closed her eyes, willing away her visions of disaster. There was nothing to be gained by worrying. The High Council would know that she had been closeted privately with Rebeke for the longer part of a day; that would stir wrath and questions enough without her borrowing trouble.

She opened her eyes. One look at Rebeke and doubt ate away her resolve like acid. Rebeke no longer sat straight on her cushion, the egg pressed to her brow. She drooped, her tall cowled head bent so far foward that it nearly brushed the floor; the blue fabric of her robe was damp and Cerie smelled the musk of her sweat. The tray of wine and food that Rebeke would need when she came out of trance sat untouched beside her. Cerie tried to remember if she had ever heard of any Windsinger holding the trance this long. It was an effort of will, comparable to gripping a razor-sharp blade and holding it as someone tried to wrest it away. But there was more to using the egg than merely enduring the pain. One had to have the will to ignore the pain and direct the egg, to command it to one's own bidding. That sort of will took training to shape. Rebeke claimed that she had been able to train herself, working from the old writings of the Windsingers. Cerie wondered. Perhaps Rebeke sat lost before her, her mind jerked free of her body by the egg's questing, taken to some far place it would never return from. That had happened before. There was a hall maintained for them by the High Council where they sat in honor for their service, speechless, sightless, neither alive nor dead. Rebeke would not look well among them.

Her heart began to beat faster as she wondered if Rebeke were already lost. Yet to touch her, to speak to her, would be certain to shatter her concentration and lose her to the egg. So Cerie sat motionless, gripping her hands together.

A sound came, a gurgle of breath drawn with difficulty. Rebeke slid sideways like jelly, and Cerie sprang hastily to her feet. But even as Rebeke collapsed, her hand reached to deposit the egg safely in its nested cushion. Cerie heard the slight hiss of it against the silk, and saw a tendril of near-colorless smoke rise from it. Heaving a sigh of relief, she knelt by Rebeke and picked up the pot of healing unguent that would soothe the peculiar burns of the egg. Rebeke sprawled limply, allowing Cerie to smooth it into her blistered hands and ease it softly over the circular mark on her forehead.

"Wine?" Cerie asked, and Rebeke's eyelids fluttered slightly. She raised Rebeke's head and held the cup to her lips. Rebeke took two tiny hesitant sips, and suddenly her blistered hands rose to clasp the cup on their own, heedless of pain, as she drained it off. Her eyes opened and her trembling hands snatched at the food on the tray, cramming the cakes into her wide mouth, gulping like a feeding Harpy. Cerie turned her head aside. It did not disgust her. Too often had she returned from the trance of the egg, and felt the savage hunger of a body mercilessly drained. Even before Rebeke had finished, she rose to go to a side table, bringing back with her a large bowl of fruit, and a basin of scented water with a small towel soaking in it. Still Rebeke did not speak as she laved her hands and sponged her face. But she sighed as she reached for the first piece of fruit, and her eyes finally met Cerie's.

"I spoke to them." Triumph vied with exhaustion in her voice. And something else; an unidentifiable emotion that jabbed at Cerie's fears.

"Were you able to strike a bargain?" Cerie demanded.

"No." Rebeke poured herself more wine. "Or perhaps I should say, not yet. I hope I have left them little choice."

"Tell me." Cerie poured wine of her own. She glanced at her comfortable throne longingly, but Rebeke had not moved from the carpeted floor.

"We began well enough. Very flowery courtesies they employ. They were surprised to hear me; Yoleth had told them she was the only Windsinger powerful enough to speak to them. They were very wary of me. I told them there had been a grave mistake; that we wished Ki and Vandien returned, and that we would return the two from their world. The Limbreth politely said it was impossible." Rebeke hesitated. "It is difficult to speak of them. There is such a sense of many in one, that I did not know if I dealt with one mind or many. Very distracting. Tell me, has Yoleth said aught to the Council of a calling gem? The Limbreth claimed that it had given her one as a final sealing of the bargain."

Cerie's eyes narrowed. "Perhaps that is the secret satisfaction behind her smile these days. What can it do?"

"I don't know. The Limbreth uses it through a Keeper to call folk into its world, or to summon folk from its own world into its service. The Limbreth claimed no knowledge of what Yoleth would use it for; she asked for it and got it. I had the strangest feeling that they were disclaiming responsibility for it."

"So Yoleth's wind blows strongest this time. I am sorry, Rebeke."

"Yoleth wins nothing," Rebeke hissed. "I did not give up so easily. I asked them what was possible, then. They were quick to offer me Vandien and a Brurjan for their own folk, or any two I wished to be rid of. I received the distinct impression that Vandien has made a nuisance of himself over there. Of the Brurjan I know nothing, except that she is no use to them, being unsuitable for their visions, and having a nasty temperament as well."

"I know nothing of any Brurjan sent through."

Rebeke smiled sourly. "I wonder how much Yoleth has done that the Council is unaware of."

"Did you agree to the exchange they offered?"

"Certainly not. If Vandien annoys them, all to the better. It may make them more willing to strike a bargain. I told them that without Ki, I would make no trades. I bid them ask of me what gifts they would to make the trade possible. They refused me totally." Rebeke fastened her strange eyes on Cerie. "Sending Ki through has had a side effect Yoleth scarcely planned. The Limbreth is exceedingly pleased with her. Its contacts with Humans in the past have been rather limited. Who can say when last that Gate was used? The Limbreth has had to be contented with what was offered; rather ordinary folk, if villainous. But in Ki they have found the exceptional, and they won't surrender her. Guess what it is about Ki that intrigues them so?" Rebeke challenged wryly.

"I'm sure I have no idea. A commoner person I couldn't imagine." Cerie sipped from her glass.

"On the surface. But if she were truly so common, Yoleth would never have put her through the Gate. The Limbreth senses in her the aura of a Windsinger, and delights in her unconscious sensitivity to the network of life and power around her. The Limbreth looks forward to consuming a Wind-singer."

Rebeke fell quiet, but Cerie looked more uncomfortable every moment.

"Rebeke," Cerie ventured. "Why not let it go? Are the Romni teamster and her man worth all this effort? Show your displeasure with the High Council in another way. Deny them access to the Relic. Charm the winds away from them. Send a peasant-killing wind to rage through their holdings."

"No!" Rebeke's refusal was vehement. "That would teach

them nothing new. They already know that to cross me means my ill will. What they must learn now is that they cannot cross me, cannot infringe on my will in any matter. I said the Romni teamster would be allowed to roam in peace, and so she will. Ki will be returned to this world. They shall learn what the power of a full Windsinger is.''

The might and majesty in her voice had grown to fill the chamber. A chill ripple of wind rose from the very floor, fluttering the robes of the two Singers. Rebeke breathed harshly for a moment; then she drew in a deep breath and with it her temper.

''I am sorry, Cerie. I should not vent my anger on you, who has given me more than an egg and a place to use it. I know what the Council will say of our little consultation. I know it will not go easy on you. But be sure you have made the right choice. My cloak will be over you, and my winds will be at your back, when I am come fully into my own.''

''I believe you, Windsinger.'' But somehow the belief was small comfort. ''Yet you say that Ki will be returned. How?''

Rebeke measured her carefully. When she spoke, her words came slowly. ''I threatened them. I told them first that they could name a price for the return of Ki. They demurred. Then I told them that they would return Ki and Vandien, or pay my price for them. I threatened to go to the Gatherers.''

If Rebeke had suggested going to the moon, Cerie's look could not have been more incredulous. ''They will know it for an idle threat. It is impossible.''

''No. It is not. I can and would do it. A speaking egg, I have come to discover, has more ability than we have guessed. Its possible range was suggested to me when I wished to make contact with the Limbreth, and now I am sure my source was correct in his claims. I could inform the Gatherers of the Limbreth's Gate-making.''

''And us? Do you believe we would go unscathed?'' A rising note marred Cerie's controlled voice.

''No. I don't think that we would. But that is the chance I would take, just as Yoleth put us all at risk when she helped to open the Gate. I cannot let this pass; I cannot let Yoleth believe she can dare more than I. She—no, all the Council—must see me as as ruthless as herself. Let them respect me for the danger I can create, if not for my skills.''

"And until then, we all hang in the balance." Anger vied with fear in Cerie's voice, and Rebeke put a steadying hand on her shoulder.

"We will not dangle for long. I urged the Limbreth to decide swiftly; three of our days I gave him. The Limbreth scoffed at me, of course. I was told that I misjudged the importance of myself and my world, if I supposed the Gatherers would even be interested. But in the same breath, the Limbreth claimed suddenly that any trade was impossible, because of the state of the Gate. They fear to use it, they said. I gather that they have opened it in that location too many times, and Vandien tore it when he went through; what is left of it is like an old, reopened wound, thick with scar tissue. But I believe they can open it one more time. My will is very strong, and I could help more than any other ever has in the making of a Gate. We can open it, even if it may be for the last time; in fact that suits me. If I can force this trade, I want no chance of future ones. I do not fancy Limbreths with an acquired taste for Windsingers. Let the Gate between our worlds heal and scar over permanently. I shall not mind at all." Rebeke picked up her glass of wine and drained it, refilled both their glasses and drank again. "I am still wearied, Cerie. And I ask myself, do I have the courage and the will for this struggle? The closer I come to it, the more I question myself. A Windsinger, I believe, should be above this sort of skullduggery; but I am not a full Windsinger yet. Some of my weakness I can blame on my coming to my training late in life, and some I shall blame on my youth's companions. But most I shall blame on the times we live in. Perhaps by my ruthlessness I can create a world and time when Windsingers can be all they should be. Perhaps the girls who now wear white and lisp their platitudes by rote will someday say, 'Rebeke, she was a wicked old thing, but the first true Windsinger in a long time!'" Her tone was as light as a jest, but Cerie did not smile. She clasped her hands inside her sleeves to still their trembling and agreed, "These are, indeed, dreadful times to be living in."

SEVENTEEN

THE road had gone bad. Vandien leaned forward on the seat, peering past the sweating greys. But he couldn't see what had caused this sudden marshy stretch, nor how far ahead of him it lasted. Hollyika, of course, was nowhere in sight.

Vandien sent shivers of encouragement down the traces to the team. There was an irony to this, he realized, as there had been to all his journey beyond the Gate, but it didn't make him smile. Usually he was the one who got impatient with the wagon's slow pace and galloped ahead to spy out the lay of the land, while Ki sat on the high seat and sweated the team through the tough spots on the road. Now he sat with his shirt sticking to him as the greys slogged forward through sucking black mud.

The road had taken them down the length of the Limbreth valley, past their soldierly row and then around a shoulder of the hills; after that, with every plodding step the team took, the road seemed to get worse. The grass and moss on either side of this part of the road were yellow-grey, withering away. It was the first blight that Vandien had noticed in the Limbreth world. He chewed at the ends of his untrimmed moustache as he watched the greys hunch their shoulders against their collars. The road had been hard and good, right up until the moment they passed out of sight of the Limbreths. Their gems still glowered dimly in the sky behind them. One wheel lurched suddenly down into a soft spot. ''Damn!'' roared Vandien, but the team dragged on steadily and the wagon walked up out of it. Vandien wiped sweat from his forehead and peered up the road. It was veering back to the hills in a steady climb; that grade and the softening roadbed might be more than the team could handle, and there was no sign of the road getting better.

The black horse reappeared, loping easily toward him, clods of turf and mud flying from his scarlet hooves, Hollyika riding high and graceful. The Brurjan's head was canted back to peer over her shoulder.

"Hollyika!" he called to her. "I'm going to pull up for a bit and let the team breathe."

She made no reply, but brought her horse in a graceful loop to pull up beside the plank seat of the wagon. The weary team snorted gratefully at the stop. Vandien put his face into his hands and rubbed his eyes. The eternal dimness of this place made him feel permanently sleepy. Just once he would have liked to see this place under a ray of sun. "How long is the road this bad?"

She shrugged and flashed a Brurjan grin on him. "Not far. Then it gets worse where the road starts to really climb." Black shifted his feet, making wet plopping sounds. "The sides are no better than the road itself," Hollyika replied to his questioning glance. "Underground stream, maybe. I can see your wheels sinking even as we talk."

"Limbreth mischief, I think."

"Whatever." She tossed her broad shoulders again. "It doesn't matter what causes it, it's what we have to go over."

"Yes." Vandien looked deep into eyes on a level with his own. They were keen, dark, and wise in their own hard way. Vandien asked abruptly, "Why is she going on? To what?"

"To whatever the Limbreth told her to do."

"But what about me?" He could not stop the hurt and outrage from slipping into his voice. "As if she had never known me, or worried about these horses, she just goes on." His own dark eyes bored into Hollyika's. "When she was with you, did she speak of me at all?"

Hollyika shifted slightly in her saddle. "If you would let me," she began in a low and reasonable voice, "I could take you inside that wagon, put you on your back, and make you forget all about Ki. For a time, anyway."

He turned his eyes from her, shaking his head in consternation. "That's not what I want," he said, not knowing how to explain.

"I didn't say I wanted it. I was simply saying that, given the opportunity, I could do it. I could keep your mind and your senses so full of me that you wouldn't for that time think of Ki, no matter what you felt for her. Afterwards, she would come back to your mind. Perhaps.'' The hard flash of teeth again. ''Right now, the Limbreth fills all her mind and senses. What she felt for you in the past is covered up, blotted out by another presence. Can you understand what I am telling you?''

''I think I do. I think you are saying, very politely, that Ki never even mentioned my name.'' I'll never say Brurjans are without courtesy again, he thought sadly.

''Hell, who was listening? We were both full of the Limbreths, speaking only to them, though we thought we conversed with each other. I don't remember half the things *I* said, let alone what the Romni babbled. When the Limbreth filled me, everything else was just background. I felt good. All through me. When I thought of things I had been fond of in the past, like Black, I was grateful the Limbreths had enlightened me as to the nature of love, and how I must let him go his own way, if I truly loved him. And I must go mine, on to the Limbreths, to be fulfilled and find peace. Do you get the drift of it? But I believed it then, and Ki is still full of it. This is more of that think and feel crap you Humans wallow in. Look, Vandien, she's gone away from you. You know that. You know what she is doing. She is getting further away from you. You know what you want. You want her to be with you. So you know what to do. Go and get her. It's all so much simpler without the 'I think' and 'I feel' shit.''

''But what about what she wants? Aren't I supposed to care at all about what she desires?''

''Hell, no. Ki can do that for herself. When we find her, you can say, 'I want you to come with me.' If she says 'no,' you can fight with her. Whoever wins, wins. It's simple.''

''It must be nice, being a Brurjan.''

A strange look, and then the flash of teeth again. ''It's nice to be anything, when you are it, instead of thinking about it. Look, we don't have time for this. Need any help with the harness?''

Vandien sat up straight and ran his eyes over the team. ''It looks fine to me.''

''Sure it's fine, if you don't plan on going anywhere.''

Vandien looked over the side of the wagon; the wheels had

sunk still deeper into the muck. He measured it with an experienced eye. "It looks bad, but the greys can still manage. It'll be slow, but they'll do it."

"Through that?" Hollyika was skeptical as she pointed up the road.

"I think so, and I'm willing to try it. I've slogged this wagon up worse hills than that."

"Have you? And I've charged through formations that offered more resistance than that. But even together I doubt that we can do both at the same time. Look at them."

Vandien followed her gaze. At first the darkness baffled him; he caught a movement of light so faint it seemed a trick of his weary eyes. He squinted and then made them out by the gleam of their hair and the flash of their eyes: a group of farmers with some kind of long tools over their shoulders. "They must be a harvest party, going from farm to farm."

"No." Hollyika's voice was flat. "I rode right up to them, calling greetings they didn't answer. But as soon as I came within range, they started swinging those rods. You want to drive a wagon up a muddy hill through that?"

Vandien's eyes went from the farmers to his wheels. A sickness touched his heart. He looked down: the mud touched hubs now. No mud could sink a wagon that fast! But it had. Given levers, brush, and a lot of time, he could have gotten it out; but he had none of these. "I can't leave the wagon," he said stubbornly.

"Why? Has your ass grown tight to the seat? Those farmers are moving faster than you might expect. You either leave the wagon, or your body. Hell, we'll be lucky to get the horses through." Even as she spoke, she had dismounted and begun to free the team from the wagon. Vandien watched her, his fists clenching and unclenching at his sides. The colors of the gaily painted wagon were dim under these skies, and it looked only awkward, uncomfortable, out of place. But this awkward uncomfortable thing had somehow become his home; too many things had happened inside its tiny cuddy for him to leave the wagon here. But he had to leave it, and the knowledge wrenched and clawed at him. Then he set his teeth, took a breath, and let it go. Silently he turned and went into the cuddy, and as he looked around its crowded homeliness, the pain tried to grip him again, but he ignored it. His rapier. There was that to take, and food for them both, and the waterskin, and a set of clothes for Ki. He resolutely ignored the trinkets and gewgaws of their life together. Practicality made light luggage. To what he had he added one sack filled with grain from the back of the wagon, and loaded it all onto the suspicious Sigurd. Hollyika had fashioned a lead rope for Sigurd and shortened the long driving reins on Sigmund's bridle. As he scrambled up onto Sigmund's back, Hollyika nodded grudgingly. "At least you learn fast."

The figures of the approaching farmers were no longer veiled by dusk. Vandien counted eight of them, men and women, as they strode resolutely on. Their faces were tranquil, their eyes fixed before them. They didn't call to Hollyika and Vandien, or speak to each other. They came on silently as dreams.

"They don't look too formidable," Vandien grumbled softly. Anger began to heat in him; had the Brurjan tricked him into abandoning Ki's wagon?

"Follow me," she growled. She leaned forward in her saddle and the black leaped suddenly to a gallop. Straight toward them she rode. Much heel-thudding nagged Sigmund into a ponderous canter, the disgruntled Sigurd trailing behind. The warrior pulled steadily away from them.

And the farmers came steadily on down the road. Vandien fixed his eyes on them as he clung to his mount. They had raised their staves. But they did not scatter, nor even take up a defensive stance. No light of battle changed their eyes or faces. There were no cries of fury or challenge. Bunched in a group, they strode down the road to meet the charging horse.

"Make way!" Hollyika roared, but they only waved their staves. Then she was among them and Vandien was sickened. The horse crashed through, silent bodies flung to either side, though he heard a few whacks as blows of the staff struck the rider. Two figures sprawled in the road, but no outcry arose. Those standing milled for a moment and began to close ranks. Vandien was too far behind Hollyika; now they were ready to meet him, eyes cold. Sigmund threw up his head and tried to wheel aside from this Human barricade. A staff came down solidly on Vandien's shoulder; he clung to Sigmund's mane, realizing he was the only target, not the horse. Another blow smote his hip, numbing his leg to the knee. The farmers surged around him. Then Black and Hollyika crashed suddenly through the press. "Ride on, stupid!" she screamed at him. He had a fleeting impression of flying scarlet hooves felling farmers. Then Sigmund took charge, leaping into the gap she had cleared and surging forward under Vandien; Sigurd crowded behind. He and the greys were clear and fleeing down the sodden black road.

He heard the splattering hoofbeats of Black as Hollyika caught up with him. Vandien glanced over at her, but kept a tight grip on the flying grey mane before him. The ponderous gallop of the beast below him was thunder in his ears. He did not know much of Brurjan facial expressions, but he thought she looked grim and ill. When they crested the first long rise, she pulled in the black. The greys dropped their pace to match with no signal from Vandien. Hollyika kept them all at a striding walk. Just as Vandien opened his mouth to speak, she turned to him. "They won't be following," she said bleakly. He shut his mouth.

The road ran on. At first they rode on the margins of the road, until the already soggy mosses and grasses turned to morass. The lands on either side of them as they struggled up the hillsides were wild places; the road and its banks were swamps now right up to the edge of brush that prickled and stabbed the horses when they tried to ride through it. "Ki could never have come this way," Vandien asserted, to which Hollyika replied, "She must have." So on they went, and on, until finally, incredibly, they reached the top of the final hill and looked down into a grey valley full of shadows. Vandien's body told him they were deep into night.

In silent accord they halted, looking down at the valley full of dusk before them. The road was straight from here, still flowing with mud, true, but implacably straight. It cut through woods and pasture, field and meadow, now clear, now veiled, until it finally emerged to intersect with the far black ribbon of another road. And gracing that stretch of road was a bridge. No, the bridge, the one he had so admired the first time he had seen it. No road had intersected with that road then; he was sure of it. "But it does now," Hollyika observed aloud. "Limbreths."

She urged her black and they began their descent, the horse's haunches braced under him, half walking and half sliding as he went. Vandien let a space develop between them, and then took the greys down. It was steep for only a short way, then it gave onto the gentler slope of a hillside pasture, grazed by some tiny hooved beasts that thundered off into the trees at their approach. The far road and the bridge were hidden from them again in the more immediate barrier of brush and trees, the brambly trees edging ever closer to the road. Water flowed over the top of the muddy path and the horses' hooves slid and squelched in it. A short distance more, and the trees began to arch over the stream that the horses now followed. If Hollyika noticed the change or found it alarming, she said nothing. Vandien did not deign to speak either. She was right. Sometimes it was simpler just doing, without worrying about what came next.

The trees thinned and then gave way. With a tingle of uneasiness, Vandien realized that the stream led them now through cultivated fields. The gleaming red fruit hung in shining globules on the vines. Sigurd snatched at the foliage hungrily, snorting with weary displeasure when Vandien jerked him on. The greys were dispirited, heads adroop, moving with slogging steps. Even Hollyika slouched in her ridiculous saddle. Vandien found it more and more difficult to keep his eyes open. Sigmund's trudging stride rocked him gently and he swayed with it. With a jerk he pulled his head up again. He rubbed his eyes and looked around, trying to wake himself up. A dark hummock far off across the rows of crops was a farmer's cottage. He stared at it and the milling of folk around it. "Hollyika!" he called softly.

She reined in her black and dropped back to be even with him. "Pay no attention to them," she commanded in a harsh whisper.

"They're staring at us."

"They look both more and less than angry, don't they? Pay them no mind. Five dark trespassers must be an unusual sight. Don't borrow trouble ahead of time. Keep riding."

Her black pulled ahead of him again, and Vandien, alert now, stepped up Sigmund's weary pace. He tried to look at the cottage and the shining folk gathered there without turning his head. There was quite a group of them, their hair lambent in the soft twilight, and in every hand stood a tall stick. His stomach turned over. He could not blot from his mind the silent sprawled figures they had left in the road; he wanted no more of that.

Black hesitated, and then stepped awkwardly down into a gully. Vandien brought Sigmund to the brink of it and waited. Hollyika sat lightly on her horse's back, moving like a part of him, swaying with him as he placed his hooves and clambered up to the other side. They had regained the original road and it was sound under his hooves.

Vandien nudged Sigmund on, and the draft horse went down like a landslide. He had barely lurched and staggered into the ditch before Sigurd came down behind them; then with another lurch they had all regained the road. Vandien glanced back the way they had come: the passage they had made through the crops was plain behind them. He sneaked a glance at the farmer's hut. The crowd was gone. Vandien twisted around, trying to see them.

"They went back inside," Hollyika informed him. Her eyes were red-rimmed, her face sagging with weariness. For a Brurjan she was grotesquely gaunt; it gave her face a Human cast. She needs food and rest, Vandien thought. She's running on a thin edge of endurance. The amount she had eaten when they had the wagon might carry her a day or so, but not well. He reached for the food bag without speaking. He parceled out dry fish for her, which she took silently, and a handful of dried fruit for himself. He would have liked the fish, but this would sustain him, whereas it would do nothing for Hollyika. He felt her eyes on him as he rolled and tied the bag shut again.

"We've got enough to make it," he told her with more confidence than he felt. She nodded slowly and put a whole stick of fish into her mouth. Her jaws moved four times and she swallowed. Her dark eyes flashed suddenly to his like a battering ram. "Stop looking at me like you want to take care of me," she snarled. "It makes me more nauseous than this fish. You should never eat anything after the blood clots."

"I'll remember that," Vandien told her meekly, and was rewarded with a savage grin.

"On to the bridge," she told him, and kneed her black gently.

Ki firmly compressed the living earth in her thin hands. She closed her eyes and with the enchanted awareness of the Limbreths, she felt the potential life in the organic matter she held. Egg of insect, seed, tiny life forms smaller than imagining lay there. And more. The more that the Limbreths had given her. It was like a tool in her mind's hands. And she, who had never been a carver of wood or a painter of pictures, began to create. This was to be the first blossom in her garden.

She had tilled the spot she had chosen by crawling over it on her knees, turning the soil with her hands. The area had taken her some time to select, for she had wished to complement the bridge while taking nothing from it. She had decided finally that the garden would be visible from the arch of the bridge, and the swell of the bridge would be glimpsed from the garden. But between the garden and the bridge itself would be a section of the road where one would walk and see but one or the other. Thus each could be viewed in its purity, or as a complementary whole. She had made the Limbreths aware of her desire and they had given their approval. They had marked out the necessary limits of it in her mind for her, and she had begun her toil.

The softening and turning of the earth had been a long task. Dirt had become embedded beneath her nails, and then her fingernails had worn away from the constant grubbing. The lines of her hands were stained with the black soil and her fingers cracked now and bled sometimes, but the Limbreths kept the pain from distracting her. She had concentrated on the next task, the moving of earth a double handful at a time, to create a harmonious rise and fall. The softly sculpted earth was ready now and waiting for her.

Ki closed her eyes and opened the new ones the Limbreths had given her, the ones that looked in. She chose memories of awesome beauty from her past; the Sisters revealed to her in the silver shining glory of the mountain pass; the light-speckled spaces of the void she had leaped with Dresh; the face of Dalvi, the oldest Romni man of the tribes, wisdom gleaming from his undimmed eyes; a scarlet Harpy stooping to its kill: these images, and dozens more of her sharpest impressions she chose, and then let melt together. She reached for that essence of them that had caught her breathless between terror and wonder, and the tool of the Limbreths found it for her, and in Ki's mind it shone.

It sprouted from the double handful of soil she held, it took shape and grew cupped in the warmth of her two hands. Ki saw it growing within her mind, held her breath as it came to fulfillment and perfection in her hands. She had a moment of disbelief. It could not be. Not from her could come so wondrous a thing; it was beyond the skills any mortal might possess. "Do not doubt," the Limbreths chided her. "To doubt is to freeze the creativity. Cast it from your soul, and be absorbed in doing." Delighted, Ki obeyed.

The flower sparkled, the brilliance of it cutting into her soul. It renewed in her the awesome beauty she had sought to recall. She treasured the miracle in her hands, experiencing wave after wave of blissful astonishment.

"Enough!" the Limbreths whispered to her. Ki sighed. She knelt and lowered it gently into the soft cup of earth that waited to receive it.

"Grow," she bid it. It obeyed, a scintillating streamer of life, uncoiling to fill the indicated curve of bed, no stray leaf overreaching, no glistening facet of petal drooping beyond the space Ki had visualized. That one was done.

Ki had to pause. A little tongue of weariness brushed against her. She felt, for an instant, drained; some part of her had been emptied. But when her puzzled mind groped for it, she found only the warm reassurances of the Limbreths. She was fine, all was well, and the garden begun. She did not want to cease being without completing it, did she? Of course not. So she must go on at once, without resting. It was begun so well. What was her next choice?

Ki took a few steps until she felt the rightness of the place. Stooping, she raised another double handful of earth. Again she felt all the potential that lurked within it, and she relaxed, knowing already what she would imprint on it. Warmth; her mother's soft breast against her cheek, filling her mouth with sweet milk; a litter of kittens asleep in her skirts; fresh berries picked and devoured while still warm from the sun.

"Ki!"

She started at the call, the cupped soil slipping between her fingers, the vision lost. Slowly she turned, blinking her eyes as if awakened by a strong light. For long moments she saw no one; then her eyes picked up movement, and finally shape. They were so grotesquely dark. Names came to her with no feelings attached to them. It was Hollyika the Brurjan bestriding a horse, and Vandien riding another as he kept a third prisoner on a lead line. Ki felt dismay uncoil within her at the sight. They came on toward her, dragging their darkness closer. Vandien was smiling, teeth white as a dog's snarl, as if he delighted in the discord he brought to her garden. The burdened animals' hooves left deep pock marks in her dirt. Her nostrils caught the sweat smell of the weary beasts, and her heart went out to them.

Pity. That was another one. "Show us," begged the Limbreths, and Ki took up more dirt. She composed herself over it, sorting her memories for ones that were pure and strong. There was the Romni woman who had lost seven children and her man to fever, untouched by it herself; and—it was no good. Her traitor eyes flickered open at the thudding hooves, darting to the intruders. "Go on," begged the Limbreths. "Don't mind them. They won't dare to disturb you. In a moment they will have to go; we have provided for them. Go on about pity."

There had been the fighting dogs in Kalnor, kept in tiny cages and teased until released to fight to the death in pits, and that tiny, frail baby with . . .

"Ki? Ki—talk to me. Gods, look at her, Hollyika. You can see the shape of the bones in her hands. Ki!"

Her eyes fluttered but she kept them closed. She refocused her mind. She could feel the invaders standing close by, looking, but not daring to touch her. It was as the Limbreths had promised. She could not see Vandien's arms folded tight against his chest and clutched to still their shaking. He stared about him at the garden, strangely repulsive in its beauty. It touched too many strings in his heart too sharply. He did not understand what he saw, and didn't want to; he did want Ki to be aware of him. He needed to hold her tightly, and feel her arms go about him to hug him with her quick strength. He was afraid to touch this haggard woman; he feared he would break her brittle bones. Some terrible illness gnawed at her, he told himself. She would be all right when he got her safely through the Gate. She twitched as if pain spasmed her, and he stepped closer to catch her if she fell. But she kept her feet.

From her cupped hands and the earth had sprung a wonder and a marvel that captured Vandien's eyes. Awe gripped his heart painfully as he watched it unfold. It reminded him of something, stirring long-buried feeling; but it cut him too close and his heart denied it. He raised his eyes from the plant to Ki's face and gave a bleat of horror. Lines of agony appeared and deepened in her face as the flower grew and blossomed; in seconds the flesh melted on her bones, leaving her face thinner yet, the bones of her wrists knobbing from her arms, her ribs stretching her skin like the ribs of a wagon under canvas. She stooped to set the thing in place. He watched numbly as she stepped to a new spot, her ravaged body staggering, and yet she picked up more earth with care and precision.

Vandien turned anguished eyes to Hollyika who still sat her horse. "What's the matter?" she asked grimly. "Did you forget what you wanted, or change your mind?"

"Damn you," he said evenly. He moved quickly to Ki, taking her wrists gently but firmly. With a shake he tumbled the soil from her hands; a questing tendril browned and died as it fell. Ki turned her face up to his and her eyes opened to him with a drowned gaze.

"I came for you. Ki, I'm Vandien. Don't you remember?"

"Vandien." She looked up at him long, hearing no guiding whisper from the Limbreths. Without their direction, she fumbled on alone. "Vandien. I cared for you so much. You were impetuous and quick, tempering my caution. Yes, you belong here." She looked down at the half a handful of dirt that remained in her hands. "Yes. I will take the way you smell when I put my face in the hollow of your shoulder, and the look of your eyes at night when the moonlight fills them, and the sudden brush of your lips and moustache across my eyes when we meet after long weeks apart on the road. I will take the soft invitation of your hands in the night."

Vandien followed her blinded gaze to her hands. In after times he could never recall to himself exactly what he saw sprouting there. The beauty of it made his eyes ache, but there was also the sense that things held dear to him had been snatched away and sold to a stranger. The secret trove that tempered his days with sweetness was being spilled out for all to see, and it was not for other eyes. "No!" he roared in a sudden jealousy, and shook it from her hands and put his boot upon it.

"Finally!" Hollyika observed, and spurred the black horse forward. His scarlet hooves wreaked carnage in the beds, trampling them to a lush ruin of black soil and severed leaf. Ki

shook like a palsied scarecrow, her mouth working but giving
forth no sound.

"Ki!" Vandien began urgently, trying to catch her flying
wrists. She struck him in the face, no slap, but the impact of a
fist that smashed his lips against his teeth and bloodied her
knuckles. He threw up an arm to guard against her furious
onslaught, surprised at the strength she had left. He ducked
away from her, flinching from blows that intended to do serious damage; but it was over in a flurry like an autumn wind.
Vandien felt her stamina give out; this Ki was not in the physical condition of the woman he was accustomed to ride with.
He lowered his arms from his face, taking her feeble blows on
his chest and arms, scarcely feeling them. Her face crumpled
like a child's when punished; he knew she was close to collapse.

Hollyika rode up beside them, felling Ki with a fist blow to
the side of her neck that was savagely efficient. Ki sank down
limp and didn't even twitch. Vandien's incredulous stare went
from the frail woman on the dark soil to the Brurjan looking
down at him slit-eyed.

"No time for it. Talk her into it later. Right now, you load
her up while I hold them off." She wheeled Black as she
spoke, calling the last words over her shoulder.

They had come silently, the fair-haired host from the
farmer's cottage. They came, stony-faced and lambent-eyed,
staffs and hoes and scythes swung to shoulders. But as Hollyika bore down on them, these clumsy weapons came to the
ready and were swung with amazing skill. They cried out not at
all, nor did they look particularly interested in what they did.
They moved efficiently, their line fanning out to flank the lone
Brurjan and her horse.

Swift as a heartbeat, he saw it all. Stooping he lifted Ki,
swinging her limp thinness easily over his shoulder. To get her
on a horse was more difficult; Sigurd was not used to such
burdens, and objected to this one. But as Hollyika had pointed
out, there was no time for niceties. He flung her between the
grain bag and the food sack, and swiftly and securely roped her
into place. His mind and body raced with adrenaline. He scrabbled atop Sigmund, and looped the lead rope around Sigmund's neck. Once settled on that broad back, he drew his
rapier from its sheath and lifted it to the ready. He had never

fought from horseback before and suspected that a staff would clear him from Sigmund's back long before his rapier came within range of anything.

Drumming his heels against Sigmund's broad sides, he broke him into a shambling trot. Hollyika had already rearranged the battle to her liking; her black had broken through the line in two places, leaving squirming bodies on the dark turf. Black's eyes shone, and Hollyika's were red-rimmed with her excitement. The horse was a magnificent weapon in his own right as he wheeled, striking out in all directions with his scarlet hooves. The whacks of the staffs he ignored, though his dark coat shone wet in two places where scythes had scored him. Hollyika swayed in her saddle, moving with him as deftly as his hooves moved under him, rocking her balance to match his as she struck out with her heavy sword. Wherever it touched, flesh bared bone, but her victims gave no cry. They fell before her sword as silently as they writhed beneath Black's hooves.

Vandien made his ponderous charge, and hoped his rapier looked impressive as it danced in his hand. But before he fairly reached the battle, the great horse underneath him smelled the blood and reached his own decision. Snorting, he threw his great head and lunged in a wild shy that nearly unseated Vandien, and fought against the bridle when Vandien tried to make him obey.

"The damn horse . . . is smarter . . . than you are!" Hollyika's words came in gasping shouts. "Get . . . the hell . . . out of here! You're in my way!" In a single warrior foray she proved her words, charging past him so closely that she nearly swept him from the saddle. The flying hooves of the black struck in their battle dance against two farmers who had come up behind him. The sharp copper smell of fresh blood under his nose was all the confirmation Sigmund needed. He lunged about, nearly colliding with Sigurd, and broke into a heavy gallop. "Get over the bridge!" Hollyika called needlessly after them as the greys found and took the road.

"As if I had any say in it," Vandien muttered, clinging to the grey mane and trying to grip the barrel body. The grey horses devoured the road, the shocks of Sigmund's hooves jarring Vandien with every stride; the big greys could move when they wished to. The only sound of the battle had been

Hollyika's gasping Brurjan curses and the whack of sword meeting staff, and these faded behind Vandien quickly. There was a brief thunder as they crossed the magnificent bridge, then more road. Vandien was flying into the night down the smooth black road. Darkness cupped him under her hand and hid their passage from all eyes.

Eighteen

Ki's skin was cold beneath his hands as he eased her down from Sigurd's back. "Ki?" he asked of her staring eyes, but they focused on something past him. She was on her feet and standing, but when he took away his support, her body slowly folded. Catching her, he moved her away from the horses and eased her to the ground.

Vandien shook his head over her as he chafed her icy hands and feet and glanced once more to where the road unwound like a dark ribbon. He didn't want Hollyika to ride past his hiding place in the dark. He flattered himself that he had chosen this grove of trees well. Their silvery trunks camouflaged the grey hides of the team. They were safe here, for the moment.

He crouched again over Ki, proffering the loose robe he had packed from the wagon for her. "Come on. Let's get you into this and warm you up." She still made no reply. Her open eyes stared past him at the ever dark sky. He sighed, thinking of the stiff blow Hollyika had dealt her. Was she witless, or too angry to speak? But her body was limp beneath his touch, and she didn't resist him as he bundled her into the robe; he found it harder to put hose and soft low boots onto feet that were equally limp. Dressed, she appeared a little more like the Ki he knew, though the looseness of the robe exaggerated her emaciated condition.

"How about some food?" No answer. He went to the food sack anyway, taking out dried fruit and hard traveler's bread. She didn't move when he put it before her, but when in exasperation he waved it under her nose, she turned away with an exclamation of disgust.

"Well, at least you've remembered how to talk," he commented sourly. He moved closer to her. "How's your head?"

"Why did you bring me here?" she demanded, low and savage.

"I'm taking you back to the Gate. To our own world, where we belong, so that Jace and Chess can come back where they belong."

"This is my world now." Leashed fury in her voice. "This is where I belong. I have a task to do here, a creation to unfold. In this world, I can make my existence mean something. I have no desire to go back."

"I don't suppose you do, right now." Vandien kept his voice reasonable. "You are not yourself at present; you are still under the Limbreth's sway. After a time without their water, and some proper food in you, you'll come back to your senses."

"You mean I'll sink back to your level." Ki sat up, running skeletal hands through her disheveled hair. She hissed out a breath. "Look at me. Already you've brought me back to anger, one of the basest emotions of the Human race. I had managed to free myself of that, Vandien, before you came back. Why did you have to spoil it all? Can't you see? You had your place in my life, and filled it sweetly. I am grateful to you for all that you were to me and all that we shared. But that time is past, and I have moved beyond you. Do not take it hard; I appreciate you now as I never did before. I have looked back at every memory I have of you, of every moment we have ever shared, and from each I have taken the gold and left the dross behind. I have purified your touch on my life. Now you would come back to soil it all again. I beg you not to. Leave me and go on, let me return to my work, and keep of you what was good."

Vandien had remained silent before her impassioned plea. Now he forced his clenched hands to open. He rose and stepped away to give her space. A practical voice inside him assured him that it was the Limbreth speaking, not Ki. She had been poisoned by their water, drugged by their visions. But that small demon of insecurity that sleeps in the best-loved of men sent forth a poisoned dart. She was done with him. She had taken of him all he had to offer her, and now she would carry it away with her. What had he to offer that could compete with the vision of the Limbreths? He coughed out a sigh and walked to the horses, to annoy them by thoroughly inspecting their hooves. He chewed his bitter choices. He could bind her like an animal and keep her at his side. He would be ashamed to treat a dog so. He could plead with her to come with him. He could let her go.

"You have my love, Vandien," she said to his hunched shoulders. "I leave it with you. You don't need me always by your side to possess that. We have cared for one another. But I am not a vine, to twist my life and twine about a strong column like yourself. Rather we have been as two strong trees that grew side by side, but must eventually lean apart from one another. You would not have me in your shade, would you, stunted and misshapen? Let me go."

"I am not holding you." The words were ripped slowly out of him, like torn pieces of flesh. He crossed his arms on his chest and held himself tightly, but there was no comfort in that solitary hug. The warm rich scents of the forest flowered up around him as it breathed out as peacefully as a sleeping child. The horses cropped the short grasses growing from the moss in contentment. No wind disturbed a single leaf; peace walked the night in velvet slippers. Vandien felt himself as a gaping red wound in the tranquil night as he watched Ki rise with difficulty. She was so painfully thin, so weakened by her fast. It was the water, he told himself vainly, the enchantment of the Limbreths that had brought them to this parting. But he could not wholly believe it. They had but brought Ki to an earlier realization of a truth he had always secretly known, that he needed her more than she needed him; that there were things waiting for one so capable and strong that could not be shared by a reckless vagabond like himself. In a thousand nightmares he had stood by the road calling after her as her wagon dwindled out of sight. Now she was going, her wagon lost to them both, and he did not call. She walked as hesitantly as a new-born fawn, picking her steps with caution born of weakness. Her robe was dark, and so was her hair; in no time the road swallowed her from sight. He stepped back into the sheltering trees, suddenly aware that his traitorous feet had nearly followed her. Let her go, he told himself sternly. Within the copse, he sank down, letting his dark head rest on his knees. He wondered what he would do next.

How long he sat he couldn't guess. He heard hoofbeats coming at an easy lope down the black road. He would have to go out of the copse and call to her, or she would pass him by in the dark. Not that it mattered much. Belatedly he recalled that he had all the food, and to Hollyika that would matter. He rose grudgingly, but before he could step out into the open, the greys had whinnied to Black and he had answered. Vandien heard the sound of his hooves change as he slowed and turned off the hard road onto firm turf.

Horse and rider looked bad and smelled worse. Vandien had heard rumors of the Brurjan battle musk, but had never smelled it before. He judged it a weapon at least as potent as her sword. He stepped forward to catch the reins of the spent horse, but he went jigging out of his reach; Hollyika pulled the horse's head sharply away.

"You're a damn fool!" she growled at him.

"I'm glad to see you, too."

She didn't even pause. "You don't muffle your horses' muzzles; how did you know it would be me coming along? Then you step up in front of a warhorse fresh from battle, waving your hands like a target; and lastly, you seem to have dropped this on your way."

"This" proved to be Ki, slung casually behind the Brurjan on her horse, and almost invisible behind her bulk.

"What the hell?" Vandien exclaimed in dismay. He stepped again to take her from the horse, remembered in time, and jumped back from the feint of Black's hooves.

"Quit spooking him!" growled the Brurjan and leaped from the saddle like a cat from a fence. She turned and went casually up to her horse, who stood docilely for her. She unslung Ki, dumping her to the ground unceremoniously. Vandien hastened to kneel beside her. "Is she hurt?"

"Not as bad as I am." For the first time, he noticed the dark drip from one of her muscular forearms. A passing scythe, he decided, and rose again, anxious for both of them.

"Let her flop." Hollyika read his thoughts. "I whacked her again, and down she went. She'll keep. She won't be up for a while, at any rate. Rip the sleeve off your shirt for a bandage." She worked her tongue around in her immense mouth, and then put her lips to her wound. Vandien watched in awe as her black tongue moved carefully down the length of the slash. Two tugs had his sleeve free of his shirt. He began to rip it into strips.

"You don't say much," Hollyika observed when she had finished licking her wound. "Not a 'thank you, Holly, I dropped her off the pack horse and never noticed' or anything."

"I didn't drop her off the pack horse." Vandien stepped up to take her arm in his hands. He split one end of his long strip to knot it firmly but not-too tightly above the wound. With a gentle touch he began to wrap the strip firmly in a long spiral down her arm. She gave no sign of pain.

"So how did you lose her?" she pressed.

"Are you asking me what I think you're asking me?" Vandien asked spitefully.

"No. I'm asking what stupid thing you did, that's all."

"She didn't want to stay with me. She wanted to go back to the Limbreths. I let her go." The words were clipped, but he resisted the urge to snug the bandage tighter around the wound.

"Stupider than I thought. I figured you had taken a nap and let her wander off. Don't you want her, after all the trouble we've gone to?"

"Yes. No. Hell, get off me! I don't want her if she doesn't want to be with me."

"Now he decides that. Wonderful. Beware of 'ifs,' Human. They dilute your purpose and spoil your drive. Consider your decision with no 'ifs.' You want her. You have her. Keep her after this."

"That's easy for you to say. You don't care about her. You won't wonder if it's right for her, good for her."

"I'd get more sense out of talking to Black. Look at her, fool! Does she look like the Limbreths are good for her?"

"There are other things besides being alive and healthy," Vandien began in a low voice, but the Brurjan cut him off with a hoot of laughter. "Name one thing worth having that you can get without being alive and healthy," she demanded.

"She wants to leave a mark on this world, a memorial to her passing."

"Sort of like a pile of horseshit in the road." Hollyika gave him her Brurjan snarl-grin. "You're funny, Human. I've laughed more since I met up with you than I have in years. Come here, Black."

The horse wheeled and came to her call. Vandien watched her in curiosity, then saw her set her mouth to his wounds, cleansing them with her tongue. "Taste good?" he asked her as rudely as he could, and received another snort of laughter from her.

He knelt over Ki, seeing for the first time that the Brurjan had bound her, wrist and ankle. Perhaps subduing Ki had not been as swift and easy as she had claimed. Her parting words still cut through his mind. Letting her go once had been hard enough; why did he have to face this twice? "But I promised you, long ago, to never ask anything of you that you were not willing to give. If you are no longer willing to give me your companionship, how shall I force it from you? I don't think you are doing what is best for you; but it is not my right to decide that for you." He reached to unfasten the rawhide thongs that bound her.

Hollyika's short knife thudded suddenly into the turf beside him. "Thanks," he muttered, and reached for it to slice the bonds. But, "Hands off her, Vandien. Next knife won't be a warning."

"You don't understand, Hollyika. I don't want her like this."

"Perhaps not. But I do. I caught her, I bound her, and that makes her mine. You had your chance at her. You let her go, knowing she was going back to her death. So now she's mine, and you'll keep your hands off her."

Vandien's dark eyes snapped as he pinned her with them. "Do you really think I'll sit back for that?" he asked in a cold voice.

She laughed. "As if it mattered what you did! Human, I told you. And I'll only tell you once. Look at me. Do you think you could defeat me if we fight over her? I'll tell you an old Brurjan custom. Kill your captives before you let them be rescued. If I had believed you had any chance of cutting her loose, that knife would have been in her. Now, hands off and go back to your own business."

Vandien remained motionless, calculating. He was no match for a Brurjan, even one as weakened as Hollyika, unless he could take her by treachery. Ki was in no position to side with him against her. He glowered at Hollyika, demanding, "Why?"

She reached under her armor to scratch. "Because I want to. It doesn't suit me that she go back to the Limbreths. Maybe I bear them hostility for finding me unworthy of their confidences and leaving me to die on the road. Maybe I think she'll sell for a good price on the other side of the Gate. Maybe I think I owe her something. Or you. But maybe I'm doing it to spite you. Remember what I told you before, Vandien? You don't need to know what I think or feel. Only what I do. And I do leave her tied, and I am taking her with us. Get me some food, will you? If Black hadn't already been bled by those farmers, I'd have him again myself.''

"The food's in the sack. Get it yourself," Vandien snarled.

She strode over to pluck her knife from the turf. She loomed over him, and then with a bark of laughter gave him a cuff that sent him sprawling. He was still recovering from it as she took food from the bag. ''Vandien,'' she called over her shoulder in an affable voice, ''you may yet be worth something. At least you growl well, even when you know you're beaten. Want anything to eat?''

"I'm still chewing my pride, thank you," he muttered as he rose to dust tendrils of moss from his clothes.

"It's too late for you to eat anyway," Hollyika observed calmly. ''Time for us to be riding on. I'm loading her back onto the nasty grey. If we meet more farmers, I don't want her hampering me. You'll still lead her horse, but don't get any stupid ideas.''

"Have I ever had any other kind?" Vandien asked bitterly, and moved to help load Ki. She was too light in his arms. He placed her as comfortably as he could, but she still looked as fragile as the flower he had stepped on. As he secured her in place, the rain began. No warning patter preceded it; it came down like a curtain, chill, soaking, relentless.

In the time it took him to get to Sigmund's back the horse was already drenched. He didn't want to move out of the grove's shelter, but Vandien pressed him on. Hollyika and Black were a sable shadow in front of him. The road was theirs again, empty of pursuit for as far as Vandien could see in the driving rain.

The spattering drops drowned all other sound. His hair soaked to his scalp, and then rivulets of water began to trickle down his face. His moustache was like a damp rag pressed to his mouth. He shook his head to clear the tickling drops, but the water clung like oil. He resigned himself to it and fixed his eyes on Hollyika's back as she plodded along, past meadows and marsh and field. At least she looked as uncomfortable as he felt. Wherever her fur was exposed, it was soaked into dripping points. Her sodden crest flopped to one side, ruining her warlike appearance.

"Vandien!" The long wailing cry cut through the rain noise and reached him. Vandien in his turn called forward to Hollyika and reined in his mount. Sigmund was glad of the rest. The road, once so fair and hard, was now softening again into a sucking muck that gripped hooves when it did not slip beneath them. Vandien was shivering, rain running down his bare arm on one side and soaking his sleeve on the other. He could not remember a more miserable night.

"Ki's awake," he told the Brurjan as her black horse picked its cautious way back to him. "With your most gracious permission, I'll cut the bonds on her ankles so she can ride upright."

"No." Hollyika's voice was flat. "I know of what I speak. She'd find a way to turn that beast and set heels to it. It's her horse, after all, and used to taking the commands of her voice. No, she rides well enough the way she is."

A slow anger began to burn inside Vandien as he looked into her grim face. He glanced again to the rain dripping from Ki's lank mop of hair. "Look at her," he said flatly. "You'll kill her. Who knows when she last ate?"

"No. She's tougher than she looks. Even I know that, as short a time as I have known her. She last ate before I met her on the riverbank; I would wager on that. And she has drunk only the Limbreth water since then. But don't worry about that. Romni can go forever on a sip of water and a gnawed bone—I should know, I've rousted enough of them. She'll be fine. You think you are trying to aid a friend, but you're only dancing to the Limbreth's tune. She is theirs. They have all her thoughts; she doesn't care for her own well-being or comfort. So we won't either. Let her ride belly down; it's the least bother to us."

"Listen to me!" Ki gasped out the words, spitting aside strands of hair. She was panting with the effort of speaking while face down across Sigurd's back. "I have words for you."

"Say them," Hollyika ordered tersely, and silenced Vandien with a glare.

"The Limbreths speak to me, and through me to you. They bid me make their will known to you, unenlightened as you are." Ki paused, and Hollyika rolled her eyes at the dramatic wording. But Vandien leaned closer, brows knit, for the voice that spoke was strangely unlike Ki's, as if someone else did speak through her mouth. Though, he reflected quickly, he had not often spoken to her while she was flung over a horse like a sack of grain.

"The Limbreths have decided to grant you their mercy. It grieves them, for you both turn aside from the graces and knowledge they offer, and from a chance to make more of your lives than merely a time to eat, rut, and sleep."

"They left out fighting." Hollyika grinned over to Vandien.

Ki drew breath. "You may go. They will make it very easy for you to regain the Gate. *If* you set me free to return to them and to finish the task we have begun. They do not desire to hamper you in pursuing your petty goals; all they ask is the return of their consecrated servant, that she may finish the task she set herself."

"And if we don't? What if one of our petty goals is taking her back to the Gate with us?"

"Then you will fail. Do you think the road is bad now? Defy them, and see what it becomes. The folk of this land will rise up against you, in numbers you cannot ignore, and the road will forget the way to the Gate and lead you only to your destruction. And mine also. So you see, you cannot save me for whatever end you had in mind. Better to release me now, and go on to the Gate unmolested, than to stubbornly follow a path that leads to all our deaths."

Hollyika snorted merrily. "Lovely logic. We should set you free and go our way, so we all get what we want. The only thing they do not mention is that you are to run back to your own death at their hands. So, it's all one to us, whether you die doing the Limbreth's bidding, or by being spitted on a farmer's staff. Vandien. Pass me the waterskin."

He unlooped it from where it was strapped on Sigurd's back. Hollyika took it from him, and slid from her horse, her boots sinking deep in the muck. "Drink or drown," she told Ki. As Vandien opened his mouth to protest, Hollyika stared him down with baleful eyes. "If you get off that horse, I'll break her neck. This is no worse than that sludge you forced down

me. Where was your sensitivity and mercy then? Look the
other way, if you must.''

But he couldn't. The Brurjan moved close to Ki, trapped her
head at an awkward angle in the bend of her arm, and forced
the neck of the waterskin between her teeth. She pinched Ki's
nose shut and squeezed the waterskin. Ki gasped and spluttered
as best she could, choking, and then gulping the water to clear
the way for air to her lungs. But another spurt of water followed before air, and most of it went down. Hollyika released
her. Ki choked and gasped and sneezed violently. ''Too bad
we can't get food into her the same way,'' Hollyika observed
calmly. ''It might bring her to her own senses again. But we've
no time to stop, and no dry wood or pot for you to use to brew
up another of your disgusting messes. The longer we stand
here, the more time they'll have to carry out their threats. Let's
be on.''

''The Gate can't be far,'' Vandien agreed wretchedly as he
eyed Ki. Her eyes had sagged shut and the rain dripped from
her face. ''I remember that I ran from the Gate all the way to
the bridge on foot. We've come a good gallop from the bridge
already. I think the Limbreths know we are nearly out of their
reach, and are trying to bluff us out of our captive.''

''Come on.'' Hollyika remounted. The black slogged ahead
of them and Sigmund fell in behind him, and a tug on the lead
rope brought Sigurd at their heels. Vandien tried to sit so as to
make no shift of weight that would throw the great horse off
stride in the dangerously mucky footing. The rain streamed
down endlessly upon them from a blacked sky and the road
dwindled to a trail of mud between trees. In vain Vandien
looked for some sign of the fragrant flowering trees that had
arched his path when first he came through the Gate. All was
blackness ahead, no sign of the Gate's red mouth. The trees
that hedged the road now were black leafless things with long
raking thorns jutting from their reaching branches. The path
was narrower than Vandien remembered, and not well trodden.
Roots humped up in the middle of it to make the weary horses
stumble. Twice swift running streams crossed their path. They
had cut deep gouges in the trail, so that the big horses lurched
down into them, and then awkwardly lunged up again, their
wide hooves slipping and squelching in the bad footing. On
they rode, and on. The trail became a track, and dwindled to

less than that. Soon the horses were breaking through vines that twined across their path from tree to tree. Vandien was damned if he knew what signs Hollyika was following; there were not even any stars to give them a heading. They could be endlessly circling. But the black horse ahead of him kept plodding on, and he kept the greys in its tracks. He could think of nothing better to do, even though he knew they should have reached the Gate long ago.

Slower and slower they plodded. Sigurd bunched up on Sigmund's heels, and Vandien became aware of Ki's voice speaking. How long she had been talking he didn't know, but she was speaking to him. Her tone was calm and reasonable, her words weighted and barbed.

". . . Dragged me from one of your impulses to another. Never content to let me live my own life in my own way, were you? In the Pass of the Sisters, you turned death aside from me, even though I was ready to accept and even welcome that end. But no, all-seeing Vandien decided it wasn't right for me then. You moved in on me, upsetting my life and routine, making me more than ever a stranger among my own people. You with your loud and rowdy ways, never aware of when a man should be silent or when gravity is more seemly than a callous laugh. How often have your foolish ideas slowed me when I had a goal to hasten to? You with your fine words of companionship and sharing; do you call this respect for one another's wishes? The only reason you want me is so that there will be someone to play mother to the child you still are. Someone to be responsible for your silliness, to look to the morrow and make your decisions for you. There is no caring in that."

Vandien bowed to her words and to the rain. They fell on him, eroding him. The greys plodded ever slower; he could not keep his eyes from darting back to her. Every word fell coldly and clearly in his ears, demoralizing as the rain. The pain was almost hypnotic. Much of what she said he could not deny. He absorbed the abuse numbly.

"You damn fool! Do I have to put a lead on your horse too, so we all go like a line of blind beggars?" Hollyika pushed her horse into his, and gave him a quick shot to the ribs that was neither gentle nor jesting. "Wake up! I'm as weary as you, but we have to push on. I looked back and couldn't even see you in this muck. Do you want to get lost?''

"Aren't we already?'' Vandien asked dully. Hollyika didn't answer. She had become aware of Ki's low monologue and was listening in fascination. "She's come back to herself a bit,'' she said as Ki paused for breath. "Seems a bit sharper and nastier than what a Limbreth would inspire her to say. A bit more personal, too. When you're in their hands, personal memories blur to a mist. But she seems to recollect your times together well enough. Whew! What a bastard you've been to her; wonder why she kept you. Listen, you!'' This last was to Ki in a grim voice. "Shut your mouth for a minute and listen to me. You hoped to get him to slip you loose, didn't you? A few kicks in the pride like that, and most men would let go. But I don't have any pride for you to trade on, and I'm the one who holds you. Pass that on to your Limbreths. And pass them this, too. I've thought things out rather thoroughly, riding through this crud. Here's the offer. They let us find the Gate, then we let you go. But if we don't find it damn quick, I'm going to start taking blood from you. I'm hungry, and my control slips when I'm hungry—and from you, too, if you try to interfere. Get your hand off that rapier hilt. I'll take the lead rope now. If you don't pay better attention, the only thing you'll lose is yourself. Move!''

Vandien didn't. His hand remained on the hilt where it had lightly fallen at the beginning of Hollyika's threat. He still gripped the lead line. He turned eyes on her that were darker than the blackness around them.

"Don't get stupid on me now, Vandien. It's the only way out.''

Vandien swallowed but remained silent and motionless, waiting for her to make a move. His heart hammered as he tried not to figure the odds against him. She was closer to Ki than he was. Her knife would be in her before he could move, unless he could figure a way to draw the attack to himself first.

"Vandien.'' Ki's voice was as hoarse as it had earlier been clear. "Please. Don't. You'll only get us both killed.''

"And that matters to you? First sensible thing we've heard out of you. A little more water might do you good, if we had the time. But we don't. And you, with the rain running into your mouth and soaking into your skin. Try to use your own brain. Listen to her. Don't be stupid.''

Vandien's grip on the rapier had firmed. He strained his eyes, trying to be aware of every small move the Brurjan made. But the night was dark, the falling rain muffled the softer sounds of her movements, and her horse was shifting restlessly under her. As her stout forearm lashed out and cleared him from his horse, he realized belatedly that she had been guiding her horse in with small commands from her heels. He lit in briars and mud, struggling to rise and draw his weapon at the same time. But Hollyika's horse was already between him and Ki, its eyes shining wickedly. "Did you tell the Limbreths yet?" Hollyika pressed Ki, and when there was no reply, she leaned down to grip her by the hair. "Did you tell them?" she snarled, yanking her head up so she saw the bared knife before her eyes.

"Yes!" Ki gasped. "I don't need to tell them. They hear all, they know all."

Vandien had stepped lightly as they spoke, working his way around her horse. But Hollyika swung her attention back to him, and with a curse sent her beast lunging at him. He retreated, the treacherous briars tripping him. He fell heavily onto his back, clutching his rapier before him. The horse was coming on, but Ki's voice suddenly cried out, "The Gate! The Gate!"

Vandien waited for death, the rain splashing on him, his rapier a tiny sting that would only madden the horse that loomed over him. But the Brurjan had checked at Ki's cry. She glared angrily down at Vandien, and glanced back to Ki. Ki shook her head to fling the wet hair from her face. "Over there!" she cried, tossing her head in the direction.

"I'll be damned. They came around pretty quick."

The Gate was visible as a red shining through the trees. The light was dim, a blackened red, but in this place of darkness it shone like a beacon. Hollyika's teeth flashed suddenly at Vandien in a menacing smile. "Get up!" she laughed at him. "We're getting out of here."

"What about me?" Ki gasped. "Let me go. At least, let me sit up."

Hollyika appraised her silently as the rain fell all around them. "Let her up," she grunted at last to Vandien.

He scrabbled to his feet, still keeping an eye on the black horse, and moved to Ki. Sheathing his rapier, he drew his belt knife and cut the bonds at her ankles. He eased her down onto

her feet, holding her upright until she could take her own
weight. She gripped the torn shoulder of his shirt to keep her
balance.

"Water?" he asked her softly.

She shook her head slightly. Then she sighed and nodded
regretfully. "The rain is only enough to tease. My throat is so
dry I'd drink anything. All my ribs feel cracked."

"Bruised is all, more likely." He grabbed the waterskin for
her and unstoppered it. Hollyika sat her horse sullenly, watching Ki sip, and then take a mouthful. She pushed the skin back
abruptly into Vandien's hands. "Tastes like swamp muck,"
she complained, but her voice was stronger.

Vandien opened his mouth to speak, but Hollyika cut in.
"Put her back on the horse." She had already taken Sigurd's
lead line and was toying with the end of it. Vandien boosted Ki
up, but she had to scramble for her own seat among the bags
strapped to the big grey. Ki gave a nod when all was settled,
and Vandien moved to Sigmund.

"I think Ki is feeling . . ."

"Oh, shut up!" Hollyika snapped. "What you think and
what she feels have no bearing on anything. The Gate is there.
Follow me."

It proved to be farther off than expected. Or perhaps, Vandien mused to himself, it is retreating before us as we go. The
fancy didn't please him. They followed the light like a kitten
after a string. Was the Limbreth toying with them to gain time
to muster a large force of peasants? He had no inkling of just
how far the powers of the Limbreth reached. Had they, as
Hollyika suspected, sent the rain that drenched them, in the
hopes of discouraging them into obedience? The road had certainly fallen to their will, and the farmers. He crouched low
over Sigmund's neck, trying to keep clear of the low branches
that threatened to sweep him off. They followed no path at all
now. Hollyika led them in and out of thickets; the horses
stumbled over roots and pushed through low brush. The red
light grew ever larger, but was always slashed by tree trunks
and branches. Vandien stared ahead at it, until he saw it even
when he blinked.

Nineteen

"You heard me, Rebeke. They don't wish to go back now. Neither of them. You don't have to believe me, though. You can ask them for yourself, as long as you're careful not to tire Jace. She's the sickly one now. The boy has come around fine. He's a quick learner, that one. You should see the place he's made for himself down cellar. Remember how you used to knead the dough for me? Well, that boy . . ."

"Where is Jace?" Rebeke cut in smoothly. She was in no mood to be reminded of a past that was no longer connected to her present, but Mickle marked the worry lines alien to the smoothness of her Windsinger countenance. Changed as she was, he could still read the weariness and tension that weighted her.

"Have a cup of tea first," he suggested boldly. "Or a sip of wine."

Rebeke almost turned to the caring in his voice. Why shouldn't she? A cup of wine at table with the old man, forget for just a while about Limbreths and Gates and the balancing of worlds. No. Time was power, to be seized now or surrendered forever. "I cannot, Mickle," she said in a soft but fully melodic voice. "For a moment we could pretend, but in the end we would both regret it. There is no recapturing the past. Let me see Jace now."

The last words were uttered in the tone of the Windsinger that would take no refusal. The old man's shoulders slumped. He gestured toward a door. "She's within. Let me tell her you want to talk to her."

She watched the door hanging drop behind him and wondered what he would say to her. That an old friend of his had come to call, or that a Windmistress had come to question her? Did it matter? Only when she came here did she feel these twinges of regret for the choices she had made and the thing she had become. Dresh had never made her rue her decision, though he sometimes wished he could understand it. But here? She didn't want Mickle's admiration for all she had made of herself, let alone his awe at her powers. He was the only one who ever made her wish to be loved because she was Rebeke. It was a mistake to come here.

He was back in an instant, swinging the door hanging aside and waving her within. Jace, pillowed in luxury on Mickle's wide bed, reminded Rebeke of a pressed flower. The color was still there, in the hair and eyes and skin, but she was drained to a papery dryness. Her aristocratic hands had only the strength to cling to the edge of the coverlet. Mickle stood over her, easing her back onto yet another pillow. The eyes she turned to Rebeke were dull, incapable of being surprised by anything.

"Now don't be asking her too many questions, now. You can see how she is; scarcely the strength of a drowned kitten. But she'll come back to herself; Mickle will see to that." He cocked his head to address Jace in bed. "This is the Windsinger I've told you about, my Rebeke. Now she wants to ask you some questions, and you do your best to answer. But all you have to do is let me know when you're tired and we'll stop." Having finished plumping the pillows, he was now fussily smoothing the coverlet, twitching it into precise flatness over the bed as if it were a tablecloth he was smoothing. From that he went to pour her a fresh glass of water from a pitcher at a stand beside the bed. He peeked over at Rebeke as he did so, kept his eyes on her as he carefully put the glass within reach of the invalid, and she stared back at him levelly. Finally he straightened up with a sigh and stood before her. "Well, aren't you going to ask her?"

"Aren't you going to leave so we may talk privately?"

Mickle bristled. "Rebeke, be you who you may, this is my house and Jace is my guest. I won't have her badgered about and made to say yes when her answer is no. I know that tongue of yours from old, and it has lost none of its powers. Even when she was a sassy little miss, she could talk the best buns off the shelf and into her pocket!"

"Mickle!" Jace broke in as Rebeke glared at him. "If you would . . ." She took a breath and he was all attention as he bent over her. "Just a little wine, perhaps, to wet my throat and help me find strength to speak?"

"Of course. Of course, my dear. It won't take a moment." He was gone in a bustle of hurry that all of Rebeke's commands could never have wrought. Both women looked after him for an instant with some fondness, then Rebeke advanced hastily to lean against the foot of the bed. Her knowing eyes summed up Jace's health quickly.

"Mickle tells me that you no longer wish to go through the Gate back to your own land."

Jace replied slowly, stopping often to breathe. "It's true. I know we cannot go back. Not now. Chess. You would not understand. He no longer belongs there. He is of this world now, for all that he cannot abide your light. I could not take him back. Nor could I go alone. So we will stay."

Rebeke paced a swift turn around the room. "I won't say that I agree with your reasons. There's little that can be done to a boy of that age that can't be undone, with a bit of care and time. You speak as if a toy were broken, instead of your son being injured, and needing the healing of his own land."

"You don't understand." Jace was adamant. "We are poisoned now. Who would take such knowledge into unsullied homes? We are outcasts, doomed to spend our lives here, and find peace again only in death."

"Let's not be dramatic." Rebeke's voice cut. "Try for a moment to think of this. There are others at stake. Ki, who went through believing that her friend needed her, for that much Chess has told Mickle. And Vandien, who went through not only for Ki, but on your behalf, to try to carve a way back for you. Unless you enter your world again, they cannot return to theirs. Would you break faith with Vandien?"

"Having seen our side, would he choose to leave it? I think not. There he would find soothing for the rough edges of his spirit and learn better ways. I don't harm him by remaining here. Indeed, it may be the only good to come out of it."

Rebeke paced another circuit, scarce hearing Jace's words. Her mind bit at her problem, seizing it from another angle. "You have seen this world. And you speak of the Limbreths as one who knows much of them. Of all you have seen in this world, what would please the Limbreths most as a gift?''

Jace was silenced, taken aback by this sudden diversion. Her face went blank. Her eyes rolled up suddenly and she convulsed. But even as Rebeke sprang to the door to call Mickle, her eyes opened again. They looked at Rebeke with intelligence, but seemed singularly uninhabited.

"At last you get to the soul of the trading," Jace said in a toneless voice. Her eyes wandered past Rebeke to rove the room listlessly. "You seem torn between gifts and threats. Or was your contacting the Gatherers but a foolish boast?"

Rebeke's mouth had dried cottony. She started to speak then sealed her lips together. The Limbreth, somehow, was here. She was not ready to deal with that, so the less she said, the fewer weaknesses she would bare in her position. But the Limbreth Jace remained silent and impassive, waiting. Rebeke ventured a question. "How do you speak through Jace?"

"Jace. That is what this one calls itself. Perhaps you would understand my position better if I did explain. Jace is but a manifestation of myself. All things in my world are, though I don't endow all with that self-knowledge. She, of course, perceives herself as a separate organism. I once thought that arrangement would be amusing and might lead to diversification. It wasn't and didn't. She is still an intrinsic part of me, as much as the trees, the road, or the water. We are one. And if I have chosen physically to express myself as a multitude, it still does not change it. You Humans have two words for our condition. Lonely. Bored."

Rebeke expelled her breath harshly. "I do begin to understand. If all within your world is yourself, then any new mind would be welcomed. But these two you have no use for."

"Nor for Vandien and the Brurjan. Most intractable creatures. They will not surrender themselves to me. Ki, however, has been a revelation. Her mind is not a closed box to be emptied, but a web stretched to all points she has ever touched. You know the awareness I speak of. You have it yourself."

"All folk of power do," Rebeke admitted unwillingly.

"So I have come to realize; and Ki's gift for it is small compared to yours. So we will come to a bargain; but not because of your foolish threats. A few Humans in my world is of no more concern to the Gatherers than a few doves among your chickens would be to you."

"Then why do you bother to balance the Gate?" Rebeke demanded. She perched on the edge of Mickle's clothes chest and locked eyes with the creature in his bed.

"Esthetics," it extemporized, and Rebeke guessed it lied. "And to give me eyes in your world. Not that I find it very satisfying. I have been always with my own thoughts and reactions and impressions. You can create no stimulus for me here that I could not duplicate more intensely in my world. 'An eternal masturbation'—a few of your decades ago, a Windsinger sent me a poet who annoyed her. That is how he expressed it when I sought to make him understand us so he could make new songs for us. But he went mad and failed. They all go mad or die; they survive so briefly. Even Ki. She will die soon. But she lasted longer than we expected, so we studied her, and now we know something we didn't before. It's the power in her. One trained to use that power might last indefinitely with us. A pleasing idea."

"It doesn't please me." Rebeke held her body still with an effort. She cursed Yoleth silently, fearing the direction this talk was taking.

"It should. For now we are willing to trade. Vandien and Ki for two of trained power. One we have already selected. She will come when we call, regardless of her own will. One we ask you to find. Only one."

"One is too many. There is no one I would feed to you."

"A pity. But I will give you the same courtesy you gave me. You have a little time to think. If you change your mind, come tomorrow of your nights, and help to open a Gate. Perhaps this knowledge will ease your choice. If you do not come, a Gate will still be opened, and we will still call the one we have selected; for we can open a Gate by ourselves, though Jace may not find it pleasant. If you force us to that, we will still have taken one of yours, but all you will have received will be that demented Brurjan."

The knowledge sickened and silenced Rebeke. She saw Jace dropped back on the pillows like an abandoned puppet. Well, and what else was she? Her musing was interrupted by Mickle's entrance. He swept the hangings aside and backed into the room with a laden tray. Beside the glass of wine was a platter of freshly sliced fruit, tiny wedges of cheese and small tender biscuits. He put the tray down and his eyes darted from Jace to Rebeke. He began to arrange the tray sullenly as he accused her. "Look at her. You never had any self-restraint. Worn to whiteness, and all but unconscious. I knew you would ask too much of her. You've had her answer, have you?"

"Yes." The word was clipped. "We have spoken. She does not wish to return."

"Exactly as I told you. But no, you have grown too wise to believe an old man, even if he . . ."

"Even if he is as blind as a bat. Look at her, Mickle, and stop your clucking. That body suffers from no more than the water flux, as might any stranger to Jojorum. Take away your tray. Give her nothing but water, boiled and cooled, and small bits of cheese for a day or so. Then start her on a coarse bread with milk that has been brought to scalding and cooled for the rest of the week. She will be fine and hearty by the end of that time."

She turned her hawk's gaze back to the woman in the bed. Jace had roused slightly, but from her eyes peered only a sick and weary woman. She was ignorant of what she was, if Rebeke was not. Best leave it that way. Rebeke's mind chewed at the enigma of it, and fancy moved her to ask, "You won't change your mind about going back?"

Jace wearily shook her head, but Mickle boiled to his feet. "Enough!" he rumbled. "Enough. She has given you her answer, and now I give you mine. She won't go through the Gate. She and the boy won't go away."

"From this world, or from you?" Rebeke's words stopped him cold, but in a moment he lunged on recklessly.

"From neither. Here they are and here they'll stay, where things are good for them and they're cared for. I mean what I say, Rebeke."

"I don't doubt that you do," she replied, and let the door hanging fall behind her.

TWENTY

REBEKE stood by the Limbreth Gate. A dark wind keened loudly through the streets, bearing a burden of dry dust to confound the eyes and ears of any folk who might be abroad this night. Rebeke herself wore a new robe, of the darkest blue the dyer could produce, one shade short of black; its midnight blended against the shadowed wall. Beside her another stood, draped in black, awaiting her summons.

Rebeke closed her eyes and her sensitive fingers traced the crack that was all that remained of the Gate. It was all darkness within, no more to the casual glance than any of the faults slowly developing in the ancient walls. Rebeke dropped her hands to her sides. Within her mind she quested subtly, reaching with the powers of a now extinct race; and within the recesses of her transmuted brain, a knowledge less a memory than an instinct stirred. Again, she felt the edges of the Gate, but this exploration had nothing to do with physical touch. She could see it, this odd twist in the web of the worlds that brought two places so far apart into a strange conjunction. Even more complex were the processes that had opened a Gate between them; it bordered on making the unreal into reality. Rebeke quivered at the sight of such deep magic, and trembled again, with foreboding, when she saw on what a flimsy knowledge it was based. The Limbreths made this as children might dig a tunnel into a sand bank, seeing only how easily the digging went, and not how ominous the collapse might be.

She balked at the thought of opening the Gate again; but it was too late. With her or without her, the Limbreths would do it. Yoleth had given them a hunger, and they would sate it. The

Gatekeeper, immune to such knowledge as Rebeke possessed, had already begun. She felt the Limbreths reaching through his mind to clasp thoughts with her, and then the flood of the Limbreths entering them both. To resist them now, to cry out of danger, would only be to make the collapse certain. Instead she bowed her will to theirs, and let them tap her strength. She sensed their pleasure as they reached into her and found a well of determination such as they had encountered nowhere else. At first it was all she could do to hold herself open to their demands, but gradually she was able to see the direction their labors took. Slowly she eased a measure of control back to herself; she sensed their outrage but ignored it. Deftly she began to twist and spin, even as they did, but with a difference. She followed them, shoring up what they had undercut, strengthening where their deep delving had weakened. But even so, even with her added insight, the Gate was a flimsy thing, little more than a wish in the night. Vandien's passage had done more damage than the Limbreths appreciated; Rebeke sensed the skewed pressures he had brought with him, and the crookedness of their mending patch. Yet it was atop this very patch that they had to open the Gate anew. Let it hold, she begged the moon, for one night more; and for no more than that!

It came, with a glimmer, and then a warm glow of red, opening and stretching the night to make a place for itself. Wider and taller it went, and the Limbreths were more satisfied with it than she was. She stood, eyes closed, muscles singing with tension, but fearful when they were ready. Could they not see; could they not feel the fragility of this thing? A Gate did they call this gap? More like to a pinprick in a bladder. But they were finished, and their gatekeeper was stepping within, using his presence to maintain the gap between the worlds. A brave soul, Rebeke thought with admiration. Then, no; she saw an ignorant, expendable bit of the Limbreth, and almost pitied him.

"The Gate is open!" Pride glittered in the voice of the new Keeper. Its squat head swiveled as if it could truly see. "Where are those who would use the Gate? Let them step forward."

"I am Rebeke of the Windsingers," Rebeke began in a gravely formal voice.

"That is known, that is known!" the other cut in sharply. "My Masters have told me all; and we await you. Have you brought what you have promised?"

"I have brought no one. The one that comes, comes of his own will. Your master will have to call whatever other one he chose."

For a moment the Keeper bowed its head, seeming to listen. "Yes, that is right. That is as agreed. It is not as it is usually done, nor as they first trained me. But they are the Masters; the Limbreths do I serve, in whatever fashion they say. So we are ready."

"Are the ones I bargained for ready as well?" Rebeke pressed.

"They approach even now. They have been brought to you with some difficulty, and my Masters would have you appreciate that. Far easier it would have been to destroy them. At first they sought to do violence against my Masters' folk. But they have been shown the light and might of my Masters, and brought to their knees. They shall come as they are bid, and we have made them anxious to use the Gate. All will go as you desire."

"Might I see them?" It was a polite nothing. Even as she asked, Rebeke sent her Windsinger senses questing through the Gate. Almost immediately she touched Ki's aura, a shape familiar to her and yet subtly changed. She hoped it was but the distortion of the Gate. She tapped Ki's senses, and became aware first of Vandien and then of some other creature, no doubt the "demented Brurjan" the Limbreths had told her of. She wondered what they would do with it, and then dismissed such speculation as childish. She would not waste her time trying to understand a Limbreth. She drew back into herself and became aware of the Keeper telling her, with polite regrets, that he could not show them to her until the moment when they entered the Gate. She stifled her impatience. She would have Ki and Vandien soon enough. "Then let us begin. The night of my world wears on, and it were best if we were finished before dawn."

"Agreed. Bring forward the one, and we shall summon the other."

Rebeke's heart skipped. She thought she had hardened herself to this moment; nay, she thought she had convinced herself that it was the greatest good for all involved. Her throat constricted and she could not voice the word that would bring her offering forward. She stepped into the shadows and with a touch made her will known.

He stepped lightly out. She looked on his dreaming features beneath the blue Windsinger bond twisted about his brow and cursed whatever demon had inspired her to dress him so. The short black cape was in the style he had always favored, the shirt of pale silken grey, open at the throat to expose his pulse beating warmly. The shirt was the same shade as his eyes, so tranquil and unfocused under her bonding. His face was unlined; he looked for all the world like a boy on the turn of manhood, unroused from a sleep of sweet dreams. She reached to remove her bonding.

"My Masters say that they can take him through the Gate like that. He may give less trouble that way."

"No!" Rebeke's voice broke harshly. "No, he goes in knowing what he faces, and who sent him to it." The Keeper is blind, a small voice within her whispered, and it might be the last kiss you would ever wish to bestow. But she did not. With a twist of her wrist, she slipped her bond from his mind, but left intact the sky rune, wrought in silver and pinned to his cloak, that kept his body's will tied to hers.

"Rebeke?" Dresh glanced about with wondering eyes, but adapted quickly. "A fine night for a stroll through old Jojorum. I'd take your arm, if I could move mine."

"The last night we shall share, Dresh. Yet I would have you know, I do not act with malice. I could never be without fear of you, if I set you free. Yet keeping you in a well like a book on a shelf demeans us both, and me not the least."

A smile twitched his lips. "But why do you bond me? You gave the decision to me. At least I shall exist. That is true?" He addressed this query to the Keeper.

"My Masters have given their word that it shall be so, and they do not lie," the Keeper intoned ponderously. "They touch this one, and find him all that they desired. He is acceptable for the exchange."

"But . . ."

"Hush," Rebeke told him, not harshly, and a touch of her will stilled his lips. She looked away from his face, refusing to meet his eyes again.

The Keeper crouched in the center of the Gate. Rebeke could feel the power whistling through him like wind through a cracked door. He was the channel for it as it flowed through the Gate, and went seeking, seeking, until it found the crystal that could focus it and make it irresistible. The command was as acute as a scream in the night. Rebeke's honed senses winced from it and she was glad it was not addressed to her.

Its target was far away. All waited in silence. Rebeke tried for amusement to pierce the Gate with her own eyes, but with no success. Her other senses confirmed that Ki and Vandien were on the other side, nearer than they had been and hastening toward her. She tried to take comfort in the thought, and to forget the silenced wizard beside her.

She came on a wind from outside the realm of night, traveling from her hall to this Gate by the paths and steeds that only a Windmistress could command. Rebeke's honed senses felt her first as a breeze and then as an anger hanging in the moving air, poorly masking a frantic struggle.

The beast, invisible to untrained eyes, dropped her in the street. Her cowl was awry and her features stiff with hate. Yoleth of the Windsingers did not come with a good will. She was not taken sleeping or drunk or in the madness of grief. But she came. She came by the strength of the calling gem that clung to the skin of her hand and made demands in a stony voice. She advanced, stiff-legged, to the Gate. It was justice, Rebeke told herself. Yoleth's frantic resistance took all her will but availed her nothing, and terror silenced her.

"Are you pleased with the gift your skills wrung from the Limbreths?" Rebeke asked her in a voice as flinty as the gem. "Come to the place you have prepared for yourself."

With a light touch to Dresh's shoulder, Rebeke moved him to her side. They stood like a bridal couple in some blasphemous ceremony. She stroked the soft hair back from Dresh's eyes, and this time she did not resist her impulse. She set her scaled lips cooly to Dresh's smooth cheek in a farewell kiss. She wondered who, if anyone, it comforted. She freed his voice.

His grey eyes met and clung to hers. "Come with me." His voice was soft, untinged by any of his skills. "In that world, perhaps we could be what we once were."

"There is no world in which we could be together and be at

peace. Neither of us was made for that. But I wish you well."
She turned away from him. "We are ready now," she told the
Keeper.

"As are we. Let them enter."

A touch of Rebeke's hand and a spur from the gem set them
in motion. At the last possible moment, her hand darted out to
rip the rune from his cloak. For an instant he struggled, but the
pull of the Gate was already upon him, and slowly he entered.
"Upon the other side, you shall feel the touch of my will no
longer," Rebeke said, knowing her words could not carry into
the Gate.

She peered into the rosy haze of the Gate, and stiffened as
the Brurjan loomed suddenly into view.

The rain had never paused. Although the Limbreths might
be willing to show them the Gate, they did not seem to wish
their journey to be short or pleasant. They had come out of the
last shred of forest into a deeply grassed meadow, and Hollyika
had cursed in the savage Brurjan tongue at the sight of a Gate
that seemed no more than a red crack in the night. But as they
rode toward it, the crack had widened and assumed regular
outlines, an arched red portico that beckoned in the night.
Hollyika had reined in before it, and given a tug on the lead
rope that brought Sigurd up beside her black. Vandien rode up
beside Ki. He glanced across at her. Her face was unreadable,
the red light giving it a glow that would have seemed whole-
some, had not her face been worn to bones.

Vandien stared into the Gate, at the Keeper like and yet
unlike the one he had overpowered to come through. His back
was to them and Vandien wondered to whom he spoke. The
Gate at last, as they had so long sought it, and in his heart there
was no joy, for it was parting time. He drew his knife to cut the
bonds on Ki's wrists.

"Leave that be!" Hollyika hissed.

"You gave your word," Vandien reminded her. He did not
know enough of Brurjan expressions to read the look on her
face.

"What is a word given to one you have not shared hot blood
with?" Hollyika whispered imperturbably. "Bite your wag-
ging tongue, and be ready to do all exactly as I say, or your
Romni friend pays for you."

Ki turned to him, and their eyes met. They pleaded, but her lips were dumb, and he did not know what she asked of him. He bowed his head, turning his eyes away from her. The Keeper had put his attention upon them.

"We're coming through," Hollyika announced before he could speak.

"Yes. Yes," the Keeper agreed. "You and the man. All has been prepared, all will balance. Be ready to come forward when I give the signal." His eyes flickered over Ki with casual interest. "You may take the animal she bestrides as well. My Masters have no use for it."

"Neither do we," Hollyika asserted. The loop of lead rope fell from her hand to the wet ground. Vandien caught his breath. Ki sat still as stone.

"Then enter now," the Keeper bade them, and turned his sightless head toward the other side. "As are we," he answered to some unheard comment. "Let them enter."

Hollyika cried out in Brurjan to her horse, and Black sprang forward as if stabbed. The lead rope loop, so showily dropped, jerked tight, and Vandien saw the loose end of it knotted to the pommel of Hollyika's saddle. Sigurd screamed at the rude jerk, but surged forward all the same. Sigmund could ignore Vandien's frantic blows, but not his team mate going without him. He too pushed into the Gate.

It met them like a rising tide. Vandien was stifled by the pressure of it. The horses struggled like trapped cattle in a mire. Black was furious, his bit foaming pink, his angry hooves seeking targets. The thick atmosphere frustrated him, changing his killing blows to floundering. Dimly Vandien was aware of a Windsinger going down before him, and rolling, to begin a slow crawl to the Limbreth side of the Gate. Her face was twisted in despair, and he had a half instant in which to wonder what drove her on. A dark-cloaked man with a hauntingly familiar face slipped nimbly through the midst of the scuffle, moving toward the Limbreth side without reluctance. Ki sat the plunging Sigurd as if she were glued to him, and Vandien saw the nudge of her knee that pushed him into the gap Hollyika had cleared.

Hollyika had seized the hapless Keeper, who wriggled like a rabbit in her grip. "I'll balance your damn Gate for you!" she roared in a voice made sodden by the heavy air. With one arm she jerked him from his feet and held him aloft. Impending disaster howled in Vandien's mind. Sigmund beneath him sensed it as well, and with a shouldering shove that pushed his brother through the Gate, he plunged out as if he were coming out of a flooded river fording. But Vandien was not quite clear of the Gate when he felt the red air within it grow suddenly thin. He had a brief image of the Keeper flung back to the Limbreth side, tumbling through the air, to suddenly wink out of the Gate. For a second he heard Hollyika's roar of laughter and saw the flash of her grin.

Then agony crushed her. Blood started from her ears and nose, and the black horse screamed like a woman. The Gate was falling, collapsing in a ruin that was both more and less than stone. The very blackness of the night fell in on itself, making a darkness that no light could pierce. Hollyika's aggressive determination alone was not enough to hold the Gate in existence; but it was barely enough to drive Black on, to spring nearly clear of it before he sank to the ground. Rocks the size of clenched fists rained down upon them. A choking dust of ancient stone filled the air; Vandien couldn't see Ki. He sprang from Sigmund and gripped Hollyika, but even the strength of terror was not enough to drag her free. A rock between the shoulders flattened him onto her and he became her unintentional shield against the debris that followed. For a small eternity the wall fell, and then a silence as heavy covered them with mercy.

"Did they get through?" A voice as loud as a roaring wind was in Vandien's ear and shaking his shoulder as well. He rolled to face it, and then recoiled from the inhuman visage so close to his own. He had seen those blue and white eyes before; the memory didn't reassure him. He opened his lips to speak but coughed rock dust instead.

"Did they get through?" The voice persisted, but Ki's voice, calm as a summer's day, was the one to answer. "I caught a glimpse of them on the other side, before she threw the Keeper at them. They were clear, and Dresh was farther from the collapse than we were."

Vandien rolled over slowly. Rebeke straightened up from shaking him, and gave him enough space to come to his feet. Ki just looked at him, without a touch or word, but her sunken eyes were full of regrets.

"So they're through. And the Gate can never be reopened. I suppose I am relieved." Rebeke's words seemed almost Human; uncertainty gave the tuned instrument of a Windsinger's voice a mortal tone this night.

Ki stepped forward, and Vandien watched her eyes roving over the fallen masonry. A whole section of the wall had gone down, exposing a flat expanse of yellow plain, with a few straggly trees. The pile of rubble did not seem enough to account for such a gap.

Belatedly, he recalled Hollyika. The horse was groaning, but she was still. To his surprise he found Rebeke helping him to drag her from the saddle. Relieved of her weight, Black made an attempt to stand. It was pitiable to watch, but he finally levered himself upright, his head drooping down until his nose nearly touched the street. He trembled and sweat began to stain the black coat; but he seemed, miraculously, unhurt.

"Is she alive?" Vandien asked Rebeke as the Windsinger stooped over Hollyika.

"You ask that question about a Brurjan?" Was that a trace of humor in the trained voice? "They're nearly as hard to kill as Romni. She's stunned, and her hearing will never be the same. But she will live to let you know she feels no debt toward you."

"I'll never understand why she did it. What did she gain by bringing Ki through?" He stopped at the strange look Rebeke gave him. "They weren't going to let Ki through, you know. That was their bargain with us. That we could pass the Gate if we left Ki behind."

"Was it? A great one for bargains, the Limbreths. I hope they think this one has been shrewd, for it is the last one they will make with this world."

"What was your role in this?" Ki asked suddenly in a flat voice.

"One that need not concern you, for I had no wishes for your well-being. You were a pawn in someone else's gambit, as usual." The words were slighting, but they held one another's eyes. Rebeke moved toward Ki, to free her still bound wrists.

Hollyika's eyes slid open. With a roar she clapped her hands

over her ears and rocked back and forth. Rebeke glanced about
the streets. Dawn was not far away; the less evidence left, the
better.

"Bring her horse," she told Vandien sharply. With a
strength he found incredible, the slender Windsinger pulled the
Brurjan to her feet and began to walk her away.

TWENTY-ONE

MICKLE's kitchen was a friendly place of well-worn comfort. In the oldest of Human traditions, it was a separate room of the house, closed off from the bedlam that currently raged through the rest of it. Vandien sat in a darkened corner of it and tried to shut his mind off.

He could hear Jace and Chess down in the cellar as they dragged about beds and chests to make room for Jace to sleep. Rebeke had banished them there, insisting that Mickle kindle enough lights in the rest of the house for her to work by, and commandeering his bed for Hollyika. Hollyika and Mickle were currently engaged in a shouting match over whether she would drink the milk and eat the nourishing stew he had brought her, or whether she really would get up out of the bed and break his neck first. Vandien was betting on Mickle at this point. The old man's determined nagging brought a tiny smile to his face, but it died there.

Ki sat at the table, staring down at her hands. Vandien looked at her, and then away. Mickle had insisted that they all must eat, in his dismay and delight at a houseful of folk coming in at dawn, and had so laden the table that there was scarce room to sit at it. In all the bustle and shouting, Vandien alone had marked how Ki had drifted from room to room in the house, now looking at Hollyika as Rebeke worked over her, now wandering through the kitchen and out into the courtyard, to stand staring at the dawn breaking over the city. Long had she stared up at the streaking colors of the sky, until Mickle had found her and, taking her arm, brought her in and put her at the table. Then she had eaten, fruit and bread in tiny bites, as

if she had forgotten how to eat. She ignored the slice of meat
he forked onto her plate, disdaining even that part of the bread
that had soaked up its juices. But wine she had taken, one
glass, and then a second, and again, until Mickle wisely and
silently left the bottle at her elbow.

Vandien too had eaten, but in quantity more than pleasure.
He felt the weight of the food in his stomach. Like a sated
wolf, his body now bade him curl up and digest. Sleep beckoned seductively as a time free of thinking. He watched Ki
pour another glass of wine, her eyes following the last red
drops into her glass. Not by word nor touch nor flicker of eye
did she acknowledge him. He sought out the dawn in the
courtyard.

A high wall surrounded it, and the grey of early day filled it.
A great oven, monument to Mickle's days as a baker, squatted
in a corner of the manicured garden. A few cherished fruit trees
were already drooping in the early heat. Full sun this day
would be scorching.

Vandien sat down beside the door and leaned back against
the wall of the house. He tipped his head back so full light fell
on his face, shining dimly through his closed eyelids. It was
warm on his face, and he willed his mind to blank sleep.

A voice jarred him from it. Rebeke was speaking inside the
kitchen. "I'd take it as a favor if you went far from this place,
and spent the rest of your life being inconspicuous."

"I don't know that I owe you any favors." Ki's voice was
slow, not drunk but softened. "I recall that you said it was not
goodwill toward me that got you involved."

"No. It wasn't. But it was definitely the ill will of others
toward you that started the whole chain of events, so perhaps
you owe me for stopping them."

"Perhaps I owe the Windsingers a lot, favors not among
them. Do you know what I am?"

"Do you?" Power lashed through Rebeke's voice. Ki was
silent. "Far away and inconspicuous. And no children, Ki, by
anyone."

Ki made a wordless sound of contempt and fury. Another
sound followed, like a thud against wood. Rebeke's voice was
calm when she spoke. "That's coin, to settle for the wagon,
and for Vandien's horse. You've no excuse not to move on.
And there's something else in there as well. I got it back for

you, after Chess told Mickle about it.'' Her voice suddenly
changed, and it was woman speaking to woman that Vandien
heard. ''I'm giving it back to you. If you've an ounce of sense
in that thick Romni skull, you'll give it away again.'' Vandien
heard her steps cross the kitchen to the other door. It was a
Windsinger that warned, ''I've come to power now. Wherever
you go, my eyes will see you. Don't give me a reason to look
for you.''

The silence in the kitchen congealed. A muscle spasmed in
Vandien's back. He would sleep, and then he would go on,
away from Jojorum. He wondered for a moment what had
happened to his horse, but let the thought go. The fruit trees
came to his mind, and the promised heat of the day. Beneath
them there would be enough shade to save his skin from burning, and enough heat and light to keep dreams of the Limbreths
from his mind. He rose with a creak of joints.

''Where are you going?'' Ki spoke softly, but Vandien
started at her voice. She stood framed in the doorway beside
him.

''To sleep.'' He gestured vaguely at the trees.

She sighed. ''I'm not tired. Not sleeping tired.'' She looked
at him, but he could not read the look, and after a moment she
went on. ''I'm tired in muscle, and too tired to eat more than a
bite at a time, but I feel as if I could do anything except sleep.
I've had enough sleep to take me to the end of summer.'' She
walked back to the table and sat down again. She kicked out a
chair for him, and her glance flicked up to his and away. He
padded softly into the kitchen, looked at the chair, then sat
down feeling numb. He reached for the wine bottle, but found
it empty. Gravely she offered him her glass, but caught it back
from him before he could drain it.

''There's a lot of explaining I have to do.'' She stopped his
voice by putting the glass back to his lips. He took it from her,
looking at her over its rim.

''A deal,'' she proposed gravely. ''You don't ask me about
things I said to you; I won't ask you where the hell my wagon
is.''

He nearly smiled. ''But it's not that simple, Ki. I need to
know, in Human folly Hollyika tells me, what you feel, now,
and what you felt. I have to ask.''

"All right, then." Ki's eyes challenged him. "But I'll start first. What the hell happened to my wagon?"

Silence fell. Ki's face was grim. Vandien shifted uncomfortably. "I lost it," he muttered, going red-faced.

"And now about my feelings. I lost them." Ki picked up a peach from the table and bit into it.

"And now," he pressed.

"And now I have regrets. Not only for things I said to you, but for all the things I have never said to you. But also for what I found over there in myself, the potential that will never be more than that. I could wish I had never known."

"You've changed."

"I won't be eating meat anymore, if that's what you mean. I've come to feel my kinship with all moving living things. And I won't be taking my time for granted anymore. I won't ignore the fact that the span of my days is short."

He could not smile at her. The relationship so carefully built seemed crumbled; he dared no longer trust the weight of his heart to it. "It's more than that," he said heavily. "It's not going to be the same between us."

Ki looked deep into his eyes, troubled by what she saw there. "The same as what? When was it ever the same between us, from day to day? When did we ever want it to be?" She paused. She smiled at him, hopefully, and her face looked less thin. "You know, of course, that I could have jumped from Sigurd's back in the confusion. I didn't have to come back through the Gate."

He swallowed, and suddenly sighed out the tension, and did not hear Ki's answering sigh. He was eased, and incredibly sleepy. She reached to touch his face, then got a good grip on the nape of his neck. Bending his head toward her, she warned him gruffly, "Next time don't be so damned careless with the things I give you." The chain went cold around his neck and the hawk thudded lightly against his chest. A look of wonder came over his face, and he reached to touch it with one finger. Rising, he pulled her up and against him. "I'm going out under the trees to sleep," he told her. "Right now, I crave light and heat against my skin."

Ki stretched within the circle of his arms, and spoke with her face in the hollow of his shoulder. "I'll come out under the trees with you," she offered. "But not for the light and heat. And not to sleep."

BEST-SELLING
Science Fiction
and
Fantasy

☐ 47809-3	**THE LEFT HAND OF DARKNESS,** Ursula K. LeGuin	$2.95
☐ 16012-3	**DORSAI!,** Gordon R. Dickson	$2.75
☐ 80581-7	**THIEVES' WORLD,** Robert Lynn Asprin, editor	$2.95
☐ 11577-2	**CONAN #1,** Robert E.Howard, L. Sprague de Camp, Lin Carter	$2.50
☐ 49142-1	**LORD DARCY INVESTIGATES,** Randell Garrett	$2.75
☐ 21889-X	**EXPANDED UNIVERSE,** Robert A. Heinlein	$3.95
☐ 87328-6	**THE WARLOCK UNLOCKED,** Christopher Stasheff	$2.95
☐ 26187-6	**FUZZY SAPIENS,** H. Beam Piper	$2.75
☐ 05469-2	**BERSERKER,** Fred Saberhagen	$2.75
☐ 10253-0	**CHANGELING,** Roger Zelazny	$2.95
☐ 51552-5	**THE MAGIC GOES AWAY,** Larry Niven	$2.75

Prices may be slightly higer in Canada.